THE OBSIDIAN ASCENT

EMERALD CITY DRAGONS - BOOK 1

WES GRANDMONT III

The Obsidian Ascent : Emerald City Dragons - Book 1
by Wes Grandmont III
Published by Steamfire Studios
(an imprint of Wesley Grandmont III)
www.wesleygrandmont.com

Hardcover Edition v1.0.0
ISBN-13: 978-1-73208-444-5
ISBN: 1-7320844-4-0

To my family and friends,
This story is for you.

1

THE HUNT BEGINS

ALLEY

It had been a year since Alley Ward last killed someone.

She chewed her thumbnail and stole another glance out the plate-glass window of the café. The man across the street had been watching her for two days. Did he know she'd been responsible for the accidents? Nothing linked her to the events except the fact that she survived them all.

He was tall with wavy black hair and wore a dark leather jacket with a fleece collar. There was a relaxed intensity to his body. It reminded her of the way a cat acted when it was pretending not to watch its prey.

He looked up at her from his phone. Alley's heart raced. She tried to find something to focus on inside the shop.

Her coworker, Brent, tilted his head towards the windows

as he wiped steamed milk off the spout of the espresso machine. "Should I call the cops?"

Alley stared at the cash register. What had she been doing before her mind wandered? "Not yet."

"He's bothering you."

"I'm fine." She lied.

Brent fit a plastic lid on a drink and handed it to a customer at the end of the counter. He shuffled over to Alley. Spatters of milk and coffee stained his green apron. He crossed his thick tattooed arms and stared out the window. "I can get rid of him."

Alley rolled her eyes but offered him a smile. "When I need a bodyguard, I'll call you."

A headache clawed at the sides of her skull. The coffee on the bus ride into work wasn't enough anymore. She pressed her hands on the cold counter to steady herself. The flesh toned polish that hid her nails had chipped off in a few places. Most people wouldn't notice the odd maze-like pattern that darkened them or would assume it was decoration—if only that were true.

The morning rush of customers had thinned out. The coffee shop was now full of people on laptops sipping at their drinks. Some were drawn together around tiny circular tables. Soft jazz filled the gaps in their murmurs. Alley knew many of them. The regulars. Working in the café was like having her finger on the pulse of the city. It made her feel connected. More than anything, it made her feel normal.

Brent called to her as he cleaned one of the blenders. "How's your biology paper going?"

Alley grabbed a bag of coffee beans and pulled at the top of the sealed package. "Good. Research is done, and I've got the first draft. Still needs work though."

"Cool. Cool. So, there's a party this weekend at Jack's place. You want to go? My band will be playing."

Alley had gone to one of their practice sessions a month ago. Brent played guitar and sang backup vocals. He was good. Really good. The kind of good that made you wonder why he was working four days a week at a coffee shop. The rest of the band was okay, but Brent's guitar playing was magic.

She pulled harder on the bag of coffee. It was refusing to open. Then it ripped. Beans spilled across the counter and out onto the floor. Heat rushed to Alley's face as people in the café looked up from their screens.

Brent dried his hands and retrieved a broom and dust-pan. "Let me help you."

"Thanks," she sighed as she dragged a waste basket over to the mess and swept beans off the counter into the trash. "I'd love to hear you play again, but I can't—"

Brent bobbed his head as he swept. "—Yeah. No problem. I figured."

Alley touched his arm. "It's my dad. You know—"

"Yeah, no, it's cool. Family first. I respect that." He ran his fingers through his sandy hair and carried the dustpan to the garbage.

Alley reached for another bag of coffee and pulled at the top. This one opened without incident. She poured it into the espresso machine's hopper.

This was the fifth time that Brent had asked her to one of his band's gigs. It was obvious he was interested in being more than friends. There wasn't anything wrong with that. She liked talking to him—liked working with him, but her life was complicated in ways that made relationships difficult. Her schedule was packed between her job, classes and caring for her father. But it was the other stuff that made it really hard. The things she couldn't open up about.

Brent put away the broom and rejoined her by the counter. "So, if a party is out of the question, how about a cup of coffee?"

Her head was still throbbing. Coffee was probably a good idea. "Sure."

He reached for two paper cups and shook them with a grin. "What'll it be?"

"Espresso." It got rid of the headaches faster than drip coffee.

"Coming right up!" He pulled shots of espresso into the cups and gave one to her.

Alley's hand shook as she took the drink. A stab of pain lanced through her head. Her cup dropped to the floor. She squeezed her eyes shut and pressed her thumbs into her temples. She hadn't had an episode in over a year. Not since the last accident. Alley squinted at the digital clock above the carafes. Three hours. It normally took at least seven before the effects of her morning coffee started to wear off.

Alley felt Brent's hand on her elbow. "Are you okay?"

She didn't know whether to nod or shake her head. Usually, she could regain control, but it could get worse. Much worse.

"Can I get you something?" he asked.

Alley gritted her teeth. "Coffee. I need more coffee."

Squinting, she glimpsed wispy, golden ribbons of power leaking from her head. They poured out of her in surges that coincided with the stabs of pain. The energy was invisible to everyone else, but that didn't make it less deadly. The snack displays on the counter rattled. A stack of cups beside the register toppled to the ground. The beans in the hopper danced and skittered like kernels of corn popping. Alley pushed on her temples harder. An image exploded in her mind.

She was standing on the peak of a wind-swept mountain covered in snow at the edge of a dark precipice. It was night, but moonlight made the snow sparkle. Orange embers drifted up from the blackness carrying the smell of sulfur. A voice echoed from below. "Join me, child."

"Alley, drink this!" Brent's voice pulled her back.

She grabbed the offered cup and gulped it down. The

bitter liquid burned her throat. It hit her stomach. The pain melted away and the rattling in the café subsided.

Alley rubbed at her face. Only Brent seemed to have noticed the episode. Espresso was spreading into a wide puddle around the fallen cups at her feet.

Brent's face was lined with worry. "Are you okay?"

"Yeah, I'm fine now. Thanks."

"Does that happen a lot?"

If only he knew. "It's nothing."

Brent looked down at the cups. "Right. Look, whatever it is, you can trust me."

"There's nothing to say. I get migraines sometimes. Coffee helps. End of story." But the hallucination was new. And it had been so vivid.

Brent lowered his voice. "Migraines don't make things fall off counters."

"It was probably just a tremor." He didn't look convinced.

Alley swallowed.

Brent bent over and tossed cups into the recycle bin. "Look, if you want to head out early today, I'll cover for you."

She grabbed some paper towels and crouched down beside him. Maybe it was a lack of sleep—the research paper had been keeping her up late. "Thanks. It probably wouldn't hurt for me to lie down." Why did he have to be so nice? It would be easier if he were a jerk. Someone she could push out of her life without feeling guilty. But he wasn't. She hated and appreciated him for it.

Alley pressed the towels into the brown puddle. "You know on second thought, if I can wrap things up with my dad early on Saturday, maybe I can meet you at Jack's."

Brent smiled. He stood and tossed the last of the cups into the bin. "I'll make sure you have the best night of your life!"

She smiled back. "I'll hold you to that."

"I'm serious about covering for you. Get out of here and get some rest."

Alley looked around the café one last time, then glanced out the front windows.

Her stalker was gone.

Alley felt someone watching as she pushed through the front doors of the coffee shop and out into the cold air. The Seattle morning commuters usually thinned out by noon, but Westlake Plaza was still bustling with tourists fresh off the monorail. She looked back, expecting to see the stalker following, but the street was just a blur of unfamiliar faces. Alley hitched her backpack higher onto her shoulder and walked faster down the street. Her phone said it was almost 10:00. If she hurried, she might catch the next bus.

The stop was a block and a half away. As she moved further from the plaza, the crowded sidewalk thinned out. Her auburn ponytail bounced in time with the pace of her footsteps. A chill October wind blew up the street, blasting her in the face.

Someone's gaze was burning a hole in her spine. Half an empty block back, a man in a red hooded sweatshirt was following her. It wasn't the guy who had been watching her the past few days. This was someone new.

He met her gaze.

Alley swallowed. There was something unnatural about his eyes.

She ran.

Up ahead, a line was forming for the bus.

The sidewalk pounded against her feet. She glanced back. The man in the sweatshirt was in pursuit.

Alley faced forward just in time to glimpse a person stepping into her path as she slammed into them. An old man in a tweed trench-coat.

He caught her arm, saving her from falling. "Is everything okay, Miss Ward?"

Alley's lungs burned. The stalker in the red sweatshirt was going to catch up. She turned, but couldn't see him. Alley scanned up and down the street. He had vanished.

"Miss Ward?"

She faced the old man. He peered at her over the wire rims of spectacles perched on the end of a pointed nose. He was thin with short white hair and piercing gray eyes.

Alley struggled to catch her breath. "Sorry—who are you?"

He smiled as he reached into his coat and withdrew a business card. "My name is Leopold Rakman. I'm a colleague of your father, Benjamin Ward."

Alley took the card. It was black with *Rakman & Associates* printed in silver lettering. The office address was in the Columbia Center. Alley looked up. "I'll tell him we met."

The bus arrived at the stop. There was still no sign of the man in the red sweatshirt.

"Please do. And if it's not too much trouble, will you deliver a message for me? Tell him, the Council can't wait any longer. We're taking matters into our own hands. He'll understand what that means."

"Okay." Cryptic, but whatever. The vehicle doors opened. "I'm sorry—I have to catch this bus." Alley pocketed the card and glanced up and down the street again as other passengers boarded.

Rakman pushed his spectacles up the bridge of his narrow nose. "It was a pleasure bumping into you, Miss Ward. I look forward to our paths crossing again."

She smiled and nodded. "Yeah, sorry about that. I'll deliver the message."

He waved with a gloved hand as she ran towards the bus. The doors started to shut. Alley jammed her foot into the narrowing gap.

The driver frowned as the doors hissed back open. "Next time, get here earlier."

Alley nodded as they clamped shut behind her. She

grabbed at the metal railing overhead and made her way to an empty seat in the back as the bus pulled away. Out the window, the old man receded into the distance. Something about his presence had spooked the stalker. She swung her pack off her shoulder, sank into one of the blue seats and wiped moisture off her brow with a sleeve.

Alley pulled out the black business card. *Leopold Rakman.* She felt bad about almost knocking him down. She'd never met anyone that worked with her father. Dad was secretive about the classified projects in his lab. A few times each month, a shuttle would arrive to take him there for the day. She could remember going as a small child, but hadn't been back in a long time. He said it was for her safety—that she'd already been effected enough by the place.

The bus was mostly empty. Alley unzipped her pack and put on her earbuds. A song with a mix of classical violin and electric baseline streamed out of her phone. She leaned her head against the seat and closed her eyes. Her mind drifted.

Cold. Nighttime. Moonlight glinting off fresh snow. Glowing embers. She was standing at the edge of the dark precipice again. Heat and the smell of sulfur wafted upward as a gust of wind blew her hair away from her face.

The silky female voice she'd heard before came from the dark. "Join me, child."

Alley squinted, trying to see what lay in the blackness. Two glowing lavender orbs appeared. They blinked. Eyes. Enormous eyes. Alley swallowed and tried to step back. Her feet were encased in ice.

"There is nowhere you can hide from me."

A high-pitched chime sounded in her ear. Someone had sent her a text message. Alley's heart raced. Her forehead felt damp. She could still feel the cold grip of ice around her ankles. The bus was on the 520-bridge crossing Lake Washington. Back to the Eastside. To Redmond. To home. She took a deep breath and slowly let it out. The sky was clear. Across the lake, Mt. Rainier's massive peak rose to the south. Every time she saw it, the mountain seemed bigger than she remembered. She rubbed her eyes and tapped the message on the phone.

It was from Elek. "*Hey Al. Back in town. Want to hang?*"

Alley couldn't help but smile. She typed a reply and hit send. "*Been a while. Where you been?*"

A moment later Elek replied. "*Long story. You know me.*"

Alley smirked and tapped a response. "*Thought you found a new best friend.*"

"Tried. Failed. Guess you'll have to do."

She stifled a laugh as she typed. "*Your failure pleases me.*"

A new message appeared. "*LOL. So you interested in catching up?*"

She did, but she needed to rest. She sighed as she responded. "*Been a rough day. U going to be around long?*"

His answer came a few seconds later. "*A bit.*"

"Got time tomorrow night?"

He answered. "*Yeah, I should be around.*"

She smiled. "*See you then.*"

Alley clicked on her photo album and scrolled back through a year's worth of pictures. She tapped the first one she saw of Elek. She'd taken it the day they graduated from high school. His green gown and cap were in a pile on the stone wall beside him. He was wearing a gray shirt and black jeans. His lanky arms were crossed. His dark eyes peered at the camera through a mop of tousled black hair. Elek was the closest thing she had to a brother.

What had he been up to for the last year and a half? She swiped through a few more pictures. Shots of them hiking in the Olympics, a bonfire on a wide flat beach roasting marshmallows. Skiing. Covered in scrapes from a wipe-out on a mountain bike. A shot of him swimming after an oar. They'd had some good times growing up, but they'd lost touch over the last year. She'd gotten busy with classes and work. He'd started a night job that meant he was sleeping whenever she was awake. They still sent texts, but it wasn't like the old days. It would be good to see Elek again.

Alley pushed the power button on the side of the phone as the bus pulled into the Redmond Transit Center. She got off and boarded the second bus. Fifteen minutes later, she was walking up the tree-lined street to her house. A nap would be good. Hopefully one free of dreams.

Autumn was turning the trees to shades of flame. As Alley approached the house, fallen leaves skittered across the cracked concrete of the driveway. Moss grew on the roof of the porch. The white paint on the clapboards was peeling.

And the front door hung open.

Alley swallowed. Her tongue was dry. Was her father okay? She ran up the creaky porch steps and entered the house.

Inside was silent except for the ticking of a clock in the living room.

"Dad?"

No answer.

Her pulse quickened. Alley dropped her backpack, shut the front door, and moved down the hallway to the back of the house. The door to his study was closed. She tried turning the handle. It was locked from the inside. She rapped her knuckles on the polished wood. "Dad?"

No answer.

She rattled the knob and pounded on the door with her fist. "Dad! Are you in there?"

Still no answer.

Alley ran into the kitchen, opened the cabinet under the sink and pulled out a rusted red toolbox. The lid squeaked as it flopped backward. Tools clattered against each other as she searched for the crowbar. She lifted the heavy iron rod out of the box and ran back to the study.

The flat head of the bar fit into the edge of the door frame near the locking mechanism. How much force would be needed to break through the lock? Alley's heart pounded.

Suddenly, the knob to the study turned, and the door swung inward. Alley dropped the crowbar.

"You're home early!" Her father was seated in his wheelchair. His thinning white hair stuck out at odd angles. His blue eyes were bright and peered at her through glasses that enlarged the wrinkles around his eyes. He pulled a pair of headphones off, wrapped them around his neck and ran his finger and thumb along his white handlebar mustache.

Alley bent down and hugged him. Her cheeks felt wet.

He wrapped his arms around her, his voice was quiet. "What's wrong?"

Alley let go and stood, brushing the tears away. She forced a smile onto her face. "You weren't answering. I thought—"

A lump formed in her throat. She looked away blinking.

Her father's warm hand rested on hers. "I'm sorry, Buttercup. I didn't hear you. You usually aren't home so early. Is everything alright?"

"I had a headache. Took the rest of the day off."

The lines deepened between his eyebrows. "Must have been a bad one."

Alley chewed her lip. "Yeah—it was one of those. I'm okay now."

He squinted at her, then turned his wheelchair and moved back into the study. She followed. The room was lined floor to ceiling with dark polished wood shelves packed with books. Some were old leather-bound tomes, cracked and falling apart, others were newer volumes on science, math, biology, politics and other subjects. Wedged between the books were odd knickknacks. At the back of the room was a workbench strewn with scientific equipment and electronic parts.

Her dad wheeled himself behind a giant oak desk in the center of the study where more books and papers were piled around a flat computer monitor. "Was anyone hurt?"

Alley shook her head and tried to block out the mental images from the last time it had gotten out of control. Her father rubbed a hand across his forehead. She could feel a lecture coming.

"Have you considered increasing your coffee dose?"

Alley raised an eyebrow. "Dad."

"I just want you to be happy—happy and safe."

She walked around the desk and hugged him. "You don't need to worry. I can handle this."

He smiled with sad eyes. "Your mother used to tell me that."

Alley glanced at the framed photo of her mom on the desk. They had the same auburn hair. The same amber eyes. Twelve years she'd been gone. The explosion at her parent's research lab had almost claimed both of them. Almost. She stared at her reflection in the polished chrome of her Dad's wheelchair. The accident hadn't just taken her mom and maimed her father. It had destroyed her mother's research notes.

Alley straightened. "I wish Mom had told you more." It was hard to believe that they'd worked in the same lab and her father had so little understanding of her mother's work. Her dad only knew that Alley had accidentally been exposed to something and her mom had been trying to find a way to reverse her condition. At least he'd known enough about her mother's findings to suggest that coffee could dampen the effects.

He looked away. "Me too."

Alley fished the business card out of her pocket. "I met someone you work with—Leopold Rakman?"

Her father reached for the card with a shaky hand.

"He asked me to deliver a message."

Her father's thumb rubbed across the silver foil letters on the card. When he spoke, his voice was low. "What did he say?"

"Something about the Council taking matters into their own hands?"

"Did he say when?"

"No, that was it. I feel bad. I literally ran into him."

Her father placed the card on the desk. He massaged his hand between his thumb and forefinger.

Alley picked up a small stone statue, engraved with detailed patterns. "Does he know about me?"

Her dad nodded. "He knows enough. You can trust him."

"Then why do you look so concerned?"

"It's probably nothing."

She put down the statue. "Should I be worried?"

"I have to make a few calls. We can talk later."

"You sure?"

He touched her arm. "You should get some rest, Buttercup. I love you."

"I love you too, Dad." What wasn't he telling her? She walked into the hall and bent down to pick up the crowbar. "Holler if you need anything."

He nodded as he picked up his phone.

Alley moved back into the kitchen and put away the tools. The message had rattled him so much that she hadn't had a chance to talk about the stalker. Or the dreams.

A pot of coffee from earlier in the morning was warming on the coffee maker hot plate. She pulled a mug out of the cabinet, filled it with the dark liquid and carried it upstairs to her bedroom.

Afternoon sun poured in through the window spilling across her desk and bed. Alley took a big sip of coffee and set the mug down on the night table. It tasted burned. She sat down on the edge of the bed and kicked off her shoes. What a crazy day. Her research books were stacked on the desk next to her laptop. Her biology project was almost done, but she couldn't focus on it right now. The morning had been so stressful. It had been a long time since she'd had an episode. It could have been bad.

Her scrapbook rested on the corner of the desk. She picked it up and set it in her lap. The cover said, *"Never Forget..."*

She opened to the first page. A photocopy of an old newspaper clipping lay beneath a thin layer of plastic. The headline read, *"Child lone survivor in highway bridge collapse."* She brushed her finger across the words. *I'm sorry.* Her chest ached.

She turned the page to another newspaper clipping. *"Bus crushed in rock-slide, students survive with minor injuries."* She felt her eyes watering. *I'm so sorry.*

She flipped past a dozen more pages to the clipping on the last page. *"Prom night turns deadly."* She skimmed the familiar report. *"—the bodies of the three students were found in the debris. It's not certain at this time what caused the collapse of the east hallway. Investigators will be examining the rest of the school over the weekend to determine if it is safe for students to return to classes next week—"*

A tear splashed on the plastic page of the scrapbook. Alley wiped at her face, then reached for the coffee mug and took a huge gulp. She couldn't lose control again. She'd start doubling her coffee intake. Whatever it took.

Alley closed the scrapbook and put it back on the desk. Someday she'd find a way to make-up for all the harm she had caused. To help people instead of—she shook her head. One step at a time. She had to complete her pre-med courses, and right now that meant finishing her research paper.

But first, her chipped nail polish needed fixing. It kept people from asking questions she didn't know the answers to.

Alley opened the drawer to her nightstand, pulled out a bottle of pink polish and shook it. She twisted the cap off, brushed a coat onto each of her fingers and blew on them gently until they were dry. Better. Alley closed the bottle and pulled her hair out of its ponytail. She flopped back onto her pillow. Nap time. Brent was a lifesaver. She owed him one.

Her eyes slid shut.

Cold wind clawed at her hair and clothes. Alley clutched her arms tight across her body. The snow was up to her knees. The moon shined high overhead, painting the mountainside in silvery light. Ahead a ridge rose, black against the night sky. Hundreds of dark forms moved towards her down the slopes.

Alley felt her stomach twist into a knot. She turned and started running. Air from her lungs formed cold clouds of vapor as she high stepped through the thick snow. Alley glanced back over her shoulder. Some of the things had reached the base of the mountain and were bounding through the drifts. She couldn't see what they were, just a mass of darkness thrashing against the shimmering white.

Ahead, the snow thinned and gave way to jagged rocks and gravel ending at a small peak. Alley ran up the slope. Her thighs and lungs were burning. Loose stones slipped beneath her feet. She stumbled forward, pushing herself upward. Alley turned as she reached the summit. The small peak was surrounded by snowy slopes. From every direction came a swarming mass of scaly black bodies.

She was trapped.

A deep female voice echoed across the valley. "I am coming for you."

The creatures crawled over one another in their haste. Alley clenched her hands into fists. They reached the bottom of the slope and made their way upwards. All she could see were their eyes, hundreds of eyes the color of jewels. And then their claws. Teeth. Dark Scales. Her heart thundered inside her chest.

The monsters leaped towards her.

Beep! Beep! Beep!

The sound of her bedside alarm clock brought her back. Alley turned it off and rubbed at her face. She squinted at the digital display. Four in the morning. An hour to catch the bus to work. Ugh. She hadn't planned on sleeping that long. Alley swung her legs onto the floor. Her body proceeded on auto-pilot going through her morning routine of showering, dressing and wandering downstairs.

The smell of freshly brewed coffee filled the kitchen. Dad was awake and had pulled his wheelchair up to the round breakfast table.

"Good morning, Buttercup!"

"Mmmm." She nodded at him as she shuffled towards the coffee pot. Alley grabbed a mug and filled it.

"You slept right through dinner. I thought you'd be starving." He gestured towards the stove. "I made pancakes and eggs. Your favorite!"

Alley set her mug down, pulled on an oven mitt and opened the door to the stove. Inside a plate of pancakes and scrambled eggs was warming. "Thanks, Dad." She brought it over to the table, then returned to the counter to retrieve her coffee and a fork. She came back and sat down across from him.

"I made some calls while you were sleeping. We need to talk this evening. There's some people I need to introduce to you."

Alley nodded her head as she chewed on a mouthful of eggs, then stopped. She'd told Elek she'd have time to catch up with him tonight. She swallowed. "Elek is back in town. I said I'd be around this evening."

Her father frowned. "It's not something I can put off any longer. Elek will understand."

Alley took a big gulp of coffee. "Okay. I'll let him know I'll be late." She cut into the stack of pancakes with the side of her fork and pushed a chunk into her mouth.

Her dad shifted in his seat and adjusted his glasses. "Is everything okay? You slept a long time."

Alley took a sip of coffee and checked the wall clock in

the kitchen. Fifteen minutes to catch the bus. "I had a strange dream."

Her father steepled his fingers. "Would you tell me about it?"

"Standard nightmare stuff. I was being chased by monsters."

Her father leaned in. "What else do you remember?"

Alley pushed the eggs around on her plate. "It was snowing, and there was a voice."

"What did it say?"

"That it was coming for me."

Her dad started massaging his hand. "You should call in sick."

"I feel fine." Why was he stressing about a dream?

"Please. It would give us a chance to talk."

Alley got up from the table. "I'd love to Dad, but Brent covered for me yesterday. We'll talk tonight. I promise."

He sighed. "Be careful."

Alley gave him a hug. "I'm careful every day." He still looked stressed, but she was going to miss the bus. She poured the rest of her coffee into a travel mug, grabbed her backpack and headed down the hallway towards the front door.

Her dad blew her a kiss. "I love you, Buttercup."

She caught it and blew one back. "I love you too."

Alley stepped off the bus onto 5th and Pine. The gray sky brightened as the morning sun tried to burn through the clouds. Commuters bundled in fall jackets and scarves rushed to work. Everyone seemed to be going somewhere, and there was no sign of her stalker. Dry leaves crunched under her sneakers as she walked along the red, black and gray bricks of the plaza. The plate-glass walls of the single-story coffee shop sat ahead on the corner of the block. She walked faster, reached the front doors of the building and yanked them open. Heat and the aroma of fresh coffee washed over her.

There were a few people inside ordering. Brent waved at her from behind the counter. He smiled as she came around to join him.

"Morning, Alley!"

How was he always so cheerful? She forced a smile on her face and glanced out the windows of the store. No stalker. Alley entered the prep room, dropped her bag and jacket in a locker, pulled a green apron over her head and tied it behind her back. Maybe everything would be back to normal today.

"Tall medium roast for Gwen." Brent handed Alley a paper coffee cup. "So, you feeling better today?"

"Yeah, a bit. Thanks for yesterday."

"Oh yeah, it was no problem." He lowered his voice. "I'm here if you ever want to talk about—you know—*stuff*."

She'd hoped Brent wouldn't mention the episode. "Thanks." Her voice came out flat.

Brent's face flushed. He seemed to sense that he had crossed a line. "So anyway—tomorrow night is going to be awesome!"

Alley glanced out the window. "Yeah, I'm looking forward to it."

Brent followed her gaze. "He's a no-show today."

Alley nodded, then turned to him. "Can I ask you a favor?"

"Anything."

"Would you mind walking me to the bus stop at the end of my shift?"

Brent's eyebrows raised. "Of course." He crossed his arms and squinted at her. "Is everything okay?"

She swallowed. "There was this guy in a red sweatshirt yesterday. He chased me down 4th street. Freaked me out."

Alley could see the muscles in Brent's forearm flex. His eyes swept across the store and out through the walls of plate-glass. "Thanks for telling me. I'll make sure no one bothers you."

A group of people came in through one of the sets of doors. Alley smoothed her apron. She felt a little relief knowing that Brent would be watching her back. "I'll take orders for a bit."

Brent nodded. "Cool."

Alley smiled as she took the first guests' order. She handed cups to Brent and heated up baked goods. The line grew as more people entered the café. Alley stole glances out the windows. No one was watching her, but her head was starting to ache. She should have more coffee. No more episodes. When they got to the end of this group, she'd pour herself a cup. Alley counted the people in line. Some faces were familiar, people she knew by name. Others were first-timers. The last person—Alley's heart skipped a beat. It was him—the guy that had been watching her the last few days. He was wearing the same dark leather jacket.

He smiled.

Alley realized her mouth was hanging open and clamped it shut. What was he doing in here?

She looked at the next person in line. "What can I get for you?"

Alley half listened to the reply, jotting the order on the side of a cup. Should she ask him why he'd been staring at her? Was he dangerous?

Alley took the orders of the next few people in front of him. Sweat trickled down her spine. He moved up to the counter. He smelled like cedar and rosemary.

Her hands were shaking. She clasped them together. "What can I—"

Before she could finish, he placed a folded piece of brown paper on the counter, turned and walked out of the café. Written in the center of the scrap in black flowing ink were six words:

You are in danger. Leave now.

She read it again. Her heart was beating. Should she call the police?

"Alley, everything okay?" Brent was at her side. "Was that who I think it was?"

"Yeah, he gave me this." She handed him the paper.

What kind of danger was she in? She looked around the shop. There were the regulars and a few new faces. No one looked dangerous. A movement in the back corner caught her eye. A guy sitting at one of the small tables. Bald, with pale skin and a dark goatee. He was watching her.

Brent saw where she was looking. "You think we need to worry about him?"

"I'm not sure—maybe."

The next person in line moved forward, blocking her view.

"Could I please have a tall, dark-roast." It was a short elderly woman with bifocals. Her white hair was tied up in a bun, and she wore a blue shawl around her shoulders.

Alley picked up a cup. "Room for cream?"

The elderly woman shook her head. It swiveled oddly, moving too fast and then slowing too quickly.

Alley blinked and rubbed at the bridge of her nose. "Sorry, was that a no?"

"That's right, dear."

Alley punched in the order. "That's a dollar fifty."

The woman reached into her purse and placed two bills on the counter. Her fingernails were long, black and splintered. Alley tried not to stare. The words on the crumpled paper screamed in her head.

You are in danger. Leave now.

Brent set the coffee on the counter.

As Alley reached to take the bills, the old woman's hand shot out and grabbed her wrist. It was like a vice. Tight, painful. She tried to pull her arm back, but the woman was too strong. Her head started to throb. *Not now!* She'd had coffee this morning. It was too soon for the effects to have worn off.

Alley gritted her teeth. "Let go!"

You must come with me. The sound of the woman's voice echoed in her head, but her lips weren't moving.

Brent grabbed the woman's arm. "Take your hand off her."

A growl rumbled in the old woman's throat. It made a spike of adrenaline surged through Alley's veins. The sound wasn't human. It was like a lion—or something worse. The old woman reached across the counter with her other hand and shoved Brent. He flew as if he'd been hit by a car, slammed into the back wall and collapsed to the floor.

The shop erupted into chaos. People yelled and ran towards the glass doors.

Brent!

He wasn't moving. Alley had to help him.

There was a metal stand holding a display of mints and candies beside the register. Alley grabbed it with her free hand and smashed it against the old woman's arm. The lady's face contorted into a snarl. Her lips peeled back to reveal sharp black teeth. Alley's heart raced. The woman yanked the stand from Alley's hand and flung it across the shop.

Alley felt her feet leave the floor as she was dragged across the counter. Her body knocked over the coffee cup. The hot liquid soaked into her shirt, burning the skin on her stomach.

A wave of dizziness washed over her. The room went out of focus. Energy leaked from her mind like a dam giving way to flood waters. Everything in the store began to rattle. Metal spoons beat a staccato rhythm against ceramic cups and saucers. Bags of coffee tumbled from shelves. The vibrations intensified as invisible tendrils of energy poured from her mind. A picture dislodged from the wall of the shop and smashed to the ground. Shards of glass skittered across the floor. The store windows fractured and cascaded onto the sidewalk. People in the street were shouting and screaming. Metal crunched as cars collided outside.

Alley's knee hit the floor as she was pulled off the counter. A stab of pain shot up her leg. The old woman was dragging her towards the shattered doors.

Golden ribbons of energy whipped and snapped outward. They tore at the steel beams overhead. Alley could feel the metal bending and tearing. Cracks formed in the ceiling, raining dust and plaster down.

Time seemed to slow as a support girder broke free from

the ceiling and swung downward. It crashed into the old woman. She let out a roar as she was knocked down and pinned beneath its weight. The skin on the woman's face peeled away revealing black scales. Alley recognized it—one of the monsters from her dream. It let go of Alley as it tried to push the enormous steel girder off its body. The beam didn't move. The creature howled in frustration. Its black teeth snapped at the air like an angry dog.

Alley scrambled away from the beast. Dust choked the air. The high-pitched hiss of escaping gas was coming from a nearby broken ceiling pipe. The sweet tang of it filled her nostrils.

She had to get Brent out of here.

Alley staggered around the counter. Brent lay where he had fallen. Blood flowed from his ears and nose. He was covered in a layer of debris. She knelt and touched his cheek. *Cold.*

No.

She pressed her finger to the inside of his hand.

Please don't be dead.

Seconds that felt like minutes slipped by. Nothing. Alley shifted her fingers and pressed again.

There was a weak pulse.

A tremor rocked the shop as more energy flowed from her body. A section of the ceiling on the other side of the counter collapsed sending a plume of dust toward them. Alley coughed as it filled her lungs. When the air cleared, a bundle of torn electrical wiring hung from the new hole in the ceiling.

She grabbed Brent under the armpits and tried to drag him. The muscles in her thighs and back burned as she strained to pull him across the floor. The smell of gas was getting stronger. The frayed ends of the exposed electrical wiring swayed back and forth in slow motion. She pulled harder. They had to get out. Another tendril of energy flowed out of Alley. It traveled into the ground, rocking the building. The torn wires swung wildly and brushed by one another. A tiny blue spark jumped between them.

No.

The inside of the shop exploded in a white-hot fireball.

Alley squeezed her eyes shut as a wave of searing heat blasted her skin. Every pore of her body screamed in pain. The oxygen was ripped from her lungs.

Darkness engulfed her mind.

2

MAGE LAW

NADJA

Nadja twirled the ornate knife in her hand. The runes etched into its surface emitted a soft green flickering glow. She tucked a stray lock of blond hair behind her ear as she walked around the man shackled to the iron chair. The seat was bolted to the floor. Old scorch marks blackened the concrete walls. High above, on the wall opposite the chair, stretched a long window. Behind the thick glass, twelve figures sat in shadow.

A voice echoed through speakers embedded in the ceiling. *"Why were you following the girl?"*

Sweat glistened on the man's bald, pale scalp. His dark goatee was streaked with flecks of gray hair. He wore jeans, a plaid shirt, and a sky-blue fall jacket. He was good at pretending to be human.

The man strained against the metal straps binding his wrists and ankles. “I broke none of your Mage Laws.”

Nadja stopped twirling the knife. Her abdomen tightened as she looked at the back of its head. She tried to keep her face calm. It was like standing next to a poisonous snake. A quick move and there would be one less of them to watch. The thought made her smile. Nadja pressed the tip of the blade against the creature’s cheek. The runes on the metal flared bright green. “Answer the question,” she said.

He tilted his head away from the knife and whispered. “Or what warden? You’ll kill me? Your masters up there won’t like that very much.”

Nadja gritted her teeth and looked up at the window.

The voice crackled over the speaker. *“Cooperate and you’ll be rewarded, if not, there will be—consequences.”*

Nadja dragged the blade across the man’s cheek. The green energy from the knife tip left a line of blisters along his skin. She whispered in his ear. “I don’t care what you do. Either way, we get something we want.”

The man’s back stiffened. He looked up at the window. “I told you. I was just having coffee. I wasn’t following anyone.”

“We know you are trying to organize a rebellion. Tell us who else is involved.”

“I don’t know what you are talking about!”

“Nadja, please help jog our guest’s memory.”

Nadja rolled her shoulders and felt her bones make a

satisfying crunch. Her thumb rubbed against the cold metal of the wedding band on her left hand. She tried to picture the faces of her husband and the girls before the attack, but all she could recall was the sight of their broken bodies in the yard when she'd come home, the house ablaze. Her fist clenched. They were gone. She couldn't bring them back, but she could make this one pay. Nadja held the knife in front of the thing's face and turned it. The gleam of the ceiling lights danced across its surface.

"This is a *scryth*—it means 'Truthseer' in ancient Elvish. It was forged in your world of a rare metal and etched with a pixie dust infused weave, toxic to your kind."

The creature turned his head toward her. "I'm not part of any rebellion."

"No?"

Nadja moved her arm in a practiced blur of motion. The blade tip arced downward and pricked the skin on the back of the man's hand. He roared and thrashed against the restraints. The skin around the knife point turned to ash and flaked away revealing glossy black scales. The edges of the scryth crackled with a green fire.

"Get it away from me!" he yelled.

Nadja twisted the tip of the blade against his scales. They glowed orange where the point pressed against them. A thin line of smoke curled upward. Nadja whispered into the thing's ear again. "If it breaks through your scales, it will cause a chain reaction. You'll burn from the inside out. It won't be pleasant."

The man gritted his teeth. "She told us to watch the girl. I did nothing! I hurt no one!"

Nadja pressed harder on the scryth, turning the scales to ash. The man thrashed against the chair. His face contorted and transformed. Dark black nails burst from the ends of his fingertips. He roared in a rage, black fangs sprouting from his open mouth.

The overhead speakers crackled to life. *"Who told you to watch the girl? Srira?"*

The creature thrashed in the chair. "You are not worthy to speak the Queen's name, mage!"

"What interest does your queen have in the girl?"

The creature roared. Its voice sounded distorted. Not human. "Make the warden stop!"

"Will you answer our questions?"

"Yes! Just make her stop!"

Behind the window, the shadowy figure in the center nodded at Nadja. She withdrew the blade. The creature whipped its head to the side and glared at her. Black horns had pushed through the pale skin along its cheekbones and brows. Its eyes had turned golden yellow. Nadja stepped behind the chair.

"Why did Srira have you follow the girl?"

The creature stared at the floor. "She said the girl is the key."

"The key to what?"

It pressed its lips closed.

Nadja crossed her arms. Her dark olive riding jacket pulled tight across her shoulders. "Answer their question."

"The Queen did not tell us."

The speaker crackled. *"We don't believe you."*

The thing strained against its bonds. "There's no more to tell."

The room was quiet. Nadja looked up at the window. The shadowy figures were in discussion behind the sound proof glass.

The creature shook its head. It looked at the ceiling, tears rolled down its face. It closed its eyes and nodded as it muttered to itself. There were rumors they could telepathically communicate. Was this one talking to one of its kind?

The creature took a deep breath. Its yellow eyes snapped open. Its lips peeled back revealing the jagged zigzag of dark fangs. "I was there."

Nadja furrowed her brow. "What are you talking about?"

"I watched your children fall from the sky."

The fingers of Nadja's right hand tightened around the handle of the scryth. Her left hand curled into a fist. Her wedding ring bit into her skin. She lunged forward and pressed the point of the blade against the thing's temple. "Don't talk about my family."

The voice crackled over the speakers. *"Nadja, step back."*

It whispered. “They screamed for you to help them when they were falling.”

Nadja’s hand trembled. Her face flushed with heat. She clenched her teeth. This thing had been there. It had helped kill them. She felt her eyes getting wet.

“Nadja, step away from the prisoner!”

It laughed. “They bounced when they hit the ground.”

Nadja’s mind went blank. Her muscles tensed. She slammed the knife into the side of the creature’s skull. A ring of green fire exploded outward from the scryth. Flames swept through the thing’s body, hissing and sputtering as it turned flesh to ash. Its clothes collapsed, kicking up a cloud of dust. The glow from the blade faded, then disappeared.

Nadja sheathed the weapon beneath her jacket and rubbed her palms on her black denim jeans. That had been counter-productive. Unprofessional. She looked up at the window. “He confessed to taking part in killing humans. A clear violation of our Laws.”

“Under the circumstances, a delay in execution would have been prudent, warden. He had more to tell us.”

She stared at the pile of ash and clothes in the chair. Good riddance.

“Control your emotions if you wish to continue serving the Council.”

“It won’t happen again.” Probably a lie.

“See that it doesn’t.”

She held her fist to her chest. It showed respect she didn't feel. "Thank you."

The mage nodded. *"Rejoin your partner and protect the girl. Her power is great, but wild and untrained."*

"Can she help us?"

"She shows great promise, but if you think she is planning to betray us—do not let her live."

3

SECRETS

ALLEY

The darkness lifted.

Alley was lying on a soft surface—it smelled familiar. Something squeaked nearby—her father's wheelchair.

"Dad?" Alley rubbed her eyes. She was in her bedroom.

Her father rolled up to the edge of her covers. An old leather-bound tome rested in his lap. "I'm sorry to wake you, Buttercup." He brushed a lock of hair away from her face.

"What happened? How did I get here?"

"You were rescued. You've been unconscious all afternoon."

She sat up, wide-eyed. "What happened to Brent?!"

Her dad clasped his hands around hers. His palms were warm. "Was he at work with you?"

She nodded. "He was knocked unconscious by something"—her hand gripped his—"It was a woman, but she turned into something horrible, a monster. I tried to save him, but there was an explosion."

He looked away. "Alley, you were the only survivor. I'm sorry."

Her hand trembled. She should have paid attention to the stalker's warning—should have left the café when she'd had the chance. "He's gone?"

Her dad nodded. Brent was dead. Alley pulled her hand away and covered her face. Her shoulders shook as a sob escaped her throat. Tears poured down her cheeks. Her father reached forward and wrapped his arms around her. She buried her face in the crook of his shoulder. Brent was dead and there was nothing she could do about it. Her condition had caused the building collapse—had caused the explosion.

"He's dead because of me!" Her muffled voice sobbed into his shoulder.

"It wasn't your fault, Alley."

She pushed away. "You know that's not true. It's just like the other times. This energy inside me—it destroys things. It hurts people."

"I know, but it's not your fault."

She paused, looking at him. "How can you say that?"

"Because it's my fault."

"That's crazy." He'd had nothing to do with any of the

accidents. She wiped the tears from her face.

Her father shook his head. "It's my fault because I should have helped you a long time ago."

"You tried. If you hadn't known that coffee would help, I might have hurt more people." She fought down the lump forming in her throat. If she'd had a few shots of espresso, the café might still be standing. Brent might still be alive.

"There's more I should have told you." He touched her cheek. "I wanted you to have a normal childhood. After the accident at the lab—losing your mother. I became such a burden to you—"

"You've never been a burden."

He shook his head, then peered at her over his bifocals. "You spent the last nine years of your childhood caring for me. I never wanted it to be this way. I had planned to help you understand your ability. The years just slipped by—I didn't want to take any more of your childhood away than you'd already sacrificed."

What was he talking about? "What else do you know about my condition?"

Her dad pressed his lips together. "I was afraid—afraid of what revealing the truth would mean for you."

"What truth? Do you know what's wrong with me? How to stop it?" She leaned forward. Her heart was racing. The swirl of emotions was almost too much. The loss of her friend made her chest ache, but now a wave of hope swept through her body.

He looked down at the old leather book in his lap. "I have to tell you something, but before I do, I want you to know how much I love you. You have been, and always will be, the very best thing that has ever happened to me. I'm so proud of the woman you have become—so honored to have been able to raise you."

Wrinkles formed between her brows. "What is it?"

He stared at his lap. "—it isn't easy for me."

He wouldn't look at her. Why? What was he so afraid to tell her?

"What do you remember about your mother?" There was sadness in his eyes.

"Lots. I remember her laugh—the way she smiled. Her stories. The warmth of sitting in her lap." She remembered her parents dancing in the living room. How happy and carefree her dad had been back then. She squeezed his hand.

Her dad smiled. "She did tell the best stories"—his face went still—"but there's one story neither of us shared with you. The story of your birth."

Alley's gaze drifted to the framed photo of her parents on the bedside table. "What story?" Dread filled her heart. Something about the fear in his eyes almost made her not want to know the answer.

Her dad bowed his head and took a deep breath. "Alley, you are something special—unique in this world. You are so special that we were afraid of what you would become if we told you the truth before you were ready."

"What truth?" Her pulse pounded in her ears.

"Your mother and I were not able to have children. Nineteen years ago, we had an opportunity. We were assigned to a highly classified research program. We had access to equipment and resources beyond imagination. It allowed us to do something we never thought would be possible. To fuse our genetic code and conceive a child—you."

"I was grown in a lab?" The idea was revolting. It made her feel like a freak. Alley pulled her arms into her body and hugged herself.

"Not exactly. You were born naturally, but your abilities were not an accident. They were engineered. They were the goal of the program." He touched her arm.

Engineered. Her fists clenched. She glared at her dad. "You did this to me? Why?" Anger surged through her veins. Her father had been right. Brent's death—the other accidents —they had all been her parent's fault.

"We could never have moved forward if we weren't also pursuing the project goals."

"What goals? To cause disasters? Kill people?"

"Your abilities are meant to protect, not to harm."

"Well you messed that up!" Images of the accidents she'd caused flashed through her head. She could still feel Brent's weak pulse against her finger tips. A lump formed in her throat.

"Alley, I'm sorry. I've been afraid to tell you for so long. I was a coward—afraid you would never forgive us—forgive me." His eyes were wet.

She stared at him. Sorrow and rage tore at her heart. He had lied. People had died because he hadn't helped her. Alley wasn't sure if she could forgive him. "Can you help me get rid of this—condition?"

"There may be a way."

She swallowed. "How?"

"Coffee. The same substance that controls it—if taken in a large enough dose—may cut you off from the power forever."

Alley covered her mouth. "Why didn't you tell me years ago?" She could be cured—live a completely normal life.

"That much coffee could also kill you. I already lost your mother—I couldn't lose you too, Alley." Tears flowed down his cheeks.

Was it worth risking her life to be free? What if she died trying? She looked in her father's eyes. This was her parent's fault. If her father loved her, then he would ensure the dosage wouldn't kill her. "You have to help cure me."

He wiped at his face. "I'll help, but only if you first understand what you are giving up."

Anger flared inside her again. What kind of game was he playing now? "I know what I'm giving up. I don't want to be responsible for anyone else's death."

He grabbed her arm. Fear filled his eyes. "That woman—that *monster*—that attacked you. Your ability is meant to protect the world from her kind—and worse. You need time to understand your power—how you can help the world—before you choose to abandon it."

Her anger evaporated, replaced by a cold icy fear gripping her chest. "You've seen something like that woman before?"

Her father nodded. "Everything is in your mother's journal. I hope once you've read it, you will be able to forgive me for not telling you these things years ago. I had planned for us to talk about this as I trained you. Some truths are easier to digest in small doses—now I must leave that to someone else."

He grasped the thick, worn book and set it on her lap. His hands were shaking.

She stared at the journal. "Why can't you just tell me now?"

The doorbell rang downstairs.

"There's no time, Alley. Just remember that where you come from does not define you—it's the choices you make."

Her brows furrowed. "But—"

"I need to get the door. Please get dressed and pack a bag. There are people downstairs who have come to take you someplace safe. You're in danger."

"From creatures like that woman?" Alley rubbed at her wrist remembering the old lady's iron grip.

Her dad nodded as he closed the door. "There are more like her hunting for you."

4

ESCAPE

ALLEY

Alley stared in shock at the closed door as the wheels of her father's chair squeaked down the hallway. The horrible dreams had become a waking nightmare.

Brent? *Dead.*

Her lip quivered.

Parents? *Liars.*

Her chest tightened.

Dangerous condition? *Could have been cured.*

Her fingers twisted the blanket as they balled into fists.

One more thing. *Monsters pretending to look like humans are hunting you. Maybe you should pack a bag.*

Alley smashed her face into her pillow and screamed. Why was this happening? Why now? She took a deep breath.

Her throat felt raw, but she felt better. Alley tossed the pillow aside.

The weight of her mother's journal pressed into her lap. She pulled up a stack of pages with her thumb and flipped through them. They were filled with notes, strange diagrams, and scientific notations. If the truth about her past was in there, the details were buried amongst years of research. She turned to a random page.

"April 12 —

Another long debate with Forester this morning. He wants to understand our methods so he can begin a parallel program. I enjoy his energy and passion, but if he continues to press on this, Ben and I will have to speak with the Council. For obvious reasons, we can't reveal our entire process. The political fallout would be immeasurable for Ben. I can't even contemplate what it would mean for our family.

We went hiking yesterday. Ben and I considered taking Alley to the Upper Caldrun (I thought she might have an interesting reaction to the place), but the trail had washed out. Perhaps another time.

The Council wants an additional report submitted next week. We sent them one last month. Don't they have their own projects to attend to? They should understand by now that moving too fast may damage natural development. Alley requires special care."

Special—because she had been created in a lab. They'd messed with her at a genetic level. They'd caused the strange patterns to form under her nails. They'd made her this way

—had intended for her to have this power, but given her no control over it. All for what? To protect the world from things like that old woman? Alley shuddered as the memory of the lady's skin peeling away flashed through her mind. What was it? It was like something from a horror movie. How was she going to protect people from that? She couldn't even protect herself—or had she?

Alley glanced at her exposed arms. The searing heat of the gas explosion had been the worst physical pain she'd ever experienced. It had killed Brent, but she didn't have a burn or scratch. How was that possible? Had the energy protected her body—or had it healed her injuries? She wished she could remember.

The next page of the journal was a hand drawn table with a series of measurements neatly printed in the rows and columns. It was meaningless. Dad expected her to read all this to get answers? He couldn't just take the time to tell her what she needed to know? She slammed the book closed and shoved it off her lap.

The wheelchair lift whirred as it lowered her father down the staircase. He wanted to send her somewhere? Someplace safe? How could he have put off her training? Especially after all the accidents and knowing there were creatures in the world like that thing? Brent's face surfaced in her mind. He had been a bright spot in her existence, had filled the void left as she and Elek had started to grow apart the summer after graduation. If her father had trained her—or cured her condition—Brent would still be alive. Now he was gone. It made her chest ache and brought fresh tears to her eyes.

Alley retrieved the framed picture of her parents from the bedside table. "Why did you lie?"

They'd tried to protect her, but they'd only made things worse. Her hand trembled as a knot grew in her throat. More tears flowed down her cheeks tracing cold trails under her chin and down her neck. They could have prevented all of it. Alley slammed the picture down on the nightstand. The glass shattered.

She wiped the tears from her face, pulled back the covers and swung her feet onto the cold hardwood floor. The lack of warmth focused her mind. None of it made any sense. She slid the photo out from under the glass shards. Her parents smiled back. Wasn't experimenting on kids illegal? Who did they work for that would fund that kind of research? And what role had Leopold Rakman played in all this if he knew about her ability?

Alley stood and paced around the bedroom. The oval rug on the floor beside her bed was warmer than the cold hardwood. Her toes sank into the soft purple shag. Autumn air leaked in through a bad seal on the window. Goosebumps rose on her arms. She hugged herself.

Dad had always loved her, always encouraged her. After the accident that killed her mother and left him without the use of his legs, he had continued to be a source of strength. He had comforted her as she'd grieved and tried to bring a sense of normalcy back into her life. Each day was a struggle for him, but he never complained, never gave up, never expressed anger or frustration at the loss of his freedom. Her father had shown that nothing was impossible to overcome. He was her only family. It didn't change her love for him, but she had to understand—why had he allowed this to continue when he saw what it was doing to her? What were these things he wanted her to protect the world from?

She heard the front door open and the sound of heavy footsteps. And who were these people that had come to take her away? Could she trust them? Could she still trust her father?

Alley felt the urgent need to get out of the house. Everything was happening too quickly. She pulled on some running clothes from the closet. She needed space and time to think—to be with someone she could trust—not a bunch of strangers.

Alley eyed the phone on her nightstand as she tugged on her sneakers. Elek's house was still on speed dial. He was the only person she'd ever told about her secret. He would understand. She dialed his number and waited.

Elek picked up on the second ring. *"Alley, are you okay? Your dad called me a few hours ago and told me what happened."*

"Can I come over? I need to talk." She fished an old duffel bag out from under her bed. Dust bunnies and lint flew into the air as she shook it off. She cradled the phone between her cheek and shoulder as she worked on unzipping the top of the bag.

"Maybe I should come over and pick you—"

Alley cut him off. "I can handle a three-block walk."

She pulled open her dresser drawers and stuffed clothes into the bag.

"I'm worried about you, Al. You were just in a serious accident—"

"I'm fine. I just need to talk."

Alley glanced at herself in the mirror above her dresser. *Ugh.* Her eyes and nose were red. Her skin was smudged with ash. Her hair was a tangled mess. She grabbed a brush and attacked the knots.

Elek cleared his throat. *"Okay, but—"*

She cut him off again. "Look, I'm not sure when we'll have time again to meet in person. I'm heading over." Alley hung up, pulled her hair back into a ponytail and secured it in place with a black elastic band.

Her father was arguing with someone downstairs. She crossed the room and pressed her ear against the door. His muffled words became clear. "—too risky to go back to the city, you could lead the dracun straight to the College. You need to go a different way."

A male voice answered. It was calm and warm. "We can take this route, here. It's remote. Less chance of them tracking us. We could be there in a few hours."

"That looks like a better option," her father replied.

"Arün, Nadja—take good care of her, please."

The man responded. "We will Ben, but we need to go soon. We should have left already."

"She's packing now. I wish we had more time."

A new voice, this time a female. "If we're lucky, they'll show up and we can end this."

Her father's voice grew stern. "Don't risk her life over a vendetta, Nadja—"

Alley had heard enough. It was time to go. Her mother's journal lay on the bed. She picked it up, then set it back down. It would take hours to read. Right now, she needed a friend. She'd call her dad later. He owed her answers.

She shouldered the bag and moved towards the door. If she went downstairs, they'd probably try to stop her from leaving. Alley turned and headed over to one of the windows. Cold air spilled into the room as she pushed up the sash.

The sun brightened the overcast sky, but it was fading fast. An unfamiliar, beat-up truck was parked in the driveway. Alley crawled out onto the roof of the porch. Green moss clung to the decades-old asphalt shingles. She'd been thirteen the last time she tried this on one of Elek's stupid dares. It was even more slippery now. She crept toward the corner where she knew she'd be able to climb down.

As she edged forward, the moss broke free. Her leg slid out. She felt her body falling. The roof hit her hard on her right side. Pain lanced through her shoulder and gravity tugged her head-first down the mossy slope.

5

FALLING

ALLEY

Alley clawed at the shingles. The slope ended in a twelve-foot drop. How far was she from the edge? Her fingers dug furrows through the thick matted surface, but her momentum didn't change.

Time seemed to slow as she tumbled out into space.

Her eyes clamped shut. There was nothing she could do. Alley held her breath and braced for impact, but instead, she landed in the warm, yielding embrace of someone's arms. The person smelled of fresh-cut cedar and rosemary. They set her gently on the ground. She opened her eyes and turned to face her rescuer.

He smiled and regarded her with deep green eyes. "You okay?"

Alley took two steps back. It was the stalker. The guy

from the café. The one who had warned her to leave. He wore a dark leather jacket over a green faded t-shirt and jeans. He looked like a model from a magazine cover. Black hair, angular features. The only flaw was the scar through his left eyebrow, but even that looked good. She tried to guess his age, late twenties, thirties? It was hard to say.

She shook her head. Focus.

He was blocking the walkway. Could she outrun him? Maybe. Maybe not. "Who are you?"

He raised his palms. "Look—I won't hurt you. My name is Arün."

"What are you doing here?" she asked.

"I rescued you from the café this morning."

Alley straightened her clothes and took a breath to calm herself. If he'd wanted to hurt her, he could have let her hit the ground. The roof had left a patchy wet streak of moss down her side. She brushed at the stain. "How do you know where I live?"

"I know your father."

She needed to get to Elek's house. "Are you one of the people he wants to send me away with?"

Arün stepped forward. "We're here to protect you—to take you someplace safe."

She wasn't going anywhere with him, but he had saved her—twice. Alley thrust out her palm. "Thanks for your help, but I have other plans."

He shook her hand. There was something weirdly electric about his touch. The hairs on Alley's arm stood on end. Arün glanced down at their clasped hands. A startled expression passed over his face. Had he felt it too?

He released his grip and reached for the strap of the duffel bag hitched over her shoulder. "At least let me walk with you?"

Alley eyed him suspiciously. "You're not going to try to stop me?"

Arün shook his head. "I saw what you did yesterday. I'm not going to drag you somewhere you don't want to go."

Alley looked away and tried not to think about Brent lying in the destroyed café. "Okay."

She let Arün take the duffel bag then led him down the front walkway and across the street. The sky was overcast and darkening. Their feet crunched on the brilliant red leaves that carpeted the sidewalk. "You always stalk people before you rescue them?"

He laughed. "Only you. Your father asked me to watch out for you."

Alley chewed her lip as they walked in silence. Her father had had her followed? She hurried up the sidewalk and waited in a pool of light cast by one of the street lamps. "I changed my mind. I don't need a babysitter or a chaperone."

Arün stopped beside her. His brows furrowed as he wrestled with whatever he was about to say. "Your father and I work for people that are very interested in your personal safety."

Alley crossed her arms. The shadows grew deeper outside the circle of light. She squinted at him. "Why do they care so much about me?"

"Truthfully?"

"Yeah, I'd prefer that over lies."

He shifted his weight to the other foot and adjusted the duffel bag on his shoulder. "They know you're special and want to keep you safe. They want to help you learn how to use your gift."

Alley stepped back. "You knew I was in danger from that woman?"

Arün peered into the growing gloom and lowered his voice. "Those creatures have an unhealthy interest in you."

Her voice got louder. "You know what that thing was?"

He looked up and down the street then leaned towards her. "Alley, you just have to trust me. I've kept you safe so far. These things are excellent trackers. If we don't get you out of town, they will find you again."

Alley studied the broken asphalt of the sidewalk under her sneaker. An ant made slow progress down one of the long cracks. "What are they?"

"If I told you, you wouldn't believe me."

"So you won't tell me?"

"I don't have clearance to say more."

She was sick of the mysteries. "Arün, you seem like a nice guy. But, I don't need anyone to watch my back. I've been taking care of myself for a long time."

"Alley, please—"

She held out her hand. "Bag."

"I'm under orders—"

"No. If I'm in that much danger shouldn't we be calling the cops? Wouldn't they be able to handle this better than you?"

He sighed, slid her duffel bag off his shoulder and handed it over to her.

"Tell my dad I'm visiting my friend Elek. I need time to think." She counted to ten in her head as she walked away into the dusk. When she stole a glance over her shoulder, the soft glow of the street lamp illuminated an empty sidewalk.

Alley clutched the duffel bag to her chest and ran towards Elek's house.

6

OLD FRIENDS

ALLEY

Alley could feel it. She was being watched. Was it Arün or someone else?

The house where Elek Mori and his parents lived was close. It was a two-story white craftsman bungalow. The front porch light was a beacon in the darkness. Alley ran toward it, her lungs burning.

She passed a driveway—and another. The cold night air raked at the back of her throat. Alley banked and ran the remaining few yards up the cement walkway to the porch steps. She jammed her finger on the doorbell and heard the chime inside.

Darkness loomed behind her. A few lights shone in the surrounding houses, but no one was outside. Fog was starting to roll in. It was quiet except for her ragged breathing. She needed to get more exercise. Maybe when life was less crazy. Maybe when fewer people were dying around her.

Alley turned at the sound of the latch being pulled back. Elek was barefoot and wearing gray sweats and a black tank top. It looked like he'd been working out. His pale, wiry arms were crisscrossed with old scars and new scabs. Evidence that his thrill seeking hadn't let up in the last year.

A big grin split his face, crinkling the skin around his dark eyes. "Alley! Man, it's good to see you." He pulled her into a bone-crushing hug.

"Good to see you too, El." And it was.

Elek waved her into the house. Alley hurried inside. He peered out into the night, then shut and locked the door. He frowned at her moss-stained clothes. "Rough night?"

"Yeah, turns out the porch roof needs cleaning."

He grinned. "Sorry I missed that. I bet it was epic."

"Probably not as epic as that," she pointed at his arms, "You'll have to tell me about where those came from."

He winked at her. "It's an awesome story. I'll save it for later."

Alley glanced at one of the Mori's family photos in the foyer. It was a picture taken when Elek had been two feet shorter. A green lake stretched behind them and at the far edge sprawled a rambling mountain resort composed of an eclectic mix of buildings. They looked happy. Elek's dad was a pediatrician. His mom was a professor at a local college. There were other framed photos in the hallway, a younger version of herself grinned back in a few of them. It made her smile.

The scent of fresh-baked cookies wafted down the hall from the kitchen. "Your mom and dad around?"

"They went to Leavenworth for Oktoberfest."

She nodded, feeling the smile slip a bit from her face. Elek's mom gave the best hugs.

"There's not much food, but I made cookies."

She raised an eyebrow. "You made cookies?"

He chuckled. "They won't be like that time. I promise."

Alley pursed her lips. "Mmhmm."

"Okay skeptic, follow me."

Alley dropped her bag as they walked down the long hall that connected the foyer to the kitchen at the back of the house. A trio of Japanese Bunjinga prints adorned the right wall, a graduation gift to Elek from his father's parents back in Japan. She'd been at the house when Elek had unwrapped them. They depicted a bunch of sword-wielding samurai battling an enormous serpent in a forest at the foot of a waterfall. Alley liked the way the artist had painted the water, swirling lines cresting in frothy wave caps.

"Nice location."

Elek laughed. "I wanted them in my room. Dad insisted on a more public spot. I think he's just trying to make sure I don't feel too comfortable—motivate me to get my own place or something. Not sure why he cares. I'm almost never here."

Alley smiled. The struggle between Elek and his dad had

started when they were eight and had been raging ever since. It seemed to be tied closely to Elek's extreme disregard for rules, reckless actions and general dislike for anything that might be leading him towards a normal life.

"So, if you're never here, what have you been up to?"

Elek had had no interest in college. He told his parents he was going to get a job and explore his options which, as far as Alley could tell, had meant spending most of the summer after graduation sleeping.

"Did I ever tell you I was interning for a while during our senior year?" he asked.

"You never mentioned it." Which was odd, she thought.

They entered the kitchen. Elek checked the lock on the door that led to the backyard and then set out two mugs.

"You still like green tea or is it all coffee all the time?"

"Coffee, please."

"I thought so, just brewed some." Elek brought over a pot of coffee and filled their mugs.

They sat down at the round granite topped table at the center of the kitchen. Alley's stomach growled at the sight of the plate of chocolate chip cookies resting on the black stone. She grabbed one. Alley needed to tell Elek about everything, but for a moment she welcomed the distraction of his latest cooking attempt. He tended to burn things, but these looked promising.

"You never mentioned interning. How the heck did you find time for that?" Alley bit into the cookie. It was still warm and melted apart on her tongue into buttery, sugary goodness.

Elek waited with a ridiculous smile on his face, nodding like he was waiting for a gold star or something.

She rolled her eyes. "Okay, they're really good."

"Ah, thank you." He bowed his head like he had just finished an Oscar-winning performance.

She set the cookie down and laughed. "Internship?"

"It was an evening internship, so I was able to do most of it after school mid-week. Anyway, they contacted me after graduation. Wanted to bring me on full-time."

"Doing what?"

Elek scratched his neck before glancing up. "Security stuff at night. Satisfies my need for adventure and they don't care about how I dress."

Alley had known Elek since they were four. During their sixteen-year friendship, she had learned to tell when he was hiding something. He wasn't telling her the whole story. "That's awesome. Sounds like it suits you."

What had he really been up to? Growing up, the Mori's had treated her like a second child, and it occurred to Alley that maybe it was because they hoped some of her maturity would rub off on their son, or at the very least help keep him from doing something stupid. The trick had always been getting Elek to reveal his plans before they spun out of control. It took time though and couldn't be rushed.

"Thanks. Yeah, I'm really enjoying it. How about you though? What happened today?"

Alley spooned sugar into the cup and added cream. It billowed into a milky cloud within the black liquid. She lifted the cup, blew across the surface, then sipped. It soothed her throat. He was changing the subject. It was okay. This was why she'd come. She needed someone to listen.

"It was like the other times, Elek. I really thought I had it under control."

Steam curled up from the mug.

Elek waited for her to continue.

"This woman came into the café. It was scary. She turned into something. I don't know what it was. It was trying to take me somewhere, but then my energy went out of control."

Alley stopped. She could feel a lump forming in her throat and choked it down. "I—destroyed the shop. There were people in there Elek, Brent—"

She covered her mouth with the back of her hand. It was shaking.

Elek's brows furrowed. "It wasn't your fault."

Alley closed her eyes and shook her head. She wiped at her face and took a breath before continuing. "You're right. My parents did this to me. My dad said they made me this way to help protect the world. He could have helped me learn to control it, maybe even cure it. But he did nothing." Her hand tightened around the mug.

Elek took a sip from his cup. "Did he tell you that?"

Strange—Elek didn't seem shocked. She tilted her head at him. "He said he already knew about that thing that attacked me. That there are more out there. Can you believe that?"

Elek reached across the table and held her hand. "I'm so sorry, Alley. The café, your friend, the thing that attacked you—it all sounds awful. I wish I had been there to help."

"I have no idea what's going on, Elek. It's freaking me out."

"Your father is a good guy. If he kept things from you, I'm sure it was for a good reason."

Why was Elek acting like what her father had done was okay? She lowered her voice. "He's had people watching me—following me."

Elek squeezed her hand. "He cares about you, Alley."

This wasn't the Elek she knew. The one who saw a conspiracy around every corner. Who questioned everything. The Elek she knew would have already come up with three theories about why her father had lied. She squinted at him. "Dad said I was in danger. There are people at our house that are supposed to take me somewhere safe."

Elek glanced at the locked door. "Let's get out of here. You and me. We can drive up to Vancouver tonight."

Alley leveled her gaze at Elek. "What's really going on here. You know something, and you're keeping it from me."

He let her hand go and tapped his fingers on the side of

his mug in a staccato rhythm. "Al, we've been friends a long time—done a lot of crazy stuff together. You trust me, right?"

Alley nodded.

"Your dad told me there were some people after you. I totally get why you don't want to be taken out of town by strangers. But we should get out of here. We can make a vacation of it. Catch up on the past year."

He wasn't talking about a vacation—he was talking about hiding. That wasn't a plan. How would she ever know if she was safe? "I don't want to be on the run. We should call the police."

"You sure that's a good idea?" Elek had a long history with the local police department.

"Why not? If someone is after me, they'd be the best people to protect me, right?"

"Al, they're the cops, not bodyguards. They won't give you an escort everywhere you go, and they'll ask lots of questions. They'll want to know why you think you're in danger. What are you going to tell them? You were attacked by a shape-shifting old woman?"

"That happened." She needed Elek to believe. He was the only person left that she trusted.

Elek shook his head. "I believe you, but they'll write you off as paranoid or insane. If by some chance they do take you seriously, they'll open an investigation. They'll do a background check on you. They'll find out you worked at the coffee shop downtown and that you were working there today. Then they'll want to know how you managed to survive without a scratch. Why you disappeared from the scene of the accident? If they have any reason to believe it was a bomb that destroyed the shop, you'll be a suspect. How much protection do you think you'll get then?"

Elek's logic made sense, but she still didn't like the idea of being on the run. "Fine, no cops. Did my dad tell you anything else?"

"I'll tell you everything, once we're on the road."

Alley sipped her coffee. "He told me there's a cure for my condition."

Elek raised his brows. "What?"

Alley leaned forward. "I want your help to try it."

Elek lowered his head and rubbed his temples. He seemed to be having an internal tug of war. "What's the cure?"

"He said if I drink enough coffee it might permanently block the energy."

Elek took a long sip of his drink, then set it down. "I have a confession, Al."

She cocked her head to the side. Finally, some answers.

"Those people your dad had watching you—the ones that showed up at your house—I work with them."

"What?" Elek knew them?

"They're good people."

Alley's mind spun. "Who are they?"

"Part of a covert group that protects this region. Your abilities could help us. Help the world."

"Help? I destroyed a café yesterday. I killed my friend." Her throat tightened as she gripped her mug. She shook her head. "I never asked for any of this, El. I never had a choice—until now. Help me be free of this."

Elek reached across the table and touched her hand. "Give me twenty-four hours to get you somewhere safe. Then I'll help you try this cure."

Alley gritted her teeth and avoided making eye contact with him. Would one more day make a difference? Probably not—if she drank enough coffee to keep the power at bay. She took a deep breath. Her hair reeked of smoke from the explosion. "Fine. You get one day, but I want your word you'll help me after that."

Elek nodded. "I promise."

She gulped down the rest of her coffee. "So, what happens now?"

"I need to pack a few things, but then we should leave."

Alley set the empty cup down. Ash and dust had mixed with sweat from her run. Her skin felt disgusting. "Is there time for me to take a shower?"

"Yeah. Upstairs bathroom is free."

Alley stood. "You owe me a lot of answers, El."

He scratched at one of the scabs on his arm. "I know. Let's save it for the drive."

Alley grabbed her bag and headed upstairs. A few

moments later, she was standing in the shower. Hot water cascaded over her body, washing away sweat, grime and ash. She leaned against the tiled wall and quietly wept—she didn't want Elek to hear. She'd killed and injured so many people and all this time there might have been a way to stop it. Now Brent was dead too. There was no way she was going to let it happen again. She'd drink a barrel of coffee—even if it killed her. There would be no more death on her hands.

Alley finished washing, toweled off and dressed. She was pulling her wet hair back into a ponytail when she heard a soft knock. Elek whispered through the door. "Get out here, we have a problem."

7

UNWANTED GUESTS

ALLEY

Elek's voice was barely a whisper, but the urgency and fear were unmistakable. Alley opened the door. "What's wrong?"

"Grab your shoes." He headed towards the guest bedroom at the end of the hall. Alley unlaced her sneakers as she followed him.

"What's going on, El?"

Elek entered the room, moved towards the window and peeked around the drawn shade. He had changed into jeans and a t-shirt and wore a leather biking jacket. Alley pulled on her shoes in the dim light from the hallway and then crouched by the window beside Elek.

He mouthed the word "look" and pointed outside. Alley raised the bottom of the shade. From the second-story window, she could see across the top of the porch to the front yard and street. Low fog clung to the ground. Everything was quiet. Still.

She felt Elek's breath near her ear. "Oak tree, left side of the driveway."

Alley squinted. Movement caught her eye. Someone was standing with their back to the tree watching the house. Her pulse quickened. Was it her stalker, Arün, or someone else?

Elek whispered to her again. "Right side, hedges."

Alley strained to make out shapes. Nothing. She heard the distant sound of a car coming down the road. A moment later headlights painted soft shadows and bright light across the foggy lawn.

Alley's breath caught in her throat. A figure was crouching by the hedges. There was the one by the tree and two more heading around the side of the house. The last was climbing onto the roof of the porch only a few feet from the window.

She leaned toward Elek and whispered. "Who are they?"

Elek held a finger to his lips, then motioned for her to move back from the window. But when she tried to stand up from her crouched position, she lost her balance. Her grasp on the shade caused it to unroll as she fell. It slipped out of her fingers and shot up with a loud snap.

They stared at the now uncovered panes of glass. Maybe the figures outside hadn't noticed.

A shadow slid past the window.

Elek jumped up and pulled her toward the bedroom door. "Move!"

Alley stumbled forward. The hallway was clear. The stairs to the first floor were right in front of them. Elek pulled the bedroom door shut.

"Follow me." He moved down the stairs, and Alley hurried to catch up.

The sound of breaking glass came from inside the bedroom. Seconds later the door exploded in a shower of splintered wood. It rained down on them as they reached the landing at the bottom of the steps.

"Keep moving!" Elek headed towards the kitchen.

A dark figure filled the top of the staircase. Alley sprinted after Elek. Who were these people? What did they want?

Elek was moving towards the kitchen door that led to the backyard.

"We need to get you out of here." As he reached for the handle, the door creaked, buckled and then disappeared with a ripping sound as something outside the house tore it off its hinges. The door landed with a crash somewhere in the blackness of the backyard.

A low rumbling growl made the hair on Alley's arms stand on end. It was the same sound the woman in the café had made.

Elek backed up as something huge filled the space where the door had been. He reached into his coat and pulled out an ornate knife with glowing green symbols etched into its surface. Alley had never seen a knife glow. It looked as if it was lit from within. Fine smoke drifted off the surface like the plume of a blown-out candle.

"Stay behind me," he said.

Elek stabbed the blade at the shape in the doorway. It roared—a deep booming sound. An enormous dark arm shot out of the blackness and flung him sideways across the room. He hit the cabinets above the sink and crashed to the floor. Elek groaned but didn't get up.

Alley's muscles locked as her brain was torn between running and fighting. The thing had to duck as it stepped through the doorway into the kitchen. It was like what the old woman had become, only bigger. It was nearly eight feet tall and smelled of sulfur and rotten meat. Muscle and sinew rippled and flexed under jet black scales with hints of subtle blue patterning. It moved towards her back-lit by the dim bulb above the kitchen stove. Its bony, pie-wedge head swiveled on top of a long thick neck. It locked its golden eyes on her. A blue tongue tasted the air from between powerful jaws lined with sharp teeth. It raised a clawed hand and pointed.

You cannot hide.

The words pierced her mind like shards of ice. The thing hadn't made a sound.

Alley stepped around the small granite table in the center of the kitchen and backed into the hallway. The creature followed. It shoved the table aside with a swipe of its hand, cracking the stone top in half.

Her heart was racing. There was nowhere to run. The thing standing in front of her shouldn't exist—it was the stuff of legends and campfire stories. The creature extended its arms and raked its claws along the hallway, shredding the wallpaper as it drew closer.

Alley glanced over her shoulder. Something even bigger filled the foyer behind her. She was trapped.

A high-pitched whirring sound like a dentist's drill came from the kitchen. It was followed by a series of sharp metallic coughs. The creature in the kitchen door arched its back and howled as flashes of green light lit up the walls behind it. The sound repeated, and the beast dropped to one knee.

A woman with short blond hair stood in the kitchen entryway. She wore a deep green hunting jacket and black pants, and she was holding a hi-tech handgun, the source of the strange mechanical noises, pointed at the creatures back.

The monster dug its claws into the walls and struggled to stand. The woman pulled the trigger of the gun. It whirred loudly and emitted another cough as the muzzle flashed green. The creature fell to the floor.

The woman stepped forward, pulled a glowing green knife like Elek's from under her jacket, and slammed it into the creature's side. An inhuman scream burst from the monster as a wave of green flame swept across its limbs, turning them into glowing charcoal. The woman withdrew the blade and what was left of the thing crumbled into a formless pile of ash.

The woman swung the gun towards Alley. "Get down!"

Before Alley could react, she felt cold hard claws clamp around her neck. She reached up and tried to pry the scaled hand open, but the grip was like iron. Stars started to form in her vision. Her heels scraped along the floor as she was pulled backward toward the front door.

The woman sheathed her knife and pulled a second gun from a shoulder holster.

She aimed them at a spot above Alley's head and yelled, "Let go of her!"

Alley couldn't breathe. Her vision was narrowing. She heard the whir of the two guns and saw the green flash of their muzzles. She felt the shock-wave of the bullet impacts through the claw gripping her throat. The woman fired again. The creature's grip loosened and Alley sucked in a lung full of air.

Her feet bumped down the porch steps as she was dragged into the front yard. The woman followed, firing rounds into whatever had a hold of her neck. Alley felt the beast crouch and leap upward. The lawn fell away. Gusts of wind tossed her hair. She clung to the scaled claw. Her body bobbed up and down through the air in time with the beating of huge wings. If it let go, she'd never survive the fall.

Movement in one of the second-story windows caught her eye. Elek crouched in the opening. He was holding a compound bow and had an arrow drawn back tight against his cheek. Alley had never seen him fire a bow. It looked like he was aiming right at her.

His fingers released, and the arrow shot upward, trailing a thin black nylon cord. It passed just above Alley's head and buried itself in between the creature's scales. Elek wrapped his end of the rope around his waist and jumped off the roof. The nylon cord went taut as he dropped from the roof and swung out across the lawn. The creature howled as the extra weight pulled it toward the ground like an enormous kite.

They side-slipped across the yard losing altitude. The creature crashed into the oak tree in the front yard, throwing her sideways. Alley gritted her teeth and held tight with her hands to keep her neck from snapping. Autumn leaves and broken oak limbs fell as the thing thrashed, trying to get clear of the branches.

Elek landed on the lawn and sprinted towards the tree. "Let her go!"

He scrambled up the nylon rope and stabbed the creature with his glowing green blade. It roared and released its grip as its scales ignited.

Alley fell to the ground and collapsed against the trunk of the oak gulping air.

Elek slid down the rope, landing beside her. "You okay, Al?"

She nodded, not yet able to speak. Above, green flames lit

up the darkness. Chunks of smoldering ash rained down around them.

More of the monsters were moving across the lawn. Green muzzle flashes from the woman's guns were keeping them at bay. Alley spotted Arün on the other side of the walkway firing the same kind of weapon at another group of the creatures.

Elek pulled Alley to her feet and yelled, "Run!"

8

INTO THE FOG

ALLEY

The fog was thick as they ran across the lawn. Behind them, the whir-cough of the strange gunfire and the roar of the creatures filled the night air. They reached Elek's hatchback parked on the side of the road. Alley yanked the passenger door open and dove inside.

Elek slid behind the wheel, jammed the key in the ignition and revved the engine. "Buckle up."

The tires squealed. Alley was pressed back into the seat as the car raced out onto the street. She pulled the seatbelt across her chest and clicked it in place. "What are those things?!"

Elek glanced at her. "Dracuns. They're like a smaller version of a dragon."

"What?!"

Elek floored the gas pedal, putting distance between the car and the house. "I found out about them during my internship, after your dad asked me to start Tyro training to become a warden—to help protect you."

"You're kidding?" she asked, but how else could she explain what had just happened? The things that had attacked her had been real.

"I'm not kidding, Alley. You wanted to know how I got those new scars? You just got a first-hand look."

Alley rubbed at her bruised neck. "If those were small dragons, what's a big one look like?"

"I've never seen one, but from what I've heard dragons make dracuns seem like pet lizards."

Elek blew through a red light and swerved onto the main road.

Dracuns. Her dreams had come to life. The dark forms that had been chasing her on the mountainside were real. Did that mean the voice in her dream was also real? And Elek had been training to protect her from them?

"What's a warden?" she asked.

"They make sure the dracun follow the Mage Laws."

"What laws?"

At the foot of the hill, Elek yanked the steering wheel to the left, and they skidded out onto Avondale Road. In the morning, the street would be clogged with commuter traffic trying to get on the 520, but at this hour it was deserted. The engine strained as the speedometer edged upward. "The laws created when they were exiled here—"

A whooping siren cut through the fog. Red and blue lights lit up the interior of their car as a police cruiser roared out of a side street.

Alley grabbed Elek's arm. "Stop, they can help us." The police would have weapons—could call backup to help protect them.

Elek sighed, slowed the car and pulled it over to the side of the road. The cruiser stopped thirty feet behind them. The officer snapped on a powerful floodlight and Alley watched in the rear-view mirror as he approached the car, flashlight held high and the other hand on his holster.

Elek rolled down his window.

"Where you headed in such a hurry?" The officer shined the beam into the car, making Alley's eyes water.

Elek squinted up at him. "We're being chased."

"Not safe to be driving that fast, especially not in this fog."

The officer looked at Alley. "Miss, what happened to you?"

She shaded her eyes. "I was attacked by—the person who is chasing us." Alley wanted to tell the officer exactly what had happened—but she might lose credibility if she went into detail.

"Are you okay now?" he asked.

She nodded her head.

The policeman focused the light back on Elek. "I need to see your license and registration."

Elek handed them to the officer.

"Please remain in the vehicle." He walked back towards the cruiser.

Alley could hear him speaking into the walkie-talkie clipped to his shoulder. "Possible 242, related to a 505 headed west on Avondale."

Elek made eye contact with her. His hand was moving towards the ignition key.

She shook her head and glared at him. "Don't do it. They can protect us."

Elek dropped his hand into his lap. "Fine, let me know if you change your mind."

Alley looked in the rear-view mirror. The officer was silhouetted against the bright floodlight and pulsing cruiser lights.

The next instant he was gone.

Alley blinked. How was that possible? People don't vanish.

Seconds passed.

Something drifted down through the fog and landed on the hood of their car. It was the officer's wide-brimmed hat—splattered with blood.

Alley's eyes went wide. "I changed my mind. Go!"

Elek turned the key in the ignition and stomped on the gas pedal.

Alley grabbed the door handle as the car leaped forward. The hat tumbled off the hood. The cruiser lights receded into the mist as they hurtled down the road out onto the 520 headed west.

Something bright and orange lit up the fog above them. A second later the car was rocked as a ball of flame caused the pavement behind them to erupt. Asphalt and dirt pinged against the trunk of the car.

"What was that?!"

"Fireball." Elek's knuckles were white on the steering wheel. He snapped off the car's headlights.

Another fireball lit up the fog and the surrounding road. Elek swerved to the left, crashing into the barricade as the ball of flames left a crater in the road where the car had just been. Elek straightened the vehicle out.

"Where are those coming from?!"

He glanced at Alley. "Some dracuns have glands that produce chemicals they spit. When the stuff mixes and hits the air, it becomes explosive."

"What?!"

The left side of the road erupted in a geyser of flame and pavement. Chunks of rock and dirt rained down on the roof of the car as they swerved around the hole.

"If we're lucky, it'll empty its glands before it hits us."

Another fireball exploded beside the car. The passenger window blew inward, and shards of glass tore into Alley's skin. Flaming goo coated the side of the vehicle and spattered her arm. Alley tried to wipe it on the door, but it only spread. Her skin sizzled like bacon cooking. Pain slammed into her senses in sickening waves. Her ears rang and then she felt a headache hit. Tendrils of invisible golden energy poured out from her body.

No. She couldn't let anything happen to Elek. She couldn't lose him too.

The car rattled and shook.

Around them, the pavement fractured into thousands of pieces and rose into the air.

The car rocketed upward.

Alley's eyelids fluttered. The burning pain was intense. She had to make it stop.

Elek was yelling something, but she couldn't hear the words. The world around her moved in slow motion. Sounds were muffled. Her eyes slid shut.

She was in the middle of a forest clearing amongst immense pine trees. At her feet, a patch of white flowers grew. As their petals opened, they released a cloud of golden sparkling dust. It floated in the air around Alley and tickled her nose. The scent was intoxicating. It was better than any flower she'd ever smelled. Was this where the energy came from?

A movement caught her eye at the edge of the woods. Someone was watching.

The car shook. Alley opened her eyes. They were at least fifty feet above the ground, driving on a floating carpet of fractured chunks of road. Alley glimpsed invisible cords of energy binding the pieces together in a mesmerizing web of light.

Elek was frantic. "Alley is this you? Are you doing this?"

Another fireball shot past, exploding far below. Through the red haze of pain Alley saw one of the creatures swooping around them. What had Elek called it? *A dracun*. It was trying to kill them. She felt the muscles in her jaw tighten as she fought to focus. It was in front and below them. Black as night, with wings that must have been forty feet across. Alley closed her eyes. She wanted to crush the monster with the car. To destroy it. To protect Elek.

She was back in the clearing. The sky had grown dark. Thunder rolled in the distance. The tops of the trees swayed and creaked in the wind. The patch of flowers was growing larger. New buds were blooming at an unnatural speed. They filled the air with sparkling dust.

If they were the source of the energy, then she needed to stop them to drop the car on the monster. She held her breath and stomped the ground—crushing each new bud that appeared before it could bloom. The storm carried the remaining golden dust away.

Alley took a breath. The air was no longer filled with the scent of the flowers.

She cast an angry gaze toward the edge of the clearing. A little girl in a white sun-dress stood in the deep shadows of the forest holding a small bouquet of the flowers in her hand. She stared in horror at the crushed blossoms.

Alley's eyes snapped open—the web of energy outside the car evaporated.

The car lurched and plummeted, slamming into the dracun's back.

Elek raised his arms to protect his face. All Alley could do was clench her fists. Pain and rage consumed her.

The car rammed into the ground. Alley heard a satisfying crunch as the dracun was sandwiched between the three-thousand-pound weight of the vehicle and the unyielding highway. The car skidded forward and crashed into the concrete barricade.

The last thing Alley saw was the dashboard coming up to smack her in the face. And then the pain was gone.

9

RECOVERY

ALLEY

It was just a pinch, like the bite of a small insect, but it forced Alley to find the strength to lift her eyelids. White acoustic paneling hovered high above her head. She could feel something blowing air into her nose. Tape tugged at the hair on her right hand. Her head rolled to the side. She was in a hospital bed. Sheets were pulled up under her arms. Someone was standing over her—a female doctor with blue scrubs and a white lab coat. Elek lay in the next bed hooked up to some machines. *Elek?* She tried to call to him, but all that came out was a wheeze.

"Good. You're awake." The doctor had an Irish accent. It sounded nice. She was drawing blood from Alley's arm into a vial. "I'm sorry to disturb you. There were some strange results with your bloodwork, so I'm sending another sample to the lab."

Alley squinted up at the woman.

The doctor pulled the needle out of her arm and pressed a gauze pad against the puncture, fastening it in place with some surgical tape. "You and your friend were very lucky. The team that brought you in said the accident was serious. There are officers here who need to ask you some questions. They've been waiting for one of you to wake."

Alley struggled to sit up but found that her wrists and ankles were tied to the bed with soft buckled restraints. Her body ached all over, but nothing felt broken.

"Too tired," she croaked.

What would she tell the police? Had they found the body of the dracun smashed into the highway? Were they going to ask about the bloody hat and the abandoned cruiser? Were they going to accuse them of some horrible crime?

Alley felt her pulse quicken. The heart rate monitor next to her sped up. The distance between the spikes growing closer and closer.

"Relax. It's just some routine questions."

Alley was sure that the doctor was lying. The massive damage from the fireballs probably made the highway look like it was shelled. *No.* There was nothing routine about the accident or what had happened to the officer that had stopped them.

She had to get out of here. Alley pulled against the

restraints, but she couldn't get free. The heart rate monitor started beeping.

"Miss, you need to relax." The doctor pulled a syringe out of her coat pocket and uncapped the needle.

Alley's eyes went wide. "What's that?"

The woman grasped the IV drip cord that ran from the suspended bag of saline down into Alley's right hand. "I'm just going to give you something to calm you down and then I'll send in the officers."

"You don't need to do that—I'm calm." But she wasn't. Alley strained against the bonds. If she could get her teeth around the IV cord, she might be able to rip it out of her arm in time. Too late. The doctor slid the needle into the med-port on the cord and depressed the syringe's plunger. Alley's body felt heavy. Her head sank into the pillow and her eyes slid shut. *No!* She needed to get out of here but her limbs refused to respond.

A gasp caused Alley to look up. The doctor was bent backward—a hand clamped over her mouth. Elek had wrenched the syringe from the doctor's hand and had jammed it into the woman's neck. He injected the remainder of the sedative into her as he whispered. "Sorry, Doc—I can't let you do that."

The woman's body went limp. Elek dragged her over to the other bed. He took off the doctor's lab coat and scrubs, then quickly pulled the heart rate monitors off his body and affixed them to the woman's chest. He patted her cheek.

"Can't have the alarms going off at the nurse's station—can we, Doc?"

Elek put on the doctor's uniform, then reached under the bed and grabbed the plastic drawstring bag containing the clothes he'd been wearing before the crash. A wheelchair sat in the corner of the room. He hooked the bag of clothes to the back.

Alley watched it all in a daze. She knew she needed to get up, to get her clothes on, but her body wouldn't cooperate. At least she was conscious. She wanted to help Elek, but she couldn't muster the drive to do anything other than smile at him.

Elek pulled the oxygen tube off her head and removed the IV from her arm. He unbuckled the restraints on her wrists and ankles, then peeled off the heart monitoring electrodes on her chest and stuck them to his chest. He turned around and quickly affixed them to the doctor's chest in the other bed. The heart rate monitor sounded a brief alarm out in the hall during the transfer. Elek waited, listening for a moment, but no one seemed to take notice. In the silence, Alley drifted off.

"Al, snap out of it." Elek shook her body.

"El"—her voice came out slurred—"how'd ya get out of the 'cuffs?"

"Dislocated my thumb. Hurts, but I'll be fine."

Elek looked bruised and scratched up, but not bad considering they had just been in a car accident. Alley could feel herself relaxing. Part of it was probably the drugs, but most of it was knowing she hadn't killed him. She smiled and felt her eyelids slide shut.

Elek patted her cheek again. "Al, we need to get out of here. Can you walk?"

She tried to stand, but her knees buckled. Elek held her up keeping her from crashing on the cold linoleum tiles.

"Need socks," she mumbled.

Elek sighed and muttered to himself. "Perfect—just perfect."

He pulled a bathrobe off a hook on the wall and helped Alley get into it. It was warm and made her feel like sleeping again. She staggered backward, Elek caught her around the waist.

"Stay with me. Let's get you to that chair."

"Cops outside." She could barely move her lips.

"I know, Al. One thing at a time."

They stumbled across the room to the wheelchair parked in the corner. Alley flopped into it, her body a loose collection of bones stuck together with rubbery bits. She slid downward. The terrycloth bathrobe offered little friction against the black plastic-coated seat cushion. Elek struggled to flip down the metal footrests on the chair and plant Alley's feet against them. The cold metal made her feel more alert. Elek found socks and slipped them onto her feet, then grabbed her clothing bag and hung it on the back of the wheelchair with his own bag.

"Thanks, El." Alley struggled to keep her speech from slurring.

Elek nodded, then went over to the door, cracked it open and peered outside. Alley's stomach was growling. She hadn't eaten since breakfast.

"Need pancakes." She could barely form the words.

Elek nodded. "I'll get you food as soon as we get out of here. The cops are by the nurse's station a few doors down the hall. Their backs are to us. I'm going to wheel you out of the room, and we're going to go the other direction, away from them. Let's hope they don't notice. Stay quiet."

As the wheelchair moved, Alley felt her body sliding off the seat again. She tried to push with her feet against the footrests but had no strength. If she said anything to Elek now, it might attract the officer's attention.

Elek backed her out into the hallway. Off to their left stood two policemen talking to someone behind a tall counter decorated with cardboard cutouts of smiling jack-o'-lanterns. One officer held a plastic bag with Elek's weird blade, driver's license and car registration inside. The cops whirled out of view as the wheelchair pivoted and Elek pushed her down the hallway in the opposite direction.

One of her feet slipped off and slid along the waxed hallway floor. She was going to fall off.

"Elek!" she hissed in a barely audible whisper.

"Not now, wait till we get around the corner." Elek whispered back just above her head.

Alley's other foot slipped off, and she felt her body slide completely out of the chair. The wheelchair clattered as Elek bumped into her. Down the hall, the officers turned to look their way. One of them put his hand on his holster. "Hey!"

Elek heaved Alley off the floor and threw her into the chair. He tilted it back and ran down the hall.

"Stop!" The officer's footsteps pounded on the tiles.

Elek turned the wheelchair to the right, and they headed along another corridor. Far down the hall, Alley saw a security guard approaching. There was something strange about the way he moved. Alley's memory flashed back to Elek's house, to the thing—*dracun*—as it had approached her in the hallway. This guard was moving in the same way.

Elek hissed, "Oh—that's bad." He must have noticed it too.

He spun the chair around and sprinted back towards the approaching officers.

Behind them, something roared.

10

LONG HALL

ELEK

Elek had to get his scryth from the cops. It was the only way they were getting out of the hospital alive. His feet slipped on the smooth linoleum floor as he struggled to keep the wheelchair tilted back at the perfect angle so Alley wouldn't slip off.

The dracun behind them roared again. Elek looked over his shoulder. It had transformed. The security guard uniform hung in shredded rags off its massive body. It might have been a rhino charging down the halls, but it wasn't—it was a dracun. The tiles on the floor cracked and popped up under its weight. Its scale covered back and wings scraped against the ceiling, breaking the fluorescent tubes and plunging the hallway behind them into sputtering flashes of darkness.

Elek pivoted around the corner they had just come from

and braced himself for the inevitable collision with the two cops. They were only a few steps away.

Elek yelled. "Run!" But, they ignored his warning. One cop grabbed the wheelchair.

The world moved in slow motion as the other cop reached for Elek's shoulder and months of warden training instinctively took over.

"Elek!" Alley's voice sounded distant and muffled. The cops were going to get them all killed.

Elek closed his eyes. *Breathe. You've prepared for this.*

Don't think, react.

Stay calm.

His left hand went to his shoulder grasping the cop's hand that held his scrubs in a fist. He twisted sharply, rotating his body up and into the man's chest. He tensed his legs and in one smooth motion pushed upward and around.

The cop was pulled off his feet, went sailing around Elek's body and landed on his back. Elek was still grasping the cop's hand, causing the man's elbow joint to lock in a painful hold. He punched the man in the neck and groin. It would buy him a minute—or at least that's what Nadja had told him each time he had practiced the move.

Elek felt like he was dancing under water. He felt alive.

"Watch out!" Alley's voice called to him through the combat haze. Elek released the man's arm and whipped his head around. The other cop was drawing his weapon as he moved toward Elek.

The hall behind them exploded in a slow-motion blast of dust, broken tile, acoustic paneling, and drywall. At the center of the storm, the dracun's black body gleamed like a freshly polished car crashing through the building. The cop ducked and turned towards the sound. His gun came up, and when he saw the creature, he fired.

The shots sped up time for Elek. Released from his trance, he could see that neither cop had his blade. They must have left it at the nurse's station. Elek grabbed the handles of the wheelchair and sprinted down the hallway.

Alley's drugged body slumped in the seat. Her head flopped back and looked up at him. Her eyes were full of fear.

"Can you stop it?" she asked.

He loved her eyes—even when they were full of worry. There wasn't anything he wouldn't do for her. "Don't worry. We're still getting pancakes," he said.

Alley managed a lopsided smile. He missed that smile. *Focus, Elek, or you're going to get her killed.*

They approached the elevated desk of the nurse's station. The nurse on duty was craning her head, looking in horror at the chaos behind them. The scryth was resting on the counter in a plastic bag. Elek reached out to snatch it as he raced by, but then his hand grasped at empty air. The nurse had pulled it off the counter at the last second and was now holding it behind the desk. Her other hand was cradling the handset of a phone.

"Send security! There's—"

Elek grabbed the cord connecting the handset to the phone base on the desk and yanked hard. The handset shot from the nurse's ear and clattered on the desk.

"Give me the knife!" The woman was going to get them all killed.

The nurse backed away from the desk. The cop Elek had knocked down was standing. He noticed the dracun for the first time. The second officer was still firing his weapon into the huge creature. The pop of the gunfire made Elek want to duck even though he knew the bullets weren't aimed at him. The policemen wouldn't last long—humans without training rarely did.

Elek vaulted the desk and landed on the floor in front of the nurse. "Give me my blade so I can help them!"

She clutched the plastic bag. "Stay away!"

Elek grit his teeth. "That thing will kill us!"

One of the cops screamed in pain. The nurse flinched, and when she did, Elek lunged forward and ripped the plastic bag from her hands.

He pushed her to the floor. "Stay down, and you might live."

Elek ripped the glowing scryth out of the plastic, pocketed his license and registration, then vaulted back over the counter. Down the hall, one cop, or what was left of him, was lying on the ground. Blood dripped from the ceiling. The other officer was grasping at his throat. The dracun lifted him off the ground with its huge black clawed hand and threw him against the wall. The cops had lasted longer than most people.

Elek gripped the scryth and resisted the urge to look back again. The elevator doors gleamed brightly at the other end of the hall. He pushed Alley toward them as fast as he could. They seemed miles away. Thundering vibrations ran up his legs. The building shook. The dracun was pursuing them again.

Elek skidded to a halt in front of the elevator and tapped at the down button.

Alley weakly pointed at the elevator door. "It's coming!" The polished steel showed the distorted reflection of the approaching monster.

"Don't worry, Al." He hoped he sounded convincing. What had Nadja told him? The eyes—go for the eyes if you can. Next the fire glands. Stay away from the claws and the teeth—that one had always seemed obvious.

Elek turned his back to the elevator door and stood in front of Alley. The scryth felt cold in his sweaty palm. His thumb ached where he'd popped it out of joint. He hoped it wouldn't affect his grip too much. Elek met the monster's gaze. The dracun caught sight of the glowing blade and slowed, stopping, just out of reach.

"Give me the girl." Its voice boomed deep and hollow. Its breath was hot and blew the hair back from Elek's face. It reeked of rotten garbage and ash.

He shook his head. "You can't have her."

It laughed and swiped a massive claw to brush him aside. Elek ducked, rolled forward and slashed at the things neck. It roared and recoiled backward, clutching at the wound that sizzled where the knife had sliced into its scales. The elevator dinged. Elek glanced over his shoulder.

He realized his mistake too late. In that instant, the monster lunged forward. It wrapped its cold claws around his neck and yanked him from the floor. Elek dropped his blade as he grabbed at the claws. He felt his pulse throbbing in his head as the dracun's grip tightened, cutting off the flow of blood to his head. The elevator doors were opening. Elek's vision narrowed and darkened.

"Put him down!" Alley was screaming at the thing, trying to push herself up from the chair.

The familiar whirring of a Warden issued Drak-9 pistol pierced the darkness enveloping Elek's mind. It fired three times, sending high-velocity, scale-piercing rounds into the air. The monster released its grip on Elek's throat and he fell to the ground struggling for breath as the world came rushing back. The creature roared as it retreated down the hall.

Arün stood in the elevator. "Get her inside!" he yelled as he shot over Elek's head at the dracun.

Elek grabbed his scryth from the floor. Keeping his head down, he pushed the wheelchair into the elevator while Arün continued to fire at the beast.

Elek jammed the lobby button and waited for what seemed like an eternity for the doors to a close. Arün sent one last shot through the crack before the elevator sealed shut and moved downward.

Above them, the building shook.

11

THE DROP

ARÜN

Arün reloaded his gun. Screeching metal echoed through the ceiling of the elevator as the dracun tore open the fourth-floor doors to the shaft above them. The elevator's digital display chimed as they passed the third floor.

There hadn't been an incident this bad in over a decade —not since the lab breach. The Council wouldn't formally call it a revolution, but it was too organized to be anything else. The Obsidian Clan had to have been planning for years, weaning themselves from the cocktail that the Wardens administered to lock them into human form. Maybe Nadja was right. Maybe they had just been putting sheep skins on wolves and sending them out into the flock. He hoped she was wrong.

Alley slouched in the wheelchair. She raised her head. "Is Elek okay?"

Elek was slumped in the corner massaging his neck. His body shook beneath the white lab coat. Arün put his hand on Elek's shoulder. "He did well. Better than most full warden."

The elevator slowed. Arün looked up at the display. It said they were on the second floor.

Elek struggled to his feet. "We're stopping?" He jabbed at the buttons trying to get the elevator to keep going.

The panel chimed, and the doors slid open. A graying janitor pushing a cleaning cart tried to barge inside. Elek held out his hand and forced the cart back into the hallway. "Get the next one."

The old man looked up, noticing them for the first time. He scowled at Elek. "I am sick of how rude you young people are getting. There's plenty of room in there."

He shoved the cart forward.

Arün held up his gun. "Sir, you don't want to get on this elevator." *You really don't*, he thought.

A roar echoed down the shaft. Everyone looked up. The janitor stepped backward as something heavy landed on the roof of the elevator denting the ceiling inward. Arün had a brief view of the old man, hand raised to his mouth in shock, before he felt his stomach rise into his throat. His body went weightless as the elevator plummeted.

They landed hard. The walls dented and crumpled,

sending a metallic screech through the air. The lights flickered, then went out. Long gashes formed in the metal above them as the dracun tore through the steel, allowing the emergency lighting in the shaft to seep into the elevator.

Arün shoved a gun into Elek's hand. "Cover us!" They had to get Alley to safety.

He pulled at the edge of the doors. The metal bit into his skin. The ceiling wouldn't last long the way the creature was tearing through it.

The dracun's voice boomed in the confined space. "Give her to me!"

The metal doors squealed on their tracks as Arün pulled them apart. The panels had bent on impact and didn't want to open all the way, but he was able to create a gap wide enough for them to slip through. It was all they needed.

Elek fired at the ceiling. "I've got this! Go!"

The whirring of Elek's gunfire and the roars of the dracun filled the air as Arün pulled Alley out of the wheelchair. She felt fragile. If he hadn't seen what she could do, he never would have understood why she was so important. They had to get her to safety. Cradling her, he stepped sideways through the broken doors out into the bright hallway. His skin tingled from their closeness.

Arün glanced back to check on Elek. The dracun reached down through the hole it had made and Elek slashed at its arm with his scryth. It hissed and jerked its limb back into the ceiling.

Arün called to the Tyro. "Forget the dracun. Follow me!"

Elek grabbed the clothing bags off the back of the wheelchair and ducked through the doors. The elevator groaned and creaked as the dracun resumed tearing through the ceiling.

A few yards ahead a sliding glass door with a green exit sign led to the parking lot. They ran towards it.

"The truck's outside!" Arün yelled.

The night air was cold as they left the building and ran across the empty lot. Nadja stood in the bed of their rusty pickup truck parked by the entrance. *Almost there.*

Arün shot a glance over his shoulder. Elek ran a few paces back, the white lab coat billowed around him. *Run faster, kid,* he thought. Nadja would never forgive Arün if something happened to her Tyro. Beyond Elek, the sliding glass doors shattered into a million pieces. The dracun emerged like a locomotive.

Elek turned and fired. The gun coughed, flashing brilliant green in the darkness. The dracun slowed but kept coming. Arün's heart raced. "Run, Elek!"

They reached the truck, and Nadja waved them towards the cab. "Hurry! Engine's running!" she yelled.

Arün yanked open the passenger door, dumped Alley onto the seat, ran around the front and slid behind the wheel.

Elek vaulted into the bed of the pickup and pounded on the roof of the truck. "Go! Go! Go!"

Arün threw the vehicle into gear and slammed his foot down on the accelerator. The old truck leaped forward knocking Elek and Nadja into the bed where a bunch of loose metal pipes rattled around.

Alley struggled to sit up. "Is it gone?"

Arün checked the rear-view mirror. The dracun was catching up. "Not yet."

Elek pushed himself up against the window of the truck cabin and fired at the creature as it charged towards the tail of the pickup.

They skidded out onto the main road. Arün reached behind and slid the rear window open. "Can you get rid of it?"

Nadja grabbed one of the long metal pipes rolling around in the bed of the truck. "I think so. When I tell you to —brake hard."

Arün nodded and steered the truck onto the 405 interstate on-ramp. He didn't know what Nadja was planning, but he trusted her. She was one of the best wardens in the Guild.

He checked the rear-view mirror again as he sped out onto the highway. The dracun was charging after them, tearing up chunks of asphalt as its feet dug into the road. Nadja lashed something onto the far end the pipe—her scryth. It crackled with green fire lighting up the bed of the truck. She was making a spear.

Nadja called through the window. "Slow down a little."

Arün took his foot off the accelerator.

The dracun gained ground as it bounded towards them.

Nadja braced the butt end of the make-shift spear against the corner of the truck bed behind Arün and yelled, "Brake!"

Arün slammed his foot on the brake pedal and the truck skidded to a stop.

The dracun tried to slow down, but it was moving too fast. Nadja raised the end of the pipe with the glowing blade lashed to it and the creature slammed into the back of the pickup impaling itself on the spear. Its yellow eyes went wide. It howled and clawed at the pipe as a wave of green fire swept across its body.

Arün pressed the accelerator. The creature crumbled to ash behind them. He knew the sense of safety was an illusion —dracun hunted in packs.

12

GETAWAY

ALLEY

Alley's skin tingled strangely where Arün's hand rested against her arm. It was like a million tiny electric charges danced between them. With each passing minute, her head became clearer, and more strength returned to her limbs. She brushed her skin where the dracun's fireball had scorched her arm—it was smooth and unblemished now. Strange.

She flexed her hand and looked over at Arün. "Do you feel that?"

The warden focused on the highway. He didn't answer. Alley figured that he must not have heard her over the roar of the truck's diesel engine. Behind them, Nadja and Elek sat in the bed of the pickup. She wondered if they were cold. At least the sun was coming up—the darkness giving way to the new day. Hopefully, a better day. She closed her eyes and enjoyed the sensation of her body returning to normal.

Arün finally replied. "Yes, I feel it."

Alley opened her eyes. "Any idea what it is?"

Arün glanced at the rear-view mirror. "I'll tell you later."

Her heart raced. She turned to look back down the highway, half expecting to see another dracun in pursuit. "Are we safe?"

"For the moment, but we need to keep moving."

She and Elek were lucky to be alive. The truck was headed back to Redmond. Cars trickled onto the interstate, the first hint of morning traffic.

"Those monsters—*dracun*—whatever. Where do they come from?"

Arün opened his mouth as if he was about to say something, then stopped. He was quiet for a moment and then continued. "Far away. Exiled here by the Mages after the Ash War."

"Mages?" She raised an eyebrow. "Like the kind that cast magic spells?"

Arün chuckled. "Some people would call what they do magic, but they consider themselves scientists. Your father is one of them—part of a secret Order of explorers who have dedicated their lives to progressing and improving humankind."

"My dad is a wizard?"

"Mage."

She rolled her eyes. "He's part of this Order?"

Arün smiled. "Yes. He's on the Council."

She already knew he was a scientist, but she'd never been clear about his exact field of study. He seemed to dabble in everything, but she'd never guessed that included magic. Rakman had mentioned a Council—was he a mage too? And what about her mom? Alley raked her fingers through her hair. So many secrets. They would have to wait—she needed to understand the immediate threat. "These dracun things are dangerous. Why are they allowed near people?"

"They aren't all bad. We have strict laws they must follow, and every one of them has a warden handler."

"That doesn't seem to apply to the ones chasing me."

Arün's grip tightened on the wheel. "The Obsidian Clan. Yes—they've become a problem."

"But, you hang out with the rest of them?" She couldn't imagine how a dracun could be safe to have around.

"We don't *hang out*. We monitor them to ensure they are blending in well—contributing to human society. We also give them one of these each month." Arün reached into his jacket and withdrew a small vial filled with clear purple liquid.

Alley took it. Something golden sparkled and swirled inside the mixture. "What is it?"

"An insurance policy."

"What do you mean?"

"It locks them in their human form. As it wears off, it

becomes very painful. When they meet with their warden, they get another dose, and they can go on living their lives as a human."

"Sounds cruel."

"There's no pain if they follow the Mage Laws and meet with their warden on schedule."

Alley handed the vial back to him. "Doesn't seem to work on the Obsidians."

Arün shook his head. "Maybe they altered the formula. Maybe they stopped taking the doses and survived the withdrawal. It doesn't matter—they can transform now, and it's a problem."

"Great—and they've been living around us for how long?"

"More than a century."

Alley raised an eyebrow. "In all that time no one has noticed them?"

"Some people have. We have ways to help them forget."

"What does that mean?"

"We don't hurt them—we alter their memory. It doesn't come up often. Most dracun try very hard to blend in. The penalty for exposing their true form is death."

Alley looked into the windows of the passing cars—everyone looked human. It was strange to think some of them weren't. She turned back to Arün. "Why did the Mages exile them here? Seems like an unnecessary risk."

"Their decisions have always been motivated by a desire to improve mankind."

Alley rolled her eyes. "Thanks for that vague non-answer."

Arün laughed. "I'm certain you'll have a chance to ask them yourself."

She shook her head. Why did everything have to be a mystery? She needed to get home. Dad might answer her questions, and she could grab her mom's journal. Alley wished she could call him but she'd forgotten her phone while escaping Elek's house.

"Everyone's keeping secrets from me," she murmured.

Arün looked over. "Sometimes people keep secrets to protect the ones they care about."

"I don't think deception is a good way to express love."

Arün focused his attention back on the road. "Sometimes there's no choice."

Alley pressed her hand against the faux-leather upholstery of the truck interior to steady herself. It was tan and cracked from years of service. "Do you have a choice about answering my questions?"

"I swore an oath to your father and the rest of the Council. There are some questions I can't answer—at least until you're safe."

Alley breathed a heavy sigh and glanced over her shoulder at her friend. Elek huddled in the rear of the pickup, the autumn wind whipped his hair around. He'd been training to be a warden for the past year. How long could he survive against these things? What kind of life would that be?

She turned to Arün. "This seems like a dangerous line of work."

He shrugged. "We train for it and the Mages have made us stronger and faster. And like I said earlier, most of the dracun don't give us a problem."

"I'm worried about my friend."

Arün glanced in the rear-view mirror at Elek. "Don't—he's the best Tyro we've ever trained."

"What's a Tyro?"

"Just another word for an apprentice. Elek has progressed to a level that other Tyro take five times as long to reach. He'll be fine."

Alley wanted to believe the warden, but she'd seen the police officers get torn to pieces in the hospital and Brent and Elek get thrown like rag-dolls. You couldn't train for that. You had to be lucky enough to survive. She chewed on her nail. "How did you get involved with all this?"

Arün was quiet for a moment. "I was running from another life and a man took me in. I didn't know it then, but he was a mage. He saw something in me I hadn't known was there."

"Do you enjoy it?"

"Sometimes I wonder how things would have gone if I'd made different choices."

"Ever tried to do something else?"

Arün half smiled and ran his hands along the top of the steering wheel. "Sometimes you keep doing a thing, not because you enjoy it anymore, but because you've gotten good at it."

"If you aren't happy, why don't you do something about it?"

Arün took a deep breath and blew it out. "I'm surprised to hear you say that."

"Why?"

"This ability you have. It hasn't brought you happiness and yet you have done nothing to improve that situation."

Alley crossed her arms. "Before you stalked me I was doing something about it."

"You were hiding from it."

Maybe he was right. She'd been trying to suppress her abilities for years. Every time they'd emerged it had been a disaster. The only safe option had been to try to bury them. Alley pressed her lips together. "Well, I'm doing something about it now, but you'd have hidden from it too."

Arün nodded. "We're all hiding from something."

Alley squinted at him. "What are you hiding from?"

His grip on the steering wheel tightened. "One day I might tell you."

A blast of cold air rushed into the cabin as the rear window slid open. Elek's head filled the opening. "There's a breakfast place up ahead. I promised Alley pancakes!"

Arün yelled back. "That's not a good plan."

Alley felt her stomach rumble at the thought of food. She touched Arün's shoulder. "Please. I'm starving, and I've got to get out of this bathrobe."

Arün checked the rear-view mirror. "What do you think, Nadja?"

The other warden poked her head into the window. "It's dangerous, but we need to get her some coffee. I don't want her having an episode while we're traveling."

Arün nodded. "Okay, but eat quickly—I've got a bad feeling about this."

13

THE MAP

ALLEY

Alley eyed Nadja across the table. "You going to tell me where we're headed?" She stuffed a forkful of syrup-soaked pancake into her mouth. Normally, she'd have enjoyed the warm texture of the buttery, sugary bite dissolving on her tongue, but all she could think about were the poor cops back at the hospital and the uncertainty of what would happen next.

They were crammed into a booth with red vinyl cushioned seats at a diner off Redmond Way. Dawn lit the overcast sky a steel gray as the morning breakfast crowd drifted in. The diner was thick with the smell of fried bacon and maple syrup.

Nadja pushed her plate out of the way and smoothed an old map out onto the table. "You should drink that coffee." She nodded toward the mug in front of Alley's plate.

Alley swallowed her mouthful of pancake and took a long sip. The coffee was weak. Hopefully, it would be enough to prevent another flare up.

Arün sat next to Nadja with a phone cupped against his ear. He had called the Council to get a repair crew out to the Mori's house and was listening to someone on the other end. The creases between his brows were deepening with each passing moment. Elek was keeping watch next to Alley. His eyes darted around the restaurant, then out to the parking lot on the other side of the big glass window in a steady sweep.

Alley pointed with her fork at the yellow creased parchment that Nadja had spread across half the table. It was an old map of the Pacific Northwest that looked like it dated back to the Gold Rush. "That looks a lot like a treasure map," she said.

"This is where we are going." Nadja tapped a location in the middle of the wilderness. "There's someone there that can train you."

It was deep in the heart of the Cascade Mountains. There was nothing on the map that showed there was anything there, but the margin of the paper had a strange set of symbols drawn along the edge. "What does that mean?" Alley pointed at the writing.

"It's how we open the entrance."

"The entrance to what?"

"The place we are going."

Alley paused, her fork midway to her mouth. She looked at the marks then back at Nadja. "Like what? An underground bunker?"

"Not quite. Look, I know this isn't easy, but you will have to trust us. Right now, the less you know, the better."

Alley lowered her voice and squinted at Nadja. "I don't have to do anything. I want to know where you are taking me."

Elek leaned over. "Al, you can trust them. Besides, I'll be with you."

She didn't like it, but she trusted Elek. He was maybe the only person she trusted. She took another sip of coffee.

Nadja looked over at Elek. "You're going back to the College."

Elek's body stiffened. He lowered his voice. "I kept her safe last night."

"You acted recklessly," she shot back.

Alley set her mug down. Nadja was irritating her. "Elek is coming with me. I'm not going to a mysterious place with people I just met. Besides, he and I have a deal." She just needed to get through this day and then Elek would help her with the cure.

Nadja's hand clenched into a fist. "This isn't up for debate."

Alley smiled at her. "I agree. He's coming with us."

Nadja's eyes narrowed. She was about to say something

when Arün rested his hand on her arm. They exchanged a look. Nadja let out a long slow breath. Her hand unclenched. "Fine. You can come, Elek, but I want you back in training as soon as this is over."

Elek nodded and kicked Alley's foot under the table. She could tell he was struggling not to smile. Alley turned her attention back to Nadja. "Thank you."

Nadja cast a sharp glance at Elek. "He needs to learn to follow orders."

Alley wanted information, not to get into more arguments. She pointed to several places on the map. "Can you tell me what these symbols mean?"

Nadja scratched at the side of her face. She looked like she was trying to decide whether she would answer. She pointed to one mark. "This first one is Mt. Baker. One of the dracun clans lives in the caverns inside the mountain. The Obsidians. They are the ones hunting you."

"Those things live inside Mt. Baker?" Alley couldn't believe it.

"Only the Obsidian Clan lives beneath Baker. The other clans nest beneath different mountains. They like the geothermal heat produced by volcanic activity. It's also the only place the Mage Laws allow them to live in their natural form."

"There's more than one clan?"

"Yes, these other symbols are their lairs." Nadja pointed to the other markings on the map.

Alley counted six mountains including Baker and Mt. Rainier marked with dracun symbols. Six clans. It was hard to believe there were so many and that nobody had noticed them.

She looked over at Elek and raised her eyebrow. He shrugged. "Al, after what you went through yesterday and last night, does it seem that far-fetched?"

Alley turned back to Nadja. "Why are the Obsidian hunting me?"

"It has something to do with your ability. The Council suspects that either they see you as a threat to their rebellion and want you dead or they want to try to use you. We don't know which, and we're not staying around to find out. Obsidian attacks have been occurring daily over the past few weeks. The media believes they're suicides—people jumping off buildings to their death. Except they didn't jump—they were dropped."

Elek nudged Alley. "If you can learn how to control your power, you could help stop the dracun rebellion—you'd be saving lives."

Alley shook her head. "I'm only one person." How could she deal with them all? She wasn't a soldier. She'd never even been in a fight.

Nadja smiled. "The Council has confidence in you. If they didn't, we wouldn't be going to all this trouble."

Alley chewed on a forkful of food. She didn't want her powers. She didn't want to be hunted. Alley didn't want to deal with any of this—especially if there was still a chance she could be cured. "I don't want to hurt people," she said.

Nadja's hands balled into fists. "These things aren't people. They are a threat to humanity."

Alley tilted her head at Arün who was still on the phone. "He said not all dracun are bad."

Nadja looked at the wedding band on her left hand. "They're all bad—some are just worse than others."

Alley changed the subject. There was something about the wild look in Nadja's eyes that made her think it would be a bad idea to tell the warden she wasn't interested in helping. "What's this last mark?" she asked.

Nadja tore her eyes away from her ring and focused on where Alley was pointing in the depths of the Cascades.

"Glacier Peak. It's a prison for the Banished. Only Mages get in or out."

Why would they put a prison deep in the mountains? It gave Alley a bad feeling. "What are the Banished?"

"Dangerous prisoners of a war that happened a long time ago."

"You mean the Ash War?" Arün had mentioned the war, but provided no details. Strange that she'd read nothing about it. When had it happened and where?

Nadja nodded. "That's enough questions for now. When we've gotten you to safety, we can talk more."

Alley scooped up the last bite of her pancake and chewed on it as Nadja folded up the map. She'd gotten lucky when the dracun was crushed in the café and when she'd dropped the car on the other dracun. She wasn't like Elek—she didn't want to be training to fight. She just wanted to learn how to control her ability or get rid of it. "I need to go home and see my dad."

Nadja paused mid-fold. "We have to keep moving."

Alley pointed her fork at Nadja. "Let me put it a different way—we will go see him after we eat."

"Don't be foolish. You were attacked only a few blocks from that house."

"I need to talk to him, and I need to get something he gave me." She never should have left the journal behind. Somewhere inside might be the specific information that explained the cure.

"It's not safe." Nadja finished folding the map and jammed it into an inside coat pocket. The corner of her left eye twitched.

Elek scanned the parking lot. "Maybe Alley can just call him?"

"No El, I need to go there. There's something I have to get." Alley didn't look at her friend as she spoke. She traded stares with Nadja across the table.

Arün turned off his cell phone and regarded the standoff. "Alley you can't go back, especially given the news I just heard."

"I don't care about the risk!"

A few of the diner's early patrons turned towards their

booth as she yelled. Elek glared at them until they looked away.

Arün leaned in and lowered his voice. "There's been an attack at your house. The warden stationed there was able to *ash* the dracun before it could get to your dad, but there'll be more. Staying mobile is the best way to throw them off. We can't leave you in any location for too long."

Her heart raced. Dad was attacked? She couldn't lose him too. Alley slid out of the booth and grabbed the plastic hospital bag with her clothes. Her hand was shaking. "I'm going to change." She glared at them, turned on her heels and stalked off towards the restrooms.

"Al, wait up!" Elek jogged to catch up as she weaved between the tables.

Alley slowed as they approached the restrooms. "I need space, El."

"No worries. I'll just hang out here and make sure no one bothers you."

People were staring. The bathrobe made her look like she'd escaped from a mental hospital. Any of those faces could be something they didn't appear to be—it gave her the creeps.

"Thanks, El," she said.

Her dad was in danger. That changed things. Alley couldn't just leave him behind. She needed time to think—time to find a way to make sure her dad would be safe.

14

VISIONS

ALLEY

Alley shouldered the bathroom door open and shuffled over to one of the two sinks against the left wall. She dropped the plastic bag on the tiled floor and leaned against the counter. Her reflection stared back at her in the mirror. Tangled, greasy hair framed her face. She looked terrible.

Alley breathed into her palm. The smell made her nose wrinkle. There was a dish of mints near the cash register. She needed a double helping. Alley turned on the hot water. As it warmed up, she changed into the clothes Elek had rescued from the hospital—jeans, a black tank-top, and her favorite gray turtleneck sweater. As she dressed, images of the last day flashed through her mind. Brent's limp body. The dead cops. The dracuns. Now they had attacked her dad. He couldn't run from them—he couldn't even walk. What if more came—what if the warden guarding him couldn't handle them all? She had to protect him. Her dad was the only family she had left.

The water was steaming, coating the large mirror with a layer of fog. Alley cupped her hands, closed her eyes and splashed hot water on her face. The heat penetrated her pores. It felt good.

She heard the bathroom door open. Elek wouldn't have let anyone inside, maybe he was just checking on her. Alley wiped the water from her eyes. When she turned around, no one else was in the bathroom. She reached down into her duffel bag and found the handle of her plastic hair brush. Alley turned off the water and attacked the knots in her hair. The fogged mirror made it hard to see if she was making any progress. She rubbed the glass clean with the sleeve of her sweater.

As she pulled her hand away from the mirror, she saw a tall figure standing behind her in the reflection. Her heart jumped. Alley whirled around. She was alone. Was she seeing things? Maybe it was a side effect of the sedative? Alley turned back around to finish brushing her hair. In the mirror, the woman appeared, standing behind her. She was blurry, like an out-of-focus picture. Tall and pale with black hair. She wore a dark dress that floated in the air like she was under water. Only her eyes were in focus—they were lavender.

Alley glanced over her shoulder once more. There was no one in the bathroom. She turned back to the mirror. The figure was still there. Waiting. Alley rubbed at the glass again.

"Hello, Alley." The woman's voice was foreign. Alley couldn't identify the accent, but she found herself captivated. The woman's hair billowed around her in slow motion.

"Who are you?" Alley's words echoed in the empty bathroom.

"I've been watching you, child."

Alley tried to speak, but she couldn't get her mouth to form words. She tried to turn around but found that she was frozen in place. The woman's eyes were the strangest shade of purple. She moved to stand beside Alley and leaned forward to whisper in her ear.

"You and I will do great things."

The woman reached into the mirror and it rippled like a pool of water. Alley felt herself being drawn toward it. The reflection of the bathroom distorted and transformed into a sweeping vista.

She was flying above Seattle. The city lay in ruins. Dark shadows flew amongst the jagged remains of steel and shattered glass. Fires billowed smoke from the rooftops, darkening the skies. Glowing embers and ash swirled through the air like burning snowflakes.

Something that looked like a giant raven was perched atop the remains of the tallest building. Alley felt her body fly towards it at incredible speed. It wasn't a bird, but an enormous dragon with black scales. A woman stood on its massive head, the wind sent chaotic ripples through her dark hair and black coat. She reached out with her hand towards the ruins of one of the neighboring skyscrapers and clenched her fingers into a fist. The building swayed then collapsed in on itself. Dust and debris billowed up from the empty canyons of the city.

Alley looked to the north. In the distance, she could see that Mt. Baker had erupted. A huge plume of fiery ash rose into the sky. Flashes of lightning illuminated the heavens revealing for an instant an army of dracun soaring within the smoke.

The woman raised her hand. The ground shook. To the south, the top of Mt. Rainer exploded blasting lava and ash into the sky.

The woman turned. She had Alley's face, but it was transformed. Soot smudged her skin like war paint. The ends of her auburn hair were blackened as were the whites of her eyes.

"This is our destiny. We will conquer the world."

No! Alley tried to close her eyes, to hide from the destruction, but her eyelids wouldn't shut. Her heart raced. She was hallucinating. She had to wake up, but the woman seemed to have a hold on her mind. She pushed back, tried to force herself to imagine something else.

"Do not fight me, child."

The swirling ash turned to snow. The flakes grew heavier and thicker. Her feet felt cold. When she looked down, she was standing in an ankle-deep drift. She was in an icy cavern. The crystalline roof rose like a frozen cathedral high overhead. Weak sunlight filtered through the frigid walls bathing the room in a soft blue light. In front of her was a mountain of ice and snow.

She stumbled as a tremor rocked the cavern. Cracks formed in the giant mountain of ice. Large chunks tumbled away. Alley's gut clenched as she felt hot sulfurous air rush towards her from the pile. The sound of a thousand ice cracks echoed through the hall. The frozen mound rose upward.

Alley realized she was looking at the snow encrusted head of a dragon whose skull must have been at least as big as her entire house. Sheets of ice fell away from its scalp revealing cold, wide-set eyes. They slid open and locked onto her. Steam rose from its massive snout. Hundreds of sharp horns protruded from its jaw and head.

It opened its mouth and inhaled, pulling the air from the chamber like an enormous vacuum. Alley gasped and tried to take a step backward. She couldn't. Her feet were frozen into the ground. She was trapped.

Alley heard the woman's voice again. "Death comes to those who oppose me."

She watched in slow motion as the monster dragon roared and an expanding ball of orange fire surged toward her like a tidal wave. Alley threw up her arms to block the intense heat. It was all around her, burning her body. She screamed as she was blasted backward.

"Alley! Alley!" Elek was shaking her.

Where was she? Her eyes snapped open. Alley swiveled her head around. Elek was cradling her on the floor of the bathroom.

"Al, thank God. You scared me."

She reached up to the sink and tried to stand. "W—what happened?"

"You tell me. I came in here a minute ago. You were convulsing on the floor."

Alley splashed cold water on her face and looked in the mirror—grateful to only see the reflection of herself and Elek. "I don't know El, maybe it was the drugs from the hospital?"

She wasn't sure if she should tell him all the details. At least not yet. She needed time to sort out whether it meant anything. The experience had been more real than any dream she could remember. Alley looked down at her hand. It was shaking. Was she capable of that kind of destruction? She hoped not. The possibility made her knees weak. She gripped the edge of the sink and closed her eyes. She inhaled and breathed out, then looked at her hand again. It was still shaking. "I'm scared, Elek."

He squeezed her shoulder. "Me too, Al. We'll get through this."

Alley looked at him in the mirror as she dried her face. "I need to go home. I need to talk to my dad—make sure he's safe. And there's something there that I think might help me."

Elek made one of his mischievous lopsided smiles. "Let's go. We can be there and back in twenty minutes. It'll be another five before they notice we're gone."

Alley turned and hugged him. She felt like crying.

He held her tightly. "I'll always have your back, Al."

"I know," she murmured. Alley realized at that moment just how much she loved Elek. She released him, then put her hair up into a ponytail.

Elek held the door open. "Well let's move, I've got a truck to hot wire, and I'm pushing my luck hanging out in the ladies' room."

Alley smiled and glanced back at the mirror. She couldn't shake the feeling that something was watching her from the other side of the glass surface.

15

SMOKE

ALLEY

Elek sparked the ignition wires, and the old truck engine roared to life. Alley slid into the passenger seat and looked back. The wardens were still in the diner. As the vehicle pulled into traffic, she let out a breath she didn't realize she'd been holding. The house was just a few minutes away. She wanted to flop into bed and sleep for a week.

Alley turned to Elek. "Thanks for helping me."

"No problem, Al."

"Nadja will be angry," she said.

Elek waved his hand. "She's in a perpetual bad mood."

"Why?"

"Her family was killed by dracun nine years ago."

Alley sucked air in through her teeth. After the night's events, it was too easy to imagine the horrific details.

Elek continued, "She hates them all—even the law-abiding registered ones, but she's an amazing warden."

Alley shook her head. "I can't believe she wanted to risk having a family in her line of work."

Elek shrugged. "She wasn't a warden before the attack. She used to be a software engineer. Made a lot of money during the tech bubble and got out before everything collapsed. She owns a big farm around here. Used to do software contracts from home."

"Why did the dracun attack her family?"

"She thought her last job was a standard defense contract, but it was a project commissioned by the Mage Council. Rogue dracuns wanted to put a stop to it. Arün saved her life, but wasn't able to save her family."

The truck passed giant sequoia pines as they headed up a steep winding section of Union Hill Road. "Do you trust Arün?" she asked.

"He trained most of the highest-ranking wardens," Elek replied.

"There's something strange about him though, right?"

Elek ran a hand through his jet-black hair. "The only thing that's a little weird is that he doesn't look as old as he must be. There are old black and white photos of him and some mages in the halls back at the College. They all look the same as today. Weird, right?"

"Yeah. Anything else?"

"He had a fianceé, but never married."

"Had?"

"She died. Nadja never told me the details."

Alley chewed on her nail. So Arün was probably still dealing with that. She felt a little better knowing more about the people protecting her. There was still something strange about Arün. The way her body reacted to him being nearby was bizarre.

"Al, they may both have personal issues, but they're committed to protecting you. We're taking a monster risk going back to your place without them." Elek. He loved puns. Mostly bad ones.

She forced herself to laugh. "Thanks for doing this."

"You said something at your house might help you?"

"I'm hoping Dad can answer some questions and I need to get a book he gave me yesterday."

"A book?"

Alley hoped she could trust him. "My mother's journal. He said it holds answers to my past."

"Sounds interesting."

"It's too much to read through right now. I'm hoping he can give me the highlights."

Alley cracked the window and leaned against the door. The crisp morning air played with her hair. They turned into her neighborhood.

She gasped. "Oh no—"

Thick black smoke rose above the trees that lined the street. Something was on fire.

It was her house.

Her pulse raced.

Flames licked out of a huge hole in the roof. The sound of distant sirens drifted through the air. It had to be a dracun attack. They'd come back. They'd burned her house. Her jaw clenched.

Elek slowed.

She opened the door and jumped out.

"Are you crazy, Alley? Get back in the truck!"

"My dad might be in there!" She sprinted across the yard. The neighbors were out on their lawns pointing and shouting at her. She ignored them and bounded up the walkway. The front door was ajar. She pushed it open and went inside. The interior felt like an oven.

Alley covered her nose and mouth with the sleeve of her sweater. "Dad!" she yelled.

No answer.

She checked each room on the first floor. There was no sign of him. Flames clawed up the walls and at the ceilings. In the kitchen, the body of a man lay on the floor in a puddle of blood, still gripping one of the strange looking warden guns. His face and neck had been slashed. She tried not to be sick.

Alley took the stairs to the second floor two at a time, afraid of what she might find, but unable to stop herself. The smoke was thicker. It made her eyes water. She had to crouch to keep from choking.

Alley made her way down the smoky hall towards her bedroom and stumbled into her father's empty wheelchair.

Please be alive, she thought.

The wallpaper in the corridor had been shredded by clawed hands, but there was no blood. What happened? Was he on the floor somewhere up here? She crouched and scrambled to his bedroom. A wall of smoke and flame knocked her backward.

"Dad!" Her yell came out weak and raspy from the thick smoke.

Still no answer.

The fire was devouring the house. She backed down the hall and staggered into her bedroom. The hallway floor collapsed. Her room was engulfed in smoke. The bed was a bonfire. Orange flames rose to the ceiling leaving black scorch marks. The journal rested on the edge of what remained of her mattress. Fire nibbled at the leather-bound tome.

Alley grabbed a slipper and batted the journal onto the floor. She knelt and folded her shag throw rug over the book to extinguish the flames. From the bottom drawer of her dresser, she grabbed a sweatshirt and wrapped it around the scorched volume.

Burning pieces of the ceiling broke free. Alley needed to get out of the house. She coughed into her sleeve. The floor beneath her knees was hot to the touch. If she could get onto the porch roof, she could climb to safety.

The house moaned, then shuddered. There was a loud cracking sound. The floor sagged and the burning wreckage of her bed disappeared as it fell out of sight. Flames and embers shot upward through the new hole, filling the room with thick black smoke. She covered her eyes and face, trying to filter air with the sweatshirt wrapped book.

Where was the window? Her heart hammered in her chest and her head throbbed in pain.

The house shook.

Not now, she thought.

Energy flooded her head. It was happening again. One of her episodes.

Alley gritted her teeth and tried to stop the flow coursing through her mind. She crawled toward where she thought the window was. She had to get out before her power, or the fire tore the building down around her.

Alley found the sill and dug her nails under the edge. The sash was stuck. Pain ripped through her head like she'd been hit with a hammer.

She was back in the middle of the forest clearing. The ground was cracking open in front of her. Flowers pushed their way upward. As the blossoms opened, they sprayed golden dust into the air.

She had to stop them before the energy collapsed the house on top of her.

Alley rushed forward ripping the blossoms from the ground

before they bloomed. For each one she picked, another grew up in its place. Her arms overflowed with buds.

In her haste, she tripped and fell into a huge patch of the flowers. A giant cloud of sparkling dust kicked up from the blooms. In the forest, she could hear a child laughing. Alley gasped and inhaled a lungful of the dust.

Energy split her mind open and poured out of her like a dam bursting.

No, she thought. *Not now!*

It was unstoppable.

16

FIRE

ALLEY

The second story of the house exploded outward. Splintered wood, broken glass and chunks of drywall rained onto the lawn. Alley fell forward through the place where her bedroom wall had been and landed on the porch roof.

She gasped. Fresh air poured into her lungs.

Somehow, the energy had saved her. The headache was gone.

Alley slipped on the moss-covered shingles, but this time she controlled her slide, jamming her heels into the rain gutter to stop herself from falling off the edge.

Elek ran toward her across the debris-littered yard. "Alley!" he yelled.

Heat pressed against her back. The interior of the house

was a wall of flame and smoke. "I'm okay." She said it to herself as much as to Elek. Alley hooked a leg over the edge of the roof and dropped the remaining few feet to the ground.

Her body went into a coughing spasm as she backed away from the house. Dad wouldn't have left without his wheelchair. If he'd been trying to escape without it, she would have seen him. He had to have been taken—probably by dracun. Alley wiped at her eyes. They could have protected him if they'd come back to the house instead of going to eat.

Elek slowed and caught his breath. "I should have gone in with you."

She shook her head. "There was nothing you could have done."

The wail of approaching sirens filled the air. Elek looked towards the street. "We need to go before the fire department shows up."

Neighbors crowded on the sidewalk. They called to Alley and Elek to step away from the blaze.

Alley looked at the house. This was where she'd spent her entire life. Tears traced lines through the ash and soot on her cheeks. It was all gone now. The dracuns had destroyed it. They'd taken her father. They'd taken everything. She gritted her teeth. Her hand tightened into a fist. Somehow she'd make them pay for what they'd done.

Elek put his arm around her. "I'm so sorry, Alley."

She let Elek guide her through the wreckage on the lawn. Glowing embers swirled around them. As they passed through the crowd, she heard concerned neighbors asking if she was all right—if her father was safe. *Safe?* Alley didn't even know if he was alive. She clutched the journal to her chest like a life preserver. Elek led her back to the truck. She heard the pickup start. It lurched into motion as the flashing red strobe lights of emergency vehicles lit up the street behind them. She stared out the windshield, not focusing on anything. Dad had to be alive. He had to be. Alley took a deep breath and relaxed her grip on the sweatshirt wrapped book. Wherever they had taken him—she would find him.

Elek handed her a tissue. She wiped the ash from her face. "Dad's wheelchair was upstairs, but he was gone."

Elek sighed. "Thank God. I was afraid to ask."

Alley continued, "There was a dead warden downstairs. It looked like a dracun had clawed him."

Elek clenched the steering wheel. "His name was Byron. He was my Recon and Tracking instructor at the College. Nadja told me he would keep an eye on your father."

"I'm sorry, El," she said.

"Don't be. Every warden knows the risks. Sounds like Byron went down fighting. It's what he would have wanted."

Traffic was thick with morning commuters. They sat in silence for a while.

"I'm afraid my dad might have been kidnapped by dracun."

"We'll find him, Al," Elek answered.

"Have they ever taken anyone before?"

Elek met Alley's gaze for a moment. "I don't know, but the fact that you didn't find his body is a good thing."

Alley nodded. She ran her hand over the old fabric of the sweatshirt in her lap. It was the tattered one she always wore when she was feeling sick. She unwrapped its folds. "At least they didn't find this."

Flakes of ash blackened the fabric as she peeled it away from the journal. The front cover was charred. The margins of the pages had been eroded by flame and smeared by soot. Alley blew the burned bits off the top of the book.

Elek cracked the window. Fresh air flooded the cabin. "I hope that was worth risking your neck for. Nadja and Arün are going to kill us."

Alley flipped through the book. A folded note slipped out from between the pages at the back of the journal. She opened it. Inside was her father's familiar handwriting:

"My dearest daughter,

I hope you can forgive an old man for his misjudgment — for trying to preserve your innocence for too long. I have only ever wanted you to know happiness. No matter what you think of me, know you have always been my greatest love and my greatest blessing.

I know you have many questions. Some of which will be answered in the pages of this journal. For the rest, you can trust an old friend of mine, Bezo, to provide many answers and Elek's parents know many things as well. The rest of the Mages, I fear, may lead you astray. Be careful seeking their counsel.

Good luck with your training.

All my love until we meet again, Your father, Ben"

She folded the note and slipped it back between the pages, then opened the book to a random entry written in her mother's long-hand.

"*—was correct, at some point, we will have to inform the Council about this new development. Alley started calling me 'Mom.' I never thought we would have children. She makes me feel both young and old at the same time. She is bright and seems to be growing like a normal child. I would have expected some differences, but she has been hitting the standard developmental milestones. Lab results show interesting anomalies in blood work, some expected, other's a surprise. We must send them over to Dr. Mori for further analysis. There are other factors we will continue to monitor—*"

Alley looked up at Elek. "Did you know my parents and your father used to work together?"

Elek furrowed his brow. "What? My dad is a pediatrician—"

She interrupted, "—who must have worked for the Council or maybe still does."

"He's said nothing to me."

"Maybe it was his idea to recruit you to be a warden."

Elek fell silent. It didn't look like he liked that idea.

Alley flipped to the back of the journal. The final entries

were dated around the time when she'd turned ten—just a few months before the lab accident.

"I woke up in the middle of the night. Everything in the house was floating. When I checked on Alley, she was sleeping. I don't think she knows anything happened. The presentation of this new ability might be linked to puberty, but we'll need more tests to confirm. The dracuns will sense it. We must determine a safe way to suppress this until she learns control. We have to explain things to her soon.

Forester is recommending we move back to the labs, but it would be detrimental to Alley's development. She needs to grow up in a home. She needs to understand love and compassion. Without that she could do more harm than good. Forester told Ben I've lost sight of the project goals. He wouldn't be saying that if it was his daughter. He wouldn't say that if he knew the truth."

Alley ran her finger across the indentations in the page where her mother's pen had pressed into the paper. *Mom.* A lump formed in her throat. She couldn't remember the night her mother was describing, but it was interesting that she thought the dracuns might have been able to sense her power. Was that how they could track her now?

The next entry was two months later. The handwriting was different—her dad had added this one.

"My sweet Laura is dead. Forester is dead. The lab was destroyed. Arün rescued me from the wreckage. I was pinned under a beam for two hours. Thankful to be alive, but the doctors say I will never walk again. Rakman proposed some experimental

therapy to repair my spine, but I can't risk my life anymore. Alley is still in shock. I've done what I can to ease her memories, but I couldn't remove it all. I don't know what would happen if she experienced another loss right now—it could make her unstable. Laura and I should have already begun her training, but I'll wait a little while longer. She's been through too much—we both have."

Arün had mentioned that the Wardens had ways of making people forget—had her father changed her memory of the accident? She'd hoped that the journal would help her find a way to cure herself. Maybe it still held that answer, but now it was raising more questions. She had a horrible feeling that learning to control her ability might be her only chance at helping rescue her dad. If he was alive, how much time did she have to learn before it was too late?

Alley wrapped the journal back up as Elek pulled the truck into the parking lot of the diner. Nadja and Arün were outside. Arün's gaze bore into Alley almost as if he had been watching them approach from a mile away. Nadja paced back and forth with her cell phone pressed to her head. Her face was flushed. It was clear she was yelling.

Elek ran his fingers through his hair, and half smiled at Alley. "Brace yourself, I don't think this will be pretty."

Alley shook her head. "There's nothing they can say that will make this day any worse."

17

FALLOUT

ALLEY

Nadja jammed her phone into her pocket and ran to the truck as Elek pulled into one of the empty spaces. A vein on her forehead looked like it was ready to burst. She yanked at the handle of the driver-side door, but Elek had locked it.

"I cannot believe you did this!"—her muffled yell pierced the glass—"the sheer stupidity, immaturity"—Nadja launched into a string of incoherent profanity. Bits of spittle sprayed the window. She pounded her fist on the door to emphasize each point—"you risked Alley's life and went against your oath as a warden!"

Elek unlocked the door and pushed it open with his foot, shoving Nadja backward. He squared his shoulders and jabbed a finger at her. "As you're so fond of reminding me, I'm not a full warden yet. I've only taken the Tyro Oath and yes, I broke that, but you've broken the Warden's Oath more times than I can count," he jerked his thumb at Alley, "She's been my friend far longer than I've been in training. She needed me."

Nadja crossed her arms and cocked her head to the side. "You jeopardized the mission."

Elek's hands balled into tight fists. He looked ready to yell again.

Arün finished walking across the parking lot. He stood beside Nadja and scanned the clouds.

Alley got out of the truck. She'd had enough. They were wasting time. "We have to rescue my dad!"

Arün looked down from the sky, concern etched into his face. "What happened?"

Elek unclenched his hands. "Alley's house was burned. Byron is dead. We don't know what happened to her dad—Alley thinks he was kidnapped."

Nadja stepped back. Her shoulders sagged as her arms went slack at her sides. Her anger drained away. She leaned against the hood of the truck. "We never should have left Byron on his own. Not with the dracun hunting."

Arün nodded. He kicked at the gravel, sending pebbles skittering across the parking lot. The rush of the passing cars filled the silence. Alley wanted to yell at them to hurry, but she resisted the urge. She understood the loss they were feeling.

After a moment Arün spoke. "He was a good warden. Let's make his sacrifice count."

Nadja turned to Elek. "He died fighting?"

Elek nodded.

Nadja rubbed the back of her neck and looked up into the sky. "There's a good chance they left a lookout behind at the house," she leveled her gaze at Elek, "I'm reporting your insubordination—"

Alley cut her off. "He was protecting me."

Nadja gave her an icy stare. "He'd have been lucky to last half as long as Byron if you'd been attacked."

Elek rolled his eyes and vaulted into the back of the truck.

Arün moved to the driver-side door. "We need to keep moving. They could be watching us now."

Alley got back in the truck. Arün slid behind the steering wheel and looked over at her. "We'll search for your father soon, but we need to get you to safety first."

Alley clutched the sweatshirt wrapped journal to her chest. She could feel his genuine concern as if she were inside his mind. He reached over and wiped a smudge of soot off the curve of her jaw. Electrical sensations rippled outward from his touch. The burning in her lungs from the smoke she'd inhaled subsided.

He looked at the cloth bundle. "Did you find what you were looking for?"

His eyes were so green. "Yes and no." She lowered the journal into her lap. "I mean—I need time to study it."

Arün put the truck into gear. "I think whatever you find —you should keep to yourself. Some secrets are best left hidden."

"What does that mean?"

"It depends on what book you've got wrapped up in there —your dad had a lot of rare volumes."

Alley rubbed her hand across the journal. This one *was* rare. A book of information that her parents had kept secret from the Council—a book about her.

Nadja slid the rear window open and poked her face into the truck cabin. "We need supplies for where we're heading. There's a warden safe house off Route-2. You remember the one I'm talking about Arün?"

"Yes," he replied.

"We'll resupply there, then get back on the road. If everything goes smooth, we can be at the trail-head before noon."

Alley raised her voice above the rush of the wind outside. "Where are we going?"

Nadja looked over at her. "I told you already. We're taking you to someone that can train you. It will be a hike." Nadja slid the window closed and slipped on a pair of black sunglasses.

The truck's tires crunched on the parking lot gravel as it pulled out onto the road. Alley stared out the window and picked at a piece of cracked vinyl on the door jamb. Another headache was building at the back of her skull. She'd need more coffee soon. Alley wished her dad hadn't tried to protect her for so long. If she'd learned to control her ability, she could have been home when the dracuns attacked. She could have stopped them. Alley was scared for him—scared he was somewhere injured or worse. What if the training took too long? What if she failed? She didn't want to think about what that could mean.

Alley lowered her head, stretching the tight muscles in her neck and shoulders. She closed her eyes and listened to the gentle rumble of the truck's engine. Sleep grabbed hold of her bringing relief.

18

THE SAFE HOUSE

ALLEY

Alley awoke to silence and realized she was alone in the truck. Where was everyone?

Her stomach knotted. She gripped the journal against her chest.

The vehicle was parked outside a rundown single-story ranch with peeling blue paint and white trim. The driveway was blanketed in dead leaves that had fallen from the skeletal limbs of an old tree growing beside the house.

Alley's head throbbed. She needed coffee. Was this the safe house? She caught sight of Arün and Nadja moving towards the building with their guns drawn. The front door was splintered. Elek was crouched behind her in the bed of the pickup.

Arün covered Nadja as they disappeared inside. Alley held her breath expecting to hear gunshots.

Minutes ticked by.

Arün appeared and motioned for them to enter. Elek jumped out of the truck bed and Alley followed. "What's going on, El?"

"I don't know."

They made their way up the walkway and stepped through the shattered door. The inside smelled musty and damp. Long scratches had been carved into the walls and floors. The remains of furniture lay scattered everywhere. *Dracun,* she thought.

"We're in here." Nadja's voice came from the back of the house.

The wardens were in the kitchen. They contemplated markings that had been scrawled into a wooden table in the center of the room.

Alley studied the symbols. "What do they mean?"

"Nothing good." Nadja pulled her phone out, took a picture and typed a message. "Someone from the Council may be able to interpret them."

Pain lanced behind Alley's eyes. "Think there's any coffee in here?"

Elek checked the cabinets. "Headache coming back?"

"Yeah," she nodded.

The kitchen was stocked with plates, cans of soup and other non-perishable essentials. Elek found a can of instant coffee in the pantry and set it on the counter. Alley grimaced. She hated instant, but anything would be preferable to the pain in her head and the possibility of collapsing the house on them. Elek grabbed a mug, filled it with hot water from the faucet and scooped in several spoonfuls of the granules from the can. He handed the mug to Alley. “Bottoms up.”

She took the mug and wrinkled her nose. *Gross.* The hot black liquid slid down her throat and formed a warm spot in the middle of her stomach. It wasn’t as bad as she thought it would be—it wasn’t great either. She handed the mug back to Elek. “Thanks,” she said.

Nadja pocketed her phone. “Let’s get what we came for and get back on the road. The supplies are in the garage out back.”

She led them outside through what was left of the rear patio door. Alley grabbed the can of instant coffee as they left. One cup might not be enough.

Set back from the house was a small windowless detached garage that appeared to have been untouched in the dracun attack. Nadja punched a code into the combination lock on the side door and pulled it open.

Neon lights sputtered to life inside. The walls were lined with a variety of gear: tents, packs, sleeping bags, cooking supplies, rations, guns, bows, knives, munitions, clothing in various sizes, body armor, the list went on. Alley couldn’t believe the variety. It looked like whoever had stocked the place had been preparing for the end of the world. In the center of the garage sat two canvas wrapped motorcycles.

Arün pointed to the back. "Elek, find some decent clothes. The lab coat and scrubs won't cut it. You too, Alley. There should be clothing in both your sizes." While they searched, Nadja and Arün stuffed gear into backpacks.

Alley hid behind a locker door as she pulled on a pair of rugged black pants, a long dark wool jacket with a high collar and combat boots with deep treads. She took a waterproof backpack off the wall and pushed the journal to the bottom.

I'll find you, Dad, she thought.

The idea of her father captured by the dracun made the skin at the back of her neck prickle. Alley jammed the can of instant coffee in on top of the journal, then rolled the top of the pack and buckled it closed.

She watched Elek as she adjusted her pack's straps. He had selected a tight-fitting leather jacket, cargo pants and thick leather gloves.

Alley caught her reflection in the locker door mirror. The girl looking back was older and tired. She touched her neck where the dracun's iron grip had almost crushed her windpipe. There were no bruises, but she could still feel the sensation of being choked.

Arün shouldered one of the large packs. "It's time to go."

They filed out the side door of the garage. Alley noticed that Elek, and the wardens had armed themselves. Should she have grabbed a weapon? Would it even matter?

Elek stopped and pointed down the driveway. "Where's the truck?"

It had been parked near the street. Arün drew his gun and looked into the gray sky. A dark shadow descended from the clouds. "Is that the—"

It was the pickup. It rocketed downward and punched through the roof of the house with a deafening crash. Rotten cedar shingles and wood fragments shot into the air and rained down across the yard. The back end of the vehicle stuck up from the roof.

Alley's eyes went wide. She stumbled backward.

Somewhere inside the structure, a spark of electricity connected with fuel from the truck's ruptured gas tank. There was a chest pounding *thump* as the pickup exploded. The windows of the house blew outward as the entire building was engulfed in flames.

Arün raised an arm to shield his face from the heat and debris. "Back inside! Now!"

Alley's heart pounded. It didn't matter if it was one huge creature that had lifted the truck into the sky or a lot of the regular sized ones. Either way, they were in trouble.

19

US-2

ALLEY

Alley stumbled backward into the garage.

Nadja pulled the canvas off one of the motorcycles. "Elek, get the cover off that other bike!" She tossed the dusty tarp into a corner.

Arün had the side-door cracked open. "They'll be here any second to see if we're dead."

Elek uncovered the other bike and grabbed two helmets from a shelf. The vehicles were twins. Sleek black cruisers with long chrome exhaust pipes. The keys were in the ignitions. Alley had never ridden on a motorcycle. They always seemed too dangerous. Now, compared to the dracun, they seemed safer than walking. Elek handed her a helmet. She pulled it down over her head. The pads pushed firmly against her cheeks and skull. She felt safer with it on—like putting on a suit of armor.

Arün grabbed a helmet and gestured towards a bike. "Ever ridden one of these?"

Alley shook her head. "Never."

He strapped his pack onto the rear of the bike. "Guess I'm driving then. Hold on tight and keep your head down. If they follow, Nadja will cover us." He straddled the bike and motioned for Alley to sit behind him as he pulled on his helmet.

Elek sat on the other bike gripping the throttle. Nadja perched behind him, a pair of the strange warden guns hung from straps under each of her arms.

Elek gave Alley a thumbs-up. "We'll be right behind you, Al."

She nodded and swung onto the bike behind Arün. She wrapped her arms around his torso and tried to ignore the weird electrical sensation from his proximity.

Arün nodded at Elek. They kick-started the bikes. The engines roared to life. Acrid exhaust seeped through the vents in Alley's helmet. Her teeth chattered as the bike rumbled beneath her.

Elek snapped his visor down and thumbed a button that triggered the garage door opener. The hinged metal screeched and rattled as it rolled back into the ceiling. Nadja pulled the pins on two metal canisters and rolled them under the expanding gap below the door.

Plumes of thick yellow smoke spewed from the canisters. Would that really be enough to hide their escape? Before Alley could put more thought into their tactical plan, the bike tires squealed, and the cycle jumped forward into the thick mustard colored cloud. She hugged the warden tighter.

Elek's bike roared as it followed them through the smoke, past the heat of the blazing house and down the driveway. Somewhere off to the right, came an inhuman cry of rage. They punched through the smoke and banked hard out onto the main road.

Arün called over his shoulder. "Hold on tight."

He cranked the throttle and cut out onto Route-2. Alley could have reached out and touched the ground as the motorcycle angled towards the breakdown lane and shot up the road past the slower moving traffic.

Alley looked over her shoulder. Three dark shapes swooped down from the sky. They were huge—like cars with wings. Nadja filled them with glowing green rounds from the warden guns. The creatures crashed into the road behind them, thrashing in pain from the bullet wounds.

Nadja yelled to Arün. "Go faster!"

The bike roared and sped up. Blood pumped through Alley's veins. They had to be violating a half dozen traffic laws.

Something hissed and tugged at Alley's left forearm. A middle-aged balding man wearing a plaid flannel shirt and jeans. If it weren't for the lips pulled back over black gums and a mouth packed with sharp, twisted, blueish-black teeth, it almost looked human. Except it wasn't. It was a dracun, and it was running fast. Obscenely fast. Keeping up with the bike as Arün throttled it up the breakdown lane. One of the black hooked claws at the end of its almost-human fingers had snagged on the sleeve of her coat as it ran just behind the motorcycle.

It hissed in her mind, *You cannot escape.*

Anger washed over Alley like a white-hot flame. "Leave me alone!"

Her face flushed and her ears burned inside her helmet. The thing tried to get a better grip on the fabric of her sleeve. Alley's eyes narrowed. She pulled her left arm sharply across her chest. The dracun's claw ripped free of her coat. She swung her arm back hard. Her elbow smashed the creature's face.

It stumbled behind the bike—then kept coming. Its legs were a blur of motion.

Arün shouted, "Good hit!"

Beyond the pursuing dracun, Elek and Nadja followed on the other bike. Nadja sat backward on the motorcycle, a gun in each hand. Green light flashed from the muzzles of the weapons as she kept four more of the almost-human dracun at bay.

Alley's attention re-focused on the closer creature. It lunged forward. She leaned out of the way avoiding the dracun as it tried to grab at her arm again.

"It's trying to pull me off the bike!"

Arün turned his head. "Don't let it."

Alley rolled her eyes. The warden was too busy steering to be any help.

The muscles in her jaw clenched, grinding her teeth together. These things had destroyed her home. Taken her dad. She knew she should feel scared, but she felt angry. They needed to pay for what they'd done. She pulled off her helmet, gripped it around the mouth guard and waited.

Trees, telephone poles, and slower cars flashed by as they raced up the side of the two-lane road. The creature drew nearer. Its legs were moving so fast it appeared to be floating over the asphalt streaking by underfoot. Cold wind whipped Alley's ponytail into a Medusa-like frenzy as she waited.

Just a little closer, she thought.

The creature reached towards her. Alley swung the helmet around with all her strength and clubbed it in the side of the head. She hit it again—and again—and again. Every time it raised its head she brought the helmet down harder. For Dad. For Brent. For Byron. For the dead officers. For her house. Every ounce of anger and frustration in the last day poured into each strike. Tears welled up in her eyes. The wind wicked them away.

The dracun took everything she gave and still maintained its inhuman stride. Alley couldn't be sure, but she thought it smiled. She threw the helmet at its feet and enjoyed seeing the creature stumble as it lost its footing.

She hugged her arms around Arün. "Nothing hurts it!"

Before he could respond, the creature caught back up to the bike and grabbed hold of her backpack. Alley's eyes went wide.

"Try this." Arün pressed something against her hand. His glowing warden blade.

She took the handle of the weapon and swung it around in a wide arc, stabbing the tip into the dracun's arm. Its scales smoked and turned to ash.

The dracun howled. It let go of her pack and clutched its arm as it tumbled into the road-side ditch. Alley's heart pounded. Her fingers gripped the hilt of the blade so tightly that her knuckles were turning white.

Arün slapped the side of her leg. "Nice work."

Alley handed the blade back to him. "Let's not do that again."

One last dracun followed them at a distance. They needed to get rid of it. Nadja had eliminated the rest but appeared to be out of ammunition.

They were passing through Gold Bar and would be in the small town of Index soon. Alley had traveled US-2 often with her parents. Before the accident, they had gone hiking in the Cascade mountains almost every weekend. Was there some place up ahead where they could lose the creature on a side street?

A stabbing pain shot through her head. Alley winced, pressing her eyes closed. The coffee's suppressing effect was wearing off. The cheap stuff never lasted long. She had to get more soon, but there was no stopping. The dracun was keeping pace with them. That left one option—the instant coffee mix in her bag.

Alley swung the pack off her shoulder and unbuckled the top with her free hand. The flap blew open and smacked her in the face. She tucked it down and carefully pulled out the can of instant coffee. The wind buffeted the bike. She almost dropped the can. Alley peeled the plastic top off the container and pushed it into the bag. With the can pressed between her chest and Arün's back, she reached in and scooped out a handful of coffee granules. The wind caught the loose crystals and blew them everywhere—into her eyes, hair, and up her nose.

Alley sneezed violently.

She lost her hold on the can. It went skittering and bouncing along the highway. She sneezed again. Her eyes stung from the coffee mix. Pain shot through her temples. Alley buried her face into Arün's back and gritted her teeth.

Not now! she screamed in her head.

The dracun gained ground on the motorcycles as they left Gold Bar. Alley slipped her pack onto her shoulders and hugged Arün trying to focus on the feeling of the wind tugging at her hair instead of the pounding drum of pain in her head. Small spots swam just outside her vision. How were they going to get away from this one? Nadja had holstered her guns. She had her warden blade in hand waiting for the dracun to come within striking distance.

Alley clutched at her head. Strands of golden power radiated outward from her, raking at the edges of the road. Even though she knew no one else could see them, it made her feel like a freak. The nearby pine trees and bushes bent towards her as they passed. Small pebbles danced off the shoulder. They skittered and jumped behind them like an angry mob of little rock people. It would get worse if she didn't get coffee soon. The recent visions of the flowers were new. Maybe if she could get back to that place in her mind, she could channel the energy and direct it at the dracun. She squeezed her eyes shut and concentrated.

Nothing happened.

They were past Gold Bar and rushing towards the bridge that passed over the South Fork Skykomish River into the town of Index. She had crossed the bridge many times with her parents. They had always stopped in Index so they could have breakfast before heading deep into the National Forest for one of their epic hiking trips. The bridge was constructed out of crisscrossing iron beams. The metal had been coated in olive green paint years ago, but now streaks of rust stained the surfaces.

The swath of pebbles and stones bounced and clattered behind them. The trees bowed and swayed as she passed. Alley took a deep breath and tried to calm herself. She closed her eyes—tried to feel where the energy was flowing from—to follow it back to the source in her mind.

She was in the clearing again. White flowers bloomed at its center. They filled the air with golden dust.

Alley walked forward. She needed to control the energy. To use it against the dracun. But, how? The energy was pouring out—pulling at things as they passed. She didn't know how she was doing that, but maybe she could increase its strength. If she timed it right, she might be able to crumple the iron beams of the bridge and trap the creature.

She gathered a bouquet of the white flowers and then pushed her face into the blossoms and inhaled. She tried to focus on the bridge.

Pull. Crumple.

Her eyes snapped open. They were at the mouth of the bridge, a hundred-yard-long stretch of metal spanning the rocky shoals of the river. The road was clear of traffic. Her head throbbed in pain as she struggled to hold in the energy. Alley needed to time the collapse so that Elek's cycle would be clear of the bridge before she tried to trap the dracun. A tendril of energy slipped out of her head and ripped out a support beam. The bridge groaned.

Alley gritted her teeth. Just a few more seconds.

They sped across the expanse, eating up the distance to the opposite shore. She could feel the power building around her. Pain pulsed in her head like a drumbeat. The energy pressed against her mind like a breath held too long. Her body screamed to set it free. Invisible golden ribbons of power leaked out, scraping flakes of old paint from the metal beams.

The world vibrated in anticipation. It seemed ready to leap at her command. She was barely holding the energy at bay. It buffeted her mind in painful waves. She had to let it go.

Their motorcycle reached the other side. Alley gritted her teeth and looked back to see if Elek and Nadja were clear. Their bike was almost at the end of the bridge. A hundred yards behind them the dracun was crossing.

Almost there, Alley thought.

A truck passed them going in the opposite direction. Time slowed to a crawl as she looked in the driver's window. It was a middle-aged woman with her dog. Alley wanted to shout. Tell the woman to stop, but before she could form the words, the truck was on the bridge.

Alley couldn't hold back the energy any longer.

20

OVER THE RIVER

ALLEY

Alley's power exploded outward. She had to protect the truck. She strained to redirect the energy away from the bridge. Her head pounded with the effort. Ropes of golden power pulsed from her into the surrounding forest and river.

"Turn around, Arün! We have to go back!" she yelled.

He shook his head. "We can't risk it!"

The woman's truck passed the dracun halfway across the bridge. A deep gurgling thunder echoed from the water. The forks of the Skykomish River surged and formed two massive walls of turbulent foam that rolled towards the bridge from both sides. They slammed into the structure like giant liquid fists colliding. The dracun was moving so fast it escaped, but the truck disappeared in the churning wall of water and spray.

"No!" Alley screamed.

The woman and her dog were gone.

No! Please no!

She reached backward and tried in vain to will the wall of water to stop. Her body trembled. She had killed someone again.

The wave rolled up the road behind them, building and churning into an enormous, debris-filled tsunami. The dracun was caught from behind, lifted into the air and then consumed by the grinding swell.

They raced just ahead of the flood, passing under power lines that spanned the highway. The crest of the water tore at the lines sending a shower of sparks into the air. The wave tilted forward and came crashing down. They throttled the bikes, staying just out of its reach. The water hit the ground with a boom, spraying mud, branches, and rocks into the air.

Then just as suddenly as it had appeared, the water poured back into the river. Muddy debris littered what was left of the road. The bridge was gone. The dracun was gone. The truck was gone.

Arün slowed and stopped the bike. Elek pulled up beside them.

Alley covered her mouth. She'd killed the woman and her dog. There was nothing she could do about it. Her hands shook. Her chest and throat tightened. Tears pooled in her eyes and rolled down her cheeks. She felt her face pulled in different directions as she fought for control over her emotions. Alley leaned her head against Arün's back as sobs convulsed her body.

Arün looked back. "I'm sorry, Alley. There was no time to save her."

Alley heard Elek push the kickstand down on the other bike and then felt the warmth of his arms. He rested his head against hers. "You saved our lives."

"I killed her." Her stomach clenched at the thought. She bit the inside of her mouth.

"It was bad luck."

Alley looked up. "It wasn't bad luck. I was trying to stop the dracun, and I lost control."

Elek rubbed his thumbs under her eyes, wiping away the wetness. "But you saved us."

Alley shook her head. He didn't understand what it was like to watch a disaster unfold that he had caused. What it felt like to see people hurt and killed because of his actions.

Nadja got off the back of the other cycle and sheathed her warden blade. "That was impressive. I didn't believe what they said about you."

That Nadja could so easily ignore the woman's death made Alley sick. She'd shown more emotion at the news of the dead warden. Alley swallowed and tried to keep her disgust from showing. "That woman has—had family—that loved her."

Nadja ignored her. "The Council will be glad to see you're making progress."

"Will the Council be happy that it cost someone their life?"

"They'll be happy you're alive."

Alley looked beyond Nadja to the devastation. Of course, they'd be pleased. Her parents would be proud. They did this. Her fists tightened.

Arün offered her a half-smile. "You'll learn to master this gift where we're going. When you do, the numbers you'll save, will far out-weigh those who have been lost."

Alley closed her eyes and breathed the cold autumn air. "I hope you're right."

A sedan came around the bend ahead of them and slowed as the driver caught sight of the washed-out road.

Arün revved the cycle. "We need to go."

Elek and Nadja climbed back on their bike. Alley took a final survey of the mess she had created. She bowed her head and closed her eyes.

I'm sorry, she thought.

The headache was gone, but there was no way to know how long it would last.

They sped east into the foothills of the Cascade mountains. Craggy peaks rose like the spine of an enormous creature shrouded in a gray mist. Traffic thinned leaving them alone on the narrow highway.

Alley checked over her shoulder. No dracun. Cold wind stung her face and hands. They sped by a brown recreation sign declaring that Deception Falls was just ahead. Arün turned into the empty visitor parking lot and stopped the motorcycle.

Elek coasted up on the other bike and Arün tossed the keys to him. "Hide the cycles in the forest."

They dismounted. Alley blew warm air into her cupped hands and rubbed them together. The empty lot made her feel exposed. Vulnerable. A gust made the tree tops sway. Alley's family had always tried to avoid hiking in the wind. Too much of a chance that a dead limb could break off a tree and hit you.

Alley followed Arün and Nadja across the empty lot towards a wooden picnic table hiding behind a row of saplings. "Is this going to be a long hike?"

Nadja pulled out the map and unfolded it across the weathered gray boards. "Look." An electric buzz came from Nadja's coat. She fished out her cell phone and stepped away from the table to answer.

Arün withdrew four black stones from his jacket. He placed one at each corner of the parchment. Wind fluttered the corners of the map. Arün whistled a few notes and the stones spun. A crimson line traced itself across the surface of the paper from their current location towards a spot deep in the mountains.

Alley brushed the glowing line with her finger. "How did you do that?"

Arün answered, "The stones are etched with a weave that responds to a specific frequency. Their activation triggers the weave in the parchment that reveals the path."

Alley stared at him for a moment and then shook her head. "Makes total sense," she lied.

Arün smiled. "You'll understand soon enough. We'll follow the trail, then cut across the river here." He tapped his finger on the glowing line. "From there it's a few hours to the entrance. We can make it before nightfall."

Alley glanced up at Arün. "Will they find us again?"

"Not if we hurry."

Elek emerged from the woods bordering the parking lot. "Bikes are hidden. We can get going whenever you're ready."

Nadja looked up from her phone. She was tapping at the screen.

Elek nodded at her. "Checking in?"

"Encoded message to the Council. Updating them on our progress. Rakman was worried that we hadn't sent a report."

Elek rubbed at his neck. "Nadja, I'm sorry about going off-mission. I—"

"I don't have time to report your insubordination right now." Nadja hit send and tucked the phone away.

Elek looked relieved.

Alley turned to Nadja. "You work for Leopold Rakman?"

Arün picked up the stones and returned them to his pocket. The red line melted away into the paper. "We work for the Council. Rakman heads operations in this territory. This is his mission."

"Call him. I want to talk to him."

Nadja sighed. "That's against mission protocol."

"I don't care about your protocols!" Alley shouted. "He needs to send someone to find my dad!"

Elek touched her shoulder. "Al, I bet they've got wardens looking for him already. The Council won't abandon one of their own."

Alley shrugged off Elek's hand and glared at Arün. "Is that true?"

Arün squinted at a passing car on the highway. "Yes, now let's get moving. I don't want a repeat of last night. I promised your dad we'd keep you safe."

Alley hoped he wasn't lying.

They formed a line with Arün in the lead and headed down the narrow trail into the woods. Cool shade engulfed them. Through the trees on the right, green water flowed from the falls churning and spraying past slick chiseled rocks. Deep earthy smells filled the crisp air. The trail reminded Alley of ones she had hiked with her dad years earlier. There was something about the Cascades that had always beckoned her. They were huge, rugged, beautiful giants.

They wound their way around boulders and giant cedars. The shadows deepened with each footstep, and the roar of the river receded. Tiny pine cones crunched underfoot like the shells of small insects. Everywhere emerald moss coated tree limbs and dripped like wet green hair from the boughs. Pine needles and dead leaves coated the forest floor between ferns and rotting logs.

Thoughts churned in Alley's mind as she hiked. Dracun. They still hunted her, but the simple act of hiking brought a sense of calm. Perhaps it was because, unlike her future, the trail ahead was clear. She didn't need to think about it too much. Just put one foot in front of the other.

The future was a different story. She'd always had a sense of what to expect in the coming days and months. A sense that her choices and life were following a clear direction. The plan had always been to get degrees in science and medicine and then research a way to cure herself and to help others. That future seemed uncertain now.

Elek moved up to hike beside her. "I'm sorry about today. About everything. I'm sorry I didn't tell you about my involvement in all this a long time ago."

"It's okay, El. I'm glad you're here with me." She reached out and squeezed his hand.

"So, what are you going to do?" Elek asked.

"What do you mean?"

"You still want me to help you try the cure?"

"I need to save my dad. I can't help him without my ability."

Elek nodded. "And after you find him?"

"After that—I don't know." If she could learn to control the power, what would she be capable of? The vision of destruction from the bathroom was frightening. That wasn't a future she wanted. She wasn't a killer or a conqueror. She wanted to help people. She wanted to make up for the pain and suffering she'd caused.

Elek left her to her thoughts. The trail grew steeper making Alley's thighs burn, and the soles of her feet ache. No one was speaking, but Alley was too winded to talk.

Hours later, Arün broke the silence. "We're close."

They climbed a steep rise where the ferns grew thick, obscuring the trail. The plants slapped at Alley's shins leaving dewy lines in the denim. As they crested the hill, she inhaled a lungful of cold misty air. They were standing on the rim of a wide glacial sinkhole. Ahead of them, a waterfall tumbled from a cliff. It fell fifty yards before crashing over smooth rocks and flowing into a swirling green pool at the bottom of the ancient pit. A break in the clouds allowed a few rays of sun to sparkle on the falling water.

They navigated a narrow trail that clung to the edge of the drop-off. Ferns and moss crowded around the falls and sprouted from every crack and crevice. Trees had grown right up to the edge of the huge hole, their roots snaked over one another and spilled down the side of the cliff. Mist from the pounding water blew upward dampening Alley's skin and making the rock and root covered path slick and treacherous.

As they drew closer to the cliff-face beside the falls, the path ahead was paved with flat oval stones. Moss had grown between the rocks making them look like slick gray lily pads on a green river.

Arün turned towards them. "You're about to see something that only a few others have seen. Keep this place a secret."

He stepped on the stones in what looked like an elaborate game of hop-scotch. As he landed on the last stone, the granite cliff wall in front of them made a grinding noise. To Alley's surprise, a section of the wall slid open revealing a dark passageway.

21

THE PORTAL

ALLEY

They followed Arün into the darkness. The carved walls muffled the echoes of the crashing water outside. The path sloped downward. Alley's eyes adjusted to the dim light, and she saw that the tunnel ended up ahead.

Arün led them out of the stone passageway into an enormous cavern. Colorful wildflowers covered the walls and floors. Her father had taught her the names of some of them: pink monkey-flowers, yellow heartleaf arnica and purple grasswidow blossoms. On the right, a large hole in the cavern wall revealed the backside of the falls. On the left, sunlight streamed through the falling curtain of water painting a dancing pattern of golden light on a carved rock stairway that led up to a huge circular arch of intertwined vines. The arch was so big that a bus could have driven through it. Each of the mossy vines was as thick as a telephone pole and covered in thorns that were bigger than ice cream cones.

Alley's jaw dropped. "Wow." The place felt like it hadn't been visited for a hundred years. Who had built it? The Mages? Someone else?

Arün led them down rough-hewn steps to the floor of the cavern. Water dripped into a wide, stone-ringed pool at the center of the space from an opening high overhead. Green vines and roots hung down from the edges of the hole trying to reach the pool below. The air was misty and filled with earthy smells.

Elek whistled. "It's beautiful."

Arün motioned towards the thorny arch at the top of the steps. He walked around the pool and headed towards the base of the staircase. "It's a portal"—his voice echoed off the damp walls and mixed with the dull roar of the falls—"to another place. Your trainer lives there, Alley. Are you ready to meet him?"

"Absolutely," she answered. It was the 'portal-to-another-place' part that concerned her. There was nothing on the other side of the archway. Her pulse quickened. The sides of the stairway sloped away towards the cavern walls. Behind the arch was a deep chasm. Beyond that was the far wall of the chamber.

Arün's voice echoed in the cavern. "These portals are rarely used due to the unpredictable time dilation that occurs inside them."

Alley chewed on her nail. "What does that mean?"

"While we are crossing to the other place, time will slow for us. It may only take us minutes, but when we come out the other side, hours, weeks or months may have passed."

Alley squinted at Arün. "That sounds bad."

His face looked grim. "The other routes we could take are too risky now."

Nadja looked back at the passageway they'd come through. She drew her warden blade and checked the metal to see if it was glowing. Alley had noticed her and Arün do it many times during the hike. The blade was dark.

Arün nodded at Nadja and continued. "If there were a better option, we'd take it. Just get across quick. I don't know how much time we'll be able to stay there, but I hope you'll be able to learn what you need."

Alley had crammed for plenty of tests, but it seemed like this would be more like learning to play a musical instrument. Years of practice. How fast could she learn even if she had the best teacher?

Arün continued, "One more thing. There are people there that may not appreciate our presence. We need to stay out of sight, especially you, Alley. If we get separated, get back here as soon as you can. Remember that when we enter the gate to return, those few seconds of time before each of us crosses could mean minutes or hours between our arrivals here. Don't be alarmed if it takes time for the person behind you to appear on this side of the gateway."

Elek stared at the steps. "The stories about Arburaan are all real?"

Alley grabbed Elek's arm. "What's Arburaan?"

He turned toward her. "It's where the Mages say the dracun came from."

Nadja crossed her arms. "Did you think they came from here?"

Elek rubbed his neck. "I thought—I don't know, that they were something from the past. Like dinosaurs that had evolved. I thought Arburaan was a myth."

Nadja snorted. "Myth? After all you've seen? Everything the Wardens have taught you is true, Elek. We can't afford to tell lies."

Elek tilted his head. "You've been there?"

"Not me," Nadja pointed to Arün, "but he has."

Arün held out his hand to Nadja. "It was a long time ago. I need the map."

She reached into her coat and handed it to him. Arün folded it so he could read the notes written on the margin.

Alley's thighs were sore and twitched from the hours they'd just spent hiking. She hoped they didn't have too much farther to go. "This place we're head to, what's it like?"

Arün looked up from the map. "Let's go find out."

They climbed the damp stone steps towards the portal. Each one was inscribed with three different runes. Each time, Arün consulted the notes on the map, then stepped on one of the runes, causing it to glow. Alley tried to keep track of which symbols he was selecting, but by the twelfth step, she gave up.

As they reached the top, the arch towered above them. Beyond it was the back wall of the cave where an intricate pattern of symbols was carved in concentric circles. Arün walked to the center of the archway, tossed something that shimmered into the air and made a quick motion with his hand. There was a grinding sound, like massive blocks of stone rubbing against one another. Circular cracks formed around the rings of symbols on the far wall. The rock crumbled and was sucked into a void as if a powerful vacuum was pulling at it from inside the Earth.

Alley backed away. What was this? Every instinct in her body told her to run, but the wardens were standing their ground.

A dark hole formed in the far wall as big around as the vine archway that loomed overhead. Alley thought she could see stars twinkling in the blackness. A ghostly moan echoed from the vastness within the maw. It rose in pitch as if a million voices were rushing towards them.

Arün drew his warden blade. It glowed bright blue. Elek and Nadja moved forward and joined him, shielding Alley from whatever might be coming. Her heart raced. What was making that sound?

The thorny archway shuddered, shedding its skin of moss. The wardens backed away, covering their heads. Around the perimeter of the arch, thousands of smooth, leafy vines sprouted and shot towards the hole. They wove themselves together as they grew, thickening and forming a tight lattice-work tunnel. It clogged the breach in the wall and pushed its way deep into the starry blackness. Alley peered into the passageway as it filled with a white mist. The ghostly howling continued but was now muffled by the tangled walls and thick swirling clouds.

The wardens relaxed and sheathed their weapons. Arün brushed clumps of moss from his hair and shoulders and motioned them forward. "We go single file. Me, then Elek, then Alley, then Nadja. Be on your guard. Move fast till you reach the other side. The tunnel is safe as long as you keep moving."

Alley shook her head. "I'm not going in there. I don't understand what I just saw, but that tunnel doesn't seem safe."

Arün turned toward her. "You want to learn how to use your ability? You want to save your father? It's the only way, Alley."

She swallowed as she watched the fog pour out of the tunnel. "Okay," she said.

Arün nodded and then stepped into the vine passageway. His boots sank into the woven floor. It flexed under his weight. He took a step forward. Then another. The mist curled around him and then he was gone.

22

OTHER SIDE

ALLEY

Elek peered into the swirling mist where Arün had just been and then back at Alley. "See you on the other side, Al." He stepped into the fog. His black leather jacket faded into the white ether.

Alley's mouth was dry. The muffled wailing was close. It sounded like a crowd of zombies pressed against the other side of the tunnel walls. What if they broke through? She wouldn't be able to see anything in the thick fog. She pulled her wool coat tight across her body. The scratchy fabric was comforting. On the other end of this portal was someone that could help. She just had to get to them.

Alley glanced at Nadja, took a deep breath and then stepped into the tunnel. The vines felt spongy under her feet, like walking on a mattress. She took another step and peered into the fog, trying to make out detail, but there was nothing to see. The voices on the other side of the wall stopped keening. Alley had a distinct impression they could sense her presence. Were they listening? She stayed quiet. Maybe if whatever was out there didn't hear her, it would leave her alone. She took a few more steps forward and became enveloped in the white haze.

Alley's heart beat faster as she traveled deeper into the tunnel. She wanted to take a breath, but the thought of pulling the fog into her lungs was almost as disturbing as the noises from the unseen mob. The urge to run was uncontrollable.

Stay quiet. Stay calm, she thought.

The floor buckled under her feet. Something was pressing upward from underneath. Alley gasped. She stumbled and regained her balance. Below her, something made a rumbling growl. There was a sniffing sound. Fetid air blew up through the tiny gaps in the vines. It smelled of rotten eggs. Alley's stomach clenched as the rank odor filled her nose. She fought the urge to vomit by burying her face in the crook of her arm and breathing in through the thick wool of the coat.

Alley stumbled through the tunnel, her left arm groping into the mist while her other arm covered her nose and mouth. Whatever was outside followed her, thumping against the walls. Up ahead the fog glowed orange. She ran forward—felt firm stone against her feet—passed through a curtain of water, then fell off a cliff.

Alley looked about wildly as she plummeted. A lake below. Impossibly large trees. Something huge in the water thrashing around—something that looked alive.

She had just enough time to gulp a lungful of air and squeeze her eyes shut before she plunged into the cold lake. Bubbles surrounded her, tickling her skin as they rose. Alley kicked, following them upward until her head broke the surface. She gasped. Her hair clung to her face as she scanned the water. Her wet clothes and heavy boots made it difficult to stay afloat. The muscles in her arms burned with the effort of stirring the water in a circular pattern. Where were Elek and Arün?

A giant mechanical arm reared up from the lake. At the end of the multi-jointed appendage was a metal claw. Alley's eyes went wide. She slapped at the water to propel herself away. The claw descended like a viper striking and hauled her from the lake.

"Help!" she screamed.

Alley tried to reach for the power in her mind, but felt nothing. Other arms thrashed in the water nearby. One held Elek. Another had Arün. They both struggled to break free.

"Hang tight, Alley!" Arün yelled as he pried at the claw gripping his waist.

She heard a splash. Nadja's head bobbed up from the water.

Arün shouted to her. "Watch out for the claws!"

Nadja swam towards the shore. Another arm unfurled from the depths of the lake and angled towards her. Nadja ducked below the water just as it descended. She surfaced again and kept swimming. She was almost at the water's edge when it grabbed her ankle and hoisted her upside down into the air.

They were trapped. Alley looked at her guardians: two wardens she barely knew and her best friend. All three struggled to free themselves, all three determined to keep her safe. If she could control her ability, she could tear this machinery apart.

An old man shuffled out from behind one of the massive trees on the shore. White and gray hair sprouted from his head as if someone had electrocuted him. He wore a loose robe that had been sewn from many pieces of colorful patterned fabric. It was cinched at the waist with a wide leather belt where bulging pouches dangled from cords like ballast on a hot-air balloon. Around his neck, he wore dozens of necklaces from which hung an odd assortment of objects. He adjusted his spectacles and selected one of the bobbles that rested against his chest. A long thin whistle made of copper on the end of a silver chain. He scratched at the short white hairs of his beard as he squinted up at them.

Alley thought he might have been the strangest person she'd ever seen. There was something familiar about him though, but she couldn't tell what it was. Had she met him before?

Alley waved her arms in wide arcs above her head. "Help us!"

The old man waved back.

He raised the whistle to his lips and blew a short, two-note blast. The mechanical arms ceased their thrashing. In the stillness, the distant sound of strange animal cries could be heard above the spattering of the waterfall behind them.

The old man cocked his head to the side and yelled. "What brings you to Arburaan?"

Arün yelled back. "I'm Arün! We met years ago. Ben sent us, please let us down!"

"Ah yes, I remember you! Did Ben send along any chocolate?"

Arün pounded his fists on the metal claw wrapped around him. "What? No!"

"Bah. Probably just as well. Water would have ruined it."

Nadja flailed her arms, her face turning crimson from hanging upside down. "Are you going to help us?!"

"Oh yes, let me see now." The man fumbled with the copper whistle. He adjusted his glasses as he peered at the side, then placed his fingers along the length and blew three sharp notes.

The claw gripping Nadja's ankle released, and she crashed head first into the water.

"Oh dear me. That wasn't the right one." The man

squinted at the whistle, selected two different holes and blew again.

Alley's stomach tightened as the mechanical arm that held her lurch from side to side like a horrible carnival ride. Ahead of her, the arms that held Arün and Elek swiveled and plowed through the water towards the shore. They arched downward and released them. The ground rushed up towards Alley and water squished between her toes as her feet hit the grass at the edge of the lake.

They stood in front of the old man, lake water running off into growing puddles at their feet. Behind them, Nadja climbed out of the water coughing and dripping.

"Sorry about the Water Sentry. It's only supposed to activate if a dracun breaches the portal. Safeguard you know. High Court is still on edge even though the banishment was ages ago. Still, it's nice to know my work has held up after a century underwater!" A wide grin spread across his face as he gazed at the glistening machinery.

Arün shivered and hugged his chest. "We're here on the Council's orders."

"Oh yes, sorry. Introductions are in order I suppose. My name is Bezo. Bezo Berolaster, Arch-Mage of the Fifth Order, Watcher of the Seventh Gate and Baker of Fine Foods." He bowed deep, his necklaces bumped together creating a chorus of metallic chimes. He straightened. "I've grown to enjoy baking more than inventing, but don't tell the Council." He winked at Alley.

She smiled. "Nice to meet you. Thanks for getting us down."

Elek gasped. "You wrote *Magna Machina*, *Species Inventa*, and *Substantia Artis*!"

The old man grinned. "A scholar! Which mage are you apprenticing with?"

Nadja's lips pursed. She shot a glance at Elek. "He's studying to be a warden. I'm sure he has an explanation for why he's spending his training time in the libraries."

Arün cleared his throat. "This is my partner, Nadja, and her Warden Tyro, Elek. I'm Arün, and this is Ben's daughter, Alley. Ben said you could train her."

"Alley! Of course, I didn't recognize you. Welcome. Welcome, all of you to Arburaan." He smiled at them and gestured towards the huge skyscraper-sized trees.

This was the guy that was supposed to show her how to control her power? He didn't inspire confidence.

"I would suggest we get started on the path. The High Court doesn't appreciate visitors as much as I do. Usually, my guests are more discreet when arriving," he glared at Arün. "I'm afraid the Sentry activation may have alerted the elves—and you may have triggered other wards. It would be better if we were not here if they come to investigate."

Arün ran his fingers through his wet hair. "I'm sorry. It wasn't safe for us to come via the usual passages."

Bezo nodded. "We'll just have to make the best of it." He raised the whistle to his lips and blew a series of notes. The mechanical arms creaked into motion and collapsed into the water. Only a few stray bubbles floating on the surface of the lake remained to hint at what lay beneath. "Had you come the other way, it would have been far worse. The High Court would not have reacted well to your unique situation."

Alley raised her hand. "Hold on. Did you say *elves*?"

Bezo nodded. "Yes. *Elves*. Didn't your father explain anything to you?"

Alley shook her head. "He neglected to tell me a few things."

"Well, then we have much to discuss!" The mage offered her his bent arm. It was so old-fashioned that she couldn't help smiling. Alley hooked her arm through his and let him lead her towards a wide path that headed into the woods. Bezo smelled of fresh-baked bread. It made her stomach growl.

In the distance, the deep low call of a hunting horn echoed through the trees.

Bezo sighed. "We need to move. I'm afraid the High Guard could make the day rather unpleasant."

23

SCALE ROAD

ALLEY

The old mage hurried them along a path as wide as a two-lane road. It was paved with oddly shaped iridescent stones that reflected light like the shells of large beetles. Tufts of grass, moss and small flowers squeezed through the gaps between the strange pavers.

Giant pine trees grew to either side, their boughs meshing together hundreds of feet overhead to form a dark canopy. Some of the trunks were so thick that Alley felt like a mouse beside them. Shafts of sun created pockets of light along the road. Roots twisted along the ground like great worms, arching over to form tunnels. Lichen and mushrooms crusted the outside of many of the trunks. Vines and small plants clung to everything. The air smelled earthy and rich, like fresh potting soil. Insects and birds chittered and chirped in the shadows. In the distance, something large crunched through the forest. Alley wondered if the animals here were as big as the plants.

They moved fast, not quite jogging, but nearly. Alley's damp boot sole slipped on one of the strange reflective stones. Bezo gripped her arm and kept her from stumbling. "It's important to stay on the road. It is imbued with magic that keeps us safe. Also, the pixies do not take kindly to being trampled—not kindly at all."

"Pixies? I don't see anything," said Alley.

Bezo chuckled. "You won't be able to see them, my dear. They are small. The forest is teaming with their towns and cities."

Alley scanned the underbrush at the edge of the roadway. There was nothing that looked like a small city. She leaned toward Elek. "Do you know what he's talking about?"

Elek shook his head.

Bezo smiled. "They are tiny—not visible to the unaided eye. The pixies hold the key to one of the most potent sources of magic in this world."

Alley's feet itched inside her water-logged boots. Her legs, which had already been aching from the hike up to the tunnel, now burned from their speed walk. "If they're so powerful why do we need to worry about stepping on them?"

The mage snapped his fingers. "Excellent question! As the honey bee harvests pollen, so the pixies harvest energy from the world. They process it to produce a fine powder. A highly potent source of magical energy. Their small size means they can only use a tiny amount of the dust themselves. That limits their ability to perform powerful magic. So, they have adapted by enlisting elves and mages as their protectors."

"What are you protecting them from?" asked Alley.

"Dragons."

She tensed. "There are dragon's here?"

Bezo patted her arm. "Not since the Ash War. That was a long time ago."

"Can you tell me about the War?" she asked.

"It was a terrible confrontation to protect this land from the Dragon Clans. This road was built at the end of the War."

The road looked like it had been in the forest a long time. Creeping vines crisscrossed the odd stones. They passed spots where roots pushed up the edge of the roadway causing the colorful paving stones to buckle upward as if they were a long carpet that had been rolled out over the uneven forest floor.

The hunting horn sounded again. It was closer. Arün and Nadja appeared visibly tense, scanning the surrounding forest and checking the road behind them. They hadn't drawn their weapons, but they looked like they wanted to.

Alley turned to Bezo. "You said the road is magic. What does the magic do?"

Bezo squinted into the air. "Before I answer I should tell you about how it was built." The mage swept his arm up toward the shadowed canopy. "The forest here is much larger than anything you would find in our world. Life layered on top of life. Many intelligent species live here. The smallest of these species are the Pixathaliam, or Pixie. Before we arrived, the elves, and the pixies had lived in a symbiotic harmony for millennia. The elves protected the pixies, and the pixies supplied the elves with dust to fuel their magic and long life. A good arrangement for all parties until the dragons arrived"—he paused as if considering something. A smile spread across his face—"you know, before I get too far into this tale, let me share something else with you."

The old man liked to talk, which was good because Alley had a ton of questions. He reminded her a little of her father. If he really was an important mage, maybe he could help her find him.

Bezo reached into a pouch and held out his hand to Alley and Elek. Nestled in his palm were three round blue candies. "You must try one of these. I've been perfecting the recipe. It's a new treat! Don't tell me what you think until you've finished eating. I'm very interested in hearing your impressions." He took one and popped it into his mouth.

Nadja cleared her throat. "Alley, I don't think it's a good idea for you to eat those."

Bezo frowned. "Dear me, warden. If I wanted to harm you, I could have easily drowned you back in the lake. Keep quiet unless you've got something intelligent to say."

Nadja pressed her lips together and looked away. Alley could see that Arün was struggling to keep from smiling.

Bezo pushed his open palm toward Alley. "Well go on, please try one."

Alley selected a candy and Elek took the other. They looked warily at each other. Elek grinned and popped the candy into his mouth. Alley examined her piece. It was dark blue and sticky. She touched her tongue to it. The taste was sweet and sour, tart berry mixed with a honey-like sugar. She put it in her mouth and rolled it around with her tongue feeling the bumpy surface rub against her taste buds.

Bezo increased his pace. "As I was saying, the dragons arrived from across the ocean from the other side of the world. A war between their clans had ravaged their homeland. They were starving and looking for a new place to settle. The elves took pity on them and allowed them to nest within a large valley in the Upper Anduwalth Mountains—a place where they would not disturb those who already called this land home. Years passed and the dragon offspring, the dracun, grew in number and roamed outside the mountains, searching for more food and larger breeding grounds beyond the valley."

A breeze blew through the forest and blasted Alley's damp clothes. She shivered. The trees creaked as they swayed in the wind. She pulled her coat closed. Everything about the place set her on edge. If any of these trees toppled, it would be like a building crashing down.

"The memory of that time is painful for the pixies. For them, it is as if it only happened yesterday. Fire. Death. Destruction. The leaders of the clans—the dragons—were a terrible force. Cynder, Krakus and Brygar led most of the attacks. They trampled Pixie towns and villages as a child might step on an anthill. They burned and plundered the Elvish cities. Many died."

Alley rolled the candy around in her mouth. The dracun had trashed this place. And it had taken a war to stop them. That was why the Mages felt like they needed her help.

They hurried down the path in silence for a few moments before Bezo raised a fist to his mouth and cleared his throat. "It was a dark time. The pixies relied on the elves to be their protectors, but the elves were unschooled in the ways of large-scale warfare and were being slaughtered by the dragons. The pixies needed others to come to their aid. They created soft spots in the ground between our worlds. When we discovered them, we called them Caldruns. They allowed us to travel into this world. The pixies showed us the power of their dust and helped us build the Thorngates, like the one you used to come here. They granted our Order access to the dust for helping them build war machines to stop the dragons—"

Elek clapped his hands together. "I've studied all the Marionette designs, sir. They are amazing! Al, they have simulator rooms at the College where you can train on any—"

Nadja cut him off. "Elek! Enough."

Elek's face turned red.

Bezo smiled. "I appreciate your passion, son."

The candy in Alley's mouth was getting smaller and changed to a banana flavor as it shrunk. "So, you stopped the dragons?"

"The Ash War lasted years. It was not until we subdued the dragon kings and queens that the war ended. It was a hard-won victory. The leaders of the clans are like nothing you have ever seen—the most terrifying creatures I have ever encountered. The worst of them was Cynder. He laid waste to the Elvish city of F'arrowmore in a matter of hours. He and his kin turned the forests of the Upper Plateau into a barren wasteland. Nothing we did seemed to hurt these monsters. Their hides possess properties that make them impervious to conventional weapons and magics."

Alley tilted her head. "How did you beat them?" If she had to fight these things to rescue her father, she needed to know how.

The old mage smiled and touched a finger to the side of his nose. "They had a weakness. The giant dragon rulers were nearly invincible, but their smaller dracun clan members were not. Our war machines thinned their ranks. As the dracun population dwindled, the clans retreated. We even took down a few of the dragons."

"What makes a dracun different from a dragon?" Alley asked.

The mage smiled. "Excellent question. Dragons appear to be an evolved form of the dracun. Fortunately, most dracun do not seem to grow into that more mature form, otherwise we never would have won the War. Which brings us back to how this road was built and what makes it magical."

The strange colored stones glided by beneath her feet.

Bezo followed her gaze. "These dracun scales were harvested from the battlefields after the Banishing. All the roads were paved with them after the War. Predatory animals in the forest still sense and fear the magic in them. It makes traveling the roads safer. And they are quite durable!" He stamped his foot on the scales as if to prove his point.

Alley grimaced. The idea was disturbing. They had peeled scales from the dead bodies of defeated dracun and paved the road with them. She had no love for the creatures, but it seemed wrong.

"I see that look on your face, my dear. We burned the bodies, but their scales are impervious to flame. We had to dispose of them. Why bury them when they possess such valuable properties?"

It made a twisted sense. Alley tried to imagine how many dracun had died to pave the roads. It must have been hundreds of thousands. "The machines that did this—do they still exist?"

"Oh yes. Most are in storage in vaults below the Elvish Capital, but I still keep a few in service to help guard the Seventh Gate. I'll show you one later if you like."

Elek looked as if he'd just heard he'd won the lottery. His excitement made Alley smile, but she had more questions for the mage. "You let some dracun live. Why?"

"I was there the day Cynder landed in the fields outside the Elvish Capital to offer the surrender of the clans. The pixies and elves wanted to have them all put to death, but we convinced them otherwise. A species as huge and powerful as the dragons should be studied, not wiped out. We agreed to have them exiled to what was then a sparsely populated area of Earth. We made a Covenant with the pixies and elves that we would be the dragon's wardens on Earth and ensure they would never return to Arburaan—"

"Why?" Alley shook her head. "Why would you bring something so dangerous to our world?"

Bezo raised an eyebrow. "We did it for the benefit of humanity. The agreement secured a steady supply of dust. The dust has enabled us to make incredible scientific advancements."

"You brought monsters into our world."

Arün interjected. "They took precautions. They formed the Warden Guild. Set clear Laws with harsh penalties. And created a cocktail to allow the dracun to coexist in our world. The system has worked for over a hundred years."

"But you knew it might fail. That's why I'm here."

Bezo shook his head. "Not because we thought it would fail, but because we wanted additional safe-guards. You can never be too prepared!"

Alley shook her head. They were all so convinced of the benefits of having these creatures around. The elves and the pixies seemed to have known better. She didn't want to spend the rest of her life defending the world from monsters. But she did want to learn how to control her power and rescue her father.

The mage was odd, but someone her dad trusted. He designed killing machines, made candy, and by his telling, must be over a hundred years old if he was around at the end of the War. Could he really teach her?

Bezo interrupted her thoughts. "We're nearly there!"

Ahead of them, the impossibly tall trees thinned and revealed a small valley of grass and wildflower. To their left, white cataracts spilled down a towering cliff face and spattered into a sapphire blue lake. The lake fed a narrow brook that flowed down the valley and out of sight around a bend far to their right. Large, snail-like creatures the size of small cars, slid through the grass. Their blue-green, mottled shells were dotted with flecks of orange.

The scale-paved road ended and turned into a dirt path that cut through the valley, crossing a small stone bridge spanning the brook and ending at a cottage perched on the far side of the lake. A white curl of smoke rose from the structure's fat chimney. It seemed to be part building and part machine. Odd brass pipes zigzagged their way around the Tudor-looking exterior, into tanks and machinery in various states of repair around the building. A wide, welcoming porch with rocking chairs and a swing made the entire place feel like a weird cross between a dollhouse and a factory. Behind the house, in the shadow of the far away trees, rose an enormous wooden barn with a steeply peaked roof and a giant sliding door.

Bezo trotted ahead of them and turned with an expansive sweep of his arms that rattled the bobbles on his chest. "Welcome to Bel-Bendar, my home for the past century. Don't worry about the Chu'la." He gestured at one of the nearby snail creatures. "They are harmless, and their slime makes a wonderful lotion. It's all the rage with the elves." Alley imagined rubbing her face on one of their glistening bodies. *No thanks,* she thought.

The horn sounded again, reverberating off the cliffs. Alley thought she could hear the clatter of hooves behind them in the forest. Arün and Nadja turned towards the sound, but whoever was approaching on the road was still out of sight.

Arün called to the mage. "They're close. We need to move faster!"

Bezo's brow furrowed. "We'd best jog the rest of the way. I'd hoped for us to have a snack, and hear your thoughts on my new candy recipe, but I think that will have to wait!" The mage broke into a run. His robes flapped around him, and the bags at his waist danced wildly.

Alley took off after Bezo. Her wet clothes slapped against her body. Elek, Arün and Nadja followed close behind.

The mage led them past the strange house, towards the large barn set back in the trees. He pulled on the massive door. It rolled sideways with a squeal on a metal track high overhead. "Inside! Quickly!"

They crowded into the darkness. Alley's eyes could make out large boxes and lumpy forms covered in tarps stacked along the walls. Bezo led them forward. He pushed one of the crates aside, found a metal ring in the floor and pulled upward. A trapdoor opened revealing a wooden staircase that descended into darkness.

"Down. Now. And not a word until I come for you!"

Elek went first, followed by Arün. Alley went next. She felt Nadja's hand on her shoulder and the rough surface of the stairs below each of her feet. In just a few steps she was at the bottom. Arün took her hand and helped her find a place to crouch. The weird electrical tingle radiated out from where he touched her skin and the ache in her muscles from the long hike subsided.

The trapdoor creaked shut. There was a brief scraping sound as the crate was moved back into position and then footsteps receding. Finally, the distant squeal of the door. The only remaining noise was four people trying to catch their breath in the darkness and the ominous call of the hunting horn.

24

HIDDEN

ALLEY

The cellar was cool and smelled like the produce section of the grocery store. Above them, nothing stirred. Alley considered asking in a quiet whisper whether any of them had a small light. She couldn't tell how far away the walls were or whether she would bump into something if she moved from Arün's side.

Minutes ticked by.

Alley remembered what Arün had said about how time worked differently between this place and home. How much time would pass while they were here? Days? Weeks? More? Alley wished she had a watch.

The door to the barn screeched as it slid sideways on its track. Muffled voices filtered down through the boards. A deep melodic voice was speaking with a strange accent.

"—didn't come here for food Arch-Mage. You say it was a malfunction with your machine, so it is my duty to verify that other areas of mutual importance haven't gone untended."

"Preposterous! It was a fluke. A breach in a seal, I'm almost certain," replied Bezo.

"The King will want to know that I've inspected the Marion, especially if we can't trust the reliability of the Water Sentry on the gate." Heavy boots thumped on the boards above their heads.

Bezo spoke, "Very well, El'Iswald, but the King knows I take my duties seriously. I conduct operational runs twice between the moons, and the reserves are inspected each season. But he knows all this, he receives the reports."

"I'm very sorry to trouble you Arch-Mage, you have your duties, and I have mine. I expect everything will be in order as you say." The footsteps faded deeper into the barn.

"Quite right. See for yourself." There was a snap and a loud hum. Bright light streamed down in dusty sheets through the gaps in the planks above their heads. Alley blinked her eyes, trying to focus on the surrounding shapes. Crates of fruits, vegetables, and nuts were stacked around them. Something rustled above as if a large tarp was being swept aside.

"Magnificent. It is amazing to see it so well preserved and without the battle damage. I do not wish to dishonor you, but I must see it activated."

Bezo's necklaces jingled as he fumbled for something hanging around his neck. "Of course."

Five musical notes cut the air. The floor shook. Dust rained from the ceiling. It sounded like Bezo had started a huge piece of construction equipment overhead. The rumble was deafening.

Arün pulled Alley back against the crates, so she was under one of the thick beams that supported the ceiling. The floor overhead creaked and sagged as something heavy moved past blocking the light. Whatever it was, headed outside leaving the barn quiet once more.

Across from Alley, Nadja placed a finger against her lips and pointed to the ceiling. Soft footsteps sounded overhead. Someone stood just above them, their shadow blocking the light. Alley had the urge to itch her nose but ignored it trying instead to focus on shallow breathing.

The footsteps moved onward and departed the barn. After a few minutes, the engine stopped outside. Alley assumed the inspection was over but didn't dare to move.

Minutes passed.

Elek smiled at her from across the small cellar, white stripes of light from the floor boards slanted across his body. She smiled back. He seemed to enjoy this too much—like it was all a game. *At least someone is having fun*, she thought. Alley realized she was a little jealous of all three of the people crouched around her. What must it feel like to know your mission in life? To not have that feeling of anxiety that lingers when you question your purpose? Alley scratched at the dirt floor with her finger. She realized that if she didn't decide on a path, the Council, the dracuns, or someone else would try to decide for her.

Footsteps crossed the barn floor. The crate over the trapdoor was pushed away sending a shower of dirt onto the wooden steps.

The hatch creaked upward. Bezo's head filled the opening. "Hello, everyone! Our friends from the High Guard have left. Grab a few potatoes and that crate of reesel fruit." He pointed to a wooden box filled with something that looked like fuzzy plums with yellow stripes. "I think I will make a pie!"

Nadja called up. "Are we in danger?"

"That's such a relative question. For tonight, we are safe," replied the mage.

Nadja pursed her lips. "That's not very reassuring. Will we have any advanced warning if they return?"

"You are paranoid—even for a warden. I'm the Arch-Mage, Watcher of the Seventh Gate. No one enters my realm without my knowledge."

Alley and the others picked up the food and ascended the rickety steps. They emerged into the massive cathedral-like barn. Bright lights nestled high in the rafters. Machinery and tools were stacked against the walls and in the loft.

Chains and ropes hung from a complex system of pulleys in the eves. Here and there were piles covered with protective canvas and burlap.

Nadja dusted herself off and addressed the mage. "You understand that we have a duty to the Council. We have to ensure Alley's safety."

Bezo rolled his eyes and waved his hand at Nadja. "Now you're going on about duty? I get enough of that with the elves. Please spare me anymore formality for the rest of your visit."

Elek crossed to the other side of the barn and lifted the edge of a dusty tarp covering a piece of enormous machinery. The cloth slid off the equipment landing in a crumpled heap on the barn floor. The machine looked like a giant drill with tank treads.

Bezo turned at the sound of the falling canvas. "Do be careful, please! There are lots of delicate instruments in here."

Elek gestured at the huge drill machine. "What's this for?"

Nadja hissed at him. "Don't touch anything!"

Bezo waved her away. "It's all right. I love an inquisitive mind. Reminds me of when I was a boy!" He gestured at the big drill. "This is one of the original machines used to travel between this world and ours before the pixies helped us grow the Thorngates."

Elek squinted at him. "How does it work?"

Bezo chuckled. His necklaces clinked against one another as he laughed. "After we discovered the Caldruns and figured out that they were places where the ground had become infused with magic, we built machines, like this one. They allowed us to tunnel through these soft spots and safely cross the boundary between our worlds."

Elek grinned. "Cool."

The mage pulled the canvas back onto the machine. He winked at Elek. "This is nothing. Follow me." He led them towards the barn door.

Outside, the setting sun was turning the sky orange. In the field, stood an enormous machine covered in armored plating. Alley guessed it was the source of the earlier noise. It was almost as tall as the barn, rising on two thick metal legs. Its enormous limbs had an assortment of blades and what looked like giant gun barrels sprouting from them. It almost appeared to be a knight with pieces of other war machines stuck on as an afterthought.

Elek jogged ahead of them. "Oh man. Is that what I think it is? Is that a Mark IV Marion?"

Bezo's face broke into a broad smile. "Why yes, it is! Centurion class. The Marionette model that ended the War."

Elek approached the machine, stopping under its legs. He ran his hand along one of the armor plates. It looked like he was standing between the metal trunks of two giant trees.

Elek let out a low whistle. “The simulator doesn’t do it justice.”

Alley jogged to catch up to Elek. “What simulator?”

Elek turned. “The College has virtual reality simulators for all the Marion models,” he grinned, “I’m at the top of the leaderboard right now.”

That didn’t surprise her at all. Elek had always been good at video games.

Nadja called from behind. “They’re a waste of time—nothing more than glorified interactive history lessons about the Ash War.”

Elek rolled his eyes.

Bezo joined them. “The elves call her Dra’kun Duum. She killed more dracuns in the War than any of my other designs. Now she helps guard the Seventh Gate.”

Elek lowered his voice so that only Alley and the mage could hear him. “Can I try it?”

Bezo chuckled and then whispered back. “Oh ho! That would violate about twelve different codes and policies between the Council, College, and the Elvish Court—”

Elek looked at the ground and nodded.

“—but I’ll consider it. Any Warden Tyro willing to read *Substantia Artis* is worth bending the rules for.”

Elek’s face lit up.

Bezo waved his hand at everyone and raised his voice. “Let’s go have dinner!”

He ushered them toward a path that led to the strange

factory-house. Alley was hungry. The pancakes and coffee were a distant memory.

Bezo turned to Alley as they walked up the path. “Make sure you eat well and get rest. Once the moons are up, we will begin your training.”

25

DEAD LANDS

ALLEY

Alley sat on the porch with Elek, watching the two moons glint off the dark lake. She teased a stray seed from the berry pie they'd had for dessert from her back molar. The meal had been delicious. Bezo had dried their clothes and boots. For a little while, she had forgotten how awful the day had been.

She glanced over at Elek. "None of this seems real, El. I feel like I could fall asleep right now and wake up in my bed. I wish I could. People are dead. Dad is missing. All my stuff is gone. I'm jobless," Alley laughed. "You know I have a paper due in two days?"

Elek smirked. "I think you're going to need an extension."

Alley smiled and shook her head. She reached down and felt the lump of her mother's journal inside her backpack.

Hopefully, it had survived the dunk in the lake. She removed it and unwrapped the sweatshirt. The book was soggy, but in one piece. Her heart raced. She carefully peeled a few pages apart—the damage appeared minimal.

Elek glanced over at the damp journal. "Going to be awhile before you'll be able to read that."

"Obviously." Alley glared at him.

"Sorry." Elek's chair creaked as his barefoot rocked him back and forth. He was thumbing through a dusty tome Bezo had given him that described the inner workings of the Mark IV Marion. He looked up from the book. "We should have hung out more this past year. I could have maybe let you know what was going on. It might have been less of a shock."

Alley nodded. "Yeah, a little heads-up would have been helpful."

He ran his finger across a mechanical illustration. "My dad will flip out when he sees the house"—he looked over at Alley—"sorry, I know I shouldn't be complaining to you. At least our place is still standing."

She gave him a lopsided smile. "The house can be rebuilt, but I need to find my dad." Alley stared at the finely carved wooden planks that made up the porch.

Elek reached over and squeezed her hand. "I'll help you find him as soon as we're out of this place—and with the cure, if you change your mind."

"Thanks, El," she said.

The roar of the distant falls filled the silence. Elek's hand was warm. She was grateful to have his company. A piece of the familiar in a land of the strange.

"Alley, do you remember when we were kids and used to roast marshmallows over the fire in your backyard? Sitting out here reminds me of those times."

"I roasted them. You turned them into flaming torches."

Elek smiled. "They're better extra crispy."

"I don't think you've had one that's been properly roasted," she replied.

He smirked. "You'll have to show me your superior technique when this is all over."

She laughed. "Deal."

The door creaked open spilling light across the porch and down onto the grass leading to the water's edge. Bezo's shadow filled the bright entrance. "I hope you are feeling refreshed, Alley! The night is our friend! Follow me!" He stepped off the porch and made his way towards the water.

Elek let go of her hand, and she struggled to pull herself out of the chair. Her muscles had stiffened while sitting. They screamed at her in protest for setting them into motion once more. This was it, she would finally learn how to control the power. Doubt gnawed at the back of her mind. What if Bezo couldn't train her? What if he didn't understand how her power worked? What if she couldn't follow his instructions? Alley shook her head. She'd find out soon enough.

Elek held out his hand. "Give me your book. I'll get it dried out for you."

Alley passed him the journal. Then bent down and gave him a hug. "Thanks again, El."

"Good luck," he said.

Alley nodded. She jogged to catch up to Bezo's flapping patchwork robe as it receded into the moonlit murk. The mage led her along a dirt path that bordered the lake. A cool night breeze brushed Alley's skin carrying mist from the waterfall. A dock materialized out of the blackness. It jutted out into the water on short stilted legs. A small boat with a high curved prow bobbed at the end.

Alley followed Bezo out onto the wooden structure. "Where are we going?"

"Somewhere the elven High Guard won't bother us. Hop aboard."

Bezo held the boat steady against the dock. Alley stepped in and took a seat facing the stern where she could lean her back against the high prow of the craft. The mage boarded, rocking the boat back and forth. He shifted his robes around and took a seat against the transom by what looked like a mechanical rudder. He pawed through the necklaces resting against his belly and selected one with a round looking stone flute. Raising it to his lips, he covered a few of the holes and blew a long low note. Something under the boat started to make a gurgling sound, and the craft glided forward.

Bezo reached up and cast off the mooring line as they

headed out into the lake. They picked up speed as if the boat was equipped with an outboard motor. The mage grasped the rudder and guided the vessel toward a place where the lake disappeared into the towering trees.

"There's a network of waterways throughout this land. It used to be the safest way to travel before the Scale Roads. The predators don't like the sting of some of the water life."

The lake funneled down into a small river that flowed into the forest. They passed beneath enormous roots that arched into the water. The monstrous plants rose into darkness blotting out the night sky. Around them the woods were alive with sounds of hundreds of animals and insects. Spots of green, orange and purple light winked on and off—bioluminescent insects performing a midnight ritual. The wake of the small boat spread out behind them in a wide lacy fan.

"My dad said you could teach me how to control my ability. Are you like me?"

"No, Alley. You are something special. I know you have many questions, questions about your power, your past and your future. I can answer some and maybe help you find the answers to others, but there will be many that no one can help you discover except yourself."

Alley's stomach tightened. So Bezo might have no clue how to control her ability? What if no one did? She gripped the gunwales to steady herself. "So can you help me or not?"

"I don't have your exact gift, but I can help you discover a path to what you seek."

Alley rubbed her palms across her face. It was something at least, but it didn't sound like a guarantee. "So how do I do it? How do I control the energy? How do I keep from hurting people—from breaking things. How do I use it to stop the dracun? And, is there a way I can be cured if this training doesn't work?"

The mage laughed. "Cured? I don't even know where to begin with that. Why would you want to make a diamond into a lump of dirt?" Bezo frowned at her and shook his head making his necklaces jingle together. "We each have the power to create and destroy. To build up or tear down. To foster life or death. You have more of this ability than most. You've seen how easy it is to use your gift for destructive purposes. The universe is chaotic so destruction comes naturally. Creation requires just as much, if not more energy, but is infinitely more layered and complex. I believe releasing your energy towards that end may help provide the key to controlling your ability."

"Knocking things down is easier than stacking them?" she asked.

Bezo laughed. "I think it's more complex than that, but yes."

The sputter of the engine filled the air.

Bezo pushed the rudder, guiding the boat around a root that curved down into the water. It was so big they could have walked side by side up the length of it. "Do you know how a dam works?" asked the mage.

Alley looked up at him. "Yes."

"And you understand hydro-electric power?"

Alley didn't know all the details, but she knew enough. "Water from behind the dam is funneled through turbines that create electricity?"

The mage nodded. "Without the dam, the power of the water is chaotic and unfocused. With the dam, the water's power is channeled and converted into useful energy. I believe you are a raging river without a dam. I believe you need to first learn how to create a dam within your mind so that you can properly harness your power."

It was an interesting theory. "How would I do that?" asked Alley.

"An excellent question. I have some ideas for us to try out, but first we must reach our destination. You may want to rest until we get there."

Alley needed no convincing. There had been bad days in the past, but this one had to be the worst. Waking up from a car crash chained to a hospital bed. Running from monsters. Escaping from her burning house. Her father kidnapped or worse. Killing that poor woman in the truck. Hiking miles through the wilderness. Falling off a cliff into a lake. Hiding from elves. Every muscle in her body ached. She leaned back against the boat and slept a dreamless sleep as they slipped through the forest.

It felt as if she'd only just closed her eyes when they bumped against something, rocking the craft from side to side. Alley's arms flailed out. She smashed her left hand against the hull of the boat.

"Dear me. Sorry about that," said Bezo.

Alley sat up rubbing her hand where it hurt. She blinked. It was still dark. Patchy mist hung over the water. The mage was tying off the mooring line onto the charred remains of a wooden dock. The thick forest along the shoreline had been replaced by low weeds and the broken, splintered and blackened stumps of once giant trees.

"Where are we?" she asked.

Bezo climbed out of the boat and held it steady. "We are at the edge of the Upper Plateau, what was once the Fel'aloh Fields. Some of the greatest battles of the Ash War were fought here. It is now called the Dead Lands."

Alley pulled herself out of the boat and inhaled. The acrid scent of ash filled the air. They walked along what was left of the dock, taking care to avoid the gaping holes where fire had once eaten the now rotting wood.

As they stepped out onto the land, Alley sensed death everywhere. Dry, brittle grass crunched under their feet. The trampled and crushed splinters of enormous trees lay everywhere. Some were blackened by fire, others bleached by the sun. In the dark crevices, mushrooms and fungi consumed the rotting remains of the forest. Bezo picked a careful path through the debris. What kind of battle could have left the land in this state? Alley had seen dracun destruction—knew what they were capable of, but this—this was on a whole new level.

"The dracun did all this?" she asked.

The mage shook his head, "Not the dracun. This was done by dragons."

Bezo pointed towards a strange structure that lay ahead of them. It looked like the burned-out frame of an ancient hall. All that was left were the supports of the walls, arching upward in dark graceful curves that almost touched high overhead. As they approached and walked inside the massive supports Alley realized what she was seeing. Ribs. Enormous dragon ribs. She tried to imagine what a creature that large would have been like alive.

Bezo stopped and spread his arms, "This is where we will conduct your training."

"Here? Why here?" Standing inside the belly of a long dead monster would do nothing to help her relax or concentrate.

"Neither the pixies nor the elves come here. You will be free to practice unhindered and if you have an accident, well, the only person who needs to worry is me." Bezo walked ahead of Alley a few paces.

She still didn't like the place. Beyond the towering ribs, the silhouettes of other giant skeletons rose above the landscape. The place was creepy.

Bezo dug his hands into the pouches that hung on either side of his belt and turned to face her. He raised his fists.

Alley took a step backward, “What are you doing?”

“I’m sorry, Alley.” Bezo flung his fingers wide open and made a complex pattern in the air. Jets of green flame shot towards her like bolts of lightning.

26

TRAINING DAY

ALLEY

Alley screamed in pain as Bezo's green fire lanced through her exposed skin. She staggered backward trying to escape the blast. The flames stuck to her body. She dropped to the ground, rolling in the ash and dead grass. Any hope of Bezo helping vanished in a haze of agony. She needed to get up and run. Get back to the water and the boat. The fire was relentless. Seconds seemed to stretch into minutes as she screamed for him to stop.

When it ended, the pain was replaced with an irritating itch—like someone had scrubbed her down with sandpaper. "Leave me alone!" she croaked. Her throat was raw.

"The only times you've been able to manifest your ability has been under duress. I'm sorry Alley, we need to understand how to draw out your power before we can seek to control it."

"By burning me?!" Alley looked at her arms and was surprised to see that her skin and clothes were unharmed.

"You're fine. The flames cause pain, nothing more."

Bezo's hands were buried in his belt pouches. Alley stepped away from him. What little trust she had placed in him had been burned away. "Don't do it again," she said.

"Or what, Alley? What will you do?"

Her fingernails bit into the palms of her hands as she clenched them at her sides. He was trying to upset her, trying to make her power erupt, but the familiar throbbing in her head was gone. She hadn't felt it since they had entered this place. How had she been able to draw it out before? The place in her mind with the flowers. Somehow, she had to get back there.

Bezo's hands flew upward from his sides. This time Alley was ready. She dove sideways, avoiding a column of brilliant white light, and rolled behind one of the giant curved ribs. Her back pressed against the char-crusted skeleton. There were grooves in the scarred surface of the bone. They formed complex angular patterns that intertwined and overlapped. Some of the patterns were familiar. Too familiar. She rubbed at her fingernails. Under the chipped nail polish were patterns that looked just like those on the ancient dragon bone. How had the same patterns formed under the beds of her fingernails? There had to be a connection. Bezo might have the answer, but could she trust him? Did she have a choice?

"Alley, if you want to learn to control your ability, you must face me!" yelled the mage.

"Not while you're trying to kill me!" she yelled back as she peeked around the corner of the giant rib. Bezo hadn't moved, but his hands were back in his pouches.

"You must accept that there will be some pain involved. As with much in life, you will only become stronger when you meet resistance."

She could deal with pain. It was the unknown that scared her. "What are you going to do?"

"I'm going to help you discover how to use your ability when you stop hiding. Face me!" Bezo's voice boomed across the empty plains like a thunder clap.

Alley's muscles clenched. She closed her eyes trying to calm herself. This was why she'd come here? So that this crazy man could teach her? The green flames had been real pain. Intense pain. Like a dentist drill hitting every nerve in her mouth at once. Alley pressed her lips together. She had turned the course of a river, blown the wall off her house, destroyed a city block, and other things she wanted to forget. Whatever Bezo was going to do, somewhere inside her was the power to protect herself. She had to learn to control the power—without it, how could she hope to help her dad?

Alley took a deep breath. The acrid scent of ancient ash filled her nostrils.

She stepped out into the open and faced the Arch-Mage. "I'm ready."

Bezo flung a handful of something powdery into the air. He traced a pattern through the falling dust with his fingers. A whirlwind of blue and green light whipped around her body—scraping against her skin and tearing into her eye sockets. This was a new kind of pain. It ripped the breath from her lungs and brought Alley to her knees. She recoiled into her mind trying to summon the power to defend herself. She saw a flash of the clearing with the flowers. Then the pain was gone. Alley stood on shaky legs and tried to catch her breath.

"It is within you, Alley. Draw it out!" Bezo tossed another handful of dust into the air. His fingers scrawled an intricate pattern in the falling cloud. A crack of lightning shot from the sky engulfing Alley in bright purple-blue electricity. Every muscle in her body spasmed. She screamed in frustration. Something burst in her mind.

Alley was back in the forest clearing. It was filled with the strange white flowers. In the center of the clearing stood a little girl. She tilted her head at Alley and waved.

"Who are you?" asked Alley.

The girl didn't answer, she turned and walked away.

"Wait!"

Alley followed, passing through the flowers. Golden dust from the blossoms filled the air as her legs brushed by. She inhaled. The energy surged inside her chest. She felt like her lungs would explode.

Alley's eyes snapped open. Invisible golden energy shot out from her body like a cannon. It slammed across the gap between them striking Bezo and throwing him backward. Alley sagged as the power drained away. Her body felt light as if she had dropped a heavy bag after a long hike. She looked up as Bezo bounced off one of the enormous ribs knocking flakes of ash into the air.

Alley stumbled toward him. "Are you okay?!"

Bezo picked himself up off the ground and cracked a wide smile. "Such power! Such potential! Can you remember how you did it?"

Alley didn't understand how he wasn't injured. "Frustration. I got frustrated that you were hurting me and a place opened in my mind. The energy just poured out."

Bezo paced around Alley. "Frustration might be your involuntary reflex trigger. Like hitting your knee with a mallet. It just kicks on its own. We need to help you understand how to flex that muscle in your mind at will." He took a candy from one of his pouches and popped it into his mouth. "I may have been wrong earlier. You might not be a raging river, Alley. You may already have a dam holding back your energy. We just need to teach you how to open the sluice gate."

Was it possible that the power was always there behind a

wall in her mind? Alley closed her eyes and tried to find the place where the energy had entered. There was a dull ache, a fading memory of a spot. She pushed at it, but couldn't break through. She pushed again.

Nothing.

Alley opened her eyes and sighed.

Bezo placed his hand on hers. His skin was papery and dry. "In my experience, if you are trying hard and seeing no results, then you are probably approaching the problem in the wrong way. Tell me what is happening inside your mind."

Alley sighed. "There's this place where I can remember the power flowed, but I can't get inside. I might as well be trying to shoulder through a mountain."

Bezo squeezed her hand. He pulled her to the ground where they sat cross-legged opposite one another. "Stop trying so hard. You say it flowed from this place. Try instead to welcome it in."

The mage picked up a small stone and set in the ashy dirt between them. "You just threw me fifty yards. I want you to hold this stone in the air between us."

Alley nodded, trying to ignore the soreness in her muscles and the rawness of her skin where Bezo's attacks had buffeted her body. She closed her eyes and pictured the forest clearing with the flowers. She could sense it—as if it lay behind a shimmering vale. Alley thought she could see the silhouette of the little girl. She reached out and tried to push through the vale. It was unyielding. Maybe she was being too forceful? Alley inhaled and imagined herself gently parting the shimmering wall. There was a glimmer, then nothing. Alley sighed and looked across at the mage.

"Relax. Breathe," he said.

Alley glared at him. "It might be easier to relax if I hadn't been shot with flames and lightning bolts."

"I'm sorry. Perhaps if I play a little melody?" Bezo snapped together wooden pipes hanging from three of his necklaces to form a pan-flute. "Something to help soothe your mind?"

He raised the instrument to his lips and began to play. Notes flowed from the flute, echoing off the bones of the ancient dragon. It was a slow, beautiful tune that reminded Alley of warm summer evenings, of playing in the backyard till sunset, the smell of fresh cut grass, the laughter of friends and family, the smell of food being barbequed, of a time when the world was not a scary place. Alley closed her eyes and let her mind drift. The music glided through her senses. The tension in her body eased.

The softest whisper entered her mind.

Alley.

She was sitting in the forest clearing amongst the flowers. The little girl sat across from her. She smiled at Alley and handed her a single blossom.

Alley took it. "Who are you?"

"You know who I am," the little girl answered.

The girl picked another flower from the ground, raised it to her nose and motioned for Alley to do the same. Alley had no idea who she was. Someone she'd met in the past? Alley pushed her nose into the petals. The little girl inhaled gently, Alley did the same. A thread of pure energy rose out of the ground between them. It bobbed and swayed with the melody. The little girl laughed.

Bezo stopped playing the song. "Something amusing?"

Alley's eyes opened. The thread wove its way through her mind. It flowed out of her chest. A gossamer strand of radiant light that only she could see.

"I can feel it. Just barely, but I can feel it!" Alley was filled with intense joy. Maybe there was a chance she could tame it. If the energy could be guided, then maybe she could face the dracun. Maybe she could find her dad. Maybe she had the ability to set everything right. The thread started to fade. "Please, keep playing," she said.

Bezo raised the flute and resumed the song. Alley took a breath and focused on the memories and happiness that the song brought from her childhood. She smiled and tugged gently on the thread again. It brightened. Alley guided it outward across the ground. It was effortless. Joyful. It vibrated with the sound of each note. There were patterns in the vibrations. Familiar patterns. Patterns like those on her fingernails and the nearby bones. Patterns that echoed things she had only sensed before in the world around her. Connections. Everywhere. Linkages of energy and matter holding everything in place. The complexity was mind-boggling. Alley pushed the thread outward. Made it coil around the tiny rock, lifting it into the air. She felt dizzy. The thread melted away. The rock kicked up a puff of dust as it landed. A smile spread across her face.

"Excellent!" Bezo bounced to his feet. "Absolutely remarkable! Ben told me you were special, but he never thought—well, he will be proud to hear about the progress you've made in such a short time."

Her excitement disappeared. "If he's alive," she whispered.

"Your father is tough—like you. He knows how to take care of himself." Bezo scratched at his beard while smacking on his candy.

A soft breeze blew flakes of weightless ash around them like flies. The light of the twin moons bathed the wasteland in an eerie twilight. Inside the belly of the long-dead beast, the towering ribs seemed to curve in towards them to listen.

Alley bit her lip. "He hid things from me. Lied to me."

"He loves you, Alley. He thought he was doing what would be best for you."

Alley nodded. "Tell me about him? There are so many things he never shared with me."

Bezo smiled. "Ben is one of our Order's leading historians and researchers. An expert on Dragon, Elf and Pixie lore. When you were younger, he came here often for field research. I always thought he should have brought you."

She tried to picture her father roaming through the giant

forests scribbling in one of his journals. The idea seemed like something out of a storybook. "Can he do magic, like you?"

"The Order won't consider a mage for membership unless they are at least a Second Order Magician. Your father is a skilled Weaver, especially good at defensive magic."

Alley scratched at the ground with a sun-bleached twig. His magic hadn't stopped him from getting taken—or worse.

Bezo must have sensed her concern. "Ben once bested a wild Yaraboo, one of the more dangerous creatures that roam these forests. An Elvish hunting party died trying to stop the thing. Ben arrived and brought the beast down in seconds. It turned out that the animals have a gap in their plating behind the ears that he'd learned of from an ancient book in the Elvish Archives. He used a simple weave to guide a small needle into the gap and slay the beast. Ben could have been a great Battle-Mage if he didn't have such an itch to spend time in the laboratories and libraries."

Dad, fighting monsters. It made Alley smile. It was a small comfort knowing that he had some ability to defend himself. Alley looked up at Bezo. "Thanks."

The old mage examined the scratches she'd made in the ash. Without realizing it, she'd been scrawling the patterns that she'd seen on the old bones—the same ones fused into her fingernails.

"How do you know these symbols, Alley?"

She felt her body tense. Should she tell him? She'd never told her father about her nails, and her body still hurt from

Bezo's attacks. *No.* If she told him now, there was no telling what other painful experiments he'd want to try. Maybe tomorrow. "They're etched into the rib bone over there."

"And you are drawing this from memory?"

"I guess." She knew the patterns all too well. "What does it mean?" she asked.

"It is a weave, a pattern that shapes and guides magical energy." he replied.

"A weave?" Arün had mentioned them too, but hadn't offered much explanation.

"A bolt of lightning is full of electricity. If that current just travels through the air, it cannot be harnessed for anything meaningful. If it travels through an electrical circuit, then it can be made to do many useful things. A weave is like a circuit for magical energy. It guides the magic into patterns that allow the weaver to harness the energy. The more difficult the task, the more complex the weave."

"Why would someone carve something like that into a dead dragon's bones?"

"Dragons are special. Their bodies have adapted to the magic in this world. Those patterns were not carved. They grew into the flesh and bone of the creature's body as it wielded magic. An adaptation that has allowed the magic to become part of them, to pass their knowledge to other generations. If you were to look closely at the dragon scales back on the road, you would see similar patterns."

"How does that happen?"

Bezo shrugged. "I don't know. Dragon biology is not my forté. Now if you'd like a good recipe for Dreshin stew or a machine to stop a dracun—I can help!"

What did that mean about her? Had the energy that had flowed through her somehow caused the patterns to form under her nails?

"Magic"—Alley added lines to the weave in the ash —"has it ever changed a person's body?"

"Weaves have never become a permanent part of any human's body, though there have been mages that tried."

"What happened to them?" she asked.

"They attempted to tattoo weaves on themselves. It didn't go well."

Alley swallowed. "What does that mean?" She almost didn't want to know the answer.

"The magic burned them when it traveled through the tattoos. It is an unpleasant way to die. There are better ways to create weaves."

Alley shuddered. Was it possible that the energy that flowed through her could one day kill her if she wasn't careful? She tried not to freak out. "What are the better ways?"

"Simple ones can be learned and traced in the air as you have seen me do when casting. More complex applications require weaves that take time to craft. They are woven into materials like fabric, metal and wood so that they can be ready when needed."

"Like the warden's blades?"

"Yes, but those are special. Weapons like the Warden Scryth take great amounts of time, knowledge and energy to forge and charge with magic," answered Bezo.

Alley felt frustrated. There was so much to learn and so little time. "Do you think these weaves may be of use with my ability?"

"Perhaps. This one you have memorized. It is a repulsion weave."

Alley squinted and shook her head.

"It channels magic in a way that applies outward force. The dragon most likely used this ability to help with flight. If you are familiar with this weave, it may explain how you were able to throw me just now. Although it is curious that I didn't see you trace the weave in the air."

Alley added a few more shapes to the design in the ash.

A serious expression passed over Bezo's face. "May I see your hand?"

Her pulse quickened. "Why?"

"Trust me."

She held out her hand—palm up to hide her nails.

The old man reached into one of the pouches at his side and sprinkled a sparkling white powder into her palm. "Pixie dust. The source component of our magic."

Where it touched her skin, an electric tingle coursed through her hand. Her eyes went wide. It felt exactly like when she touched Arün's skin. "It feels strange," she said.

"Does it?" Bezo raised an eyebrow.

"Yes, like electricity."

"Have you ever felt that sensation before?" he asked.

Yes. Whenever Arün touches me, she thought. But she wasn't ready to trust Bezo with that information yet. He'd caused her too much pain already. Alley shook her head instead. "I—don't know."

Bezo nodded. "You can feel magic. It is unusual, but not unheard of."

The dust sparkled in her palm.

"How do I use it?"

Bezo chuckled. "Today we should try to understand the magic you already possess."

Alley focused on the dust. It tingled but provided no indication as to how the energy within it could be tapped. She turned her hand and let the shimmering particles fall on the symbols she'd drawn on the ground. They were sucked toward the grooves in the ash like iron filings to a magnet. There was a thump in her chest. Something blew her backward, lifting her into the air as if she'd been hit by a gale force wind. Bezo's body flew in the opposite direction. Alley landed on her back kicking up a cloud of ash.

The old mage got up first coughing. "That's my fault. I should have warned you to keep the dust away from the repulsion weave."

Alley sat up and brushed herself off. "What happened?"

"The magic is drawn to fresh weaves." Bezo massaged the

muscles in his neck as he walked back toward her. "It's what makes air-weaving possible.

The mage reached into one of the pouches at his side and tossed a pinch of pixie dust into the air. "Observe."

As it fell, he made a complex pattern with his fingers through the descending cloud. The dust was sucked towards the trails left by his finger movements and formed bluish glowing lines in the air. They merged to form a glowing sphere of light that floated above his palm.

Alley squinted her eyes. The sphere was brighter than a camping lantern. The pattern Bezo had used to form it had looked simple enough.

Bezo poked his finger into the light and made a simple movement. The sphere burst into a shower of tiny glowing sparkles. "It would stay lit for hours."

"Wow!" she exclaimed. He made it look easy.

"Wow, indeed." The old mage looked at her thoughtfully. "What will you do when you can control your power, Alley?"

It was dangerous, like owning a handgun that could go off at random. If she could control it, she would use it for good. "I want to help people—I'm not sure how yet."

"I'm glad to hear you say that. Power doesn't belong in the hands of those who do not seek to use it for the good of humanity."

Alley wished helping people didn't include fighting dracun. "I need to ask you a question and I need you to be honest with me."

Bezo raised an eyebrow.

"How does the Council think my powers are going to protect humanity? You already have wardens to fight dracun. What is it you see me doing?"

The mage was quiet for a moment before he spoke. "If the time comes—slay a dragon."

She looked at the massive ribs. How was she going to take on anything this big? All it would have to do is step on her. "There's no way."

Bezo smiled. "Your doubt is misplaced."

"But you said the dragons have all been imprisoned. Why do you still need me?"

"There was a time when I thought your help would never be needed, but I fear that time has passed. Something has changed. The Obsidian Clan is openly defying us."

"Just send them back here. Why keep them in our world?"

"The pixies and elves would consider it a betrayal. They would sever the ties between our worlds. We would lose access to the dust."

"So?" she asked.

Bezo shook his head. "You are asking me, the Council and most of the Warden Guild to sign our own death sentences."

What was he talking about? "No, I'm not."

"We're well over a century old because of the dust. It has

extended all of our lives. Without it we'd all be dead within a few years."

So, there was no way they'd be convinced to jeopardize their fountain of youth. "But, you have the Marionettes. You used those to kill this dragon." She spread her arms wide.

"At great cost. Many died before we could stop this one. You are far more powerful than any of my machines or any of the weapons possessed by humanity's military forces. When we have completed your training, you'll be able to take down a dragon before it can hurt anyone."

Alley felt none of the conviction that she heard in the old mage's voice. "I don't know."

Maybe there was another way. She felt ashamed asking, but she had to know. "Why don't you kill them all now? While they are imprisoned."

Bezo's eyes looked sad. "Would you do it? Would you kill those mighty creatures in cold blood? They surrendered to us. Submitted to imprisonment. Their kin live among us, work beside us—most peacefully. Right now, the Obsidian are the only clan causing a problem. If we were to kill the dragons, every clan would revolt. We don't have nearly enough wardens to suppress an uprising at that scale. It would be a blood-bath."

Alley hung her head. "I'm sorry—you're right, I shouldn't have asked that."

"It's alright. It was a fair question, one that has been

debated within the Council," Bezo reached out and touched her hand. "Alley, it's okay to be afraid."

Her gaze drifted back up to the giant ribs around them. The vision of Seattle in ruins flashed through her mind. Ash. Fire. A dracun with lavender eyes. "Do any of the rulers of the clans have purple eyes?" she asked.

Bezo leaned back and pursed his lips. "That's an odd question—"

Alley's stomach tightened.

Bezo stood in a flurry of patchwork and ash. "Where did you see the Obsidian Queen?"

"Who?"

"Queen Srira of House Styg. Ruler of the Obsidian Clan. She's the only dracun regent with purple eyes. Was it in one of your father's books?"

"No." Alley stood as well.

Bezo squinted at her.

Alley hugged her chest. "She was in a dream." Somehow it seemed too strange to admit to having a vision.

"What kind of dream?" asked Bezo.

Alley described the vision in detail. The destruction of the city. The Queen's invitation and threat. She shuddered. The Queen's lavender eyes hung in the blackness of her mind.

Bezo listened and then paced around the giant ribcage tugging at his beard and muttering. He reached into his pouch and pulled something out. "We need to try one more thing tonight. I was going to wait until tomorrow, but I see now that our time is running short." He placed the object in her hand. It was smooth and hard—some kind of strange nut?

She rolled it between her fingers. "Why? What's wrong?"

"Those weren't dreams. The dragon Srira showed you in the ice cave—that's Cynder. I think she is trying to free him."

27

THE SEED

ALLEY

Alley's heart raced. The dragon in her vision had been huge—twice as big as the skeleton they sat inside. It had roasted her alive. She squinted at the mage. "Back on the road, you said Cynder was the worst of the dragons."

"Not was—is. If he is freed, I fear you'll need reserves of power to stop him."

Alley shook her head. "What do you mean?"

"Magic can be stored." The old mage walked away from Alley. "Some weaves require vast amounts of energy, more than can be drawn out of a few handfuls of dust. It is useful to build reserves of magic in places where it can be released quickly." He motioned at the nut in her hand. "Plants have been used by the pixies for ages as a storage medium. They can house enormous amounts of magical energy."

The wind blew a swirl of ash through the giant moonlit bones. It rustled the withered grass. Alley scratched at her skin where it still itched from the mage's tests. She already had too much energy. Storing it seemed dangerous, like bottling lightning.

Bezo combed his fingers through his beard. "Channel your energy into that nut. A little at a time. Over days and weeks, the seed will become a powerful magical reserve."

Alley held the nut up, examining the strange shell. It looked like an acorn, but with odd swirls in the husk. It didn't look like something that could hold much energy. "Okay—how do I do that?" she asked.

"For me, it requires the etching of a complicated weave into the shell of the nut and a slow application of pixie dust. But I suspect your ability may be more like the pixies. You may be able to channel magical energy into it with your mind. Try." Bezo crossed his arms. The collection of chains around his neck clinked together like wind chimes.

Alley needed to re-create the thread of energy. "Will you play that song again?" she asked.

"Of course." Bezo raised the flute to his lips and played.

Alley closed her eyes and let the song take her back to the clearing in her mind.

The glade was empty this time, but she could feel the little girl watching her from somewhere nearby. Alley bent down, plucked a single white flower from the field and breathed in its scent. She felt the energy fill her body.

Her eyes opened. The golden thread of power flowed out of her chest. Alley smiled in wonder at how effortless it was compared to her past attempts. She guided the tendril toward the hull of the strange acorn. The thread twisted its way towards the nut until it came to rest on the shell of the pod. Alley gasped as the line of energy went taut. She felt a tugging sensation. The seed was pulling greedily at the flow, devouring it. In response, the opening in her mind widened. Energy poured out, funneling toward the seed in greater quantities.

"What's happening?" she gasped.

Bezo rushed forward and caught her as she was about to fall. "Stay in control!"

The seed fell from her hand and landed in the ash. Alley tried to cut off the flow. The pod's suction was too strong. She stomped on the nut. It split open. Roots dug into the dry soil, snaking out in every direction. A tiny stalk reached upward, leaf buds emerged and blossomed along its length. The stem thickened as it rocketed skyward.

Bezo pulled her backward trying to avoid the bulging cracks in the surrounding ground. "Alley, stop! Make it stop now!"

She couldn't speak. Her eyes watered as she gasped for breath. The seed was tearing at her mind, trying to pull everything it could from her. "It—won't—stop," she stammered.

What was once a small seed, was now a towering tree—

bigger than many they had passed on the walk along the Scale Road. Acorn-like nuts rained down from the boughs, peppering the soil. Alley felt weak. She struggled to stop the flow, but it was only getting worse. What was happening? How could a plant do this? She needed to get away from it. Maybe distance would break the connection to her mind. "Help me to the boat," she gasped.

Bezo pulled her arm around his neck and helped her stand. The cords of his necklaces dug into her cheek as she collapsed against him. He dragged her past the dragon ribs, now overshadowed by the enormous tree. Alley cried out as hundreds of new presences tugged at her mind—the new acorns that had fallen—they were all clawing at the tendrils of energy now. Other trees sprang up. She had to make it stop, she could feel her body growing weak.

Alley was back in the clearing. The little girl stood at its center—crying. The wind howled, and the air was filled with golden dust from the flowers. It flowed into the forest as if something deep in the shadows was inhaling it. Alley wrapped her arms around the trembling girl. She stared into the forest—her anger growing.

"Help me." The little girl whispered into Alley's ear.

Alley's anger turned to rage. She let the swirling dust fill her mind.

Power flooded Alley's body. She had to defend herself.

Alley whipped tendrils of energy towards the tree and its offspring. In her mind, she felt the plant's thirst slow. Rage filled her in a white-hot blaze. She pushed away from Bezo and dug her hands into the soil.

Bezo was yelling something at her, but she wasn't listening. She had to destroy the tree and the seeds.

Alley sent energy into the ground. Felt insects and worms obliterated by the surge of power—felt it enter the roots of the giant tree.

Up towards its core.

She would splinter it into toothpicks.

S—top.

The clarity of the voice in her head melted her anger into confusion. It wasn't Bezo. Somewhere in the distance, she could sense he was yelling something at her, but she couldn't hear what he was saying.

P—eace. The voice was like the moan of the wind through a rocky canyon. Slow and plodding, but full of power. The flood of energy left her body, but her mind was still within the tree.

Who is this? she asked in her head.

Silence. Then the deep rolling voice echoed in her thoughts. *H—elp.*

Who are you? she yelled in her mind.

Something was shaking her body, but she ignored it. Where was the voice was coming from? Was it the pixies? Something else? Could the tree itself be talking to her? Her hands clenched in the soil. Grains of dirt squeezed between her fingers.

Images flashed through her mind as if lit by bursts of lighting.

A cave with a high ceiling open to the sky. A large egg at the bottom bathed in a ray of moonlight.

A flash and now she was in a forest. Something enormous passed high overhead. The canopy above erupted in a blaze of fire. Burning leaves rained down.

A flash and she was soaring over a land bathed in flames.

A flash and she was staring into the gaze of a creature with enormous wide-set eyes, not human, but similar. A pixie? It smiled and then touched her arm. The skin on her hands turned dry and bark-like. Leaves sprouted from her fingers. She felt her joints getting stiffer. Her feet felt like they were sinking into the ground. Her heart beat frantically and then slowed.

A flash and her mind was shoved backward.

R—e—member, said the voice in her head.

Bezo was shaking her. "Alley what's going on! Wake up!"

She pushed him away and stood on shaky legs, stumbling over an enormous root that had burrowed through the ground.

Alley looked up at the massive tree looming over them. "It wouldn't stop."

Bezo followed her gaze upward. "Remarkable. I've never seen a tree grow this fast."

"Remarkable? That thing almost killed me!" She kicked at one of the tree roots. "It wouldn't stop until it thought I would destroy it!"

Bezo squinted at her. "It *thought?*"

Perhaps she'd tell him about the visions tomorrow when she'd had more time to think about everything. "It was more like a feeling," she lied.

Bezo drummed his fingers on his bottom lip. "Interesting. I've often speculated that the plants here might be sentient. I've had nothing conclusive to prove it. Just a hunch. The pixies have been very unhelpful when I've tried to investigate my hypothesis."

"I don't want to try that again," she said.

Bezo looked back up at the tree. "I think we've done enough for tonight." He turned and made his way towards the river, stepping over the tangle of roots that ran along the ground.

Alley followed. She felt fatigue in every part of her body. The giant tree scared her. She could almost sense it watching as she followed Bezo back towards the boat. It had touched her mind—had controlled the energy flowing from her better than she ever had. How had it done that? Using seeds to store power seemed dangerous—at least for her. Alley took comfort in knowing she'd been able to draw the energy out twice and it was getting easier to go back to the clearing in her mind. But she wished she knew who the little girl was and why she was always there.

Alley's toe struck something and sent it skittering ahead on the path.

It was a nut from the tree.

She bent over and picked it up. Maybe she would try

again when she had more control. Alley dropped it into the pocket of her black woolen jacket and jogged to catch up with the Arch-Mage.

Bezo had said the pixies had been using plants to store energy for years. Maybe they would have a better understanding of what had just happened. "Do you think I can talk to the pixies?" she asked.

Bezo laughed. "You can try. The pixies decide who they want to talk to and when. You may find the conversation one-sided."

They made their way back to the charred remains of the dock. The boat thumped against the decaying pylons.

"Don't you talk to them?"

Bezo held the boat so she could step in. "Occasionally, but our conversations are not always—productive. The pixies are just as likely to tease you as help you. It takes extreme patience to deal with them."

Alley settled into the seat at the prow of the boat and relaxed her tired limbs. Bezo sat in the back. He fumbled for the proper whistle around his neck to start the engine. "There is something else to consider. If you talk to them, they may alert the elves. Given your unique qualities I'm afraid that might not go well."

Was the creature the tree had shown her in the flashes a pixie or something else? Maybe she could try to talk to the tree again tomorrow. Alley fingered the seed in her pocket and stared up at the twin moons. Bezo blew a note on one of the whistles, bringing the boat to life beneath them. As her fingers rubbed across the rough husk of the seed, a gust of wind blew across the water and the tree's voice echoed in her mind.

R—e—member.

28

JEHALO

ALLEY

Alley watched Elek rise from his rocking chair as she and Bezo emerged from the gloom into the light of the porch lanterns.

"Alley, you look awful!" he exclaimed.

She managed a half smile, too tired to explain to him why her body felt like she'd been thrown down a staircase. He took her arm and led her inside the house. The interior was warm and bathed in an orange glow from the belly of a cast-iron stove squatting against the far wall. Arün and Nadja rose from their seats by a thick wooden table.

Elek glared at the mage. "What happened to her?"

"She made great progress."

"Great progress? It looks like she got beat up!"

Bezo grabbed the banister by the stairs and hoisted

himself onto the first step. "There are two guest bedrooms upstairs and one down here. You should all rest. Tomorrow is a special day." The wood creaked under his weight as he made his way upstairs.

Elek glared at the mage's back.

Alley patted her friends arm. "I'm fine." At least she was alive. She had never run a marathon but imagined that the exhaustion she felt had to be on par with how those athletes felt at the end of a race.

Elek looked at her skeptically.

Arün crossed the room and touched his hand to her cheek. She closed her eyes and inhaled. The scent of cedar and rosemary filled her nose. His touch sent electrical tingles surging through her body. He felt like the pixie dust —like magic.

It washed away some fatigue and wiped way the irritating itching that had plagued her skin since Bezo's attacks. "We were worried. Bezo refused to allow us to accompany you."

Alley squinted at Arün. He'd done it again, somehow his touch had taken away the pain. She had to find a time to ask him about it.

She stood her body no longer stiff. "Next time"—she glanced at Elek and Nadja—"I want you all to come. I don't feel safe here."

"I'll talk to the Arch-Mage in the morning," said Arün.

Elek pulled her toward the stairs. "I got your book dried out, and I brought your stuff up to one of the guest rooms."

Alley followed him, already feeling her eyelids getting heavy. Hopefully, the bed was soft.

At the top of the landing, Elek opened one of the doors. "This is your room."

"Thanks, El." She shuffled inside and turned to close the door.

"If you need anything, I'm right across the hall."

"Okay," she started to push the door closed.

Elek frowned. "Seriously. Snacks, tall glass of water. You name it—I'm your guy."

Alley rolled her eyes and closed the door. She stripped out of her ash covered clothes as she stumbled towards the bed on the far side of the room. She felt bad about getting into a clean bed still caked in sweat and soot but forgot all about it as her body sank into the soft mattress. Fatigue tugged her eyes closed.

Alley awoke to the smell of fresh bread. She smiled expecting to hear her dad's wheelchair squeaking down the hallway. Then she remembered where she was—her smile faded. She pushed herself up from the bed. Downstairs, the murmur of voices rose above the grinding and churning of the house. Alley swung her legs down onto the cold wooden planks of the floor. She stood and put on a fuzzy blue bathrobe that hung on the back of the door. It was baggy with big pockets and a "B" embroidered in gold. It wasn't as soft as the bed, but it would do. She opened the door and headed down the creaky wooden staircase. Arün appeared at the bottom landing.

"You look like you could use an assist." He took the steps two at a time to reach her side, and offered his hand. The now familiar electrical sensation moved up her arm from where their bare skin touched. It made her feel more alert.

The first floor was warm. The smell of fresh bread was even stronger. The downstairs had been decorated. Thick purple satin ribbon looped from the ceiling and around the thick wooden support beams. Bundles of grass tied with purple ribbons hung from the heavy rafters. Golden sunbeams streamed in through the open windows painting the floors and wall with hot squares of light. Everyone was seated around the large table at the center of the room which now had a white linen table cloth. It was set with square red plates surrounded by golden eating utensils and white porcelain tea cups.

Alley stared in wonder. It looked like Bezo had decided to throw a party. When had he had time to hang all the decorations?

The mage sat at the head of the table discussing something with Nadja. Elek was staring across at them, his hands clasped in front of his mouth. He looked angry, the way he used to look when his father was lecturing him after a visit from the police. Arün pulled out the carved wooden chair beside Nadja. She eased into it, trying to catch Elek's eye so she could offer him a smile.

"Everything Nadja has told me about your feats over the last few days has been impressive for such a young Tyro," Bezo said to Elek. "But it is no substitute for full training. I can't endorse the Warden Trials. Even if I did, the Trials take time you do not have right now."

Elek was as still as a statue, except for his leg under the table which was shaking up and down. It was making the utensils on the table rattle. Alley had seen him act this way in the past. It rarely ended well.

To her surprise, Elek unclasped his hands, smoothed the tablecloth on either side of his plate and adjusted the alignment of his place setting. "I—I appreciate, uh, you considering Nadja's recommendation. I'll do whatever you feel is best for the Council and the Wardens."

Alley raised an eyebrow. Impressive. She'd never seen him exercise this much self-control. He'd changed a lot during the last year.

Bezo reached over and patted him on the shoulder. "You will make a wonderful warden, Elek. You've got the right temperament. That's everything when the stakes are high."

She tried to catch Elek's attention, but he was staring at the table cloth.

The mage looked over at Alley. A broad smile cracked his face into a web of deep wrinkles. "Good morning and Happy Jehalo! I was afraid you might sleep through breakfast!"

"Uh, thanks. What's up with the ribbons?" She twirled her finger at the loops hanging from the ceiling.

"Oh, yes, yes! I've been fascinated by the Elvish High Holidays since coming here. The elves have many special days. That means many fantastic opportunities to bake! Today is Jehalo, the celebration of the Inner Gift. The elves believe each living thing has a gift to be shared with the world. Jehalo is the celebration of one's journey to discover that gift! A very appropriate holiday for you, don't you think?"

"Yeah, it's pretty special." Alley was tired, hungry and in no mood to celebrate. She hadn't forgiven Bezo for the beating she'd gotten the night before and didn't enjoy seeing Elek upset.

Bezo ignored her mood. He pushed his chair back and stood. "Yes, well, I've baked some traditional Jehalo sweet bread for our morning meal. I think it's just about cooled."

He left the room and returned carrying a large cloth-lined wicker basket filled with steaming oval loaves of golden bread. Alley's mouth watered.

"Jehalo bread is a traditional part of the holiday feast and includes the giving of gifts baked inside the loaves to remind us of the gifts hidden within each of us. I enjoy staying faithful to tradition. Please be careful as you bite into the bread." Bezo walked around the table and used a set of polished wooden tongs to place a loaf on each of their red plates.

Alley squished the loaf with her fingers and felt something hard under the surface.

To her right, Arün grabbed his bread and ripped it in half spraying flakes of crust across the table. Something fell out onto his plate. A small wooden box. The others did the same. Similar containers landed on the table in front of each of them. Each had intricate carvings on all the sides.

Alley picked up her box. It was warm from being inside the hot bread. She noticed a small latch on one edge and pushed it with her thumb. The top of the box sprung open blowing a shower of colorful glitter into the air. She nearly tipped her chair as she jerked backward.

Bezo laughed, clapped his hands and drummed them against the edge of the table. He was enjoying the reactions of his guests. The others released the latches on their boxes, filling the air with a cloud of bright sparkles.

Alley blew the glitter away from her food and took a bite of the bread. The taste of cinnamon, almonds, and butter washed across her tongue.

She peered into the box. The inside was lined with purple satin. Nestled at the bottom was a silver locket. She reached in and pulled it out by a long elegant chain. It was as big as a coin and had a clasp.

Alley pried it open with her fingernail. Inside was a swirling milky surface. She touched it with her finger. Even though it looked liquid, it felt smooth and hard.

Alley looked up at Bezo. “This is beautiful. What’s this inside?”

The mage stood and came around the table. “You are each holding a milkstone. A curious Elvish device. When you touch them together, they form a bond that isn’t broken by time or distance. The lockets will always lead back to one another. Try it. You need to do it at the same time and speak your name, so they will all be connected.”

Alley touched the locket and a troubling thought entered her head. The milkstone meant that her location would always be known by the wardens. Was it a gift or a way to control her?

Arün, Nadja, and Elek leaned into the center of the table and touched their lockets together as if they were making a toast. Elek motioned for Alley to do the same. She sighed and leaned in, touching her locket to the others. Hopefully, she wouldn’t regret the decision.

When they were all touching, Arün was the first to speak his name. “Arün.” A low tone emitted from the lockets like a tuning fork being struck.

“Nadja.” Another low tone sounded.

“Elek.” And another.

“Alley.” A final note was struck. Their raised hands were pushed apart by an unseen force from within the lockets.

Alley sat back and considered her milkstone. The silky swirling white surface now appeared to bubble in three spots along the edge of the stone, toward where Elek, Arün, and

Nadja were sitting. She touched the bubbling spot that appeared to point towards Arün. It expanded. The liquid swirls formed the contours of Arün's face. She tapped the small portrait, and it swirled apart reforming into the three bubbling spots again. She touched the one pointing towards Elek and the liquid swirled to form his features.

Alley shut the locket. "This is interesting. Thanks." She wasn't sure if she wanted it, but didn't want to be rude.

"I hope it serves you well in the journey ahead," said Bezo.

Alley unfastened the chain and clasped it around her neck. If only her father had a similar locket.

Bezo left and came back with a steaming kettle of tea. He walked around the table filling everyone's cup.

Nadja reached for her tea. "This is a nice break, but we need to figure out what our plan is for today. Time could be flying by on the other side of the gate. The dracun aren't sitting idle. Their attacks yesterday violated all our Laws. If it continues, war is inevitable."

"Ah, my fine warden. You are getting into the holiday spirit." Bezo chuckled as he sat down and sipped his drink.

"Laugh all you want. We need a plan."

"If you insist." Bezo set down his cup, his voice lowering. "Alley and I will continue training this afternoon. The rest of you can prepare for your departure this evening. You should leave under the cover of darkness. The High Guard is on alert, so we need to be careful. You can't afford to be detained and I don't need another visit from El'Iswald and his cronies. I love the elves, but the High Guard lack the civility of the Court."

"I thought you trained her last night?" Nadja pointed her loaf at the mage.

Bezo's eyes narrowed. "I did. Perhaps you are an expert now in magical training and know how long it takes?"

Alley shook her head. The mage was no expert either, at least when it came to her abilities, but she decided not to point it out.

Nadja looked at her plate in silence and chewed.

Arün cleared his throat, casting a glance at his partner. "I think what Nadja was trying to say, is that we are very concerned about getting back. Another day here could be another month on the other side."

Bezo sighed looking over at Alley. "You need more time. We've barely begun."

Alley met his gaze. She'd made a lot of progress last night. Another day could make a huge difference. "Bezo is right, I don't have full control yet, but I think I can get there soon."

Nadja shook her head and tucked a lock of blond hair behind her ear.

Arün reached over and squeezed Alley's hand. "Do what you need to do. If you aren't ready—well, then this trip, all that happened yesterday—it was for nothing."

The electric crackle of his touch traveled up her arm.

Alley looked out the window towards the sunlight glinting off the lake. She needed time to process all that had happened over the last few days, before she endured another training session with the mage. "After breakfast and a shower, I'd like to go for a walk," she said.

"An excellent idea!" Bezo exclaimed.

"By myself."

The mage's grin melted as he tapped his fingers on his lower lip and his eyes roamed the top of the table. "Oh. Dear me. No. No, that wouldn't be a good idea. There are far too many things about this world you don't know. I can't allow it."

Her hands balled into tight fists. "Bezo, I'm going."

"No. You do not understand what—"

Arün shifted in his chair. "I'll go with her. I know the dangers and can make sure she's safe."

Alley gritted her teeth. Were a few minutes of peace so much to ask for? "I don't need a chaperone!" she snapped.

Arün looked at her. "How about a friend?"

Elek rolled his eyes.

Alley's hands relaxed as she re-considered Arün's offer. If having him follow her meant that she didn't need to worry about the creatures in the forest, then maybe it would make for a more relaxing walk. "Okay, but I need space to think."

The warden nodded.

Bezo sighed. "I'm not thrilled about it, but I know you

will keep her safe. You would do well to stay on the path that runs along the lake. Do not stray into the woods."

Through the windows, the lake looked serene in the morning sun. Something big broke the surface of the water and then dived back down shoving glinting ripples towards the shore.

Alley turned to the mage. "There's something huge in there."

Bezo glanced out the window. "You would do well to avoid the water, too."

29

THE WALK

ALLEY

Wind-blown mist from the crashing falls glided across the lake. Alley closed her eyes and listened to the dull roar of the falling water. For a moment, it almost felt like being alone. She drew a deep breath of cold air and continued walking. Her boots crunched on the gravel path that ran along the shore. She could hear Arün's footsteps a few paces behind.

Massive evergreens looked down on her from the right. Their trunks towered higher than the heights of the waterfall that lay ahead. The ancient giants swayed in the breeze, whispering to one another. She felt small and insignificant in their presence, even though her power could topple them.

Alley pulled her coat closed and asked for forgiveness from the dead. Brent, the woman on the bridge—all the rest.

These people had been going about their lives; then she had snuffed them out. She couldn't fix that. A knot formed in her stomach. Her throat tightened. Tears came unbidden to her eyes.

Alley dropped to her knees. The gravel bit into her skin through her jeans. She had killed them. They were dead because of her. Arün's arms closed around her as grief shook her body. He said nothing, just held her while the sadness poured out. Alley wished their strange connection would wipe away the hurt, but this pain wasn't physical—it was worse. She barely knew herself anymore.

Alley wiped her eyes with her sleeve and stood—pushing herself away from Arün's embrace. She didn't want to turn around—to let him see the redness of her eyes and her quivering lip. She stood and resumed her walk.

Last night had been the first time she had controlled the energy. The little girl had something to do with it. Was she a part of her subconscious? The clearing in her mind was so vivid and detailed, it almost seemed like a real place. The song Bezo played, had made her feel things she hadn't felt in a long time. That carefree feeling from her childhood seemed to be the key to controlling the energy. What if the magic fed off her emotions? What if the happier she was, the more control she had? It was an interesting possibility. Maybe Bezo would have more insights during the afternoon training.

The path ended near the base of the waterfall. The cliff

soared above. The roar of the water was deafening. Large flat stones rose from the lake offering a wide platform to view the falls. Alley carefully stepped across them and stopped on the largest one. The mist blew in thick swirls, plastering strands of hair across her face. It washed away the salty tear stains. Arün followed and stopped beside her.

The morning sun shone through the mist of the falls causing a rainbow to arc across the valley. It looked as if it ended on the back of one of the giant Chu'la snails on the far side of the lake.

You've felt our connection.

Arün's voice was only a whisper, but Alley was startled by its clarity. She looked sideways at him. His eyes looked sad. Alley grabbed his forearm and shook her head at him mouthing a response. "How did you do that?" The pounding of the waterfall drowned out her words.

The other day. At the coffee shop—

Alley's eyes went wide. His mouth wasn't moving, but she could hear him as if they were talking on the phone. She took a step back, letting go of his arm.

—no human could have survived that explosion, he continued.

Alley shook her head, taking another step away, but there was nowhere to go. She had reached the edge of the rock slab. How was he talking? What did he mean?

Arün took her hand and pulled her away from the edge

of the rock. *I believe we have a connection because we are—similar,* he said in her mind.

HOW?! she screamed back.

Arün's face broke into a broad smile as he touched her damp cheek. *No need to yell, Alley.*

She blinked, his touch brought calm to the turmoil within her. *How is this possible? What are you?* she thought.

Do you know how dracun communicate?

No? She looked at him her brows furrowing as her mind struggled to process hearing his voice without seeing his lips move.

Telepathy. They can speak to each other through their thoughts.

Are you saying I'm a dracun?

No, but I believe part of you is.

Why do you think that?

Because I am part-dracun and you can hear me. Alley stiffened. He looked nothing like a dracun.

Arün saw her alarm and his smile faded, replaced by sadness. *Let me explain. I'm not a dracun. Those are young dragon offspring that magically assume a human form. No part of them is human. I am the product of a program the Mages began a century ago. A combination of human and dragon genomes.*

You think I'm part-dracun too? Alley didn't want to believe it. She looked at her hand and flexed her fingers. The question felt so strange. She didn't want to consider the answer. But the similarity between the patterns under her nails and the ones etched into the ribs of the long dead dragon already pointed to the truth.

Arün tucked a lock of her hair behind her ear. *We don't choose how we enter the universe, Alley. But we must choose how we spend our time here. I've never felt as if I belonged anywhere. Not with humans and not with dracuns. My life, like yours, has become a web of secrets and half-truths, but what you are, need not define who you are.*

Alley's mind reeled as she searched the cold, wet stone between them. I'm part dracun. I'm part dracun. She said it over and over in her mind, trying it on for size. It might explain the telepathy, but could dracuns do the things she'd done? Could Arün? She needed to know.

Do you have abilities like me? she asked in her mind.

He shook his head. *You are something unique, Alley—the next stage of the Mages' program.*

She didn't want to be unique in that way. Alley turned away and jammed her hands into the pockets of her coat.

Swirls of mist blew between them beaten up by the crashing water. It beaded up on their skin and dampened their clothes and hair. Alley couldn't tell if it was water or tears that streamed down Arün's face. He seemed to stare into the past—at something that had brought him great sadness.

The fire inside Alley cooled. Whatever she was, she was still the same person she had been yesterday and the day before. She reached for his hand and held it. His eyes closed and water dripped from the locks of hair above his forehead.

Arün whispered in her mind. *A long time ago, I thought I could be a warden and lead a normal life—that I could be happy. My fianceé, Lyla, threw herself from a cliff when she found out what I was—what I had become.* He swallowed.

Alley squeezed his hand. *I'm so sorry, Arün.*

He squeezed back, his mouth a tight line. *If you need someone to talk to—I understand what it means to be different. To not fit in.*

Alley nodded.

Arün's face looked serious. *The Council and a few of the highest-ranking wardens are the only people who know the truth. Alley, no one else can know. About me. About either of us. Especially Nadja. She would—I don't think she would handle it well.*

I won't tell anyone, she replied.

Alley thought she heard a horn echo above the roar of the falls. The water was deafening. It sounded again. Arün turned towards the far shore. A stampede of horses in brilliant liveries of orange, red, gold and brown rode across the field toward Bezo's house.

Arün spoke in her mind. *It's the High Guard. Get back on the path. We need to hide before they see us.*

30

TRUTH DISCOVERED

ALLEY

Arün leaped back across the flat rocks towards the shore. Alley followed. They crossed the gravel path and stopped at the edge of the woods. The trees swayed—creaking and cracking. Leaves rustled overhead. Alley felt like she was trespassing—as if the forest disapproved of her standing at its doorstep.

Arün handed her a small pair of binoculars. *This doesn't look good.*

She adjusted the focus. The elven cavalry had formed a semi-circle around Bezo's house. Their leader dismounted and glided up the porch steps. He was tall and slender with flowing white hair tied back in a ponytail. Long ears sprouted upwards from the sides of his head, ending in tufted points. His hand rested on the pommel of a sword that flashed silver in the sunlight. Armor glinted beneath his autumn colored tunic.

Bezo threw open the door of the house. The mage seemed angry. He was gesturing and jabbing his finger down the valley, back in the direction the elves had come from. The elf on the porch made a motion with his hand. The ones on horseback swept their gazes around the valley.

Alley felt exposed. She stepped back towards the woods. Arün grabbed her arm as she shifted.

Don't move. Elves have excellent sight.

Her muscles tightened.

One of the mounted elves pointed up the path towards the falls. The leader bowed to Bezo and then gestured to the cavalry. His hand made a chopping motion as he first pointed down the valley, then up towards their hiding spot. Half the force spurred their mounts and galloped up the path. The other half headed down the valley.

Arün took the binoculars. *Back up slowly,* he whispered in her mind.

He pulled her deeper into the forest. Large wet leaves slapped against her legs. Moss squished beneath her feet. Alley followed Arün behind the trunk of one of the massive trees, out of sight of the path and settled into a small hollow where two giant moss-covered roots branched out into the undergrowth. Arün raised a finger to his lips.

They are excellent trackers. I'll be surprised if they don't pick up our trail at the edge of the forest, he said in her mind.

What do we do? she asked.

Arün unsheathed his warden blade. *We may get lucky. If not, we fight.*

We could try talking to them.

Arün shook his head. *After the Ash War, the Elves swore a blood-oath to kill any dragon or dracun that set foot in Arburaan. They have sensitive magical wards spread throughout their kingdom. We must have triggered one of them when we came through the gate—maybe another during the walk. I don't think they will understand or care that we are only partly dracun.*

I won't kill them—she put her hand on Arün's arm—*we won't kill them. I'm already responsible for too much death.*

Elves wield magic, Alley. They are powerful warriors. We may not have a choice.

There had to be a way for them to evade the elves without fighting. Alley peeked around the tree. Through the bushes and vines, she could see the edge of the path. The elves had almost reached the spot where they had entered the woods. Alley's heart beat faster. She ducked behind the trunk.

Maybe she could grow the forest like she'd done last night. Tangle them in roots? She had to try something. Alley squeezed her eyes shut and tried to find the source of the magic in her mind—to find the forest clearing.

Nothing.

She could try humming the tune that Bezo had played

but the elves might hear. The only other times she'd been able to access the energy was when she'd been in pain.

Hit me! she yelled to Arün in her head.

Arün looked at her as if she was crazy. *What? Why?*

Pain, I think pain might trigger my abilities. Hit me!

I won't hit you.

She could hear elven voices. They were saying something in their native language as they entered the forest. Alley gritted her teeth.

Hit me!

No.

The elves were getting closer. They wouldn't be hidden from view much longer. Alley flexed her hands. What could she do?

She searched the ground and picked up a large stick. *Get ready to run.*

Alley leaned back and threw the stick in a high arc deep into the forest. It spun end over end crashing against branches and plants in the deep gloom of the trees. Elven warriors ran past their tree on both sides. Their feet barely made a sound as they darted into the woods.

Go! she yelled to the warden in her head.

Arün sheathed his blade as they jumped from their hiding spot. They slid across the soft moss that coated the root of the giant tree. Arün pushed her forward. The underbrush tore at her clothing. They broke free of the trees and ran towards the horses. Alley glanced back. Arün was right behind her. Adrenaline surged through her veins.

"Get on the—"

Arün's voice trailed off as his last word turned into an exhaled breath.

Alley heard him hit the ground. She glanced back and had just enough time to see him face down on the path before something sharp stung her neck. She reached up to where the pain radiated and felt something like a toothpick with feathers stuck in her skin. Her legs gave way.

Alley felt herself falling just before darkness enveloped her mind.

"Tis, tis, pa lachot!"

The musical voice was so close Alley thought it was whispering in her ear. The ground pressed against her back. Sharp stones dug into her scalp making her want to sit up. Alley tried to use her hands, but they were bound. She blinked against the harsh sunlight. An elven warrior stood over her—he was holding Arün's scryth.

"Dus, warden?" The elf thrust the knife in her direction.

Alley shook her head. "I don't understand." Was the elf asking if she was a warden?

He tugged upward on a cord that connected Alley's bound wrists to one of the horse's saddles. Or what looked like a horse—they had an extra set of nostrils, and their hooves were split into three parts. As she struggled to stand, she saw that Arün was tied up on the ground. The other elves had returned and were seated on their mounts.

Arün groaned and rolled. The elf jabbed the blade toward Alley again. His eyes were a vibrant sapphire—cold and unblinking. "Why were you hiding?" The elf enunciated each syllable.

What could she say that wouldn't make the situation worse? "We were going for a walk and heard something—we thought you were a wild animal."

The warrior made a sucking sound through his teeth. The other elves laughed. "A lie. Our footsteps are but a kiss of the wind upon the ground."

Arün opened his eyes. The elf yanked roughly on the silken cord binding his wrists, pulling him to his feet. "You dishonor yourself, warden." He tied Arün's cord to a saddle and jumped onto his horse. His movements were graceful. The elf spurred the animal forward, forcing the warden to stumble along the path. Arün looked back and spoke in her mind. *Say nothing, Alley.*

The horse she was tied to began to walk. The silken rope tightened around her wrists cutting off the flow of blood to her fingers. Alley jogged to keep up with the strange animal.

The trip back to the house didn't take long. Bezo was still on the porch with what Alley guessed was the Captain of the High Guard.

The Captain stepped off the porch as they approached. "What do you know of this, mage?" He gestured at them.

Bezo crossed his arms. "I told you already. I received no information about the arrival of any off-worlders."

"And yet, here they are."

The elf that led Arün handed the Captain the warden's blade. The head of the High Guard turned it over in his slender hands, examining the runes etched into its surface. "A scryth of the Duv'rath." He looked up at Arün. "You are a warden."

Arün straightened his back. "I am."

"Explain why you have not followed our customs? Why did you not present yourself to the Court upon entry into our realm?"

Arün looked down and shifted his weight. "There was a malfunction with the Water Sentry at the gate. We barely escaped. My map was damaged in the lake and we became lost."

The elf squinted at Alley. "And who is this maiden? You are no warden. No mage. Why are you here?"

Before Alley could answer, Bezo coughed and rubbed at his eyes. "My goodness! Is that you, Gretchen? You've grown! I didn't even recognize you!"

The Captain turned to face the mage. "So, you know these travelers?"

"Why, I suppose I do. Gretchen Lockwood is my sister's daughter's daughter's daughter. The last time I saw her, she was just a babe." He chuckled and scratched his beard. "Sorry for all this confusion, I suppose we can just cut them free now. We will stop by the Court this evening."

The Captain frowned at the mage and turned back to Arün. "Did anything come through the gate with you?"

Arün swallowed. "I saw nothing."

The elf looked at Alley. His iron gaze seemed to pierce her eyes and pin her thoughts to the back of her skull. "Did you see anything, Lady Lockwood?"

Alley almost didn't realize she was being addressed. "I—no—nothing, trees." *Ugh.* She sounded like an idiot. The elf shifted his gaze between Bezo, Arün and her. He tapped the flat of Arün's blade against his palm as he appeared to ponder their story. The horses snorted, growing impatient.

The Captain flipped the knife around and handed it, hilt first to Bezo, "Very well, present yourselves at Court. You may join our Jehalo Day feast. My apologies, Arch-Mage. These are dangerous times."

Bezo accepted the blade. "My thanks to you for finding my great-grandniece."

The Captain bowed and then turned toward Arün. He grasped the silken rope that bound Arün's wrists and drew an ornate dagger from a sheath at his waist. The metal flared a brilliant orange like hot charcoal. The elf dropped the rope and stepped back in complete shock as he looked from the dagger in his hand to Arün.

"Dus Dragun?!"

The mounted warriors nocked wicked looking barbed arrows into their bows and aimed them at Arün.

Alley's eyes went wide as she looked over at the warden. *What just happened, Arün!*

He focused on the glowing orange blade. *The elf knows I'm part-dracun, but he doesn't suspect you.*

Bezo stepped off the porch. "What's the trouble?"

The Captain's nostrils flared. His lips curled back revealing a disturbing number of teeth. "My blade is Drag'roth. *Dragon Seeker.* Your niece is in the company of dragon spawn."

Bezo snorted as he held up Arün's knife. "This scryth detects nothing."

The Captain pointed his knife at Arün. "Drag'roth does not lie. Your niece has violated the Pact and committed treason by bringing this thing into our world."

Bezo forced a chuckle. "Let's not be hasty."

The Captain pointed the smoking blade at Alley. "She comes with us to be judged by the High Court." He swung the knife back at Arün. "As for this abomination—the punishment is immediate death."

31

ESCAPE

ALLEY

"I command you to stand down, Captain!" Bezo's voice boomed as if amplified by an enormous speaker deep within the earth.

Dust drifted down from the ceiling of the porch as his words reverberated across the valley. From the back of the house, something that sounded like a huge diesel engine rumbled to life. Wooden hatches sprung open on the porch floor and ceiling. Silver turrets telescoped out. Each turret had a shiny metal sphere on the end that made a humming sound.

"Do not interfere, Arch-Mage. You know our laws. Our quarrel is not with you," growled the Captain.

Bezo widened his stance and thrust his hands inside the pouches that hung at his waist. "You pass judgment too swiftly and with little evidence. Do you hold life in such low regard?"

The Captain waved his smoking orange blade at Bezo. "This is all the evidence I require. There is no doubt." He raised the knife into the air and nodded to the mounted elven warriors. They drew their bowstrings tight and aimed at Arün.

Alley tensed. She had to do something.

Bezo's hands flung outward at the elves, spreading a cloud of glittering dust. He moved his fingers through the shimmering air. A spiderweb of purple lightning bolts laced out from the metal spheres on the porch, barely missing Alley as they struck the archers. Their arrows shot into the sky as they were blown off their horses. Their bodies hit the ground, muscles twitching wildly from the electrical currents.

Alley knew how the elves felt. The memory of the pain from Bezo's training was still fresh. She was starting to suspect that the old mage enjoyed shooting people with lightning.

The Captain was untouched. He looked at his warriors on the ground and then narrowed his eyes as he turned toward Bezo. "The High Court will hear about this."

Bezo stepped off the porch. "Oh, I expect they will."

The metal spheres hummed and crackled with electricity. Bezo sliced through the ropes binding Alley's hands and then freed Arün and returned his blade. Alley rubbed at her wrists—they were sore from where the cord had bitten into her skin.

Alley glared at the elf. "We did nothing wrong."

The Captain's lips pressed into a tight line as his gaze flicked from Alley to the metal spheres. The elf backed away. He drew his hunting horn and blew it. The long low moan of the horn was answered by another farther down the valley.

"The rest of my forces are close. We will not let you—"

Bezo pointed at the Captain. Bolts of electric energy shot from the spheres and hit the elf in the chest. He flew out into the field, smacked the ground and flopped on the grass like a fish.

Bezo smoothed his robes and smiled. "That was satisfying."

Alley was sure now—the mage definitely enjoyed shooting people with lightning.

Down the valley, the remainder of the elven cavalry pounded toward the house answering the call of their captain's hunting horn.

Arün sheathed his scryth. "We need to go."

The ground trembled, but it wasn't the approaching horses.

Bezo looked over his shoulder. "Yes, I suppose you're right. And look, here's your ride!"

The massive Centurion Class Marionette they had seen the day before stepped around the corner of the house. Its engine rumbled. The squeak of metal parts and hiss of hydraulics filled the air. Each time the machine took a step, the ground shook.

It stopped near the pile of thrashing elves. The vehicle was monstrous. A cross between construction equipment and a giant football linebacker with an arsenal of blades and munitions sprouting from its back like a giant pin cushion. Sunshine glinted off the Marion's armor plating.

A hatch opened at the top. Elek's shaggy grinning head appeared. "Let's go! There are rungs on the legs!"

Alley smiled. Elek had gotten his wish—hopefully he was as good a pilot as he claimed.

Arün followed Alley as she climbed the side of the machine. Vibrations from the huge engine traveled through her grip on the rungs and made her teeth rattle. Across the valley, she could see the rest of the elven cavalry getting closer.

Bezo called up to them, pointing across to where the path from his house led to the entrance to the Scale Road. "Go back to the Thorngate! I'll try to delay them!"

Alley reached the machine's shoulder. There was a hatch on the side of what looked like its head. She ducked inside. Elek was strapping himself back into an elaborate armature in front of a complex panel of buttons, dials and gauges. He looked like a human-sized marionette puppet being held in the air by a complicated tangle of metal arms and cables.

Nadja stood against the far wall. She called over to them, "Grab onto something!"

Arün closed and locked the hatch as Alley took a position against the wall.

Elek's eyes were obscured by a pair of glowing blue goggles. He flipped a switch on a panel. The engine noises changed in pitch. "Brace yourselves! I'm not sure how bumpy this will get!" he yelled.

The steel decking vibrated beneath their feet. Piping and tubes ran along the walls, interrupted by horizontal viewports that allowed light into the control room. Alley grabbed a pipe as the giant lurched forward. It picked up speed as Elek moved his legs in a running motion. Each step made the cockpit jerk and sway. It reminded Alley of standing on a subway car that was careening along an uneven track. The sweet, acrid smell of oil and grease filled her nostrils. They were going faster, metal squealed, the engine thumped and the whole room shook in a steady rhythm. Elek pumped his legs and arms and made quick adjustments on the buttons and dials. He seemed to know what he was doing.

The cockpit got darker as they entered the forest. There was barely enough room for the machine to maneuver down the road. Elek ducked the giant under massive roots and vaulted over smaller ones that crossed the path.

Were the elves following them or had Bezo created a distraction? Alley grabbed at a nearby pipe and worked her way towards the rear viewport. Behind them, the remnants of the High Guard pursued on horseback.

Alley yelled to Elek over the riot of noise that echoed in the small space. “They’re following us!”

Elek nodded. He was out of breath, running in place as if sprinting on a treadmill.

Arün joined her at the back of the cockpit. “They’ve got ranged weapons and magic. We need enough time to get out of this machine and back through the gate.” He called to Elek. “Does this thing have counter-measures? Something non-lethal?”

Elek gave a thumbs-up and pulled a lever overhead. There was a loud clang outside the machine. Alley stumbled towards the right side viewport to see what had made the sound. An enormous blade etched with runes telescoped from the right forearm of the machine. She turned to Elek. “El, that doesn’t look non-lethal!”

“Sorry, this is setup a bit different from the simulator. Let me try something else!” Elek pulled the lever again, retracting the blade and punched a green button. A buzzer sounded inside the cockpit.

Alley looked out the window to see what was happening. Serrated metal plates slid out of the giant’s wrists and closed over the machine’s hands forming what looked like giant drill bits. They began to spin. “That’s not going to help! Try something else!”

Elek pushed the green button again, folding the drills back into the arms of the machine. He twisted a dial. A low hum started below them. “I think this will work!”

Alley couldn't see anything changing on the outside the machine. "What's happening?"

Elek's mouth spread into a grin beneath the glowing blue goggles. "Watch."

Nadja, Arün and Alley stumbled towards the back viewport. The horses were close.

Elek pressed a button. Thick purple smoke poured from ports on the back of the Marion's arms, legs and shoulders. It streamed off the sprinting machine, flowing to the ground in huge curling waves. The cavalry entered the cloud. Their horses bucked wildly, throwing the riders.

Elek pushed the button again, cutting off the flow of smoke. "That should buy us a few minutes."

They burst out of the forest into the lake-filled clearing where they had entered Arburaan. The entrance to the gateway lay at the top of the waterfall that formed the right side of the dell. The Marion waded into the water and lumbered towards the falls.

Elek turned to them. "Get out on the hand! I'll raise you up!"

Arün opened the hatch. Misty air filled the cockpit as he stepped out onto the shoulder of the machine. He called back. "I'll get the portal open!"

Alley grasped Elek's hand. "You're coming with us!"

"I'll try, but get through the gate first, Al!" he yelled.

"I'm not leaving you here!"

Nadja gritted her teeth. "We don't have time for this! Get outside!"

Alley shot her a withering glance. She wasn't going to let her friend get captured by the elves.

Elek squeezed Alley's hand. "I'll be right behind you. Go!"

Alley's eyes watered. She pulled Elek's head down and kissed his cheek. "Don't do anything stupid."

He gave her a lopsided smile. "See you on the other side."

Nadja clapped her hands. "Come on! Come on! Come on! We don't want to be here when they start firing poison arrows."

Alley tore her gaze away from Elek and stumbled towards the open hatch.

Elek raised his right arm. The huge right arm of the machine extended straight out at shoulder height. Arün sprinted out along it. Alley crept forward more cautiously. The metal was slick from the mist. Nadja followed. The huge plated arm of the Marion rose upward powered by massive gears and pistons. When the hand was level with the cliff ledge, Arün jumped off and ran towards the gate.

Alley edged forward, but then the machine lurched sideways. Her heart raced as she grabbed a bolt on the armor to keep from slipping off.

Giant mechanical claws had risen out of the water and clamped onto the Marion's arm. Bezo's Water Sentry machine was activated. *Again.*

An instant later an arrow ricocheted off the metal plating inches from Alley's hand. The elves had caught up.

Nadja yelled back at the open hatch. "Elek, do something!"

The Marion's left arm swung into view. At the end of the arm was a huge Gatling gun. It aimed at the mechanical claws in the water. The deafening shriek of metal split the air. Alley's muscles tensed at the sound. A stream of explosive bullets ripped through the Water Sentry's metal claws. The Marion's right arm was free.

Alley scrambled past the elbow joint. An arrow zipped by her head. As she reached the machine's hand, she dove behind the huge hinged thumb. Nadja joined her. The spray from the waterfall blew in their faces. Black arrows clattered across the riveted metal. The side of the cliff slid past as the hand rose until it was level with the misty cave opening that led to the gateway. Alley leaped off onto the wet stone ledge.

Nadja ran toward the maw of the cave. "Let's go!"

Alley shook her head. "I'm not leaving Elek!"

Nadja pointed at the giant Marion. "He'll be fine! Look!"

Alley turned. Elek was maneuvering the massive giant to face the elven cavalry. He waded the machine out of the water spraying bullets at the clawed appendages that tried to drag the machine back into the lake. The cavalry circled the dripping legs of the Marion. One elf jumped off his horse and grabbed a rung on the leg of the machine. He climbed upward. The Marion reached down, plucked the elf off like a bug and flicked him into the lake.

Nadja touched her shoulder. "We have to go. Arün is already through. Every minute we wait could mean hours on the other side. Elek and Bezo can handle this."

Alley nodded as she grasped the milkstone locket around her neck. She wished she could talk to Elek the same way she could talk to Arün.

Be careful, El, she thought.

Nadja drew her scryth. "Go first. I'll be right behind you."

Alley took one last look at Elek and then sprinted into the cold mist of the thorny tunnel. Nadja followed close behind, but disappeared as they were enveloped by the fog. The sound of the battle was soon replaced by the haunting wails of whatever lived on the other side of the tunnel walls.

32

WINTER

ALLEY

Alley tried not twist an ankle on the thick mat of knotted vines as she ran through the blinding white mist. From far behind, came a creaking and cracking sound —like trees blowing in a strong wind. The sound was getting louder. Closer.

Her chest tightened when she realized where it was coming from—the gate was closing. The vines that formed the tunnel were retracting. Frigid wind blasted her face as a sucking vacuum tugged at her hair and jacket from behind. The chorus of moans from whatever existed beyond the tunnel walls got louder and more frantic.

Alley's heart pounded. Ahead, the mist thinned. Firm stone pushed against her feet as she exited the tunnel. She was home. The air in the cavern was cold and everything was covered in frost.

Where was Nadja? She'd been right behind Alley as they entered the gateway. Alley looked back into the fog. The vines slithered back into the archway. Gaps opened in the walls of the tunnel.

Nadja burst out of the mist, balanced on one of the retracting vines as the tunnel walls split apart. She clutched her scryth. The runes on the blade glowed a brilliant blue. Alley didn't know what it meant, but she didn't need the scryth to tell her that something horrible was close—she could hear it. The moans coming from the mist were deafening.

Nadja jumped onto the rock ledge beneath the Thorngate. She turned to face the collapsing tunnel. The last few vines snaked away from the opening and withdrew back into the huge thorny archway. All that was left now was a gaping black hole in the granite stone—the fog had been sucked into the starry maw.

"Get behind me, Alley!" yelled Nadja.

There was a grinding sound, like huge boulders rubbing against each other. Fragments of stone and rock locked together like a giant jigsaw puzzle blocking out the void.

Just before the cracks sealed, Alley thought she saw faces —horrible twisted, tormented faces with white skin, black eyes and gaping mouths. She shivered and let out a breath she didn't realize she'd been holding. The air came out in a cloud, condensing in the chill of the cave.

The blue light from the scryth faded away. Nadja sheathed the blade. "I think we're safe."

Alley pointed at the weapon. "It glowed blue. What was that in the tunnel with us?"

Nadja rubbed sweat from her brow and wiped it on her jeans. "Things that live between our worlds."

"What are they?"

Nadja shook her head. "I don't know and I don't want to find out."

"How is Elek going to get back?" asked Alley.

Nadja turned and started down the steps to the cavern floor. "Don't worry, the mage will help him."

That wasn't reassuring, but Elek seemed to know how to handle the Marion and could get back to Bezo's house. Alley took one last look at the sealed wall and up at the Thorngate before following Nadja. The warden was with her, but without Elek, she felt alone.

The grotto was silent. They had been in the other world for only two days, but on this side, months had passed. Autumn had become winter. The cave was icy and cold. The waterfall still flowed, but layers of long thick icicles covered the opening where the sunlight entered. Giant fingers of ice had formed in the center of the cave where water had dripped into the now frozen pool. The flowers that had grown around the stone wall of the pool were brown and dusted with frost. Alley made her way down the icy stone steps and across the cavern. There were no signs that Arün had passed through the cave. All was quiet except for the echo of their steps.

Nadja unzipped her jacket and retrieved her phone. She pressed the power button. The screen lit up as it searched for a signal. She waited for a moment then looked at Alley. "I can't get a connection in here. We need to get outside so I can contact Arün."

Alley closed her eyes and whispered in her mind. *Arün, can you hear me?*

Nothing.

They exited through the narrow stone passage and emerged out onto the snow-covered trail that ran around the perimeter of the upper falls. Nadja held her phone up. The signal strength was weak. Snowflakes collected on the smooth illuminated glass. She dialed and pressed the phone against her ear. Her face was etched with concern. "Arün should have waited for us at the tunnel entrance."

"Why would he leave?" Alley asked even though she thought she knew the answer.

Nadja hung up the phone and pointed to fading footprints in the fresh white powder. "If dracun were waiting for us, he would have tried to draw them away."

Delicate flakes drifted down from the gray sky. Bending

low, Nadja followed the tracks along the path stopping every few feet to listen. She quickened her pace. The trail led down to a snow dusted clearing. The tracks ended in a confusing array of footprints and scraped snow. A spray of black liquid stood out against the white ground.

Alley pointed at the stains. "What's that?"

Nadja frowned. "Dracun blood."

The warden searched the trees and sky. The snow was falling faster bringing a hush to the forest. "There was a fight here, recently"—Nadja circled the muddled trail—"I see no exit tracks."

Alley chewed on her lower lip. The snowfall was erasing the signs of the struggle. She called out in her mind, *Arün, are you out there?*

No answer.

Nadja did two laps around the clearing before stopping. She sighed. "No exit tracks means the dracun took him."

Alley was torn. She needed to find her father. She wanted to know whether Elek had made it to safety and she wanted to help Arün. She cocked her head at the warden. "So, what now? Are we still in danger?"

"If the dracun were close, they'd have attacked by now." Nadja examined her milkstone locket and pointed to the north. "They took Arün that way. If he's lucky, they won't drop him from the sky."

Alley swallowed as she considered that.

Nadja pulled out her phone. "I need to check-in with the Council." She entered a number.

"Ask them if they found my dad!" Alley exclaimed.

Nadja nodded at Alley as she spoke into the phone, "We're back. The asset is secure. My partner was captured by dracun."

Alley shook her head in disgust. She wasn't an asset. She was a person. Alley wasn't sure why the term irritated her so much.

Nadja listened to the Council's reply, then spoke, "He was captured inside the hour, west of Stevens Pass. Probably airborne."

The warden nodded as she listened and then replied, "Yes, she was trained, but she needs more time. We ran into complications."

A reply came and then Nadja responded, "We have transport. We hid motorcycles at the trailhead. Any news on the asset's father?"

Nadja nodded as she paced. "Okay, we'll be there in a few hours."

Alley fidgeted. What had they said? Was her dad okay?

Nadja tucked the phone into her jacket. "We're going to see the Council."

"What about my dad?"

Nadja jogged down the trail. "He's still missing, but they said they have more information to share once we get back to headquarters. We'd better get started, it will take a few hours to reach the parking lot."

Alley's heart pounded. The Council had more information about her father. She needed to get to them. Alley took a final look around the clearing and then ran after Nadja.

33

THE COUNCIL

ALLEY

Alley stood in the center of the Council's circular war chamber. High overhead, scraps of daylight filtered through purple cubes of scuffed glass embedded in the sidewalk where pedestrians walked unaware of the world below. They had traveled through a connected warren of tunnels and halls deep beneath Seattle's streets to get here—a city under the city. It felt like a courtroom with its old polished wood paneling and curved podium seating where the Council sat like judges presiding over a case. Seated in the center, was Leopold Rakman. Nadja had just finished recounting the details of their trip.

Rakman leaned forward. "Thank you, Nadja. It is most unfortunate that your escape required an escalation in tension with the elves, but we're glad you made it back. And welcome, Alley." He shook his head. "I wish we were meeting again under better circumstances."

Snow and ice had melted from their hair and coats, forming a puddle beneath their feet. Alley squinted at the shadowy figures seated above them. She wasn't certain, but one of the mages on the end looked like he might be Elek's dad. She focused her attention back on Leopold Rakman. "Nadja said you had more information about my father?" Her voice echoed in the large room.

The mage's glasses slid to the end of his nose. He caught them at the last second and pushed them back up. "We sent a team into the Obsidian lair two weeks ago. Unfortunately, they were all lost, but not before they sent out some information."

Rakman tugged at the white cuffs of his shirt where they peeked out from the sleeves of his black suit jacket and then picked up a remote control. He pointed it towards the wall across the room. A large display lit up spilling blue light across the polished tiled floor. "As you know, the situation with the Obsidian has been escalating."

A series of images flashed on the screen showing black and white crime-scene photos. Bodies lying in pools of splattered blood.

"The Obsidian attacks have increased in frequency. We covered-up most of the incidents, but the current rate of violation threatens the secrecy we've had in place. We doubled the warden patrols and have enlisted the help of the Opal Clan to aid us."

Nadja blinked and tilted her head. "We're working with dracun now?"

The mage looked annoyed. "The Opal Clan has provided critical intelligence and are helping us patrol the skies."

Nadja crossed her arms. "How are they helping patrol the skies?"

Leopold lowered his head and looked at her from under bushy eyebrows. His glasses began another slow slide down his nose. "I don't like your tone. Our Warden Flight program has been very successful. They've foiled dozens of dracun attacks in the last few weeks."

Nadja's jaw hung open. "I—I'm sorry. It's just—that information is unexpected."

Alley clenched her fists. "What does any of this have to do with my father?"

The mage clicked the remote. "We believe the Obsidian Clan is holding him hostage somewhere in their nest. Perhaps as a bargaining chip."

A grainy photo appeared on the screen. It was blurry and poorly lit, but Alley recognized her dad. "Why haven't you rescued him?"

"We've tried"—Rakman looked across at the shadowed faces of the other members of the Council—"twice."

Alley's stomach clenched. "What happened?"

"The warden teams never returned—they're presumed captured or dead."

Alley stared at her reflection in the puddle of water beneath her feet. She had to rescue him, but could she succeed where two teams of trained wardens had failed? It didn't matter. She had to try. Alley tilted her head up. "Send me."

Rakman took a sip of tea from a tiny china cup that had been hiding behind the podium. "We were considering it, but we weren't sure if you'd be prepared."

Alley squared her shoulders. "I am." She hoped her voice held more confidence than she felt.

Rakman raised an eyebrow. "We received no reports from Arch-Mage Berolaster on your progress."

Alley gritted her teeth. "I learned fast."

The mage smiled and quickly finished his tea. "Prove it. Stop this from hitting the ground." He tossed the cup off the edge of the podium.

It spun end-over-end.

Alley's eyes went wide. She'd never be able to draw out the energy in time. She dove forward and caught the cup before it could shatter on the floor.

Rakman's lips pressed together and he shook his head. "You're not ready."

Nadja cleared her throat. "I saw Alley turn the course of a river."

Leopold looked irritated. "Yes, we're aware of your report. You also said she lost control."

Alley took a breath and closed her eyes. They had to let her help rescue her father. What could she do to convince them? In her mind she replayed Bezo's song—let it take her to the clearing in her mind.

The little girl was there smiling as if she'd been waiting for Alley to arrive. She held out a single white flower. Alley took it and inhaled the sweet scent.

Her eyes opened. She guided a golden tendril of energy out of her body and wrapped it around the cup as she'd done with stone. The cup rose into the air. Alley used the ribbon of power to push it upward to Rakman and then released it. The cup dropped onto the table in front of him.

Alley smiled. It was getting easier.

The Council members gasped and murmured to one another. Leopold Rakman exchanged some whispered words with those around him, then returned his attention to Alley. "Perhaps you've learned enough. We may not have the luxury of waiting till you achieve full mastery."

He pressed a button on the remote. New images flashed on the screen—a schematic of a machine, followed by a looping video of the device shot with night-vision. "The same team that took the picture of your father captured this video. That's a high-range electromagnetic pulse device—an EMP weapon."

The image switched to a cross section view of a mountain

with a point highlighted below the surface. "Our intelligence indicates it's within the Obsidian lair below Mt. Baker."

The display showed a map of Washington State with concentric rings radiating out from the mountain. "We believe the EMP device is capable of knocking out communications and electronics over much of the state."

Rakman clicked the remote again. The screen changed to a worn scrap of parchment with harsh angular runes along its surface. "We received one final piece of information that has been confirmed by several sources. Srira, the clan's regent, is trying to free one of the Banished."

"We need to destroy those monsters now," Nadja yelled. "We can't let any of those things get loose!"

Rakman shifted in his seat. "Perhaps you're right, but winter snows have prevented us from reaching the prison caves by land, and we've lost every team that has flown in. We were planning to send a larger force, but when the attacks on civilians escalated, the additional patrols spread the Wardens too thin."

Nadja's face pinched as if she were getting a headache. "You realize that the attacks are just a distraction, right?"

The old man glared at her. "We will secure the prison, but the greater threat is the EMP weapon. We believe Srira will use it to throw the region into chaos, allowing her forces to attack without warning and without an organized human resistance."

The other Council members nodded in agreement.

"We need to eliminate the device. If it is destroyed, the Queen may be less inclined to start a war. The military, and our own defensive capabilities, will deter her aggression. Nadja, you will captain a small team that will infiltrate the Obsidian lair beneath Mt. Baker. Your primary aim is to destroy the EMP device. Your secondary objective is to rescue Ben, your partner, Arün, and any other wardens that may be held captive."

Nadja blinked. "What? You located Arün already?"

"We tracked his phone before it went offline. The last transmission was close to the reported location of the device."

Alley stepped forward. "So, I'm going too?"

The mage's brow furrowed. "Yes. I don't know if it is the wisest choice, but perhaps you'll help them find success this time."

Alley breathed a sigh of relief. Even though heading straight into danger made her stomach queasy, staying behind and not being able to help her dad felt worse.

Rakman gestured towards the shadows behind them. "Meet the rest of your team."

The thick lacquered oak doors swung open. Six people entered the room. Two appeared to be wardens. Nadja smiled at them and clasped hands with each one. The first, a tall brunette, introduced herself to Alley. "I'm Jenna. Nadja and I used to patrol together."

"I'm Rigel," said the second, a thin, wiry warden with a shaved head.

Nadja glared at the remaining four members of the team. Her hand moved to her scryth. One of them met Alley's gaze. He had beautiful green eyes that sparkled with flecks of gold. He was dressed in a winter jacket and jeans.

His voice echoed in her mind. *Greetings, dauthma.*

Alley's heart skipped a beat. *Dracun.* The remaining four were dracun. What if they revealed that she was part-dracun? What would Nadja do?

The man with the brilliant green and gold eyes, stepped forward and bowed to Nadja. "It is an honor to serve with you, Captain. I am Vicktor."

The creature's soft voice reminded Alley of air being let out of a tire. Nadja's face filled with disgust. She turned away from the dracun and looked up at the shadowy faces of the Council. "I usually hand-pick my team."

Rakman pushed his glasses up his nose. "There's no time for that. The dracun will get you to Mt. Baker faster than any other route. You can trust them. They have proved themselves in battle during the last few weeks."

Nadja clenched and unclenched her fists. Alley could see a vein standing out on her neck.

The Council regarded her in silence.

Alley heard the dracun whisper in her mind again. *Your friend is filled with hatred.*

She's not my friend Alley thought, but instead she answered in her mind. *Her family was killed by dracun.*

Viktor's eyes looked sad. *You have nothing to fear, dauthma. We are Opal dracun of House Halcyon. We are here to help. And we will keep your secret.*

Alley swallowed. *Thank you, but how did you know?*

Your scent is strong, dauthma. It reminds me of your mother. She is still held in high honor among the Clans.

You knew my mom?

Yes.

The dracun knew her mother. That was surprising. Why did they have so much respect for her?

Nadja's face was growing red.

Rakman shifted forward in his seat. "Nadja, do you feel unsuited to this task?"

The warden let out a deep breath and unclenched her fists. "No—I'm good. We'll make it work."

Rakman stared at her for a moment before speaking. "Good. Proceed to the Armory. We have supplied you with enough explosives to destroy the device, but decide what else you may require to complete the mission. We want you airborne in the next thirty minutes." His expression softened. "Good luck."

The Council stood as one and filed out of the chamber through an exit behind the high semi-circular desk. The door slammed behind them, reverberating in the empty room.

Nadja took several deep breaths before closing her eyes and turning around. Vicktor bowed to her again. Ignoring him, she headed out of the room, through the giant oak doors. "I don't trust dracun. If any of you step out of line on this mission, you won't be coming back. Rigel, Jenna, Alley, I'm counting on each of you to make sure our friends here don't betray us."

Nadja stalked down the dimly lit underground corridor. Alley followed, marveling at the strange labyrinth. The halls had been built like a bunker with thick steel reinforcements spaced at regular intervals between the concrete. The Mages had tried to soften the effect by adding ornate wood paneling. It made everything look old. They passed reinforced doors with carved wooden accents. The frame of each door was metal with intricately engraved weaves. Alley wondered what secrets hid behind them.

Rigel cleared his throat. "Captain, you can trust them. They're on our side."

Nadja didn't turn around to answer. "When I want your opinion, Rigel, I'll ask for it."

Alley looked over at Viktor and spoke in her mind. *How did you know my mother?*

The dracun glanced at her and then looked away before replying. *She is the reason we are not all dead.*

What do you mean?

She convinced the mages and elves to spare us at the end of the War.

Her mom had done that? She was the reason the dracun were exiled here? Why would she have pushed to bring a threat as great as the dracun into the world? Alley rubbed her face. Maybe her mom thought there was no danger? Maybe the other dracun were like the Opals?

Viktor, do you know why the Obsidian are attacking people?

Their queen is filled with anger. The clan's actions reflect her will. They have no choice but to obey.

Alley squinted. *No choice?*

Viktor nodded to himself. *The clans are bonded to their ruler's mind. Srira has stolen her clan's free will. She compels them to do these things. Even when most would prefer peace.*

But your clan leader is not like that?

No. Our queen does not rob us of our will. Urthabel is kind and gracious. Nothing like Srira. Had our king listened to her council he would not be imprisoned.

Alley stole another glance at Viktor. *Can your queen talk to Srira? Make her stop?*

She has tried. Srira will not listen.

They turned a final bend in the corridor. A large set of double doors barred their way. Two wardens stood on either side. As they approached, one of them entered a code into a keypad. The doors swung open. Nadja nodded at them as they passed through into the blue lighting of the Armory. The room was high and deep. Stacks of containers and metal crates rose against the back wall. Racks of weapons lined the sides. Their footsteps clanked on the steel plated floor.

A group of wardens stood around a polished aluminum table in the center of the room. On the table sat a collection of white backpacks and helmets. Nadja waved to the group clustered around the table, then looked over her shoulder at Alley. “The big guy is Broderick Nelson. He’s the Warden High Commander.”

Broderick was a bear of a man. Black combat fatigues covered his tall, stocky body with pads sewn into the knees and elbows. The sleeves were rolled up, exposing his thick hairy arms crisscrossed with old scars. His bushy red beard had been trimmed and his hair was pulled back into a short ponytail. He left the table and walked towards Nadja—his arms extended wide. A broad smile appeared below his rosy bulbous nose.

“Tha’ prodigal warden returns!” His voice boomed as he wrapped her in a smothering hug.

“Good to see you too, Brody.” Nadja’s voice was muffled by the folds of the High Commander’s shirt.

He released Nadja and extended a calloused hand to Alley. “A pleasure to meet ya, Miss Ward. I’m Brody. You let me know if any of the wardens give ya grief.” He smelled like engine grease and sweat. Alley shook his enormous hand. “Nice to meet you.”

Nadja crossed her arms. “Why aren’t you coming with us on this mission?”

Brody frowned. “Tha’ Council’s keepin’ me grounded. Wants my tactical input for plannin’. Blah, blah, blah. I’m not pleased, but I'll vouch for these fine 'gents." He jabbed a fat finger at Viktor. "I picked 'em myself."

Nadja raised a skeptical eyebrow.

Brody laughed. The sound echoed in the cavernous space. "Caw-mon! Let me show you the fun surprises we've put together for your lil' jaunt!" He waved them over to the table.

"We've got four packs here. Each has ten plastic explosive charges. Each one has a timed tamper proof detonator." He picked up a pack and pointed at an altitude gauge and a plastic handle attached to a cord. "This deploys the parachute. Make sure you do it above seven hundred feet." He handed a pack to Nadja and the remaining packs to Alley, Rigel and Jenna.

Alley wasn't sure about wearing explosives strapped to her back, but the parachute seemed like a good idea if the plan was to ride on dracuns.

Broderick lifted a helmet off the table. "Your flight helmets are keyed to the same secure frequency and have satellite up-link with active heads-up-displays." He switched on each helmet and handed them out.

Alley glanced at the faces of the team. They were expressionless. She wondered if they could tell how afraid she felt. They all looked battle hardened—like this was just another day at the office.

Brody gestured to the weapons racks behind him. "Grab

cold weather gear, pick your favorite toys and then meet me by the elevator."

Alley carried her pack to the lockers where the clothing was stored. She found a white form-fitting neoprene suit with integrated Kevlar armored panels, a pair of white leather combat boots and gloves. She removed the milkstone locket and placed it on the low bench in front of the locker. Wherever Elek was, she hoped he was safe. After the mission—after her dad was safe—she'd find him.

Alley took off her wool coat and then stripped off her sweat soaked clothing. Her nose wrinkled. She smelled awful. No time for a shower. Alley opened a locker and found a stick of deodorant inside. It would have to do. She rubbed some on and then placed the locket back around her neck before pulling on the suit. The spongy neoprene squeezed her body and warmed against her skin. Alley pulled the wool coat back on over the suit and then slipped her arms through the straps of the explosive-laden pack. Finally, she pushed the helmet down onto her head and stuffed her wet clothes into the locker.

Nadja handed her a holster holding one of the strange warden guns. Alley took the weapon from the warden. "I've never fired a gun before," she said.

Nadja drew the weapon from the holster. "This is a Drak-9. It fires scale-piercing rounds. Push here to turn off the safety, aim and squeeze." She shoved it back into the holster. "Better safe than sorry."

Alley buckled on the weapon. It felt strange to be wearing a gun. Nadja led them out of the Armory and down the hallway. Broderick stood by the open elevator door.

Brody winked at them. “Ready to party?” He was way too cheerful about the approaching danger.

They boarded the elevator, and the doors closed. The lift shot them upward out of the bowels of the city. A moment later they were standing on a rooftop. Thick fog obscured the surrounding buildings. They walked out onto the graveled surface.

The four dracun team members moved ahead and spaced themselves out in a line along the edge of the roof. Each stood beside what looked like an over-sized padded horse saddle. They took off their coats, arched their backs and spread their arms. There was a crunching sound like brittle ice breaking, the dracun’s bodies expanded, their clothes separated and fell away where the clothing seams had been designed to unsnap. Their human skin ripped and flaked away revealing glistening white scales. Wings and tails unfurled. They rolled and flexed their limbs, now free of their magic induced human forms.

It was an amazing sight, but Alley felt nervous. This was the plan—to jump on the backs of dracuns? She reached out with her mind to Vicktor. *Is this safe?*

Very safe, dauthma.

Alley was certain he was lying. Nothing about this looked safe.

The wardens packed the dracun's clothes into the saddle bags, then lifted the seats onto the backs of the creatures, fastening them in place with wide straps. Rigel adjusted the saddle on the back of Alley's ride while the other wardens got settled into their own mounts.

Alley's dracun dipped its massive white scaled head in a bow and lowered its body to the roof top so she could climb into the saddle. *I am Zefar, dauthma. It is an honor to bear you into battle. Climb aboard.*

Alley climbed up his side. *I've never flown like this before.*

The dracuns voice sounded surprised in her mind. *Your mother never took you?*

No, never, she replied. Had her mother flown on dracun?

Then my honor is even greater, replied Zefar.

Alley pulled herself onto the huge saddle. It had a contoured seat back that came up to the middle of her spine. She pulled the shoulder straps into place, buckled them, then secured the waist and foot straps. Up close, Zefar's scales reminded her of the white surface of the milkstone.

Brody approached. "Alley, I know this is your first-time riding so here's the deal." He reached up and touched the horn that rose from the front of the saddle. "You hold on here. Zefar will handle the flying, but if you want to give any suggestions on movement, you tilt the horn. It works pads under the saddle that help him feel which way you are pushing. Forward means down, back means up, and tilting to the left and right mean just what you might think." He patted two metal fasteners. "Your lap and shoulder harnesses can be released by pulling both latches. Hopefully, you won't need to do that, but if something were to happen to Zefar, you might need to break free in a hurry."

Zefar snorted at Brody.

The High Commander held up his hands. "I said, IF!" He stepped back and raised his voice. "Good luck and good hunting, everyone!"

Nadja called, "Let's go! Keep the lights on for us, Brody!"

Zefar crouched and beat his wings. Alley felt a sickening sensation as the dracun leaped skyward. His powerful muscles rippled beneath the surface of his scales. As the fog enveloped them, Alley hoped they wouldn't be too late—that her dad was still out there, waiting for her to come bring him home.

34

CHANGE OF PLANS

ALLEY

The wind gusted. Alley's stomach clenched as Zefar was tossed upward. Her knuckles ached from gripping the saddle. Icy sleet splattered the helmet's visor. The heads-up-display overlaid glowing blue lines across her field of view—horizontal elevation markers showing the contours of Mt. Baker's massive bulk ahead. A glowing yellow square spun on the slopes of the overlay. It marked a remote ice tunnel that Nadja said was one of the least guarded routes into the Obsidian lair.

Beyond the tactical readouts, the pale scales of Zefar's body rose and fell against a sea of white nothingness. Even though the Thorngate was far away, the thick clouds made it feel like Alley was back in the tunnel, passing between worlds. Haunting moans echoed in her mind. She blinked, shaking off the memory.

The wardens were hidden in the surrounding blizzard. The display showed their positions as bright green triangles. A voice crackled in her ear. It was Nadja. *"Five minutes to the LZ."*

The green triangles that were Jenna and Rigel blinked acknowledging Nadja's update. Alley keyed the chin switch in her helmet activating her microphone. "Got it."

Alley adjusted her legs and grip to make sure the sleet hadn't frozen them to the saddle. A few more minutes and they'd be on the ground. She took a deep breath, pulling in chilled air through the vents in the helmet. It helped distract from the sickening sensation of the choppy flight.

Garbled noise erupted from the helmet speakers. One of the green triangles disappeared from her display.

Jenna.

Nadja's voice crackled over the speakers in the helmet. *"Jenna! Do you copy?"*

Static.

"Rigel, Alley. Can you see Jenna?"

Alley winced as Rigel's yell blasted her eardrums. *"I think we have company! I'm going weapons hot!"*

Alley couldn't see anything in the storm. "There's too much snow!" she yelled into her helmet's comm.

Three red dots appeared on the visor, tracking toward their position. Alley drew her gun and checked that the safety was off. Her heart was pounding. Nadja called, *"Looks like you were right, Rigel. Get ready!"*

"Hate it when I'm right, Boss!" he shouted back.

The red dots split. One headed towards Alley's position. The others veered towards the wardens.

Alley focused on Zefar. *Do you see anything?*

Nothing, dauthma!

A black shape hurtled out of the blinding snow. A dracun with dark scales and an orange stripe along its neck. *Obsidian.* It crashed into them—its fangs sunk deep into Zefar's neck. Black liquid spattered Alley's visor as the Opal dracun's body went limp.

Zefar! she cried in her mind. The dracun didn't answer.

Alley fired at the Obsidian, it grunted and pushed away, disappearing into the storm.

Her body went weightless as they tumbled from the sky. Alley screamed into her helmet, "We're going down!"

Nadja yelled back, *"Release the harness and pull your ripcord!"*

Alley holstered the gun. She fumbled for the release latches that Brody had pointed out. Wind buffeted her body as her stomach did cartwheels. Her fingers found the metal buckles and pulled. She wiggled out of the harness and kicked away into open air.

Before she could pull the ripcord, something grabbed her pack and yanked upward. The shoulder straps dug into her armpits, stopping her fall. Zephar's body disappeared as it continued to plummet. Alley looked up. The Obsidian dracun with the orange stripe had a hold of her backpack.

Alley's heartbeat thundered in her chest. She grabbed the gun from her holster and fired up at the creature.

Foolish, child. The dracun's voice growled in her mind. It knocked the gun out of her hand.

"Nadja! One of them—"

Before she could finish, the helmet was ripped from Alley's head. Snow and wind blasted her face. She squeezed her eyes shut.

The monster growled in her mind. *No more running.*

One clawed hand grasped Alley's neck as a talon on the other hand sliced the shoulder straps of her pack and tossed it away. If the dracun dropped her now, she was as good as dead. Alley grabbed at the scaled hand around her throat. Her legs kicked empty air. It was choking her.

Can't breathe—she thought.

The dracun laughed in her head. *I know.*

Spots formed in her vision and then everything went black.

— Nadja —

Nadja screamed, "Alley! Do you copy?"

There was no answer.

Rigel's voice filled her helmet. *"Dracun at two o'clock high. Engaging!"*

The rapid pop of automatic weapons fire crackled off Nadja's starboard side.

A ball of orange flame burned through the whiteness, screaming past her head.

That was too close, she thought.

They had to break away. The mission was already a disaster, but there was still a chance of completing at least part of it, as long as the dracun didn't follow them to the tunnel entrance.

A red dot reappeared hurtling toward her position. Nadja pulled right on the flight stick. Vicktor banked hard, but it was too late. An Obsidian dracun slammed into them, its black talons tearing into Vicktor's hide.

They fell from the sky tumbling end over end as the giant beasts snapped and clawed at each other. Nadja felt like vomiting as earth became sky and sky became earth. The helmet display was a riot of glowing lines twirling across her field of vision. She tried to focus on the white scales of Vicktor's back and the black form that was digging its claws into his body.

Nadja keyed her comm. "We're going down. We've got a dracun attached to us!"

Static.

Was everyone dead?

The glowing blue terrain lines spun across her visor as they flipped through the air. There were no green triangles.

Wind and sleet pelted her body from every direction.

Vicktor couldn't beat his wings with the other dracun attached to him. They would hit the ground if she didn't do something.

Nadja released the saddle harness, unsheathed her scryth and threw herself towards the black creature's scaled body. The blade glowed bright green as she streaked across Vicktor's back. She landed hard against the Obsidian's torso and plunged her knife between the beast's ribs.

The effect was immediate. The monster howled in pain and steamed as if being cooked from the inside out. Black scales peeled off like shingles blown from a house in a tornado. Vicktor used the distraction to sink his teeth into the dracun's neck. He tore out a huge chunk of flesh. The howling ceased.

The creature fractured into smoldering chunks. The wind tore the parts into smaller pieces as they careened toward the forest floor. Nadja fell forward through the ash as the dracun broke apart. The soot blackened her visor. She was no longer connected to anything solid. Where was Vicktor? Nadja glanced at the altimeter on her shoulder. It was caked in ice. Her hand fumbled for the emergency ripcord on the chute, but she couldn't find it.

Her vision dimmed and then she blacked out.

— Alley —

A wave of nausea rippled through Alley's gut. She tried to

concentrate on the freezing wind whipping her hair across her face. Her body rose and fell like a boat bobbing in huge ocean swells. The iron grip of the dracun dug into her armpits. Its leathery wings beat cold gusts at her head. Alley felt like crying. How was she going to save her dad now? She couldn't even save herself. Her body shivered, unable to stay warm in the blasts of arctic air.

She'd glimpsed snow encrusted pines far below, but now it was impossible to tell what direction they were heading in or how long they'd been flying. Alley's muscles shook. Her teeth chattered.

An uncomfortable tingling sensation coursed through her shoulders where the dracun's talons gripped. It itched like a wool sweater and reminded her of the odd feeling when Arün was close. The dracun had spoken to her when it attacked. Perhaps it was listening to her thoughts now. She focused on the darkness above her head.

Can you hear me? she thought.

No answer.

Where are you taking me?

A growl rumbled in her mind. *Shut up, child. Get out of my head.*

What do you want?! she yelled back.

The dracun squeezed her shoulders painfully. *The Queen wishes to speak with you. I do not.*

It was taking her to Srira. The creature's grip felt as if it was millimeters from breaking a bone. Alley gasped. The dracun relaxed its hold. She needed to get to the clearing in her mind—to grab hold of the power. Would she be able to access it in time to stop the Queen? Her extremities were numb from the cold. Tears welled in her eyes and froze her lashes shut.

— Nadja —

Nadja was lying on something cold when she awoke. Her helmet was still on, but the visor read-out was dark and covered with a thin layer of snow. She tugged the helmet off. Wind and snow tossed her blond hair. A valley of frosted pines stretched out into the distance.

Vicktor sat across from her in quasi-human form, covered in white scales. His wings had collapsed into his body. He was now a sixth of his original size. His green-yellow eyes regarded her from atop his long, scaled neck.

She pushed herself up. "What happened?"

"We did not hit the ground—thanks to you, Captain." The dracun touched his brow with a clawed hand and bowed his triangular head. He'd bandaged the slash marks in his side and held a protective hand against the wounds.

"What do you mean?"

"After you dispatched the enemy, I resumed our flight to the cave entrance, but the rest of our team did not make it."

Alley, Jenna, and Rigel—all lost. Nadja stood and threw her helmet into a snowbank. She ran her fingers through her matted hair. Two more wardens lost and the girl—the person they had fought to keep safe—the person they had hoped could be a last line of defense—hadn't lasted five minutes. Why? Because the Mages failed to deal with the mess they had created. It was up to her now.

The Drak-9 swung from her wrist. Nadja unclipped it and pushed it back into its holster. Her blade had already been returned to the sheath on her thigh. The backpack with the explosives sat a few feet away in the snow. The saddle was discarded by a nearby tree. She reached for the pack. Perhaps she owed Vicktor her life? Nadja pushed the thought away. "How far are we from the cave entrance?"

Vicktor stood and brushed the snow off his scaled legs. "It's just over the rise."

She pulled on her pack. "Lead the way."

Vicktor bowed and trudged up the slope. Nadja drew her gun and followed. Her feet sunk into the drifts. Above them, massive sheets of ice and snow clung to the mountainside. Weapon fire could trigger an avalanche. Nadja holstered the gun and drew her blade instead.

When they reached the crest, she stopped next to Vicktor. The tunnel entrance was nestled below them in a shadowed crevice. Nadja pulled binoculars out of the pack and examined the opening. The snow outside was undisturbed, a good sign that no one had passed through since the last storm. "Okay, let's get down there."

They descended the slope. A few minutes later they stood

on the threshold of the cave. The walls were layered with translucent blue ice. They looked as if they had been carved out one scoop at a time. The ceiling was at least a dozen feet above their heads.

Vicktor wrinkled his reptilian nose. "I can smell the lair. The Obsidian are a filthy clan."

Nadja glanced at the dracun. Should she have him stay behind? Vicktor could have let her die, but he saved her life. He might be useful in a fight. She grimaced. Was she starting to trust one of these monsters?

"Vicktor, how quiet can you be?"

"Silent, Captain."

"Good. I'll take the lead. Keep up."

He nodded. His eyes seemed to glow with an inner fire in the shadows of the cave.

Nadja held her scryth out. It glowed a bright flickering green that cast enough light for her to see by in the dark tunnel. Normally, she counted on the blade's glow to give her advance-warning of approaching dracun, but with Vicktor at her back, it glowed constantly. At least she could see the path ahead. The ice on the tunnel floor had formed brittle sheets between the loose rock. It crunched with each footstep. True to his word, Vicktor followed and avoided making any additional sound. They inched their way down the cold tunnel.

Somewhere up ahead lay the EMP device and hopefully Arün. If the dracun had killed him—Nadja shook her head —no, he had to be alive. She opened the milkstone locket.

Three dark spots bubbled on the edges of the stone. Nadja tapped the largest one. Arün's face coalesced on the surface. He was close. She tapped the next largest and Alley's face swirled into view. Somehow, she'd survived, but she was farther away now. Had Alley been captured? The last dot was barely visible. Elek. He must still be in Arburaan. Nadja hoped he'd escaped the High Guard. She snapped the locket shut and tucked it away.

They had been hiking for a while when she noticed the smell that Vicktor had sensed at the tunnel entrance. Sickly and sweet—like rotting fruit. Nadja had been looking for signs of dracun along the tunnel path. There were occasional animal bones half frozen in the ice, but no discernible tracks. They had encountered no forks or alternate paths. How deep were they? A half mile? More? She'd been so focused on staying quiet, the distance was hard to gauge now.

They rounded a bend. The tunnel ended in a sheet of icy stalagmites that rose overhead like a giant frozen waterfall.

Vicktor approached and leaned close. "We must go up."

Nadja fought the instinct to stab his reptilian features with the blade. Instead, she leaned away. Great. She should have planned for this. No harness, no rope, no crampons, no ice picks. How were they going to scale the wall?

The dracun knelt and gestured at its back. "Climb on."

Nadja sighed. There was no choice. She sheathed her knife. Without the light from the blade, she noticed that high above, there was a soft orange glow. Where was that coming from? She grabbed onto Vicktor's shoulders and wrapped her legs around his waist.

The dracun slapped his hand onto one of the thick icy stalagmites. His claws dug deep grooves into the surface. He repeated the process with his other hand and pulled upward. They ascended the wall of ice. The glow overhead got brighter as they left the tunnel floor far below.

A few moments later, they crested the top of the ice flow. The air was warmer. Orange light reflected off glistening wet rock. Nadja let go of Vicktor and led the way down the tunnel.

Something crunched underfoot that resembled broken pottery shards. Nadja bent and picked up a fragment. It wasn't pottery. It was a piece of dracun egg shell. In the distance, she heard the guttural voices of multiple dracun and something else—a higher pitched sound.

Hatchlings?

A nest! she thought.

The dracun were forbidden from reproducing without special permission from the Council. The Mages would want to know about the size and extent of the breeding grounds. It was outside the mission parameters, but there had been lots of times she'd bent the rules for the greater good of the Council.

Nadja pocketed the egg shard and crept forward. The tunnel split. The shrill sound of dracun young echoed from the left fork of the tunnel.

Nadja had to see the nest.

Vicktor cocked his head at her and motioned toward the right fork of the tunnel. Nadja shook her head and pointed down the left fork. The dracun's face was impossible to read, but she sensed his disapproval. She didn't need his permission nor his acceptance. Nadja headed down the glowing left-hand passage. Vicktor followed. The air got hotter, and the sounds grew louder. The walls were black and smooth. They had been formed by hot magma flowing through the mountain. The tunnel ended. Just beyond, it opened into a larger, brighter space.

Nadja inched forward, staying in the shadows, and peered into the vast chamber. The cavern was hundreds of yards across. The ceiling was supported by massive black tubes of hardened lava studded with glistening red crystals. Thousands of oily black dracun eggs lay beside bubbling pools of glowing molten rock. The eggs varied in size from as small as a basketball to as big as an overstuffed suitcase. There were at least a half-dozen dracun moving through the nest. Each one about as big as a delivery truck. The creatures rotated and arranged the eggs around the lava pools. A few had hatched. The feeble cries of the newborns echoed off the cavern walls. Nadja couldn't believe how many eggs she saw —enough for an army.

If the eggs reached maturity, there would be no way the Wardens could contain them. They would overrun the world in a matter of years. This was worse than an EMP device—

far worse. Nadja felt wetness around her eyes. The dracun had taken everything from her, but she could still protect the rest of the planet. Her fists tightened.

Nadja examined the huge columns that supported the ceiling. There were three primary ones. A few charges on each column would bring down the entire cavern. Vicktor touched her shoulder. Nadja whipped around.

The dracun gestured back down the tunnel the way they had come. “Captain, we have our orders. The EMP device isn't here, we should go the other way.”

Nadja glared at him. “The Warden mission is to safeguard humanity.” The dracun’s eyes were impassive pools of green and amber. She didn’t remember having drawn her blade, but she now held it pointed at Vicktor. Surges of green energy raced across its surface.

“Please, Captain. The Council was specific—we must go now and disable the device.”

Nadja shook her head. Heat from the giant cavern radiated against her back. The cries of the hatchlings were like fingernails dragged across a chalkboard. “No. If they knew about this, they would never allow it to exist.”

Vicktor shifted his weight and took a step backward. “There is no honor in killing children.”

“Children?” Nadja’s voice was barely a whisper. The muscle above her left eye twitched. She pressed her thumb against it until the spasm stopped. How had the Wardens come to trust these creatures? Nadja took a deep breath and shook her head. "On the battlefield, you follow orders, or you die."

The dracun tilted its head to the side. Its white scales reflected the orange glow from the magma pools. "With respect, Captain. Your judgment is clouded by your hatred. I won't help you commit genocide."

Nadja's eye twitched again. Her pain and anger felt like a ball of fire in her stomach. This dracun dared to judge her? She stared at him trying to understand why she had tolerated his presence at all.

Nadja pressed the blade against the dracun's chest. Smoke curled up from the tip of the knife. "I don't need your help."

Vicktor stumbled backward away from the weapon. "This is not why we came here."

"You saved my life. Leave now before I regret returning the favor."

The dracun paused for a moment as if considering whether to say more. Nadja hoped it would give her an excuse to end its life.

It backed away into the darkness of the tunnel till she could only see its glowing eyes. "May you find peace one day, Captain." The eyes disappeared and were replaced with the quiet echo of retreating footsteps.

Vicktor's words burned, but who was he to judge her? He was a monster like the rest. No human child should ever have to live in fear of these demons. The Mages were wrong to trust them. They were not of this world. They did not belong here. Their presence threatened the safety of everyone on the planet. She was doing the right thing. If this had been a cavern filled with thousands of poisonous snakes, no one would fault her for eradicating them.

Nadja unslung her pack and pulled out the explosive charges. She would find peace when all the dracun were dead.

35

FIRESIDE CHAT

ALLEY

A female voice reverberated in Alley's mind. *Bring her to me.*

It was the voice from her visions.

Srira. Queen of the Obsidian Clan.

Alley's eyelashes were frozen shut. She couldn't feel her arms. When the dracun dropped from the sky, she couldn't see it coming. The contents of her stomach rose into her throat. The creature beat its wings, slowing their descent with blasts of frigid air. Alley's boots scraped on hard ground. The iron grip on her shoulders released. Her legs crumpled. A sharp pain stabbed into her knees as they hit cold stone. The dracun grabbed the collar of her wool coat and dragged her forward. Its claws clicked against the ground. The sound echoed back from distant walls.

Alley tried to focus on the clearing in her mind—on Bezo's song. If she could draw out the energy she could end this now. The dracun lifted her onto a warm, soft surface. Something hot was placed against her lips.

"Drink, child." The voice was smooth, seductive. Comforting.

Alley pressed her lips together. *No,* she thought.

A firm hand grasped her cheeks and forced her jaw open. Hot liquid flowed into her mouth. It burned a trail down her throat and warmed her insides. Alley coughed, but the heat felt good. What was it? More of the sweet liquid flooded her mouth. She swallowed. Eggnog? Cinnamon? Her heart raced. An eggnog latte. *Espresso.* She wouldn't be able to channel the energy!

Warm air caressed her frozen skin. Cold water drip down her cheeks as the ice crystals on her brows and lashes melted away. Alley blinked.

"Doesn't that feel better?" asked the Queen. Her lavender eyes peered into Alley's.

Srira's hair was raven black. Her lips, blood red. She looked human except that she was twice the size of a normal person. Her milky white skin was smooth, broken by ridges of small black horns that protruded from her high cheekbones. A larger row of the spikes sprouted from her forehead like a bone tiara. She wore a sleek black scaled dress trimmed with ruby red stones.

Alley tried to sit up, but her body was still numb. She was

seated in an ornate wooden chair, padded in red velvet across from the Queen. Where was she? What had happened to the rest of the team? Were her dad and Arün here?

Srira shifted her gaze to somewhere behind Alley. "Bring her a blanket." Talons clicked on stone as the dracun behind Alley departed.

They were in a huge circular cavern with a high ceiling. Fires burned in pits that had been chiseled into the floor at intervals around the room. The flames cast a flickering light across ornate bas-reliefs carved into the natural stone walls. The images depicted dragons and humans engaged in battle. Tendrils of green ivy slithered up the walls and around the room framing the entrances to dark tunnels that led out of the space. Their chairs had been positioned in the center of the chamber atop a large rug.

The click of returning footsteps echoed behind Alley. A moment later she felt a warm heavy fur draped across her shoulders.

The Queen extended the steaming latte. "I'm sorry for the manner in which you were brought here. Please have another drink." Srira pressed the mug to Alley's lips and tilted more of the hot liquid into her mouth. Alley was too cold to resist. The damage was already done. She swallowed the drink and let the warmth fill her stomach.

Feeling returned to her arms. A thousand tiny needles prickled across her skin. "What do you want?" asked Alley.

Srira set the cup on the table and settled back into her

chair. Her red lips curved into a smile. "What I want is to rule in peace. To see my people, prosper. But I imagine what you are asking is what do I want with *you*?"

Alley waited. Srira's composed manner was stiff and unnatural. Coils of tension and rage seemed to seethe just below the surface of her movements. The Queen leaned forward and brushed icy water from Alley's cheek with a human looking finger that tapered at the end into a sharp black talon. "You are special. Do you know that?"

"Yeah," she answered.

"What do you know about elves, mages, and wardens? Do you know the source of their power?"

Alley pressed her lips together. She refused to offer any information. Somehow, she had to figure out a way to escape.

The Queen continued. "Their power comes from the pixies. Horrible little parasites that infest our world. They make a dust that the mages and elves use in their magic. The bigger the magic, the more dust they need." The Queen offered her the mug again.

Alley took it. It would make a poor weapon, but it was better than nothing. "What do you want?" she asked again.

The Queen shook her head. "I am not your enemy, Alley. I have not deceived you. I have not lied to you your entire life about who and what you are."

"You're lying now. You're pretending to be human."

"I thought you would find this form less jarring, and it

allows us to talk and interact in a way that my true form would not permit."

Alley shook her head. "You should have skipped the horns if you were going for less jarring."

The Queen smiled. "You remind me of your mother."

Alley squinted at the Queen. Srira knew her mom?

The Queen looked sad. "Yes, I knew your mother—I knew her well."

Had her mother spent time with the Obsidian dracun when she was trying to stop the war?

The Queen interrupted her thoughts. "Years ago, when she told me about meeting your father, I said she was making a mistake—that she was a fool to trust any human—especially a mage. But she was blinded by love. She wouldn't see reason."

Alley's eyes went wide. "No. That's impossible. My mom was human."

The Queen laughed and shook her head. "She was my daughter."

"No." There was no way her mom was an Obsidian dracun—no way the Queen was her—

Srira smiled. "Yes."

Was the Queen lying or was it possible? Alley thought of what her dad had told her—that he and her mom couldn't have children—that they'd agreed to help with the Mages' secret research project because it allowed them to have a family.

Could their inability to have kids been because they weren't the same species or was Srira just playing a mind-game? Part of her was dracun, but had that part come from her mother?

Alley looked up at the Queen. "Prove it."

Srira's eyes narrowed. She spoke in Alley's mind. *I've already proved it.*

Alley shook her head. *This proves nothing. I've spoken to other dracuns like this.*

Srira smiled, her voice whispered in Alley's head. *Have the others spoken to you from miles away? Come to you in your dreams?*

Alley swallowed. *No.* She'd only been able to hear other dracun when they were close.

The Queen spoke aloud. "I'm bonded to the members of my clan—even stronger to those in my direct bloodline. If we were not bonded, I would not have been able to reach out to you."

Alley's hand was shaking, but it wasn't from the cold anymore. Srira was her grandmother? She didn't want to believe it. Her mom hadn't been a monster.

Srira nodded. "Your father and mother tried to hide you from me. They feared I would help you reach your true potential."

She was trying to make her hate her parents. Alley's fists clenched. "What do you want?"

The Queen leaned forward. "I want to offer you a future.

A place at my side. A place where you will always be welcome—and loved."

"You ruined my life."

"I've been trying to rescue you—to offer you something better. There is a change coming—a change that will restore balance. I need your help. In return, you will rule by my side and be reunited with your true family."

"I didn't need to be rescued and I have no interest in helping you with whatever war you're trying to start."

The Queen smoothed her dress and regarded Alley with half-closed eyes. "You will help me."

Alley spit back. "Why would I do that?"

"Because if you don't you'll never see your father again."

Alley froze. "Where is he?"

The Queen whispered. "I will take you to him if you help me."

"I won't help you destroy my world."

Srira shook her head. "I only need your help to break a seal. Nothing more."

Alley wanted to reach over and strangle the woman. She gritted her teeth instead. "What do you mean?"

"It's a lock that was put in place a long time ago."

"What happens when this seal is broken?"

The Queen's red lips curled into a wide smile revealing a mouth of too many white teeth. "My husband, Cynder, will be free."

— Nadja —

Nadja crept across the cavern floor. She stopped to rub dirt and soot over her clothes to help blend in with the rocks. The first of the massive columns supporting the roof of the nesting grounds lay ahead. The cavern was like an oven. Waves of heat radiated from the lava pools scattered about the space. A sulfurous stench filled her nose. She flattened herself to the ground behind a cluster of eggs as one of the dracun wandered past her position.

There were ten explosive charges in the pack. Hopefully, planting a few at the base of each of the three primary columns in the cavern would be enough to collapse the roof and destroy the nest.

The dracun stopped and rotated an egg near the edge of a lava pool. The creature was as big as an elephant, but with longer, more agile limbs and large wings folded tight against its black scaled body. It was incredible that the Mages' cocktail could force these creatures into a human form outside the mountain. Nadja had always been curious about the Council's strange blend of science and magic, but it was taboo for wardens to ask too many questions about their arcane practices. They only taught wardens when absolutely necessary, like the weave they'd shown Arün to open the Thorngate.

The dracun moved away. Nadja scrambled to the base of the first column. It was formed from the smooth black lava stone that composed the rest of the cavern and studded with chunks of reddish crystal that got larger where they sprouted higher up the column.

Nadja swung the pack off her back. The explosives could be manually triggered or be set to go off at a specific time. She glanced at the two remaining columns and estimated it would take her about thirty more minutes to reach each of them, plant the charges and then get back to the tunnel. She'd then need to find the EMP device and plant the last charge on it. If there was any time left, she'd try to find Arün. All told, maybe an hour. The remote detonator would be useless under the mountain. A timed detonation was the only option. Nadja reached into her pack and set the charges for a sixty-minute delay. Hopefully, it would be enough time. Moving slowly, she set three charges around the base of the first column. The creatures roaming the nest hadn't noticed her. Nadja hoped her luck would hold.

— Arün —

Arün's head throbbed. He wanted to press his fingers against his skull—to massage the ache in his temples, but his wrists were tied. He lifted his head and peeled one eye open. The other was swollen shut. A cold wind blasted his body. He was at the back of a small cave. The floor was smooth and dusted with snow. Opposite him, the cave was open to the outside. It overlooked a misty valley covered with snow encrusted pines. The edge of the cave was a sheer drop-off to the forest floor hundreds of feet below.

His ankles and wrists were bound with thick ropes to iron rings anchored into the stone. The bindings forced him to stand spread-eagle. Arün's shirt had been stripped off. His chest was covered in scabbed over cuts and bruises that had blossomed into patches of purple and yellow. His left hand was cramped from being balled into a tight fist. Inside was the milkstone. He'd hidden it in his hand when the dracuns had caught him. Somehow, he'd held on to it through the beatings.

Almost every part of him hurt. There was something else though. A new feeling. Something he hadn't felt in a long time. Arün could feel his restrained arms, but he felt another set of limbs he could move freely. They were clumsy. With his one good eye, he looked over his shoulder hoping not to see what he knew had to be there.

Arün's stomach clenched when he saw leathery wings flexing behind him. They beat against the hard stone. Pain lanced through his back. He took a deep breath and calmed himself. How long had it been? Sixty years? More? It was a part of himself that he'd buried deep. He'd been the first to sign up when the Mages had asked for volunteers. They told him he was going to be the first of a new breed of wardens. Tougher. Stronger. Faster. But the side effects had been a surprise. The Mages adapted their formula and found success with other wardens, but their initial miscalculation had forever changed him.

Arün focused his mind trying to trigger the transformation that would retract the wings. His body shivered as a blast of cold mountain air hit his bare chest. He couldn't remember how to do it—he'd avoided it for so many years. His mind drifted to Alley. How could he have been so reckless? He should have expected the dracun would track them to the Thorngate. They should have come back by through a different portal. He should have been more careful. He hoped Nadja and Elek had kept Alley safe. He had to get free.

Arün pulled at the ropes until his wrists bled, but they held fast.

— Alley —

Alley shook her head. "I'm not helping you free him. Cynder is a monster. He destroyed entire cities."

The Queen pointed a taloned finger at Alley. "He is your grandfather and your King."

"He's not my King."

The Queen pounded her fist on the arm of her chair, splintering the wood. "Cynder does not deserve to be imprisoned for an eternity!" She took a deep breath and then spoke softly. "I suspect, the Mages did not tell you why the War started."

Alley jabbed a finger at Srira. "You started it. Cynder and the other clan leaders attacked the pixies."

"That is a half-truth. You heard one side of the tale. Now I will tell you the other." She touched Alley's cheek. The cavern disappeared. Srira's voice echoed in her mind.

Long ago on Arburaan, there was a terrible war in the land of our ancestors. Our children were dying. We gathered what was left of our clans and traveled across the Great Ocean until we arrived on the shores of what the elves call Du'harloth.

Alley was flying over a blue sea. Ahead the hazy silhouette of land formed a ragged edge along the horizon. All around flew countless dracun, small and large. The setting sun glinted off their colorful scales. A moment later the vision of the ocean was obscured by clouds. The mist cleared revealing a beautiful mountain range filled with valleys of grass, waterfalls, and herds of roaming animals.

The elves welcomed us and granted us land in the high mountains. We rebuilt our life. For centuries our people prospered.

Fingers of frost crept across Alley's vision. Snow covered the mountains. The waterfalls turned to ice.

Then came the Deep Frost. A cold descended on our new home. We were forced out of the highlands to survive.

Alley was traveling amongst the dracun as they followed their massive clan leaders out of the mountains, down into the lowland forests. She could feel their desperation. Their hunger.

The forests offered us refuge from the cold and food in abun-

dance, but our clans were not built for small spaces. We cleared a swath of the northern forests to make room for our people.

Thousands of dracun knocked over trees and burned underbrush to form clearings and build shelters. Alley followed hunting parties as they tracked and killed herds of unusual creatures, dragging the biggest kills back to feed their massive dragon clan leaders. She could feel their relief. Their hope.

The elves were angered and warned us to leave the rest of the forest untouched. We did—for a time. As food grew scarce, we were forced further into the central woodlands.

Alley watched the clans move deeper into the forest where the trees towered overhead. They nested in clearings and glades as they hunted for food.

Then came the disappearances. Dracun went missing at night. There were tales of the forest swallowing them whole. It went on for years and grew more frequent.

The sun and moons flew across the sky. Clouds raced by and the seasons changed. As time passed, she saw fewer and fewer dracun roaming the nesting grounds. Alley felt their loss. She felt their fear.

The elves warned that we had angered the forest spirits, the pixies, and that we should return to the mountains. But our home was still frozen. With our numbers dwindling we did the only thing we could do to ensure our survival—we razed the forests to protect our people—to keep the pixies at bay.

The enormous clan leaders burned and toppled massive

trees to create wide roads and hunting trails through the old forest for their dracun kin.

The elves declared war. We fought for years even as we continued to lose family members to the forest.

A great battle raged across a vast plain of charred and broken trees. Giant armies of elves with glowing weapons cut into the dracun. Their bodies burned from the inside out crumbling into piles of smoldering ash. She felt the anguish of the clan leaders as their people died—felt their rage. Huge dragons, the leaders of the clans, advanced across the land burning everything in their path. Countless elvish warriors were burned alive and crushed as they tried and failed to bring down the clan leaders. The armies retreated. The dragons pursued. They leveled cities—killed thousands of elves.

We pushed the elves back to their fragile cities, but just when we thought we'd won our freedom, the Mages arrived with their horrible machines of war.

As the sun, clouds, and stars raced overhead, battle after battle between the clan leaders and waves of bizarre war machines rolled across the scarred landscape. Some machines looked like tanks, others like huge mechanical insects and animals. Each time the clan leaders ripped them apart—until a new design emerged—one that looked just like the machine Elek had piloted. A bipedal giant that was more agile and deadly than the earlier ones. It attacked the dracun avoiding the larger clan leaders. She felt fear again. Anguish.

They slaughtered our people. We had to surrender or risk extinction. Your mother negotiated a truce. The Mages exiled us to this world. Our clan rulers, including my husband, were imprisoned below these mountains.

The monstrous clan leaders donned huge collars, cuffs, and anklets inscribed with complex weaves. They followed mages in battle armor as they were led into deep mountain tunnels. The walls closed in as they were forced to crawl deeper and deeper. The tunnels were collapsed behind them. The weaves on the collars were activated sending the dragons into a deep sleep. She could feel their despair as darkness overtook their minds.

Your grandfather was only trying to save our people. He does not deserve this fate.

Srira withdrew her hand. Alley's sight returned. The dracun had just been trying to survive. The Ash War, the destruction, the death, it had all been a horrible misunderstanding between these races. If they had only taken time to understand one another, so much of it might have been avoided. Seeing the Elvish cities destroyed reminded her of the vision Srira had shown her of Seattle in ruins, but it seemed cruel to imprison the dragons forever. Alley wished there was another way to help her dad. "How do I know Cynder won't hurt my world if I help you?"

The Queen laughed. "Child, I can offer you no such

assurances. When he awakes, I will try to calm him, but his anger will be great."

Alley shook her head. "Then I can't help you free him."

The Queen motioned to the dracun standing behind Alley. "Then I'm afraid your father is of no further use to me."

Was she threatening to kill him? Alley held out her hand. "Wait. Take me to him."

The Queen spoke inside her head once more. *Will you help me?*

— Nadja —

Nadja wedged the final explosive into a crack at the base of the third crystal encrusted column. Her backpack felt lighter with only a single charge left to destroy the EMP device. She wiped her brow with the back of her hand. The cavern would be destroyed and with it, a future army of dracun—she checked her watch—in less than thirty minutes.

The trip around the room had taken longer than expected. It didn't leave her much time to locate the EMP device and find Arün. In the shadow of the towering black pillar, she pulled out her milkstone. The largest of the three dark spots showed Arün was close. She snapped the locket shut and tucked it under her armored body suit.

Nadja crept out of the shadows and headed back toward

the tunnel. She avoided the shattered remains of hatched eggs that littered the nest—stepping on one might alert the roaming dracun. Nadja was almost halfway to the tunnel, passing through a field of tall spiked stalagmites when she felt something heavy fall onto her backpack.

A high-pitched screech pierced the air. Tiny wings beat sulfurous fumes against her head. A baby dracun clung to her pack. It must have been perched on a stalagmite and dropped onto her. Nadja swatted at the creature. "Get—off!" she hissed.

The baby shrieked and beat its tiny wings harder.

Nadja unsheathed her scryth. It glowed brilliant green, brighter than she'd ever seen it. The light from the weapon erased the shadows.

Nadja froze. *Oh no,* she thought.

The adult dracuns in the cavern turned toward the light and roared. Nadja sheathed the blade and sprinted towards the tunnel. The tiny dracun held on and continued to scream in her ear. If she could make it to the exit, the dracuns would need to transform to follow. In the tunnel, she might be able to fight them one at a time. Nadja drew her gun and thumbed the safety off as she ran.

A ball of flame shot past and splashed against a nearby stalagmite. Six monstrous dracun stampeded across the nest trying to cut off her exit. Nadja fired at them. The shots echoed off the walls of the cavern and startled the hatchling clinging to her back. It flew away as she reached the tunnel entrance.

Nadja sprinted down the passageway. Dracun roars reverberated off the walls. A fireball lit up the tunnel and exploded, splattering chunks of flaming jelly into the air. Some of it landed on her body armor and burned through the suit. Nadja slapped at the flames to put them out. They wouldn't be able to breathe fire once they transformed. Pinpoints of pain blossomed on the backs of her arms and legs where she hadn't extinguished the tiny globs of flaming dracun mucus fast enough.

Nadja holstered her gun and unslung the pack as she ran. She pulled out the last explosive charge and the remote detonator. She needed to collapse the tunnel, or she'd never have enough time to rescue Arün and disable the EMP before the timed charges in the nest went off. Nadja stopped long enough to press the explosive up into a crevice in the low ceiling. Guttural dracun speech and pursuing footsteps echoed from back around the bend in the tunnel.

Nadja slung the pack onto her shoulders and ran. She had no idea what the blast radius would be or how far away the remote detonator would work in the tunnels. She plugged her ears and then thumbed the detonator switch.

Nadja didn't hear the explosion, but she felt her body get thrown forward. Her face hit something hard and everything went black.

When she awoke, she lay for a moment waiting for the pain and ringing in her ears to subside.

Get up, she thought.

Nadja pushed against the ground and stood on unsteady legs. The air was thick with dust and the acrid smell of explosive residue. Her nose and upper lip felt numb. She touched them. Her hand came away covered in blood. The haze filled tunnel looked empty. Nadja checked her scryth. It glowed faintly—there were dracun nearby, but not close.

She sheathed the blade, sat down and pulled off her pack. One of the side pouches contained a small first aid kit. Nadja took out a tiny mirror and angled it towards her face. She'd smashed her nose and scraped her cheeks, but she'd seen worse. Nadja wiped the blood away and sprayed antiseptic on her face. The mist stung when it hit the cuts. She sprayed more on the backs of her arms and legs where the dracun fire had seared through the suit.

How long had she been unconscious? Nadja looked at her watch—ten minutes until the explosives detonated. She pulled out the milkstone locket. It pointed further down the tunnel. Arün was close. If she could free him, he could help find and destroy the device.

Nadja drew her scryth and ran, letting the milkstone lead her into the darkness.

36

REUNIONS

ALLEY

The Queen repeated the question inside Alley's head. *Will you help me?*

Alley glared at her—she wanted to punch the smug look right off Srira's face. "Fine," she said.

The Queen stood. She had to be at least ten feet tall. The red gems in her black gown sparkled as they reflected the flames. "Follow me." Without waiting, she turned and strode towards one of the ivy-covered archways.

Alley pushed herself out of the chair. The fur blanket fell off her shoulders as she hurried after Srira. Her clothes were soaked from the melted ice. The heat of the flames faded as they passed under the arch and into the darkness of a long tunnel. Her breath came out in clouds as she hurried to keep up with Srira's long strides. Pangs of fear stabbed at her gut. Dad had to be okay.

The passageway ended in a giant set of double doors—thick carved wood covered in frost. The Queen placed a palm on each of them and thrust her arms forward. The doors screeched and crashed inward as if hit by a battering ram. Snow billowed into the tunnel carried by an arctic blast of air. Alley shivered and held her arms tight across her body. Her damp clothes stiffened in the cold air.

The entrance led to a stone ledge that overlooked a huge cavern. The walls were encrusted with millions of icicles that had fused together into frozen pillars. They soared upward towards the distant ceiling. Weak light filtered through the crystalline columns bathing the icy cave in a blue glow. Snow filled every crack and crevice. It swirled in the air like ash. A jolt of adrenaline rocketed through Alley's veins as she recognized the mountain of ice and snow at the opposite end of the open space. This was the cavern from her vision—the cavern with the dragon.

Uneven steps hewn from the rock led down to the snow-swept lower floor. Out in the center of the frozen hall, someone sat on a chiseled stone block in front of a small fire. He wore a tattered green coat pulled tight around his frail body.

Alley's heart skipped. "Dad!" she yelled.

She pushed past the Queen and took the icy steps two at a time, her boots crunching on the sparkling snow.

Her father turned. His eyes grew wide. "Alley?"

She ran across the cavern floor and wrapped him in a hug. His body felt weak—like a stiff breeze would blow him off the cold stone. His mustache had grown into a full beard. Tears welled up in her eyes. His hand stroked her cold, wet hair. "You shouldn't be here. It's what Srira wants."

Alley whispered into his neck. "I know, but I couldn't leave you."

He squeezed her. "I'm so sorry, Alley—for everything."

She released him and knelt in the snow beside the stone. He looked barely alive. A tear rolled down her cheek. She brushed it away with her sleeve. "Don't be."

He whispered. "Were you able to train?"

She wiped away another tear. "A little."

He squeezed her fingers, his eyes sparkling behind his cracked bifocals. "Can you use your abilities now?"

Alley shook her head. "Not well."

Her father glanced back at Srira. She was descending the icy staircase. He whispered. "Get out of here. *Now.* I'll try to create a distraction. I think there's another passageway at the far end of this chamber."

Alley gripped his hand. "I'm not leaving you."

He pointed to a chain that led from his ankle to a ring attached to the stone block. "I'm not going anywhere, and you are too important to be captured."

The Queen's voice boomed through the cave. "Enough!" The reverberation of her voice shook icicles loose. They shattered on the cavern floor, sending shards skittering along the ground.

Alley stood and faced the Queen. "Free my father!"

Srira threw her head back and laughed. Her voice boomed inside Alley's mind. *You do not get to make demands of me, child! When Cynder is free, I will consider releasing the mage.*

Alley screamed in her mind. *Then I won't help you!*

Foolish girl. Do you think you have a choice? Now that I touched your skin, I have full access to your mind. And your mind is weak.

A crushing pain lanced through Alley's skull. She squeezed her eyes shut and fell to her knees.

She was in the clearing. A storm raged in the sky. The Queen stood in the middle of the glade amongst the flowers, her black dress blowing in the wind. The little girl's body floated rigidly in the air in front of Srira—her young eyes unblinking and filled with fear.

The Queen pulled a handful of flowers from the ground and breathed in their scent. She smiled wickedly through the blossoms and whispered to Alley, "You don't deserve such power."

Srira made a fist. Alley's skin burned as if it was on fire. She screamed. The Queen hissed, "This form offers other advantages. With these human hands I don't need you to guide the magic! I only need access to your mind."

Alley felt her dad's hand on her shoulder.

"Leave her alone!" He sounded a mile away.

Inside her head, the Queen's voice purred. *You will help*

me, or the pain you just experienced will be a shadow of what will follow.

Her father's voice was closer now. "I'll do it. Just leave her alone."

Alley gasped as the pain vanished. She opened her eyes and struggled to her feet. Srira stood at the foot of the steps —smiling. Alley wanted to tear the ceiling down on her head.

The Queen pointed a black clawed finger at her father. "Draw the weave, mage."

Alley turned toward him. "What's she talking about?"

Her father peered at her over the cracked rim of his glasses. "The weave to awaken Cynder. She needs both of us, Alley. My knowledge and your power."

Alley shook her head. "We don't have to do this."

Her father traced lines in the snow. "I can't watch you suffer."

Alley grabbed his wrist. "Stop! I've seen what she wants to—"

Pain ripped through her skull, darkening her vision. It was intense. She couldn't focus on anything else.

Her father yelled. "Stop hurting her! I said I'd help you!"

The pain subsided but didn't vanish. Alley opened her eyes.

Her dad reached out and touched her cheek. His voice was barely a whisper. "Please, let me finish."

She nodded. It was all she could do. Her father's frail

arms traced a complex pattern into the packed snow—a weave more complex than anything she'd yet seen. After several minutes he sat back. "It's done."

Alley felt a tugging sensation in her head. Energy was being drawn from her mind—a small thread being pulled through the eye of a needle. She tried to cut off the Queen's control, but the energy flowed out in greater and greater amounts like water through a crack in a dam. Golden tendrils of invisible light streamed from her body into the intricate weave in the snow. It was the same attack she'd felt during Bezo's training, when the seed had sucked at her mind. Except this time, she couldn't control anything. Srira was in her head.

It was getting harder to focus. Alley needed to know the truth. "Dad, was Mom a dracun?"

Her father nodded. "Alley, I'm sorry. There's so much I should have told you—"

She couldn't form words. He was holding out his hand. Alley reached for it to steady herself as power gushed from her body. The snow in the cavern swirled and snaked towards the mountain of ice at the opposite side of the chamber.

"—I loved your mother, but our love was forbidden by her parents"—he glanced at Srira—"and by the Council. We wanted to live in peace. We wanted a family. So we hid our union from the world."

A tremor shook the cavern. Waterfalls of snow rained

down. Cracks formed in the giant mountain of ice, large chunks tumbled away. Alley gritted her teeth. Beads of sweat collected on her brow and rolled down her cheek. It was happening—the vision was becoming real.

Her father continued, "Our research pointed to a way for us to finally have the child we'd always wanted. We discovered a way to combine human and dracun genomes—a fusion of science and magic. But the process required more than just our genes. We had to use two other species to bridge the differences in the genetic sequencing—"

What? Was she more than just human and dracun?

Hot sulfurous air rushed towards them from the massive ice mountain. A cascading chorus of grinding cracks echoed through the chamber as the giant pile rose upward. Her father glanced over his shoulder and talked faster. "We wanted you to have a happy, normal childhood. To learn what it was to be human before you discovered the other parts that make you unique. We tried to suppress your power to keep your grandmother from finding you—"

A low growl rolled through the hall sending an avalanche of snow crashing to the ground. Chunks of ice fell away from the huge pile, uncovering Cynder's enormous head. It was bigger than a house, with dark wide-set eyes sunk deep beneath bony spiked brows. Steam rose from huge nostrils on either side of a massive jaw covered with rows of sharp horns.

Her dad squeezed her hand. "Alley, the only thing that matters now is that you're my daughter and I love you."

She had more questions, but she couldn't make her mouth work.

Cynder's jaws opened as wide as a hanger bay door revealing wickedly sharp teeth the size of Christmas trees. His blue forked tongue looked like the tentacle of a sea monster.

And then he roared. Every muscle in Alley's body tightened. She'd never heard anything alive make a sound so loud. Her ears rang.

The ground beside Cynder's head cracked and gave way as he struggled to free one of his massive clawed arms from its icy prison. Power surged from Alley's mind. She watched as the Srira guided the energy, crafting complex weaves in the air with her taloned fingers. The tendrils pulled at the ice and rock that encased Cynder's body. The patterns Srira used to weave the flow were simple and elegant. Alley hated herself for admiring it.

The Queen's voice pierced Alley's mind. *Arise, my King!*

How long? Answered a deep, gravelly voice. It dripped with anger.

More than a century, my love.

The ground shook as Cynder roared. He slammed his head against a thick column of ice, shattering it into pieces. The heat from his breath washed over them like a hot furnace.

What of our children? Cynder's voice boomed in Alley's head.

Some live, most have been slaughtered by elves and men.

Cynder roared again. His front claw broke free of the ice like an uprooted tree. He breathed heavily from the struggle to free his body. His scales ground together like huge stone plates. Alley could feel the Queen continuing to draw energy —breaking and loosening the ice around Cynder's massive form—using patterns that now felt familiar.

The dragon lowered its head to peer at them. *What is this? A meal after my long slumber?*

Smoke curled up from Cynder's nostrils as if bonfires blazed inside his skull.

A mage and his spawn. They are nothing.

MAGE?! Cynder roared.

She wanted to warn her father. The dragon curled back its lips and sucked air in from the room through its jagged teeth.

No! It was happening, just like in her vision. They were going to be burned alive, but Alley couldn't move or speak.

Her father put his hand on her shoulder and squeezed. "I love you, Alley. I always have." Then he pushed.

Alley felt her body falling backward. She saw her father turn towards Cynder and raise his palm. The dragon's jaws opened, its dark teeth were back-lit by white-hot flames rushing upward from its belly.

Alley heard her father yell as his hands made a complex

motion in the air. The pattern was new, but she recognized certain elements of it. The wall of flame rolled toward them, turning the snow to steam in slow motion.

She wanted to reach out to her father, but the fire was too fast. Within seconds, it engulfed him, turning his body into a dark spot in the white heat. The flames surrounded her—the pain was unspeakable.

Then there was darkness and nothing.

— Arün —

Arün hung against his bonds. His wings sagged against the ground like a cape. His shoulders ached. Dried blood covered his arms. It had run down from the cuts on his wrist where the rope had rubbed his skin raw. It didn't bother him now. His hands had gone numb. At least the view was good. The pine trees in the valley were beautiful. Beyond, the mountains stretched away until they were swallowed by the clouds. The sun had dipped below the horizon, filling the cave with deep shadows. Alley, Nadja and Elek were out there somewhere. Arün looked up at his numb hand. It was still clenched in a fist around the locket.

An explosion shook the cave sending a surge of adrenaline through his body. It had been close. His heart raced. The noise would bring the dracun back. He held his breath and strained to hear the familiar click of their talons on the cold stone.

Minutes passed. Nothing.

Just the wind whistling up from the valley floor.

Wait. Were those footsteps? Someone running?

Not dracun. They were getting closer.

The sound echoed off the walls of his prison.

Then he heard Nadja's voice. "Arün!"

He turned his head, squinting out of the one eye that wasn't swollen shut. Was it really Nadja? It was hard to see in the fading light. She stood in front of him. An angel dressed in grimy white, standing in a small pool of green light from her glowing scryth. Her blond hair was a wild mess tossed around by the wind. He couldn't tell what emotion was on her face. Relief? Fear? Concern?

She reached a hand up to touch his cheek. "My God, what did they do to you?"

He managed to smile even though the effort sent a wave of pain through his face. "Took you long enough." His voice came out rough and croaky.

"Hold still. I'll cut you down." She slid her blade against the thick rope severing the twisted fibers. His arm fell like a dead weight. She started on the second rope. Blood rushed down his veins sending pinpricks of pain into his hand. It felt good.

"How did you find me?"

"The milkstone, but you aren't the reason I'm here. There's an EMP device somewhere nearby. We have to find and disarm it."

"An EMP? For what?"

"The Obsidian plan to use it to knock out our defenses before they attack the city. They're trying to free one of the Banished. If that EMP weapon is activated the military won't be able to help us."

Her blade cut through the second rope. Arün's other arm dropped to his side. He sat down as Nadja sawed at the ropes that bound his ankles.

Arün looked out over the mountains. "So, that's why they wanted Alley." He'd never been to the prison, but he'd heard the stories about the Banished. It would take powerful magic to free one of the dragons—the same kind of power that coursed through Alley.

Nadja finished freeing his legs. "Let's hope she's not helping them. They've violated every breeding law we have. I used all the explosives in their nest."

"What? A nest? Here?"

Nadja stood. "We don't have much time before the charges go off, but it might be long enough to find the EMP."

Arün looked up at her. "I'm sorry. Give me a second. I'll be ready to go." He laughed to himself. Ready to go. That was funny. He needed a hospital.

He had to use his right hand to pry open the fingers of his left hand. The milkstone locket stuck to his flesh where the blood had dried. He peeled it out of his palm and pulled the chain around his neck.

Nadja gasped, "No—"

Arün looked up at the sound of her voice. *No?* Why would she say that? Nadja backed away, her blade pointed at him.

"No. no. no." He realized where she was staring—at his wings.

Arün held up a hand even though it sent pain through his shoulder. "Wait. I can explain."

Nadja shook her head as she backed away to the open mouth of the cave.

"It's not what you think, Nadja. I'm not one of them."

She waved her knife at him. "I trusted you, Arün." Tears welled up in her eyes.

He clutched at his bruised chest. "The Mages did this to me. They made me like this."

"Those are dracun wings, Arün! You're a dracun!" She jabbed her blade in his direction to emphasize each of her words.

"I'm human, Nadja. At least most of me. And I'm your partner!"

"I don't know what you are, Arün. All this time—you lied to me. What else have you lied about?" Nadja backed up all the way to the edge of the drop-off.

"Nothing." It came out as almost a whisper. It was happening again. This time it was Nadja, not Lyla, his fianceé, standing near the edge of a cliff. Another person in his life unable to accept this part of him.

"I don't believe you!" yelled Nadja. "How do I know you aren't the dracun that killed my family?!"

"I'm not a dracun, Nadja!"

"I don't believe you!"

"I'm sorry I never told you. After what happened to your family—I was afraid you wouldn't understand."

Nadja paced back and forth along the edge of the cliff. Arün struggled to stand. His wings flared outward as he tried to gain his balance.

She turned toward him. Her face wrinkled in disgust as she saw his outspread wings. "You're right. The Mages are responsible for all of this."

"Nadja, please. You said we didn't have much time."

"The Mages have to be stopped. Look at what they have done. To you. To our world. Someone has to end it."

"Nadja, what are you saying?"

"It doesn't matter. I have to go."

"What? Where?"

Nadja looked at her wrist. "Five minutes before the explosives go off. I hope you can find the EMP and disarm it."

"Nadja, wait."

"I want to believe you, Arün. That you aren't one of them, but I—I can't."

"Nadja, please. I'm sorry I didn't tell you."

"I am too." She turned her back to him, stepped off the edge of the precipice and plummeted from view.

Arün gasped and scrambled across the cold ground

ignoring the pain it caused him. He reached the edge and peered down at the valley floor hundreds of feet below. Old memories of Lyla's broken body splashed on the rocks overlaid themselves over his vision. Far below there were only smooth drifts of snow. His one good eye caught movement near the mouth of the valley. He squinted. Tension left his muscles. Nadja was gliding over the tree tops under the white silken canopy of a tactical parachute. He watched her until she disappeared around the edge of one of the craggy ridges.

A rumble shook the cave knocking chunks of rock loose. Had five minutes passed? Another explosion rocked the mountain. Screams of enraged dracun echoed up from the tunnels. Arün pushed himself off the cold stone and searched for something to protect his chest from the harsh mountain air. The tatters of his shirt lay in the snow. He picked it up and pulled it over his head. Another explosion rattled his teeth.

The cries of the dracun were getting closer. He'd never find the device before the dracun found him, but he might be able to rescue Alley before she could be used to free one of the Banished. Arün opened the locket. The milky surface showed Alley was somewhere toward the east, the same direction as the ancient prison under the mountain.

It had been decades since he'd last flown. Arün moved the wings on his back flexing them to try to remember the motion. It was strange but familiar. A dracun roared. It was close. There was no time for more practice. He leaped off the cliff.

Cold air filled his wings as he dropped towards the forest. The muscles in his back screamed in pain as he beat his wings to gain altitude.

Arün cleared the treetops and glimpsed hundreds of distant city lights, a welcome reminder of civilization. They burned amber and gold in the dim half-light filtering through the dense cloud ceiling. He considered flying towards them to find a hospital and a phone to contact the Council, but that would just take him further from Alley.

As he banked eastward to find her, the city lights winked out.

The Obsidian had triggered the EMP.

37

AFTERMATH

ALLEY

A*lley.*

The distant voice awoke her from the darkness.

Cold flakes tickled her face. Her eyelids fluttered opened. Snow fell towards her through a gaping hole in the icy ceiling. The cavern was empty.

Everything was quiet.

Alley pushed herself up. Her coat was singed, tattered and dusted with a fine layer of snow. The memory of her father silhouetted against a ball of fire filled her mind.

Her stomach clenched. Had Cynder killed him?

The slab of stone where he'd sat was covered in white. Alley pushed herself forward dreading what she might find. She ran her hand through the cold dusting. Her fingers closed around ash. It stained the snow gray as it passed between her fingers. Her hands trembled. Her throat constricted. Cold tears traced trails down her cheeks

Alley squeezed her eyes shut. If she had just died in the flames with him, this nightmare would be over. Her hands dug deep into the ash. Each breath shook her body and brought fresh tears to her eyes.

A moan came from the far side of the slab.

Alley gasped. “Dad?”

She scrambled around the stone block. He was lying face down in the snow. His skin was red and peeling as if he’d been lying in the sun all day.

“You’re alive!”

He coughed and tried to sit up, but then sank back down. “Shield weave,” he coughed, “I used your energy to cast it.”

Alley turned him over. Half his face was burned. She whispered. “I thought I’d lost you.”

He coughed again, wincing in pain. “Not yet, Buttercup.” His eyes slid shut and his body went limp in her arms.

“Dad?” He was still breathing, but he’d passed out.

Alley wiped her cheek with the back of her hand and noticed for the first time that her nails had turned glossy black. The skin around the ends of her fingers had darkened too. At first, she thought it was just the ash staining her hands, but no, the intricate weave that had been under her nail beds had crept up her fingers, etching complex patterns into her skin. What did it mean? Had Cynder's flames caused the change?

A voice spoke in her mind. *Alley, are you there?*

Her heart jumped. She scanned the cavern. *Arün?*

I'm close. Are you okay?

Alley looked at her transformed hands. At her father's battered body. At the chunks of ice and rock that littered the cavern in the wake of Cynder's exit.

I'm alive, but my Dad is injured.

A shadow passed overhead. Silhouetted against the frosty clouds, the dark bat-like wings of a dracun beat against the falling snow. Her fist clenched. Unbidden, the clearing flashed through her mind. Dust from the blossoms filled the air. The power surged. She sent it outward, using her mind to mimic the patterns she'd watched the Queen use. Chunks of ice and rock skittered and danced on the cavern floor. Alley wanted to crush the dracun. The debris swirled as the thread of energy in her mind became an increasing flow. She channeled it into more of the rocks and ice, into the stone slab which scraped along the ground and joined the swirling cyclone of destruction.

Alley, it's me!

Arün's voice was in her head—so close he could have been standing next to her. The dracun dropped towards the cavern floor like a demonic angel. She focused her mind pulling everything in her grasp towards the creature.

Alley, stop!

It wasn't a dracun, it was Arün, but he had grown wings? She closed her eyes. In her mind, she went to the clearing, and held her breath—cutting off the flow of energy from the dust. The tornado of stone and ice fell crashing to the cavern floor.

Alley opened her eyes and realized she was also holding her physical breath. She let it out as Arün landed.

He looked terrible. One of his eyes was swollen shut and his clothes were a wreck. Where his skin showed through he was covered in cuts and bruises.

Arün staggered towards her and dropped to his knees. "Thank God, I found you. What happened?"

She bit her lip. Fresh tears welled in her eyes as she looked down at her father. "Cynder is free." She barely got the words out before her throat constricted. Her eyes watered. "I don't know if my dad is going to make it."

"I'm so sorry." Arün knelt and put his hand on her cheek. His touch sent soothing tingles of electric energy through her body. It eased the pain. She looked up into his face and watched as the swelling in his eye disappeared. The scratches and bruises on his body closed, healed and faded. The coldness was driven from her limbs. She was left feeling warm all over as if she'd been lying in the hot summer sand on a faraway beach.

Somehow, they were healing each other.

"Alley, are you doing this?" asked Arün.

She shook her head. "I think we both are."

Maybe her father could explain it. Arün released her as she stood. Except for his ruined clothes and dracun wings, he looked healed. She grabbed his arm. "We need to get my dad to a hospital."

Arün nodded. "The Council can help him, and we need to warn them about the dragon."

Alley bent down to lift her father. "Did you see Cynder or Srira?"

"No, but I can guess where they are headed."

Alley raised a questioning eyebrow.

Arün looked toward the sky. "To Seattle, to destroy the Council."

Her dad had lost so much weight it was almost no effort for her to lift him. "We have to warn them. There's a base in Bremerton and others further south. The military must have something capable of killing a dragon."

Arün shook his head. "I don't think they know what's coming. The dracun have triggered an electromagnetic pulse device. The entire area is in the dark. No electricity. No communications. The Council and Wardens may be the only ones who can defend the city right now."

Alley cradled her father. "Then we need to go. Can you carry us?"

"Yes, but not like this," answered Arün.

"Are you still injured?" asked Alley.

"No. I'm just not strong enough like this to carry you."

Alley tilted her head. "I don't understand."

"You will. Stand back." Arün dropped to his hands and knees. His body convulsed and expanded. Emerald green scales and black horns pushed through his skin. His body elongated, ripping apart his already tattered clothing.

Alley stepped backward.

Arün's face morphed into a reptilian muzzle. His hands expanded, and his fingernails grew into thick yellow talons. Moments later, where he had once crouched, stood a brilliant green dracun.

Alley gasped, "Could you always do that?"

Arün bent low so that she could climb between his shoulder blades, then spoke in her mind. *I had suppressed it for so long, I'd forgotten how.*

Alley laid her father across Arün's back and then pulled herself up. His scales were like polished jewels. She swung her leg across his spine, wedging herself between two of the large spikes that jutted from his back. He beat his wings and leaped towards the hole in the ceiling. Alley felt her stomach lurch. She held her father to keep him from slipping and squeezed her legs against Arün's hide. The cavern floor fell away as they climbed into the sky. Moonlight permeated the clouds. The ground below was black except for places where fresh snow reflected some dim light.

Alley marveled at the scales on Arün's back. He could transform. Somehow, they were alike, but how much alike? He didn't have her abilities, but did she have his? The thought of changing her body into something not human made her shudder. Dad had said that she was only partly human. What did that mean?

What other blood besides dracun and human ran through her veins? She glanced at her glossy black nails, at the darkened skin around her fingers formed by the strange weaves that had grown into her skin. She was changing but in a different way.

Wind whipped her face, but this time she didn't feel cold. Where she gripped Arün's back the connection between them sent waves of warmth through her body. She watched the plated scales on his back glide over one another as his massive muscles contracted, pushing his huge wings through the winter air.

She reached out with her mind. *How did you forget how to transform?*

It's been a long time. It's not like riding a bicycle. It takes practice.

Alley squinted. *But you just did it?*

When the Obsidian were beating me, something in my mind snapped. Once I felt my wings, I remembered the rest. But, I'm not sure if remember how to go back.

Maybe the Mages can help? she said.

Arün sighed. *Maybe. Nadja saw me half-shifted. If we make it out of this, I need to find her. Her family was killed by dracun. I need her to understand that I'm not one of them.*

They were flying a few hundred feet above the tree tops. Everything was dark. No street lamps. Alley heard a dog barking. There were cars stalled on the roads—sounds of people shouting. She checked her dad's pulse and relaxed when she felt the gentle rhythm of his heart. She thumped Arün's back. *How much farther?*

Not long, he answered.

She spoke in her mind. *There's been no sign of Cynder. Maybe they went somewhere else.*

Arün replied. *I wish you were right—look towards the horizon.*

A flickering orange glow lit the clouds ahead of them.

Seattle was ablaze.

38

THE NEEDLE

ALLEY

They approached the burning city, skimming low over the rooftops of Fremont and Queen Anne. Green lighting laced across the sky arcing from the Space Needle to the tops of the skyscrapers in downtown Seattle. The city was ringed in fire. Flashes of green lightning and flames illuminated flocks of dracun battling in the air. Fireballs shot between the creatures, splashing onto the sides of buildings and down into the bowels of the city. Where were Cynder and Srira? Arün tucked in his wings and took them lower, angling towards the Needle.

Alley's muscles clenched as a bolt of green lightning cracked into the ground near them. "Where is that coming from?!" she yelled.

Magic defense grid. It was designed to protect the city from a dracun uprising. Arün replied in her mind.

She hadn't noticed before, but the green bolts were hitting some of the dracun in the sky, knocking them into buildings and sending them tumbling to the streets. Arün swooped upward toward the disk-shaped top of the Space Needle. His claws gripped the steel decking.

Opal dracun perched along the edge of the observation platform. An armed warden sat in a saddle atop each one. As soon as the wardens noticed them, they raised their weapons.

Arün spoke in Alley's mind again. *You'll probably need to do the talking here. The guy with the scars is named Trusk. He's the ranking Warden.*

Great, she thought and then raised her hands and yelled, "We're friends!"

The warden named Trusk had jet black hair that was graying at his temples. Three deep scars crossed the side of his face leaving furrows in his stubble. He looked at her down the barrel of his gun. "Who are you?"

"My name is Alley. This is my father, Benjamin Ward." A lump formed in her throat as she looked at her dad's limp form. She choked it down. "He's hurt. I need to get him help."

Trusk's eyes flicked to her father's prone form—recognition flashed across his face. He motioned for the others to lower their guns. "You found him!" He waved to a woman. "Beth, tell Brody, that part of Nadja's team made it back! And contact Rakman. Tell him that Alley rescued Ben." He pointed at a man, "Marc, bring me one of the healing drinks!"

The wardens scattered around the platform, running to carry out the orders. Bright bolts of magical electricity crackled and exploded above their heads. Alley blinked. Some of the dracun leaped off the Needle and raced towards the city as others swooped up wounded from the battle. A group of wardens rushed to help the new arrivals. They applied salves to the wounds of both the dracuns and their riders, passed reloaded weapons to them and gave them a liquid potion to drink. It was like watching a pit crew at a car race. As soon as they were done the riders launched skyward to rejoin the battle.

Arün, what if we can't stop the Obsidian? asked Alley.

They will conquer this region and then expand their territory.

The wardens returned. One of them handed Alley a bottle with a sparkling liquid inside and applied cream to her father's burned skin. Beth handed a scrap of paper to Trusk. He glanced at it and his brow furrowed. "Rakman says you can help us?"

Alley slid off Arün's back. "Maybe. But I need to help my dad first." She unscrewed the bottle and tilted her father's head up so she could pour some of the fluid into his mouth. He coughed and his eyes fluttered.

Trusk eyed the battle and then looked at Alley. "Rakman instructed me to brief you. We lost power across the region about an hour ago—some kind of high-power electromagnetic pulse weapon. It sends out a wave every few minutes. We've tried firing up backup generators, but they keep getting fried. The Obsidian attacked after the first outage. The defensive grid is barely holding them off. We're outnumbered at least four to one. They've killed hundreds of civilians already. About a half-hour ago, things got worse. A dragon showed up. One of the big ones. He swept flame around the city and destroyed a few blocks before he headed across the Sound. Our guess is he's attacking the military bases and will be back. We need to be ready. The Grid doesn't seem to phase him, and he shrugs off conventional firearms. We need something more powerful. They said you could stop him?"

"Maybe," Alley replied and it was a big maybe. She wasn't a hero. The wardens on the platform had fear in their eyes. These people had pledged their lives to protect humanity from the dracun, but they weren't equipped to do anything about Cynder. Could she? He was huge. Massive. A spike of fear stabbed her in the chest. Cynder could crush her in his mouth like a piece of candy. If the Queen took control of her mind, she would be helpless.

Her father raised his head. The salve the warden had applied had healed his burned skin. "Where are we?" he croaked.

Alley helped him sit up. "The Space Needle. Cynder and Srira are attacking the city."

Her father took the bottle from her and gulped down the rest of the drink. Alley breathed a sigh of relief. Except for his singed mustache, he was almost his old self. Unfortunately, the potion had no effect on his crippled legs. He shifted himself on Arün's back. "We need to stop them."

A roar split the air like a clap of thunder.

Alley cringed. A swimming pool sized fireball raced towards them from out of the clouds. The dracun riders dove away from the platform as the far side of the sky deck was splashed with flame. She could hear the screams of wardens bathed in fire.

Alley, we have to go! Arün's voice yelled in her mind.

"Get my dad out of here! Get him to the Council!" she screamed back. Her eyes watered from the smoke.

Her father yelled. "No, we go together or not at all!"

"Arün, get him out of here!" Alley cried. She'd rescued him and now he was already trying to put himself in danger again.

Arün shook his scaled head. *Get on, Alley!*

Cynder burst through the low clouds. He beat his enormous wings as he landed on the Space Needle, fanning smoke across the platform. Alley stumbled as the tower creaked and bent under his massive weight. Bolts of lightning shot into his thick scaled hide with no effect. Srira stood between two of the immense horns on Cynder's skull.

Blood surged through Alley's body as her heart beat faster. He was too big. In the cavern with half his body encased in ice, his head had been as big as a house. His full size was terrifying. How could she hope to stop him? She tried to go to the clearing in her mind, but fear kept it just out of reach.

The Queen called down from atop Cynder's head. "Child, I'm so pleased that you survived that unfortunate accident. Join us in bringing freedom to our clan."

"You're killing innocent people!" yelled Alley.

"Don't speak of innocence! These humans just killed thousands of our children!"

Alley had no idea what Srira was talking about.

The Queen continued, "You are a pawn in a game you do not understand." Srira pointed at her father. "These mages are beyond evil. Did they tell you why they agreed to imprison us on this world?"

Her father yelled. "We were sparing your lives!"

The Queen's face contorted with rage. "You discovered that our bodies produce a compound that regenerates tissue. You wanted yet another path to immortality!"

Arün broke into her mind. *Alley, don't listen to her!*

The dracun riders regrouped and banked back toward the Needle.

Alley turned to her father. "Is that true?"

He glared at the Queen. "She twists the truth. We did not want immortality for selfish reasons. We needed more time to continue our work—work to benefit humanity."

Alley shook her head. "But why did you need the dracun?

I thought the Mages' magic was fueled by pixie dust?"

Her father's face looked weary. "It's complicated. The—"

Srira cut him off. "They do not trust the pixies. They exiled us here so they could study us! Experiment on us! Find ways to extract our magic in case the pixies ever betrayed them. You do not understand the things that they have done!"

Her dad yelled. "I loved your daughter! We wanted nothing, but peace between our people. She wouldn't have wanted you to do this!"

"She was a traitor!" The Queen's voice raised in pitch.

Alley grabbed at her dad's arm. "Dad, what are you doing? You're making things worse!"

Her father's face turned red. "Tell her, Srira! Tell your granddaughter how you had her mother murdered!"

"What?" Alley turned to face the Queen.

Srira sneered. "Child, your mother betrayed us. Betrayed her own father! For a"—she hissed at Alley's dad—"human."

Cynder roared. The sound sent a spike of adrenaline through Alley's body. This was spiraling out of control.

Alley's dad yelled. "You'd all be dead if it weren't for Laura and you repaid her kindness by having her killed!"

"You should have died too! You stole her from us! Turned her against her own kind!" Srira screamed back.

Cynder's chest rumbled. Light leaked from between the gaps in his massive teeth as he sucked in a lungful of air.

Alley felt a spike of pain in her mind. The Queen's voice

echoed in her head. *This time your father will pay for what he did to our family.*

"Dad! Go!" Alley barely got the words out before pain made her collapse to her knees. *Arün, she'll kill him, go!*

Srira pulled tendrils of energy out Alley's mind. She watched as the Queen willed the energy into a complex weave that encased Alley's body in a capsule of invisible golden energy. She felt herself float into the air—could feel how Srira manipulated the power to move her body.

Arün dove off the platform. His voice filled Alley's head. *The tallest building over there—the Columbia Center. I'll bring your dad there and be right back!*

She screamed in her mind. *Don't come back! It's too dangerous!*

Alley glided past Cynder's head—past a chin covered in gnarled horns. Past jagged teeth where a wave of heat and embers assaulted her lungs. Everything in her body screamed to run. To find a small dark hole and hide. It had to be the way a mouse felt in the presence of an eagle. His body was covered with huge jagged scales that reminded her of giant slate patio stones. They had ice-caked grooves and patterns. *Weaves.* When she was level with the bridge of his nose, she saw the Queen, standing on the crown of his head. The horns that sprouted from her skin had grown longer, sharper. Her scaled black gown whipped in the winter air.

Cynder's gravelly voice boomed in her head. *Granddaughter. Now you will learn what it means to have power.*

39

PURSUIT

ALLEY

Srira open her hand and Alley's body shot toward her through the air. The Queen's taloned fingers clamped around Alley's neck. She pushed Alley to her knees and whispered, "I warned you that death comes to those who oppose me."

Cynder crouched and leaped into the sky. Alley grasped at the armored scales atop his head. Her stomach heaved as his enormous wings churned the air pushing them upward one second and then dropping them down the next.

They flew toward downtown Seattle, chasing Arün's fleeing form. Green lightning arced through the air and struck the spikes on Cynder's spine. It had no effect.

Arün landed on the roof of the Columbia Center.

wardens swarmed him, lifting her father from his back and carrying him out of view.

Cynder angled towards a nearby building and landed on its roof, shattering glass, masonry, and cement as his claws dug into the seven hundred foot highrise.

A ghostly blue mist rose from the roof of the Columbia Center and coalesced into the giant head of a sharp-featured man with spectacles. Leopold Rakman. His voice reverberated off the cavern between the skyscrapers. *"You have violated the Mage Laws! You have violated the Ash War peace terms! If you surrender now, we will spare your clan."*

Cynder let out a deafening roar. His voice thundered in her head. *MURDERERS!*

Srira yelled back. "It is you who will surrender, or we will tear this city to the ground and lay waste to your people!"

Oh no. No, she thought. Alley tried to concentrate. She had to get Srira out of her head. If she could get a hold of the energy, she could stop this.

The Queen's grip on her neck tightened. *What are you doing, child?* she hissed in Alley's mind.

The ghostly face above the Columbia Center laughed. "You were powerless against us in the Ash War. What makes you think you can stand against us today?"

The Queen's voice whispered in Alley's head. *Now we tear their castle to the ground.*

No. Her father was in there!

Alley gasped as the Queen's presence invaded her mind.

Srira dug the talons of her hand into Alley's shoulder. She screamed. The Queen's claws had pierced the thick wool of her coat and cut into her skin. Daggers of pain shot through her neck. "The Mages will appreciate a demonstration of your abilities."

The Queen reached out with her other hand and clenched it into a fist. The ghostly head evaporated as if blasted by a gust of wind. The glass windows of the Columbia Center shattered into millions of fragments and rained down on the street below. Srira twisted her fist. The entire building bent and buckled. Arün dove away and disappeared into the darkness.

Alley screamed and tried to pull away. "Stop! Please!" This was what the Queen had shown her in the vision.

Dad!

He would die if Srira didn't stop.

Alley was back in the clearing. The Queen was there and had the little girl captive again, floating in the air. Alley grabbed a broken branch at the edge of the forest and charged at Srira. She swung the branch like a bat, striking the Queen in the leg. Srira gasped and dropped to a knee. The little girl's body collapsed onto the ground kicking up a cloud of dust from the flowers. Alley swung the branch again, this time at Srira's face. The Queen's hand shot up and snapped the branch into splinters. "You are weak, child," she said.

Srira sent tendrils of power outward, wrapping it through the fabric of the building. She pulled it tighter and tighter, driving fissures and cracks between steel and stone. Alley watched the Queen manipulate the energy with horrified fascination. There was a beauty to the channel and flow of the power, but she had to make it stop. She tried to pull away from the Queen, but her grip was like iron.

The Columbia Center toppled in a screeching cloud of dust and rubble.

"Nooo!" The scream twisted Alley's gut.

A wave of sorrow and anger crashed over her.

Srira had killed her father.

She'd killed her mother.

She'd taken everything.

A wave of heat and smoke assaulted Alley as Cynder blasted the place where the building had been with a searing jet of flame.

Tears streamed down Alley's face.

The Queen laughed as she extended her hand towards another building and squeezed it into a fist. Alley felt power surge through her mind again. Ribbons of energy drove into the ground below the building and wrapped around the basement, forming lacy patterns of gold. The highrise screeched upward from its foundation, then slammed into the ground. A shock wave rippled through the structure. It toppled sideways, collapsing into a skeletal pile of girders and masonry.

Cold tears flowed down Alley's cheeks. *No more!* So many

dead. She tried to crawl away. The Queen's painful grip tightened on her shoulder.

Alley, hold on! It was Arün's voice. He was close.

She closed her eyes, blocking out the devastation—blocking out the place where father's body lay under a mountain of rubble.

There was a rush of wind, an inhuman scream, then pain in her shoulder as Srira's talons were ripped away. The Queen's presence vanished from her mind. Alley turned to see Arün's emerald form rocketing into the gap between two buildings. Srira's black gown flapped in the wind as she hung limply in Arün's claws. He climbed and headed south away from the city.

Alley stumbled as Cynder's head rose and roared at Arün. *BRING HER BACK!*

The dragon lurched skyward. Alley wrapped her arms around a horn on Cynder's skull. His massive wings carved billowing curls of air through the smoke and dust as he struggled to gain altitude and catch up to Arün's fleeing form.

Arün! Could he hear her at this distance? She wanted him to drop the Queen—let her body shatter on the ground. Srira needed to pay for what she'd done.

Snow fell and the wind picked up as they flew over Renton and sped southeast. Alley touched her throbbing shoulder and felt sticky wetness. *Blood.* At least she could still move her arm.

There had to be a way stop Cynder. She concentrated and felt the energy flow from the clearing in her mind. It was easier to draw out now—almost like exhaling. She sent tendrils of force outward. It recoiled against Cynder's scales. Whatever magic protected him from the lightning also prevented her from attacking him with the power. Cynder sent a ball of flame rocketing ahead of them. For an instant, Arün's emerald-scaled body was illuminated as he banked and rolled out of the way of the fireball, then he was swallowed by the darkness. He was still clutching the Queen.

Alley closed her eyes and tried to forget that she was riding atop a monster. She delved into her mind and breathed in more energy. Alley reached towards the ground—the tendrils of power trailed along the surface of the earth like thousands of fingers brushing through loose sand. She could feel rock, dirt, buildings, and machinery sliding past. Could she grab hold of any of it?

Alley wrapped ribbons of energy around a huge rock, but the tendrils stretched thin and snapped as they flew past. She gritted her teeth and pounded her hand on Cynder's scales. He probably didn't even realize that she was still on his head—or didn't care. If she could slow him down, she could grab hold of something on the ground and use it as a weapon against him.

Another fireball rocketed from Cynder's jaws and shot towards Arün. Alley choked as smoke blew in her face. Arün rolled, this time dodging left as the flaming liquid shot past.

The terrain below was dark, but Alley knew Arün was luring Cynder away from the city. He climbed into the snowy clouds. Cynder followed. Mist engulfed them. The only light came from the dull glow that leaked from the dragon's maw. The creature sprayed a fountain of fire, lighting up the clouds.

They were getting close to the slopes of Mt. Rainier. If they hit the side of the mountain, she'd be thrown from Cynder's head. She might have a better chance further down the dragon's back. Alley climbed back toward the place where Cynder's wings joined with his massive body. The armor plates on his back shifted and compressed as he flew. She made her way from spike to spike along the dragon's spine, hugging each one as if it were a giant tree trunk. The mist was thick. It felt like wandering in a forest at night in the middle of an earthquake.

In the darkness, Cynder's massive wings rose and fell to either side. Alley clung to a frost encrusted spike and tried to calm her breathing. The thin layer of ice under her hand gave her an idea. She'd been worried about hitting the mountain, but maybe that was what she needed to stop Cynder. The patterns she had watched the Queen utilize to manipulate the snow and ice in the dragon's prison had been simple enough. She could even see a way to reverse them.

Alley drew energy out of the clearing in her mind and sent chutes of power outward into the clouds, forming millions of tiny ice crystals. She pulled them towards

Cynder's head. In a matter of seconds, his skull was caked in thick sheets of ice.

He roared in her mind. *TRAITOROUS, CHILD!*

Cynder tried to slow his forward momentum. Alley pulled more crystals toward his body, coating his wings in dense layers of snow and frost. Her stomach rose into her chest as the dragon plummeted from the sky.

They fell fast. Cynder shot a fireball—probably in an attempt to see what lay ahead. The flames splashed against the nearby forested mountainside. The ground was only a few hundred feet away—no time to react. Cynder's head plowed into the side of the craggy peak and his entire body crumpled as the force of the impact traveled up his spine.

Alley was thrown from his back. She closed her eyes as she pin-wheeled through the cold night air.

40

CYNDER

ALLEY

Alley waited to hit the mountain, but the impact never came. She opened her eyes. Small chunks of ice and rock tumbled around her. She was encased in a luminous web of golden energy. It held her twenty feet off the ground. It was beautiful—like being an astronaut in zero gravity.

Alley recognized the pattern. It was the same one Srira had used on the Needle to float her into the air. Somehow, she'd reformed the weave to protect herself. She pushed the web outward with her mind as she remembered Srira had done and rose higher in the air. Alley used the energy to tug at the ground on her left and felt herself slip sideways. She pulled at the ground in front of her and slid forward. Despite the grief and anger, it brought a small smile to her face.

But where was Cynder? Alley spun herself around. The

nearby forest was ablaze from his last fireball. The flames cast flickering shadows across a hulking hill of glistening scales. The dragon had plowed a deep furrow into the mountain. The nearby pine trees looked like small shrubs next to his body.

Alley drifted closer. It was hard to tell if he was dead in the orange glow of the forest fire.

Cynder's spiked tail swept out of the smoke and slammed into the web of energy.

Alley went sailing across the valley. She sent frantic forks of power outward trying to slow herself. The web fragmented and she plowed into a bank of snow.

Alley lay in the drift for a moment, the cold seeped into her head and hands. She'd just been hit by Cynder—and survived! Her hands grew colder as she gripped fistfuls of snow and sat up. Her mouth pressed into a tight line. She had to stop him.

Alley reached into her mind. The current of energy opened. She wove the invisible cocoon of power around her body and rose out of the snow. Her coat and hair floated as if she were underwater. Cynder and Srira had declared war on her world—on her family. Alley clenched her fists and glided back towards the crackling flames.

A roar echoed across the valley. A massive fireball came racing at her through the darkness. Alley raised her hand, her mind quickly formed the shield weave that she'd seen her father make. The flames splashed around her like ocean waves breaking on a rock.

Alley felt calm. Creating the weaves was easy—like muscle memory—like they had become a part of her body. That was it! She looked at her hands, at the weaves that blackened her nails and now crept up her hand like a strange tatoo. Her body had absorbed the weaves she'd seen others perform—made them a part of her in the same way they'd been a part of the dragon's rib she'd seen in the Dead Lands. And now her mind was instinctively channeling energy through them.

Alley propelled herself towards the burning forest. Cynder emerged from the wall of smoke. He was bigger than the Statue of Liberty. She didn't care.

You are not worthy of our clan! Cynder's voice boomed in her mind.

Alley spread her arms wide and sent tendrils of power deep into the ground, coiling around the roots of the surrounding pines. She clenched her hands and pulled upward ripping hundreds of trees from the icy mountainside. Pillows of snow slid from thousands of pine boughs as she thrust her hands towards Cynder. The trees arced forward like a volley of gigantic lances. They sailed through the air, pummeling Cynder's body, knocking him backward—piling onto his wings, pinning him to the ground. He thrashed knocking over more trees and kicking boulders loose from the mountain.

Alley sailed forward and sent energy out from each hand grasping two huge chunks of bedrock that Cynder had knocked loose. She cocked her right arm back and drove it forward, sending one of the giant boulders smashing into the dragon's head. Before he could react, she hooked her left arm around and hit him from the other side with the second boulder. Shards of stone flew as the rocks smashed against Cynder's scaled hide. Each hit sent a thundering echo reverberating across the mist enshrouded valley. Alley hit him again and again. The boulders crumbled into pieces. She had felt so helpless over the last few days—not now. Never again.

Cynder collapsed against the mountain, dark blood flowing from gashes in his body. Alley unwound the energy from the fragmented remains of the two boulders. They fell into the snow. She moved closer. Smoke and mist wrapped around the field of energy that held her in the air. Cynder's chest moved with shallow breathes. He was still alive. She steered clear of his tail and approached his head. Cynder's eyes were half closed and unfocused.

Grandfather, she whispered in her thoughts.

The dragon didn't respond.

I don't want to kill you. Alley unclenched her fists. *But I can't let you destroy my world.*

Cynder's eye blinked and pivoted to focus on her. *The Mages murdered our family,* Cynder's deep voice boomed in her mind. He struggled to unpin his wings.

Alley shook her head. *They could have killed you. They*

didn't. They allowed you to live—allowed your people to live among us.

They stole our freedom, and you think it an act of kindness. You are a fool, little girl.

Alley reached out with the power and pulled mist and snow towards Cynder. Frost form over his scales. Thick chunks of ice coated the dragon's body. He tried to break them loose.

What are you doing?

When the Mages find us, I will help them take you back to prison. She pulled more snow and ice toward the dragon.

Srira's voice hissed in Alley's mind. *No. You will not.*

Her connection to the power was cut off. The web of energy holding her in the air evaporated. Alley flailed her arms and legs as gravity pulled her down. Her foot twisted when she landed. Pain shot through her left leg. Alley tried to stand, but her ankle refused to hold the weight. She fell to her knee.

A dark form descended through the smoke and flames. Srira had changed. Her body was still human, but her arms and legs ended in massive black scaled claws. Huge glossy black wings held her aloft and pushed the smoke away in gusts as they beat the air and sent ripples through her black dress. Her face was barely recognizable. The horns along her forehead had extended into two-foot spikes. Her porcelain skin had peeled back in places exposing glossy black scales beneath. A long tail tipped with spikes whipped behind her.

Alley felt a tug in her mind as power was drawn out. The Queen raised one of her large black claws. The ice around Cynder's body cracked and shattered. She raised her other clawed hand. The remains of the pine trees that Alley had hurled at Cynder rose into the air. Srira flicked her wrist. The trees went flying out of sight into the darkness. Cynder pulled himself up shaking off snow and rock. The wounds on his body healed shut. His movements made the ground shake.

The Queen pointed at Alley. "Your power will help us claim this world."

Alley clenched her teeth. Adrenaline surged through her veins. "I won't help you anymore," she yelled.

Cynder lowered his head and blew a cloud of embers at her. *Then I will eat you.*

The Queen landed and walked toward Alley. *No. She will help us.*

A gust of cold air blasted down from the ridge line above them. Alley shivered. The sky was glowing. The sun would rise soon. Her fingers were going numb. She jammed them into the pockets of her tattered wool coat. Alley felt the rough husk of the seed she had picked up when she'd been training with Bezo. *The seed.* A plan started to form in her head. She needed to distract the Queen long enough to grab a thread of energy.

Srira plucked a vial from the folds of her dress and sent it floating toward Alley. "Drink," she commanded.

"What is it?" asked Alley.

The Queen smiled. Her teeth had become more pointed and vicious looking. "Espresso."

The tiny vial hovered in front of Alley's face. She grabbed it from the air. Espresso. She'd be cut off from the power. Srira would be free to use it without having to worry about her fighting back. If she drank it, there would be no chance for her plan to work. Alley twisted the top off the vial and turned it upside down. The espresso poured out, but just before it hit the snow, it clumped together into a wobbling sphere of floating liquid.

The Queen raised a dark claw and pointed at Alley. "Drink it."

The blob of espresso floated up to Alley's face. She pressed her lips closed, but then her jaw opened against her will. *Get out of my head!* Alley screamed in her mind.

The liquid floated into her mouth. She could taste the sweet bitterness on her tongue.

No! she thought.

Her mouth closed on its own. Alley pressed her tongue against the back of her throat trying to keep the espresso from forcing its way down.

A roar split the air as a jet of blue flame blasted the Queen from the side. A second later a flash of emerald rocketed out of the mist.

Arün!

He slammed into Srira, plowing her through the snow

and rock.

The wall in Alley's mind weakened for an instant. She had control of her body again. She spit out the coffee and grabbed hold of a thread of energy. Alley sent power flowing into the seed in her pocket. It sucked at the energy—drawing it from her in greater and greater waves.

Cynder roared at Arün and rose on his hind legs.

The story Bezo had told Alley, about how her father had once killed a dangerous beast with a needle, had given her an idea. Alley sent the seed sailing like an arrow towards the dragon's open maw. It flew past his teeth and down his throat. She felt the seed continue to draw energy from her mind. Alley couldn't see it anymore, but she knew it was growing just as the other seed had done during her training.

Arün grappled with the Queen. Srira's face twisted and deformed into a snout. Her skin ripped away. Her neck elongated, and her body gained size as it transformed. They slashed at each other with razor sharp talons. The Queen opened a huge gash in Arün's side that sprayed blood onto the snow. He fell to the ground and tried to roll away. The Queen crushed his head into a drift with one of her massive taloned claws. Alley felt her mind cut off from the power again. Srira no longer looked human at all. Her entire body had transformed into a glistening black dracun as large as a school bus.

Cynder staggered. He clutched a massive paw to his chest and looked down at Alley. *What have you done?*

Alley cried. "I'm sorry. You gave me no choice!"

The Queen released Arün's limp body and bounded across the snow toward the towering giant. *Cynder! What's wrong?*

The dragon convulsed and looked down at his massive clawed toes. They grew longer, sprouted roots, and burrowed into the frozen ground. His scales were turned to rough bark. As he struggled, his legs and tail stiffened and fused together into a single enormous trunk. He opened his jaw to roar and leafy branches erupted from his throat, then exploded into a wide canopy overhead. In a matter of seconds, his entire body had been transformed into an enormous oak tree. The Queen threw herself at the trunk and screamed.

Her head whipped around to focus on Alley. *You did this.*

"You started this war!" Alley yelled as she scrambled backward across the cold ground, dragging her injured foot. She glanced over at Arün's still form. His scaled body was half buried in blood-stained snow.

Srira stalked forward. *I was wrong to have let you live.*

The Queen reared up in front of Alley, spreading her enormous black wings. Alley held her breath. Srira was going to crush her.

Something huge dropped out of the sky and crashed into the ground behind the Queen throwing a spray of snow and dirt into the air. Alley's teeth chattered as the mountain shook from the impact. A giant metal monster rose from the crater. A Marionette. It leaped towards the Queen. A huge silver blade carved with glowing green runes slid out of the machine's arm, drove through Srira's back and exploded out of her chest. The wall in Alley's mind disappeared as the Queen's claws clutched frantically at the blade blossoming from her sternum. The skin around the metal smoldered and flaked away.

Srira's lavender eyes locked onto Alley's. For a moment, something burned inside Alley's brain—like a lump of hot coal had been placed there. The pain vanished, and Alley heard the low hiss of hundreds of voices in her head. *He is gone... He is dead... Who will protect us?.. Who has killed him?*

The Queen gasped above the murmur. *My granddaughter has killed your King!*

Magical fire swept outward from where the giant blade sprouted from Srira's chest. Her body turned to glowing charcoal. What was left of the Queen, crumbled into a smoldering pile of ash and embers. The Marion retracted the giant sword into its arm and powered down.

Alley sank into the snow.

Her parents were dead.

And now, her grandparents were dead too.

But, it was over.

A hatch opened high on the machine's shoulder and a familiar face emerged. Elek.

The flames in the forest were dying out. Plumes of smoke drifted into the sky. The horizon glowed brighter, glinting off the Marion's metallic form and Arün's green-scaled body.

Her stomach clenched. Alley pulled at the thread of energy in her mind and wove a web of invisible power around herself. Whispers filled her head. It felt like she was backstage listening to the murmur of an audience. What had Srira done to her? Was it the voices of the clan?

Alley rose into the air and floated to Arün. Lowering herself to the ground, she pushed the snow away from his snout. He was barely breathing. "Arün, stay with me," she whispered.

Alley pulled up the sleeves of her coat and hugged her bare arms around his neck letting the electrical energy course between them where their skin touched. She felt the pain in her shoulder and ankle disappear. The deep gashes in Arün's hide closed as if they were being zipped up. Fresh scales grew over the exposed flesh.

Arün stirred. His eye opened. *What—happened?*

Alley smiled and touched Arün's muzzle. "We won."

He looked up at the massive oak tree. *Where did that come from?*

"That's Cynder—what's left of him, anyway."

You did that? he asked.

She smiled at him. "I had help."

Alley heard approaching footsteps crunching through the snow. Elek and Bezo. Behind them, the sun peeked over the mountain ridge.

Elek jogged the last few feet. His hair was soaked with sweat and plastered to his forehead. "Two things, Al. First, when did you learn how to float? And second, are you sure that dracun is safe to be hugging?"

Alley stood and brushed snow off her knees. "It's okay—this is Arün."

Elek's brow furrowed. "How?"

She looked at Bezo. "It's something the Mages did to him."

The mage shook his head. "Don't look at me like that. I had nothing to do with it."

Alley hugged Elek. "Thanks for showing up when you did."

"Sorry it took so long, Al. After Bezo received the distress call from the Council, it took a while to get the Marion to a Caldrun so we could cross over"—Elek stepped back from her and pulled out the milkstone locket hanging around his neck—"If it weren't for this thing, I don't think we would have found you in time."

The sun rose higher bathing the valley in golden rays of light. Arün stood, shaking off the snow. Alley rested her hand on his scaled arm. "Bezo, can you help him change back?"

"In time," the mage scratched his beard, "right now there's a device somewhere inside Mt. Baker, guarded by hundreds of angry dracun. It needs to be shut down to restore power to the area." He pointed at Alley. "Are you and this warden up to the task?"

Arün's thoughts rumbled in Alley's head. *Let's turn on the lights.*

41

ASCENT

ALLEY

Mt. Baker loomed ahead. Sunlight sparkled on the lower slopes. The upper peak was shrouded in mist. The voices in Alley's head were getting louder—angrier. *She killed them... She is coming... She is close...*

The scales on Arün's back were cool against her hands as he glided through the morning air. His voice echoed in her mind. *We've killed their King and Queen. Don't expect a warm welcome.*

The murmurs in her head were making it hard to concentrate. *Arün, do you hear them?*

He beat his wings and angled towards a cave opening on the upper slopes. *No, what are you talking about?*

Alley tried to ignore the voices. It was like sitting in a

stadium. The din was distracting. *The clan. I think I can hear them—all of them.*

They landed on an icy rock shelf in front of the cave entrance. Fog shrouded the mountainside, turning the nearby trees into blurry smudges. Alley slid off Arün's back. Ice crunched under her feet.

Arün nudged her shoulder with his snout. *This is where they imprisoned me. There's a tunnel in the back that leads into the nest, but this is as far as I can go. The passageway isn't big enough for me.*

"How am I going to find the device?" Her voice sounded muffled in the fog.

It will be well guarded by Obsidian dracun. Follow the smell. You'll find them.

"We should have brought Bezo and Elek."

Someone had to notify the Council, and the city needs help to rescue survivors from the collapsed buildings. Besides, you don't need their help or mine—he snorted jets of steam into the foggy air—*not anymore.*

Alley hoped that was true. The cave behind her was dark. She sent invisible ropes of energy into the entrance. The voices grew silent in her head. Alley swallowed and took one last look at Arün's green eyes before stepping into the darkness.

The cave walls were covered in ice and frost. The floor was a mixture of frozen puddles and loose volcanic rock. Alley wrapped the dark wool coat around her body and used a few tendrils of energy to help stabilize herself. She sniffed the air and wrinkled her nose. There was an odor wafting down the tunnel. It was sweet and sickening, like the inside of a dumpster. It was the smell of rotting dead things. Her stomach heaved. *Smells lovely,* she thought.

Arün chuckled in her mind. *Leftovers. They don't cook their food.*

Awesome, she replied in her mind. The idea of accidentally stepping in rotting meat made Alley's mouth wrinkle. She wrapped herself in a bubble of energy and floated off the cave floor. Better. She felt safer in the bubble. More in control. Alley pushed herself deeper into the tunnel, sliding over the jagged rocks and ice. The last fragments of morning light faded away as she rounded a bend. The whispers in her head were gone. It was too quiet. They were waiting for her.

Why was she doing this alone? Her power had failed her so many times. What if there was another Obsidian dracun like Srira? Someone capable of reaching into her mind and stealing her power? She'd prayed for years that someday she would find a way to control the energy. Now she had the ability to use it for good, but she needed more time to learn how to guard it—to prevent others from taking what she'd struggled so long to understand and control. If she were cut off from her power here, she would be defenseless.

Arün? Alley held her breath hoping he was still close enough.

Silence.

She swallowed. Her mouth felt dry. There were people trapped under rubble—people dying. The city needed electricity to help them. Alley clenched her fists. Shimmering golden threads of energy pulsed around her in the darkness. Even if there were another dracun that could invade her mind, it would have to find her before she destroyed the device. She needed to move fast and stay hidden.

Alley slid forward, letting the golden cocoon of energy glide her over the rough walls and floor of the passage. The tunnel angled downward taking her deeper into the mountain. The rotting smell grew stronger. She tried to breathe through her mouth to keep from gagging on the stench. The air got warmer and humid as the tunnel brightened ahead.

The passageway opened into a long gallery with a vaulted ceiling. Huge gem encrusted pillars of black rock held the cavern roof aloft. Iron torches had been bolted into the rock walls and cast pools of sputtering orange light on the stone floors. Around the room, shadows danced next to piles of bones. Decaying remnants of meat and fur still clung to some of them.

A large shadow moved at the far end of the hall. *Welcome, Dama.* The voice echoed in Alley's head—a frail croak.

She gathered energy and sent it out along the floor of the cavern, grabbing chunks of rock and bones to defend herself.

I mean you no harm.

The shadow separated from the wall and limped into a pool of torchlight. It was an old dracun as big as a pickup truck. It looked starved and war-torn. Where its back right leg should have been was a scarred stump. Its right eye was an empty socket and what was left of its wings dragged on the ground behind it like a tattered blanket. Its body was crisscrossed with long-healed gashes revealing the gray skin beneath its worn black scales.

The dracun tilted its head sideways to look at her with its one milky white eye. *I hoped you would come.*

Alley pushed the bubble of energy outward, creating an invisible barrier between herself and the creature. "Who are you?" she asked.

It closed its eye and bowed. *I am called Malcore. I have served the clan rulers for centuries.*

"What do you want?"

The dracun made a wheezing sound. Its body shook. It was laughing. *The mantle has been passed to you, Dama. I am here to prepare you for Ascension.*

"There's a machine in this mountain that needs to be turned off. Help me with that or get out of my way," she said.

Malcore bowed his head. *In good time, Dama. There are certain formalities we must attend to first.*

"I don't have time for this." Alley tried to push the old dracun aside, but her tendrils of energy evaporated as they touched him.

You are powerful, Dama, but you are young. There are many mysteries you do not understand. I can help you, but only if you accept the mantle.

"I don't need your help." Malcore seemed to be resistant to the energy in the same way Cynder had been.

The power you wield is strong, but your mind is weak. I have seen it fail you. I have seen others take control. I can help you.

"Why would you do that?"

The old dracun wheezed. *It was my counsel that led your mother to your father. I helped her broker the peace that ended the Ash War.*

"You knew my mother?" asked Alley.

She was my great-great-grand niece. She was beloved by this clan—by me.

It was strange to think about the Obsidian dracun being family. They had killed people. Destroyed her home. "I don't trust you."

Malcore coughed. *I do not blame you. The Queen made this clan do horrible things in the name of justice.*

Alley nodded. Viktor had explained how the leaders could force their will on their clan. And she had first-hand experience now. But the Queen was gone. The Obsidian were free to make their own choices again. "What's their excuse now?" she asked. "Srira is dead. Why haven't they shut down the device?"

They are afraid, Dama. Afraid of the Mages' wraith. Afraid the clan will be wiped out because of the actions of Srira and Cynder—because of what the Queen forced them to do.

Alley shook her head. "I won't let them hurt you if you surrender."

I believe you. You are like your mother—more than you know. We need you, Dama. Help your people. Help your family.

Alley clenched her hands. "Turn the device off and I can help!"

Malcore wheezed again. *You can make that decree once the clan has recognized you as their leader. Are you prepared to ascend to the Throne?*

Alley ran her hand through her hair. She'd always said she wanted to use her power for good—to help save people. She had the chance now—the chance to prevent more pain and suffering. She was afraid, but it felt right—it felt like what her mother and father would have wanted. Tears welled in her eyes as she thought of their smiling faces. Her heart ached. They'd sacrificed everything to bring her into the world. Now she had the chance to make that sacrifice worth something. Was she ready to rule the Obsidian Clan? No, but the Obsidian were her extended family—her distant cousins, aunts and uncles. If she didn't protect them, there was a good chance the Council would send wardens to wipe them out.

Alley wished she had more time to think, but knew she would only search for an excuse to avoid following the path her heart was already pulling her toward. She nodded at Malcore. "I'm ready."

Murmurs and whispers exploded in her head.

The old dracun bowed. *I will escort you to the Ascension chamber.*

The dracun turned and limped toward the far end of the hall. Alley floated after him. The cavern ended in a massive rock wall split by a narrow vertical crack as wide as a person. Heat and light poured out of the tall opening. Alley lowered herself to the ground.

Malcore turned toward her. *Forgive me, but I must change form to proceed.* He walked behind a column as steam rose off his scales and his limbs began to shorten. When he emerged on the other side, his body had transformed into a pale, bald, old man. He'd donned a simple brown robe tied at the waist with a rope. An eye patch covered his right eye and he held a crutch under his right arm.

Malcore scratched at the stubble on his cheek. "I don't have the energy for anything more elaborate these days." He smiled at her. His teeth were black and crooked. "The chamber is this way. The clan is expecting us."

He shuffled into the hot crevice. Alley followed at a distance. They walked for several minutes, the whispers in her head grew louder. The air grew hotter with each step. They emerged onto a wide ledge overlooking an open space lit by orange light. Acrid fumes burned the inside of Alley's nose and swirled through the air like tormented spirits. In the shadowy heights, long stalactites hung down like giant teeth. Alley peered over the edge. Below burned a lake of magma. At the center of the lake, a massive stalagmite rose like a small three-story building. The top had broken off and toppled into the lake of fire creating a bridge to the tower island. At the top of the broken stalagmite, it was flat and at the center sat an empty chair carved from stone. The walls of the cavern were covered in glistening black. Thousands of dracun clung to the walls and perched on the surrounding ledges and spikes of rock. A shudder ran through her body as she remembered the vision she'd had of being chased by hordes of dracun.

"What is this place?" she asked.

"It's the Ascension chamber," Malcore gestured with a bony hand towards the island. "Once you have ascended and claimed your seat, it will be your throne room."

The cavern was making her sweat. Alley wove a layer of energy around herself to block out the heat.

"Dama, have the Mages told you what makes a dragon different from a dracun?"

"The Wardens said dracuns are baby dragons."

Malcore snorted. "I assure you I am no child and yet I have not become a dragon due to old age."

"Okay, enlighten me," she said.

"Any dracun can elect to evolve into a dragon."

"I don't understand. Why wouldn't all dracun choose to become a dragon?"

"Dragons are powerful and grow to an immense size. It is an honor to make this transition, but it is a path only a few can follow. A dracun needs the support of their clan to help them transform. A dragon is a protector of the clan, but they are also a burden. If there were more dragons, it would be too difficult to find adequate food and living space. It is a balance between survival and defense."

"Why are you telling me this?"

"All clan rulers undergo the rite of passage from dracun into dragon when ascending the Throne."

"What?"

Malcore looked at her with his one yellow eye. "You must ascend the Throne. It is the only way our clan will recognize you as their ruler."

"Will I transform into a dragon?"

Malcore bobbed his bald head. "Perhaps not, but dragon blood flows in your veins, Dama. If it were not so, we would not share the mind-bond."

Alley swallowed and looked at her hands. Hadn't she already transformed enough? The intricate black patterns that stained the ends of her fingers were evidence that something in her had already changed. She didn't want to lose any more of herself, but she couldn't let anymore people, whether they were human or dracun, die while she had the ability to prevent it. "Tell me what I need to do."

"Very well, Dama. Follow me."

Malcore led her down a narrow stone stairway towards the edge of the lake of lava. The heat coming off the magma made Alley feel like she was standing inside an oven. The stairs ended at the bridge leading across the lake to the island.

"You must go the rest of the way alone."

"This is it? I don't need to make a speech?"

"No words are necessary now. When you ascend to the Throne, your word will be Clan Law." The old man transformed back into a dracun and limped up the stairs.

The bridge was like a giant ice cream cone lying sideways, half submerged in molten rock. The narrow part touched the shore where she stood and widened as it got closer to the tower. The top surface was curved and sloped away towards the glowing crust of lava on either side.

It was at least a hundred yards to the base of the tower. Alley floated herself into the air and moved forward across the bridge. Dracun eyes watched her from every side. Their whispers echoed in her mind as if she were inside a monstrous cathedral. *Welcome, Dama... Welcome King Slayer... Welcome Protector...*

One of the dracun detached from the wall and swept downward on dark wings. It landed in the middle of the bridge. The creature's massive body cracked the stone and sent ripples through the magma. It glittered black with an orange stripe of scales running down its neck. Alley recognized him. It was the dracun that had brought her to the Queen.

Begone, pretender. I do not recognize your claim, it hissed in her mind.

Malcore had to have known she would be challenged. He should have warned her. Alley clenched her jaw. "Get out of my way!" she yelled.

You are weak. You did not kill the Queen. It was another.

Alley sent a tendril of energy deep into the magma, clenched her fist and hooked her right arm around. A thick tentacle of lava arced out of the lake and slammed into the dracun knocking it off the bridge. It thrashed in the magma and pulled itself back up. Smoke poured off its scales. It shook its body like a wet dog sending globs of lava sizzling through the air. It swung its head towards her. *You are nothing, Whelp. I will not let you take the Throne.*

Alley could feel eyes watching—judging. She had to end this. She pushed herself forward. The creature braced its feet on the slopes of the rock bridge and inhaled. A deep rumble came from its chest as its throat swelled and smoke leaked from between its jagged clenched teeth.

It was preparing to shoot a fireball.

Alley raised her hand to the roof and sent a tendril of energy upward.

The dracun drew its head back. Its chest expanded as it sucked in air. Yellow light illuminated the back of its throat making it look like a terrifying jack-o'-lantern.

Alley wrapped the energy around the base of a stalactite hanging from the dark ceiling overhead and squeezed her fist. It broke off and hurtled downward.

The dracun opened its jaws and the light in its throat intensified as a ball of flame rose from its chest.

The huge column of stone crashed down. It slammed into the dracun like a railway car falling from the sky. The fireball the dracun had been about to expel exploded inside its body, ripping it to pieces. The remains of the creature and broken stalactite toppled into the fiery lake leaving only a blackened stain on the bridge.

Alley looked upward at the Obsidian arrayed around the walls of the cavern. There were no whispers in her head. It was silent except for the sizzle and gurgle of the molten rock. She pushed herself forward. Past the place where the dracun had stood and arrived at the base of the rock tower. She floated upward. The dracun were motionless. Thousands of unblinking jewel-like eyes watched her ascend.

Alley crested the top of the tower and lowered herself to the ground. The stone chair sat a few yards away at the center of the circular top. The throne was three times as big as what a normal-sized person would use. She walked toward the chair half expecting another dracun to detach from the wall and attack. Alley rested her hand on the arm of the massive throne. She floated herself upward onto the seat and then stood looking around at the clan. Was this it?

A voice echoed in her head. It was Malcore. *The Dama has Ascended to the Throne. She is ready.*

The dracun stirred. Orange light rippled across their scales as a thousand bodies shifted. Almost as one, the dracun pushed off the wall. The air thundered with the beating of thousands of pairs of wings. They circled the pillar in a giant swarm.

"What is happening, Malcore?!" yelled Alley.

Baptism. You will be reborn as a Dragon. You will be reborn as our Queen.

The first fireball struck her from the side. It knocked her off the stone chair and seared the side of her face. Alley landed on the ground in a puddle of burning liquid. The pain made her gasp. She was hit again from behind by another ball of flame. Alley tried to pull at the energy, but it slipped from her grasp as she was hit with yet another ball of blinding heat and fire. The dracun bombarded her. Alley crawled toward the chair to shield herself, but it was hard to see where she was going. Everything was fire and smoke. They were burning her alive. She curled into a ball and closed her eyes. Every inch of her skin screamed in pain. Alley could smell her flesh burning. How long would it take to die? For the pain to go away?

Fireball after fireball struck her body. Alley lost track of time. It went on and on. Each time she thought it was over, she got hit again. Her clothing turned to ash and flaked away. She drifted in and out of consciousness. Pain was everywhere.

It was hard to tell when it ended. One minute the sizzling crackle of burning napalm surrounded her, the next minute it was quiet. She felt a soft touch on her shoulder.

Rise, my Queen.

Alley hurt all over—like the worst sunburn of her life. She opened her eyes and slowly uncurled. Her fingers ended in sharp points—talons. Alley stood. Tatters of charred cloth barely covered her naked ash coated body. She was alive, but felt changed.

Malcore backed away with a bow.

Alley narrowed her eyes and looked around at her clan. They clung to the walls of the cavern. Their presence filled her mind. They were afraid.

A low inhuman sound rumbled in her chest. Her word was law now. The EMP device needed to be shutdown.

Alley growled in her mind. *Turn. It. Off.*

42

FOUR MONTHS LATER

ALLEY

Spring air flooded the pickup truck's cabin as Arün drove Alley into the Cascade Mountains along the cracked pavement of Route-2. She hung her arm out the window feeling the wind pass over the top and bottom of her taloned hand. Alley looked over at Arün. "How much farther?"

He smiled. "Impatient?"

"A little." The boughs of the hemlocks and fir trees blurred as they passed. Cool air tousled her auburn hair. Alley glanced at herself in the side-view mirror. Her irises sparkled as if they were made from amethyst and the whites of her eyes had turned black. They were more dracun than human now. The clan's flames had changed her in ways she was still trying to understand and accept.

"We're close. Just enjoy the ride," said Arün as he swung the truck onto an old overgrown logging road. The vehicle bounced as they climbed the rutted dirt path. Dappled pools of light danced across the hood of the pickup as they passed under the tall pines. Overhead, mountain birds twittered and sang.

Alley looked over at Arün. He'd been flying her between downtown and Mt. Baker at night. She enjoyed the rides, and it had allowed them to grow closer. He was the only person in her life who understood what it was like being both human and dracun. "Would have been a great day for flying," she said.

Arün leaned forward and looked into the sky. "The daylight ban is still in place—at least till they stop reporting on the meteor disaster."

Alley shook her head. "People know what they saw. They aren't buying the cover story."

"The boulders you planted are helping convince people."

Alley snorted. "I heard a geologist from UW on the news saying he didn't believe they were meteors."

Arün smiled. "The Mages will quiet them. The scientific community won't want to risk having their funding cut."

Alley shook her head. "Even so, the military won't be so easy to convince."

Arün rolled his window down. "The military knows how to cover things up. For decades, they've had a secret task force that we've coordinated with—they're just demanding to be more involved now."

"What does that mean?" she asked.

Arün shrugged. "The Council is sorting it out."

Alley raised her eyebrow. "All this cover-up is nice, but I've seen people's faces at the construction sites. They're all skeptics."

Arün gripped the steering wheel and shifted into a lower gear as the truck climbed a steep section of the road. "It was dark, there was no power, and most of them ran into cover when the fireballs rained down."

Alley drummed her fingers on the truck door. "I guess for people who only saw the fireballs, the meteor story works, but the ones who saw Cynder—"

Arün interrupted. "The eye-witnesses stopped talking when the tabloids picked up their story. Would you want to be quoted saying you saw a giant monster attacking the city?"

"They still talk, and they've been watching us rebuild. I think they've noticed the workers," she said.

Arün sighed, "It was your idea to use the Obsidian Clan around the clock. Normal people sleep."

"They need to fix what they destroyed—but maybe you're right. I'll slow things down." Alley reached out with her thoughts. She could feel the minds of her clan. She sought Malcore.

His voice echoed in her mind. *My Queen?*

No more double-shifts, Malcore.

But we are nearly done. This will add weeks.

Alley pressed her lips together. *Please.* She could have compelled him, but she wasn't her grandmother. She'd made a promise to the clan that as long as she was their leader, their choices would be their own.

As you wish.

Alley felt his presence withdraw and let out a sigh. The downtown buildings already stood tall once again. Even in their current state, it had to be a record.

Arün looked over at her. "Talking to the troops?"

She nodded, watching the trees pass. Up ahead, a lichen covered arch had been constructed out of two thick twenty-foot-high logs sunk into either side of the road. At the top, wide planks spanned the gap making it look like they were driving through a massive rotting door frame. Nailed to the planks was a battered metal sign that read, *"Danger: Falling Debris. Authorized Personnel Only."*

Alley squinted at the gate as they passed under it. "I thought you said this place was nice?"

"It helps discourage the public from visiting," answered Arün.

"It would have been easier to fly."

Arün scratched at his jaw. "Even if there wasn't a ban, I like driving my truck."

"But, you look good in green."

He looked over. "I feel naked in green."

Alley laughed. "Aren't scales sort of like clothes?"

"They are nothing like clothes."

The road rounded a bend. The forest opened, revealing a steep gorge. Pines clung to rocky shelves that nature had chiseled into the far slope. A rusting steel draw bridge spanned the gap. Thick cables dripping with green moss traveled from the end of the bridge closest to them up to a series of pulleys embedded into the rock on the far side. Hundreds of feet below a river splashed its way over fallen logs, and slick rocks. Arün slowed the truck as they drove onto the narrow bridge. The metal groaned and shook as they crossed.

"We're almost there," he said.

On the far side of the bridge, the road led into a dark cleft where a massive slab of rock had sheared away from the mountain. Arün flicked on the headlights as they drove into the opening. Vines covered the walls inside the tunnel. They emerged back into daylight. Thirty-foot high ivy-covered walls and a thick wrought-iron gate blocked the road. A tarnished brass plaque to the left of the gate said, "*Warden & Weaver College.*"

"This is it?" she asked.

"This is the main gate." Arün reached into his jacket, withdrew a whistle carved from green crystal and blew two notes on it. The hinges of the gates squealed and creaked as they swung inward. Arün pressed the accelerator, and the truck rolled forward.

"The campus walls are unbreachable by conventional

means, and there's a weave around the valley that blocks it from satellite imaging."

Alley looked at the high walls and gate as they passed through. "This doesn't look like it's been used in years."

"Everyone usually comes in through the portals that connect the campus to downtown."

"Why didn't we—," Alley started.

"They were damaged by the attack. They'll be fixed soon," interrupted Arün.

"Why didn't we come here when the dracun were hunting me?"

"Too dangerous. We'd have risked leading your clan here, and you had so little control that we feared you might accidentally destroy the College."

Alley nodded and looked out the window. She wished she could go back in time and explain to her younger-self everything she'd learned. She could have prevented the destruction in the city, saved her father, Brent and so many more. Her father used to say everything happened for a reason and that she needed to have faith that things would work out for the best. Had his death been for the best? How would she have handled her power if she hadn't seen the Queen using it for the wrong reasons? Would she have valued human life the same if she had never lost a friend or a family member? The temptation to abuse her power was ever present now. The death it had caused made it easy to resist misusing it.

On the far side of the gate, the road turned from gravel into red brick paving stones as it wound through mossy oaks. It was strange to think Elek had been training here since they graduated from high school and he was here now—somewhere up ahead.

The forest thinned revealing an oblong valley with a clear sapphire-blue lake at its center. The water was ringed by chiseled cliffs dotted with pines and oak trees. On one side of the lake was a sprawling structure of connected buildings that started up on the cliffs and then spilled down towards the water in an odd assortment of roof lines and turrets. Some buildings had been built in a Victorian style with high pitched slate roofs and dormer windows, these were fused into stone structures that resembled a medieval castle and then gave way to Mediterranean architecture with red-tiled roofs. Closer to the lake the buildings were built from heavy timber, resembling a Swiss chalet. Other buildings dotted the cliffs around the lake including one that looked like a large observatory with a domed roof. They were all connected by elevated walkways that seemed to have been woven from a tangle of roots that grew from the cliff sides.

"It's pretty," she said.

Arün laughed. "They've been adding to it for over a century. Can't seem to stick with a style."

Above the lake, a group of Opal dracun circled and took turns diving towards the water. They all wore harnesses with warden riders.

"What's happening up there?"

"Flight drills for the Tyros. We're expanding the test program."

They slowed to a stop in front of the main building. A wide set of steps led up to an entrance with tall ornate polished wood doors. As Alley got out of the truck, one of the dracun broke formation and came diving towards them across the lake. It beat the air kicking up a dust cloud as it landed on the bricks in front of the vehicle. The warden rider, dressed in sleek padded leather motorcycle clothes and helmet, slid off the back of the dracun and ran towards Alley. He pulled off his helmet revealing a tangle of dark hair and a familiar grin.

"Elek!" Alley hugged him. He smelled of leather, damp moss and earth.

"It's good to see you, Al. Been too long."

She stepped back from him and squeezed one of his biceps. "Working out again?"

Elek looked at the ground. "Just training."

Arün got out of the truck and slammed the door. "Just training? Elek is being modest. He is our star Tyro."

Elek licked his lips, "Well—"

A gurgle and a flash of steam interrupted Elek as the Opal dracun's body transformed into a tall humanoid creature. It stepped forward and bowed low to Alley. "I am honored to be in your presence once more."

Alley dipped her head as Malcore had taught. She recognized the dracun. He had transported Nadja on their mission.

"Well met, Viktor." She nodded towards Elek. "Is he as good as Arün says?"

Viktor grinned revealing a row of white fangs. "Indeed. Except for the time he dropped the flag during Rings."

Elek turned to Viktor. "That happened one time—"

The carved wooden doors at the top of the steps boomed as they swung open. Bezo stepped out of the shadows. "Come inside. The Council is waiting."

Alley sighed and gave Elek another hug. The Council was the most impatient group of people she'd ever met. He smiled at her. "It's good to see you again, Alley."

"You too, El."

Bezo crossed his arms. "No need to say your goodbyes. Alley, you and Elek both need to come with me."

Elek looked over at Arün and raised an eyebrow. Arün shook his head and shrugged.

Bezo turned on his heels and headed back into the building.

Arün opened the door to the truck. "I'll meet up with you later, Alley. Better not keep them waiting."

Elek extended his helmet toward Viktor. "Would you mind?"

Viktor took the helmet. "Of course." He bowed to Alley. His voice echoed in her head. *Go in peace, Dama.*

Alley closed her eyes for a moment and tilted her head toward him. *Peace be with you, Viktor.*

Viktor ran towards the lake and leaped into the air. A ripple ran through his white scales as his limbs elongated and his body expanded into a full sized dracun. His broad wings beat the air as he flew across the water.

Alley reached for Elek's hand. "Guess we better catch up to Bezo."

They climbed the stone steps and entered the building. The interior was covered in lacquered wood paneling. Ornate rugs covered the hardwood floors. Heavy wooden beams crisscrossed in the high rafters overhead. In between them, small windows allowed natural light to stream in. It felt like a mountain lodge that had been built like a cathedral.

Bezo had disappeared.

Elek pulled on her hand. "They'll be in the Grand Hall."

He led her past old paintings and photographs of groups of people, each with a tiny brass label affixed to the bottom of the frame. Glass displays held strange artifacts and weapons. Alley wished there was time to stop and examine them. They went through a series of halls and passageways before coming to a set of tall doors that were propped open.

The room they entered was shaped like an enormous half moon. It reminded her of a picture she'd seen of the United Nations General Assembly Hall. Tiers of seats sloped down towards a tiled main floor that was as big as a basketball court. At the far side of the main floor was a raised platform where the Mage Council sat behind a wide curved podium of dark wood. Deep blue carpeted steps led from the entrance down to the main floor. Bezo waited at the bottom.

A voice boomed through hidden speakers. "Welcome to the College, Alley Ward. We have much to discuss with you."

Elek's palm felt sweaty, his face was expressionless. Alley squeezed his hand, and they descended the carpeted steps. This would be her third meeting with the Council since she became the leader of the Obsidian Clan. They hadn't been happy about her new role or that she'd prevented them from punishing the Obsidians, but they'd calmed down when she'd pledged to restore Seattle and enforce peace within the clan. She'd been helping rebuild the city for months and her last contact with the Council had been a brief meeting to discuss the status of the rebuilding efforts.

Alley let go of Elek's hand as they reached the bottom of the steps. Bezo ushered them forward towards the middle of the floor.

Leopold Rakman was seated at the center of the wide podium, dressed in a black suit. His glasses were perched on the end of his long narrow nose. He had a helpful name plate in front of his microphone that said, *"Rakman."* Alley doubted whether there was anyone at the College who didn't know him. He adjusted the stem of a long thin microphone that sprouted from the podium like an insect's antenna.

"Elek Mori, The Council wishes to thank you for your role in helping stop the Obsidian revolt."

Bezo leaned towards Elek and muttered. "Sorry about this. I wanted to make it a small affair, but this lot loves their pomp."

Rakman cleared his throat. "Is there something you'd like to add Arch-Mage Berolaster?"

Bezo scratched at his beard and looked up at them. "No, no. You are doing a fine job. Please continue."

Rakman pushed his glasses up his nose and looked at Elek. He motioned to someone behind the podium and Arün emerged from the shadows carrying a carved wooden box attached to a small wooden stand. He walked across the polished floor, set the stand in front of Elek and opened the lid of the box.

Inside, nestled against black velvet was a blade—a new Warden Scryth.

Elek ran his finger along the weapon's hilt.

Rakman's voice echoed in the large hall. "Elek, your deeds have proved better than any test that you are ready to be a warden."

Bezo raised his voice, "I think he is ready for something else!"

Everyone's eyes turned towards the mage. Rakman rubbed his forehead with a bony hand. "What, pray tell, are you talking about?"

Bezo turned to Elek. "I would like you to be my Apprentice."

Elek's jaw dropped.

Alley whispered in her mind to Arün. *Did you know this would happen?*

Arün glanced at her and then back to Elek. *I'm as surprised as you are.*

The Council broke into excited murmurs. Leopold Rakman covered the microphone and leaned over to talk to one of the mages at his side. Alley realized that it was Elek's dad. A moment later he uncovered the microphone and spoke. "This is irregular. You know candidates are supposed to be reviewed by the Council."

Bezo cocked his head to the side and smiled. "High Arch-Mage Rakman. Are you saying I'm unable to judge a candidate on my own?"

Rakman stared at Bezo his right thumb drumming a quiet rhythm on the podium. The other mages watched him, some with odd smirks on their faces, waiting to see what he would say.

Rakman's hand grew still. He leaned into the microphone. "Your track record is beyond reproach."

Bezo winked and nodded. "I thought you might agree."

A few of the Council members covered their mouths, trying to hide their amusement. Rakman flashed them an angry glance.

Bezo held his hand towards Elek. "This candidate shows

more potential than any candidate"—he looked up at Leopold Rakman—"I have ever trained."

Rakman's lips pressed into a thin line. A smile spread across Elek's father's face. Alley had never seen him look so happy.

Bezo looked at Elek. "You are capable of far more than you know."

Elek whispered, "I'm honored, but I don't know if I'm smart enough."

Bezo laughed and lowered his voice, "Smart enough? I trained the clown up there running this circus. You are more than smart enough."

Arün placed a hand on Elek's shoulder and whispered, "Do it. You'll always be welcomed back as a warden if you change your mind."

Elek looked from Bezo to Arün and back to Bezo, then glanced up at his dad before nodding. "I accept."

Bezo clapped his hands. "It's done!"

Rakman pushed his glasses up his nose. "Fantastic. Now that we've concluded that business we have private matters to discuss with Ms. Ward."

Arün gave a quick nod, picked up the box with the blade and headed towards a doorway in the shadows.

Alley gave Elek a hug. "Congratulations, El. You'll make a great mage."

Elek smiled at her. "Thanks, Al. See you later?"

Alley nodded. He turned and jogged after Arün. Bezo remained at Alley's side.

The overhead speakers crackled. "Arch-Mage Berolaster. I believe your new Apprentice needs guidance—seeing as he's only recently become aware of this new opportunity."

"I will remain to hear the private matters that need to be discussed," said Bezo.

Rakman smiled. "I'm sure you have confidence that the Council will act appropriately in your absence. If we can't trust each other to operate in our mutual best interests, then perhaps we have other issues to discuss."

Bezo shifted on his feet. He appeared to want to say something but thought better. "Of course. I trust my fellow Council members. I look forward to hearing the details of the meeting later today." He whispered to Alley—"I will meet you afterward"—then left through the side door.

Silence filled the hall for a moment, then Rakman breathed into the microphone. "Alley Ward. I apologize for how little we have spoken over the past few months."

She nodded.

"Thank you again for everything you have done. We remain very sorry for your loss. Your father was a brilliant mage. We still mourn his passing."

Alley's gut twisted, and she felt her eyes getting watery. She studied the carpet, her jaw clenching as she tried to calm herself. She would not cry in front of them. She'd helped dig through the charred rubble but had never found her father's remains. Cynder's flames had turned the collapsed building into an inferno. Alley had taken some ashes from the devastation up into the mountains and scattered them along one of his favorite trails. She hoped her parents had finally found peace together.

"In recognition for your deeds, we wish to offer you a place at this College and an opportunity to take part in our ground-breaking research."

Alley resisted the urge to wipe at her eyes as she looked up. "What research?"

"Helping us continue our studies into the scientific and magical properties of the flora and fauna of Arburaan. And you would be free to hone your abilities within the safety of the campus grounds."

"I'll think about it," she said.

The mages on the platform stirred.

Rakman leaned forward. "Do you have other plans?"

Alley looked up at them. Other plans? The last four months had been a blur of crying, trying to bring order to the clan, exploring her power and rebuilding the city. She had spent little time thinking long-term. "I have duties as a clan leader. Beyond that—no plans."

"If you find the College not to your liking, you are always free to go."

The Council had already been providing her an apartment in downtown Seattle close to the reconstruction sites. "Where would I be staying?" she asked.

Rakman adjusted the microphone. "We've prepared a residence for you at the top of the West Tower. We hope it is to your liking. It used to be one of your father's research spaces."

Alley had always loved spending time with her dad in his study at home. Had they left any of his things in place? She wanted to touch something that had once belonged to him. Anything that might trigger a memory of a moment they had shared.

She wasn't sure if the College was the right fit, but it was a place that had been special to her parents and the buildings in Seattle would be completed soon. After that, there would be no reason for her to stay downtown. "All right, I'll give it a try."

"Excellent. There is one other item. There are students at the College who would benefit from your natural talent with Weaves. Would you consider mentoring them?"

Alley laughed, she was just starting to understand her abilities. She didn't feel like she'd make a good mentor. "I'm not sure. Maybe."

"Please consider it. You have much to offer. Thank you again, Alley, and welcome to the College." The Council stood and began exiting.

Alley raised her voice. "Wait." The words came out two octaves lower than she'd intended. Sometimes the dragon part of her was hard to control.

The mages froze. Their eyes went wide at the deep sound.

Alley laughed as she forced her voice back to a normal pitch. "I'm sorry. There's one other matter I need to discuss with you."

Rakman cocked his head to the side. "Please, continue."

Alley clasped her hands behind her back. "I've been meeting with the other clan leaders. We are forming a governing body for the dracuns to help provide more structure for the Clans—to prevent future escalations. We are calling it the Dragon Council. I wanted to extend an invitation for a member of the Mage Council to attend our sessions.

Rakman cleared his throat. "We don't want to encourage the dracuns to organize."

Alley squinted at him. "I'm not asking you for permission. I'm informing you of what's happening and offering you a place at our table."

The mages murmured. Rakman started to say something, but Elek's father cut him off. "I would be honored to represent the Mages at the Dragon Council."

Alley smiled. "Thank you, Dr. Mori." It was comforting knowing there was still someone on the Council who remembered her from before she was different. She turned and walked up the carpeted steps and out into the hallway before the mages had a chance to react. Malcore had impressed upon her how important it was that the Council understand she was their equal.

Sun shown through tall windows bathing the oak paneled corridor in light. The building was beautiful. It would be a different life than living in the city. She'd be able to be herself here. No more needing to wear sunglasses and gloves to discourage people from staring. Here, she'd finally fit in.

Alley walked to the end of the hall where Elek, Arün and Bezo were waiting. The old mage clasped his hands together. "Well, I hope the Council wasn't too irritating to deal with?"

She laughed. "I understand now, why you like them so much."

Bezo chuckled. "They were supposed to have made you an offer."

"They did. I'll be staying here. I guess I have a room in the West Tower?"

Bezo nodded. "Ben's old offices. That was my idea. I thought it might feel more like home."

"I'd love to see it."

Bezo started to walk down the hall. "I need to take my new apprentice on a quick orientation, but Arün knows the way. I left a little house warming gift for you."

Elek turned to her. "I'll swing by later, so we can catch up, Al."

"Yeah, don't be a stranger," she said.

Elek gave her one of his lopsided smiles and jogged down

the sun dappled hallway to catch up with Bezo. *Elek the Mage.* She would have to get used to that.

Arün scratched at his stubble. "He would have made an incredible warden."

Alley bumped her shoulder into him. "Don't get all mopey. Let's go check out my new place."

Arün rolled his eyes and headed down a side corridor. They passed classrooms, libraries, laboratories and training rooms filled with people in robes covered in hundreds of strips of cloth embroidered with magical weaves. The walls changed from paneled wood to velvety wallpaper, then to brick and stone as the architecture melted from one style into the next.

Arün was quiet.

"I'm sorry. I know it must be hard losing Elek," she said.

"It's not that. I'm happy for him—"

Alley stayed silent.

"—It's Nadja. No one has heard from her since we parted ways."

They climbed a flight of curving stairs.

"You have no idea where she is?"

Arün pulled his milkstone locket out from beneath his shirt and snapped it open. "She's not in this world."

"She's in Arburaan?"

He nodded. "I don't know why she's there, but if she's not coming back, I need to go to her. I can't leave things the way they are between us."

"Is that a good idea? According to Bezo, our last visit has raised tensions to a dangerous level between the mages and elves. They're still trying to smooth things over."

"There's a way I can cross over undetected."

"Maybe you could just send a letter with Bezo."

Arün sighed. "I've sent three already."

"I'm sorry, Arün."

They came to a landing with a heavy lacquered oak door set into the wall. Arün tucked the locket back under his shirt. "This is it."

Alley turned the worn brass knob and pushed on the door. It swung inward revealing a large circular room with a high ceiling. Tall windows looked out over the mountains and a set of glass doors opened out onto a balcony with Adirondack chairs. The room was paneled in wood and lined with shelves of books. Red carpet covered the floor. On the far side, the chimney of a field-stone fireplace climbed toward the ceiling. A brass staircase followed the curve of the wall and led to a small loft with a bed. Cushioned reading chairs and a couch crowded around the hearth. Off to one side squatted a heavy looking carved desk. The top surface was littered with pens, paper and a peculiar package wrapped in brown paper and twine.

Alley walked over to the desk and sat down. She ran her hands along the wood. Her dad had sat here. Maybe this had been the place where he and her mom had planned her birth. She pulled the package closer and untied the twine.

The brown paper slid off to reveal a white box. Inside lay her mother's charred journal.

An envelope rested on top of the book. Inside was a note.

"You left this in my house. I'm sorry it's taken so long to return it. — Bezo"

Alley flipped through the pages. They were all dry now but wrinkled from their dip in the lake. Somewhere within her mother's notes, Alley hoped there was an answer to what her father had hinted at—that she wasn't just human and dracun—she was more. Alley opened the note her father had left in the journal and read the last line.

"—All my love until we meet again, Your father, Ben."

She could hear his voice when she read the words.

Arün's presence echoed in her mind. *He was a good man. A good friend.*

Alley looked up from the journal. Arün was standing by the glass doors looking out towards the mountains. She got up from the desk and joined him. He was watching the dracun and wardens circling and diving above the lake.

Fly with them, she said in her mind.

Arün turned toward her and smiled before looking back up into the sky. *Maybe I will,* his thoughts answered back.

She nudged him. "What are you waiting for?"

His face reddened. "Can you turn around?"

"Seriously?"

He crossed his arms.

Alley laughed and held up her hands. "Should I count to thirty or something?"

"Just turn around."

She smirked as she faced away from him. A crunching sound like brittle ice breaking filled the room. Alley turned back. Arün's emerald-scaled body was perched on the balcony. His head stuck through the open glass doorway. *Thanks,* he thought to her.

She smiled at him. "Have fun."

Arün bowed his head and dove off the balcony to join the other dracun above the lake.

There was a knock on the door.

Alley called across the room. "Come in!"

Elek peeked inside. "You decent?"

"Come in, dork. I figured Bezo would have you pouring over a pile of books."

Elek entered and closed the door. He was holding a bag behind his back. "I explained to him, that I was already long overdue for a class you had offered me."

Alley laughed. "What are you talking about?"

Elek grinned. He showed her the bag and two sticks he'd brought. "Marshmallows."

"What?"

"I figured you needed to break in this swanky fireplace and you made me a deal on Bezo's porch."

Alley laughed again. "So, you've finally come to learn how to roast them properly?"

"If you have time?"

Alley motioned to the chairs by the fireplace. She sent a thread of energy out into the stack of logs, building up friction between the fibers until they ignited into a small blaze.

"For you Elek—I always have time."

They pulled the chairs close to the fire and squished marshmallows onto the end of their sticks.

Alley extended her marshmallow out over the flames. "So, you're going to be a mage?"

Elek smiled. "Yeah, I can't believe it. Bezo said I'll be the first Battle-Mage to be trained in over fifty years."

Alley reached over and pushed his hand up. "You're getting too close to the flames. Higher and rotate the stick."

Elek followed her directions.

She nodded her approval. "A Battle-Mage? Do I need to be afraid? Are you going to challenge me to arm wrestling?"

Elek tried not to crack a smile. "It's because of my warden training and experience with the Marions. Bezo says that Cynder's attack exposed a weakness in the College's mage training."

Alley nodded. "You're going to be a great mage. I owe you my life, El."

Elek blushed. "You know I'd never let anything happen to you."

Alley bit her lip and glanced at her friend. "Yeah."

They sat in silence for a moment.

Alley's eyes went wide. "Woe! Elek that's too close!" It was too late. Elek's marshmallow burst into flame. He blew on it to extinguish the fire. The outside was a charred mess.

Alley glared at him.

Elek grinned. "Sorry?"

They burst into laughter.

Alley felt warm inside, but it wasn't the heat from the fire. It was because for the first time, in a long time, she felt like she was home.

THE END

IF YOU ENJOYED THIS BOOK...

If you enjoyed reading the *The Obsidian Ascent*, I'd be grateful if you would take a few moments and leave a brief review.

Reviews help other readers, just like you, discover the *Emerald City Dragons* series!

To leave a review, please visit: **wesleygrandmont.com/books** and click on the link for *The Obsidian Ascent.*

Thank you so much for being one of my readers!

-Wes Grandmont III

GET A FREE BOOK!

I'd like to invite you to join the Emerald City Dragons Reader Goup! When you signup, I'll send you my newsletter each month and you'll receive a free ebook! Here's what to expect:

1. A free ebook edition of **The Alley of Secrets : Emerald City Dragons - Prologue**
2. Advance notification about my upcoming releases and sales.
3. Special promotions on discounted and free books.
4. Behind-the-scenes insights about the series and other surprises!

To join, visit : **wesleygrandmont.com** and click on the "START THE ADVENTURE NOW!" button.

While I hope you'll stay in touch, you are free to unsubscribe at any time!

ABOUT THE AUTHOR

Wesley Grandmont III is a writer, artist and game developer who is passionate about crafting immersive worlds for his readers. He writes stories that mix the modern world with magic—urban fantasies with the tension and pacing of espionage thrillers. His debut book series *Emerald City Dragons*, is an urban fantasy world set in and around Seattle.

A seasoned veteran of the video game industry, Wes has worked on over twenty games, most recently as Lead Technical Art Director on Microsoft's *Halo 5 : Guardians*, and Sony's *Ghost of Tsushima*.

When not crafting new stories or games, he loves coffee (lots of coffee), skiing, hiking and spending time with family and friends in the Pacific Northwest.

facebook.com/WesGrandmontAuthor

amazon.com/author/wesgrandmont

ACKNOWLEDGEMENTS

Many late nights and many cups of coffee went into the pages you hold in your hands. This book has been a labor of love that has unfolded over years, but I wouldn't have been able to complete it without the love and support of my family and friends.

Thank you to my wife, Rebecca, my sounding board and my muse. You endured the earliest drafts in all their ugly forms and helped provide feedback that pushed the story in the right direction. You were patient with my repetitive rants and supportive of my late hours at the keyboard. I love you for all that and so much more!

A big thank you to my Dad. You shared your love of science fiction and fantasy with me at an early age and provided valuable feedback on the earliest draft of the book. Your encouragement has meant the world to me!

Many thanks to my Beta Readers: Marc Marshall, Jason Carter and Patricia Black. I appreciate all the time you put into reading and providing feedback over the years! Hopefully, each of you are able to see some of your input reflected in the final pages. The story never would have been as good without all your help.

Special thanks to my sister-in-law, Christina Kostelak, for helping me with the title for this book.

I also want to thank my editor, Jodi Keller, from NY Book Editors. Your notes and feedback put the final shine on *The Obsidian Ascent* and provided me with valuable perspective that helped me grow as a writer.

Finally I want to thank you, my dear reader. For taking a chance on a new author. For coming on an adventure with me. Without you, there would be no story, just words on a page. It's your imagination, your emotions, your experiences that breath unique life into these words. I hope you've enjoyed this first book in the *Emerald City Dragons* series. Stick around the story is just beginning.

-Wes Grandmont III

ALSO BY WES GRANDMONT III

Make sure to check out all the books in the *Emerald City Dragons* series!

The Alley of Secrets
The Obsidian Ascent
The City of Ruins
The Lost Warden
and more!

For a complete list, please visit:
wesleygrandmont.com/books

www.ingramcontent.com/pod-product-compliance
Lightning Source LLC
Chambersburg PA
CBHW030540310726
48979CB00010B/1982/J

* 9 7 8 1 7 3 2 0 8 4 4 4 5 *